PENGUIN BOOKS

TOOTH AND CLAW

T.C. Boyle is the author of *Talk Talk*, *The Inner Circle*, *Drop City* (a finalist for the National Book Award), *A Friend of the Earth*, *Riven Rock*, *The Tortilla Curtain*, *The Road to Wellville*, *East Is East*, *World's End* (winner of the PEN/Faulkner Award), *Budding Prospects*, *Water Music*, and seven collections of stories. In 1999, he was the recipient of the PEN/Malamud Award for Excellence in Short Fiction. His stories appear regularly in major American magazines, including *The New Yorker*, *GQ*, *Esquire*, *Harper's*, *McSweeney's*, and *Playboy*. He lives near Santa Barbara, California. T.C. Boyle's Web site is www.tcboyle.com.

Praise for *Tooth and Claw* by T.C. Boyle

"Inside *Tooth and Claw* are Boyle's trademark taut writing, immediate intimacy, vivid language. . . . Among Boyle's gifts are his roaring intelligence and a curiosity that has led him over the years to develop a masterly range of subjects and locales."   —Annie Proulx, *The Washington Post*

"Boyle returns to mercilessly test his characters' physical and emotional endurance. . . . Each character, captured in Boyle's calculating and caustic prose, fights his or her way out of the wreckage."   —*Time*

"An impressive miscellany of styles, genres, voices, and subjects . . . at his best, Boyle succeeds in creating a world where scientific determinism plays a part, but the characters go on living as if they had a choice and a chance. That he makes their predicament not just compelling but often exuberantly amusing is a tribute to his talent and proof of John Cheever's claim that good prose can cure anything, including the common cold."
—Michael Mewshaw, *Los Angeles Times*

"Spine-freezing, guilty-giggle inducing and, oddly, heartwarming stories . . . fourteen small masterpieces of sculpture fashioned from sinew, muscle, marrow . . . heart. While unremittingly primal, they remain undeniably, and touchingly, human."   —*The San Diego Union-Tribune*

"As always, Boyle writes wonderfully about oddballs, boozers, and the terminally self-deluded. But his best work here isn't satirical. In 'Chicxulub,' he juxtaposes the history of civilization-ending asteroids with an account of a happy middle aged couple, summoned in the night with terrible news about their daughter. The impact is shattering."
—*Entertainment Weekly*

"Whether Boyle is breaking your heart or making you laugh, you just don't care because he is so darned good at it. . . . Boyle has the voice to make you smile, make you care and make you hate yourself in the morning for being taken in by such a smooth storyteller."
—*San Francisco Chronicle*

"There is little doubt that Boyle is one of the most inventive writers of our age. . . . He is at the top of his game in 'Swept Away'—wry, playful, and generous toward his tenderhearted lovers even as they are torn asunder. . . . 'Dogology' is another irresistible romp [which] deftly plumbs the inextricable conflict between man's rational capacities and his animalistic urges, a theme Boyle has been examining, in one way or another, since his debut collection *Descent of Man*."   —*The Boston Globe*

"Boyle has an impressionist's range with voice. He is adept at jerking the rip cord at story's end without leaving readers feeling they've been jerked around. And he loves the challenge of grabbing an intimidating premise and whipping it toward despair or disaster." —*The Oregonian*

"For those who are unfamiliar with Boyle's work, this collection is a perfect place to start. . . . The short story is an ideal form for his remarkable talents. He has a seemingly limitless gift for the outrageous, sometimes grotesque, often incredible situation and for compelling the reader to buy into it. . . . Many of these stories are dazzling." —*Rocky Mountain News*

"T.C. Boyle could probably spin a riveting story out of the contents of a seed catalog. He is a writer of astonishing range and imagination, fierce intelligence and trenchant wit. Those gifts are dazzlingly on display in this collection of fourteen short stories, each a fully realized world shot through with perils either natural or man-made. . . . His universe may be cruel and random, but it has a brilliant blaze." —*Milwaukee Journal Sentinel*

"Like the best episodes of the late *Six Feet Under*, T.C. Boyle's new collection of stories takes readers to the edges of life just to keep it valid. . . . Boyle keeps us hooked by injecting vivid details and dark humor into his characters' distress. His conversational storytelling also draws the reader in casually as if he is just sharing heartbreak over drinks at the bar." —*Boston Herald*

"The threat of imminent demise—whether self-inflicted or from an ungentle Mother Nature—hovers in Boyle's seventh collection. . . . The wired rhythms of Boyle's prose and the enormity of his imagination make this collection irresistible; with it he continues to shore up his place as one of the most distinctive, funniest—and finest—writers around." —*Publishers Weekly*

"Boyle has never been more enrapturing than in his seventh collection of shrewd and comic tales. He orchestrates suspenseful, ludicrous, and wrenching predicaments, and his evocation of visceral detail, great gift for supple social commentary, and ability to occupy the psyches of his perplexed male characters are extraordinary." —*Booklist*

"Vintage Boyle, and not to be missed. . . . Darker tones and an impressive range of subjects dominate this impressive collection of fourteen vivid stories." —*Kirkus Reviews*

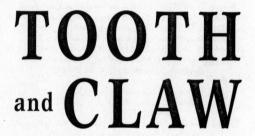

TOOTH and CLAW

T. Coraghessan Boyle

Penguin Books

PENGUIN BOOKS

Published by the Penguin Group
Penguin Group (USA) Inc., 375 Hudson Street, New York, New York 10014, U.S.A.
Penguin Group (Canada), 90 Eglinton Avenue East, Suite 700, Toronto,
Ontario, Canada M4P 2Y3 (a division of Pearson Penguin Canada Inc.)
Penguin Books Ltd, 80 Strand, London WC2R 0RL, England
Penguin Ireland, 25 St Stephen's Green, Dublin 2, Ireland (a division of Penguin Books Ltd)
Penguin Group (Australia), 250 Camberwell Road, Camberwell,
Victoria 3124, Australia (a division of Pearson Australia Group Pty Ltd)
Penguin Books India Pvt Ltd, 11 Community Centre, Panchsheel Park, New Delhi – 110 017, India
Penguin Group (NZ), cnr Airborne and Rosedale Roads, Albany,
Auckland 1310, New Zealand (a division of Pearson New Zealand Ltd)
Penguin Books (South Africa) (Pty) Ltd, 24 Sturdee Avenue,
Rosebank, Johannesburg 2196, South Africa

Penguin Books Ltd, Registered Offices:
80 Strand, London WC2R 0RL, England

First published in the United States of America by Viking Penguin,
a member of Penguin Group (USA) Inc. 2005
Published in Penguin Books 2006

1 3 5 7 9 10 8 6 4 2

Page ix constitutes an extension of this copyright page.

THE LIBRARY OF CONGRESS HAS CATALOGED THE HARDCOVER EDITION AS FOLLOWS:
Boyle, T. Coraghessan.
Tooth and claw / T. Coraghessan Boyle.
p. cm.
ISBN 0-670-03435-5 (hc.)
ISBN 0 14 30.3743 9 (pbk.)
I. Title.
PS3552.O932T66 2005
813'.54—dc22   20040655108

Printed in the United States of America
Set in Adobe Garamond

For Rob Jordan and Valerie Wong

ACKNOWLEDGMENTS

Grateful acknowledgment is made to the following magazines, in which these stories first appeared: *GQ,* "The Kind Assassin"; *Harper's,* "Rastrow's Island" and "Here Comes"; *McSweeney's,* "Blinded by the Light" and "The Doubtfulness of Water"; *The New Yorker,* "When I Woke Up This Morning, Everything I Had Was Gone," "Swept Away," "Dogology," "Chicxulub" and "Tooth and Claw"; *Playboy,* "Jubilation," "Up Against the Wall" and "The Swift Passage of the Animals"; and *StoryQuarterly,* "All the Wrecks I've Crawled Out Of."

"Swept Away" also appeared in *The O. Henry Prize Stories, 2003,* edited by Laura Furman (Anchor Books), and "Tooth and Claw" in *The Best American Short Stories, 2004,* edited by Lorrie Moore (Houghton Mifflin).

The author would also like to cite the following books as sources of certain factual details in "Dogology": *The Wolf Children: Fact or Fantasy,* by Charles MacLean; *Wolf-Children and Feral Man,* by the Reverend J. A. L. Singh and Robert M. Zingg; and *The Hidden Lives of Dogs,* by Elizabeth Marshall Thomas.

The Simiadae then branched off into two great stems, the New World and the Old World monkeys; and from the latter at a remote period, Man, the wonder and the glory of the universe, proceeded.

—CHARLES DARWIN, *The Descent of Man*

CONTENTS

TOOTH and CLAW

When I Woke Up This Morning, Everything I Had Was Gone

THE MAN I WANT to tell you about, the one I met at the bar at Jimmy's Steak House, was on a tear. Hardly surprising, since this was a bar, after all, and what do people do at bars except drink, and one drink leads to another—and if you're in a certain frame of mind, I suppose, you don't stop for a day or two or maybe more. But this man—he was in his forties, tall, no fat on him, dressed in a pair of stained Dockers and a navy blue sweatshirt cut off raggedly at the elbows—seemed to have been going at it steadily for weeks, months even.

It was a Saturday night, rain sizzling in the streets and steaming the windows, the dinner crowd beginning to rouse themselves over decaf, cheesecake and V.S.O.P. and the regulars drifting in to look the women over and wait for the band to set up in the corner. I was new in town. I had no date, no wife, no friends. I was on something of a tear myself—a mini-tear, I guess you'd call it. The night before I'd gone out with one of my co-workers from the office, who, like me, was recently divorced, and we had dinner, went to a couple places afterward. But nothing came of it—she didn't like me, and I could see that before we were halfway through dinner. I wasn't her type, whatever that might have been—and I started feeling sorry for myself, I guess, and drank too much. When I got up in the morning, I made myself a Bloody Mary with a can of Snap-E-Tom, a teaspoon of horseradish and two jiggers of vodka, just to clear my head, then went out to breakfast at a place by the water and drank a glass or two of Chardonnay with my frittata and homemade duck sausage with fennel, and then I wandered over to a sports bar and then another

place after that, and I never got any of the errands done I'd been putting off all week—and I didn't have any lunch either. Or dinner. And
so I drifted into Jimmy's and there he was, the man in the sweatshirt,
on his tear.

There was a space around him at the bar. He was standing there,
the stool shoved back and away from him as if he had no use for
comfort, and his lips were moving, though nobody I could see was
talking to him. A flashlight, a notebook and a cigarette lighter were laid
out in front of him on the mahogany bar, and though Jimmy's special-
ized in margaritas—there were eighteen different types of margaritas
offered on the drinks menu—this man was apparently going the
direct route. Half a glass of beer sat on the counter just south of the
flashlight and he was guarding three empty shot glasses as if he was
afraid someone was going to run off with them. The bar was filling
up. There were only two seats available in the place, one on either
side of him. I was feeling a little washed out, my legs gone heavy on
me all of a sudden, and I was thinking I might get a burger or a steak
and fries at the bar. I studied him a moment, considered, then took
the seat to his right and ordered a drink.

Our first communication came half a second later. He tapped my
arm, gave me a long, tunneled look, and made the universal two-
fingered gesture for a smoke. Normally this would have irritated
me—the law says you can no longer smoke in a public place in this
state, and in any case I don't smoke and never have—but I was on a
tear myself, I guess, and just gave him a smile and shrugged my
shoulders. He turned away from me then to flag down the bartender
and order another shot—he was drinking Herradura Gold—and a
beer chaser. There was a ritualistic moment during which he took a
bite from the wedge of lime the bartender provided, sprinkled salt
onto the webbing between the thumb and index finger of his left
hand, licked it off and threw back the shot, after which the beer came
into play. He exhaled deeply, and then his eyes migrated back to me.
"Nice to see you," he said, as if we'd known each other for years.

I said it was nice to see him too. The gabble of voices around us
seemed to go up a notch. A woman at the end of the bar began to

laugh with a thick, dredging sound, as if she were bringing something up with great reluctance.

He leaned in confidentially. "You know," he said, "people drink for a lot of reasons. You know why I drink? Because I like the taste of it. Sweet and simple. I like the taste."

I told him I liked the taste of it too, and then he made a fist and cuffed me lightly on the meat of the arm. "You're all right, you know that?" He held out his hand as if we'd just closed a deal, and I took it. I've been in business for years—for all but one of the years since I left college—and it was just a reflex to give him my name. He didn't say anything in response, just stared into my eyes, grinning, until I said, "And what do I call you?"

The man looked past me, his eyes groping toward the red and green neon sign with its neatly bunched neon palm trees that glowed behind the bar and apprised everybody of the name of the establishment. It took him a minute, but then he dropped my hand and said, "Just call me Jimmy."

After a couple of drinks at a bar, after the subjects of sports, movies and TV have been exhausted, people tend to talk about liquor, about the people they know who drink too much, fly off the handle, wind up wrecking their lives and the lives of everyone around them, and then they tend to get specific. This man—Jimmy—was no different. Alcoholism ran in his family, he told me. His father had died in the streets when he was younger than Jimmy was now, a transient, a bum, useless to the world and, more emphatically, to his wife and children. And Jimmy himself had a problem. He admitted as much.

A year before, he'd been living on the East Coast, in a town up the Hudson River, just outside of New York. He taught history at the local high school, and he'd come to it late, after working a high-stress job in Manhattan and commuting for years. History was his passion, and he hadn't had time to stagnate in the job like so many of his fellow teachers who went through the motions as if they were the walking dead. He loved sports too. He was a jogger, a tennis player, a mountain-biker, and he coached lacrosse in the fall and baseball in the spring. He was married to a girl he'd met in his senior year at the state university at Albany. They had a son—"Call him 'Chris,'" he said, looking to the neon sign again—and he'd coached Chris in high school and watched him go on to college himself as a newly minted freshman at an Ivy League school.

That was all right. Everything was all right. The school year began and he dug out his notes, Xeroxed study guides, looked up and down the class register and saw who he could trust and who he'd have to watch. In the mornings, before it was light, he ate breakfast alone in the kitchen, listening to the soft hum of the classic rock channel, the hits that took him back, hits he hadn't heard in years because Chris always had the radio tuned to hip-hop or the alternative station. Above him, in the master bedroom, Caroline was enjoying the luxury of sleeping late after thirteen years of scrambling eggs and buttering toast and seeing her son off to school. It was still dark when he climbed into his car, and most mornings he was the first one in the building, striding down the wide polished halls in a silence that could have choked on itself.

Fall settled in early that year, a succession of damp glistening days that took the leaves off the trees and fed on the breath of the wind. It seemed to do nothing but rain, day after day. The sky never swelled to flex its glory; the sun never shone. He saw a photo in the paper of a barechested jogger on the beach in Key Biscayne and felt reality slipping away from him. One afternoon he was out on the field in back of the school—the lacrosse team was scrimmaging with a bigger, more talented squad from a prep school upstate—and he couldn't seem to focus on the game. The assistant coach, no more than three or four years out of school himself, stepped up and took over the hectoring and the shoulder patting, managed the stream of substitutions and curbed the erupting tempers—discipline, that's what Jimmy taught above all else, because in a contact sport the team that controls its emotions will win out every time—while the clock ticked off the minutes to the half and the sky drew into itself and the rain whitened to sleet.

The sticks flashed, the players hurtled past him, grunting and cursing. He stood there in the weather, a physical presence, chilled, his hair wet, yet he wasn't there at all. He was reliving an episode from the previous year when his son had been the star player on the team, a moment like this one, the field slick, the players' legs a patchwork of mud, stippled flesh and dark blooming contusions. Chris had the ball. Two defenders converged on him, and Jimmy—the coach, the father—could see it all coming, the collision that would break open the day, bone to bone, the concussion, the shattered femur, injury to the spinal cord, to the brain. The sound of it—the sick wet explosion— froze him so that he couldn't even go to his son, couldn't move. But then, a miracle, Chris pushed himself up from the icy turf, stiff as a rake, and began to walk it off.

Jimmy awoke to the fact that someone was tugging at his arm. "Coach," somebody was saying, Mary-Louise, the principal's secre- tary, and what was she doing out here in this weather, the sleet caught like dander in the drift of her hairdo that must have cost sixty-five dollars to streak and color and set? "Jimmy," she said. "You need to call your wife." Her face fell, the white pellets pounded her hair. "It's an emergency."

He used the phone in the history chair's office, more weary than anything else. Since Chris had left home, everything seemed to set off alarm bells in Caroline's head—she thought she heard a sound in the front end of the car, the telephone had rung three times in suc- cession but nobody was there, the cat was refusing to eat and she was sure it was feline leukemia because she'd just read an article about it in the local paper. And what was it this time—a furtive scratching in the attic? Mold eating at the caulking around the tub? He thought nothing. Stared at the crescent of white beach on the marked-up cal- endar tacked to the wall behind Jerry Mortensen's desk as he dialed, and wished he could feel some sun on his face for a change. Florida. Maybe they'd go to Florida for the holidays, if Chris was up for it.

Caroline picked up on the second ring and her words burned a hole right through him. "It's Chris," she said. "He's in the hospital." There was no quaver, no emotion, no cracking around the edges of what she was trying to convey, and it scared him. "He's in the hospi- tal," she repeated.

"The hospital?"

"Jimmy," she said, and her voice cracked now, snapped like a compound fracture. "Jimmy. He's dying."

Dying? An eighteen-year-old athlete with a charmer's smile and no bad habits, heart like a clock, limbs of hammered wire, studious, dutiful, not a wild bone in his body? "What was it," I said, sounding tinny in my own ears, because his pain wasn't mine and there was no confusing the two. "Car crash?"

There had been a fraternity party the night before. The streets were slick, power lines were down, rain turned to ice, ice to snow. Chris was one of twelve pledges at Delta Upsilon, a party-hearty fraternity that offered instant access to the social scene, and it was the pledges' responsibility to pick up the party supplies—beer, vodka, cranberry juice, chips and salsa, and bunting to drape over the doorways of the big white ocean liner of a house, which had belonged to a shipping magnate at the turn of the last century. None of them had a car, so they had to walk into town and back, three trips in all, over sidewalks that were like bobsled runs, the snow so thick it was coming down in clumps, and somebody—it was Sonny Hammerschmitt, twenty-three years old and fresh from four years in the Navy and the only one of them who didn't need fake ID—suggested they ought to stop in at the Owl's Eye Tavern and sneak a quick beer to get in the party mood. Chris tried to talk them out of it. "Are you kidding?" he said, a cardboard box bristling with the amber necks of tequila bottles perched up on one shoulder while cars shushed by on the street and the intermediate distance blurred to white. "Dagan'll kill us if he finds out."

"Fuck Dagan. What's he going to do, blackball us? All of us?"

A snowball careened off the box and Chris almost lost his grip on it. Everybody was laughing, breath streaming, faces red with novelty, with hilarity and release. He set down the box and pelted his pledgemates with snowballs, each in his turn. Directly across the street was the tavern, a nondescript shingled building with a steep-pitched roof that might have been there when the Pilgrims came over—ancient, indelible, rooted like the trees. It was getting dark. Snow frosted the roof; the windows were pools of gold. A car crept up the street, chains jingling on the rear tires. Chris threw back his head and closed his eyes a moment, the snow accumulating like a cold compress on his eyelids. "Sure," he said, "okay. Why not? But just one, and then we'd better—" but he never finished the thought.

Inside, it was like another world, like a history lesson, with jars of pickled eggs and Polish sausage lined up behind the bar, a display of campaign buttons from the forties and fifties—*I Like Ike*—and a fireplace, a real fireplace, split oak sending up fantails of sparks against a backdrop of blackened brick. The air smelled sweet—it wasn't a confectionary sweetness or the false scent of air freshener either, but the smell of wood and wood smoke, pipe tobacco, booze. Sonny got them two pitchers of beer and shots of peppermint schnapps all around. They were there no more than half an hour—Dagan Drava, their pledgemaster, would really have their hides if he ever found out—and they drank quickly, greedily, drank as if they were getting away with something. Which they were. The snow mounted on the ledge outside the window. They had two more shots each and refilled the pitchers at least once, or maybe it was twice. Chris couldn't be sure.

Then it was the party, a blur of grinning, lurching faces, the music like a second pulse, the laughter of the girls, the brothers treating the pledges almost like human beings and everything made special by the snow that was still coming down, coming harder, coming like the end of the world. Every time the front door opened, the smell of it took hold of you as if you'd been plunged in a cold stream on the hottest day in August, and there would be two girls, two more girls, in knit hats pulled down to the eyebrows and scarves flung over their shoulders, stamping the snow from their boots and shouting, "A beer! A beer! My kingdom for a beer!"

Time contracted. One minute Chris and his pledgemates were scrambling to replenish the drinks and snacks on the big table in the dining room, everything reeking of spilled beer and tequila, as if a sea of it had washed through the house, from the attic on down to the basement, and the next minute the girls were gone, the night was settling in and Dagan was there, cracking the whip. "All right, you dogs, I want this place clean—spotless, you understand me? You've got ten minutes, ten minutes and all the trash is out of here and every scrap of this shit off the floor." The rest of the brothers were standing around now, post-party, working on the keg—the ones who weren't off getting laid, that is—and they added jeers and head slaps, barking out random orders and making the pledges drop for twenty at the slightest provocation (and being alive, breathing and present seemed provocation enough).

Like any other healthy eighteen-year-old, Chris drank, and he'd tried just about everything at least once. He was no angel on a pedestal, Jimmy knew that, and drinking—the taste for it—ran in his blood, sure it did, but in high school it was beer only and never to excess. Chris was afraid of what alcohol would do to him, to his performance on the field, to his grades, and more often than not he was the one who wound up driving everybody home after the post-game parties. But here he was, dense with it, his head stuffed full of cellulose, a screen pulled down over his eyes. He moved slowly and deliberately, lurching behind a black plastic bag full of wet trash, fumbling with the broom, the dustpan, listening for Dagan's voice in the mélange of shouts and curses and too-loud dance music as if it were the one thing he could cling to, the one thing that would get him through this and into the shelter of his bed in the windowless room behind the stairway on the second floor.

"Wait a minute, what's this? Hey, Dagan. *Dagan.* You see this?" It was the guy they called Pillar, a senior who wore a perpetual look of disappointment on his face and was said to have once won the drinking contest at Harry's Bar in Key West by outlasting a three-hundred-pound Samoan through sixteen rounds of mojitos. He was holding up two still-sealed bottles of Don José tequila.

Dagan's face floated into the picture. "I see what you mean, bro—the place just isn't clean, is it? I mean, would you want to operate under these conditions?"

"Uh-uh, no way," Pillar said. "Not while these motherfucking bottles are sitting here. I'm offended. I really am. How about you, Dagan? Aren't you offended?"

Dude. That was what they called the drinking game, though Chris had never heard of it before and would never hear of it again. Dude, that was all, and the whole house was chanting it now, "Dude! Dude! Dude!" Dagan marched the pledges down to the game room in the basement, made them line up against the back wall and handed each of them a shot glass. This was where the big-screen TV was, where the whole house gathered to watch the Pats and the Celtics and the porn videos that made your blood surge till you thought it was going to keep on going right out the top of your head.

It was 2:00 A.M. Chris couldn't feel his legs. Everything seemed funny suddenly, and he was laughing so hard he thought he was going to bring it all up, the beer, the schnapps, the pepperoni pizza and the chips and salsa and Cheez Doodles, and his pledgemates were laughing too, Dude, the funniest thing in the world. Then Dagan slipped the video into the VCR—*Bill & Ted's Excellent Adventure*—and gave them their instructions, serious business now, a ritual, and no fooling around ("I'm serious, people, and wipe the smirks off your faces—you are in deep shit now"). Music, a flash of color, and there was Keanu Reeves, with his slice of an Asiatic face and disappearing eyes, playing the fool, or maybe playing to type, and every time he uttered the monosyllabic tag that gave the game its name, the pledge class had to lift the glasses to their lips and down a shot—"Hey, dude; 'S up, dude"—till both bottles were drained.

Benny Chung was the first one to break. He was seventeen, a Merit Scholarship finalist, with narrow shoulders, wrists you could loop two fingers around and a head that seemed to float up like a balloon from the tether of his neck. His shoulders dipped forward as if he were trying to duck under a low-hanging limb, then his lips pulled back and he spewed all over the floor and his pant legs and his black high-top Converse sneakers. It was a heroic effort, so much of that umber chowder coming out of so frail a vessel, and Benny had to go down on one knee to get it all out. Nobody said anything, and nobody was laughing now. Up on the screen, Keanu Reeves said the magic word, and all the pledges, including Benny, hammered another shot. Benny couldn't hold it, though, and neither could Chris. Chris saw the look on Benny's face—the outrage of an entire organism and all its constituent cells—and he remembered his own legs buckling and the release the first wave of nausea gave him, and then he felt nothing more.

All the Delts were swarming the room now, expostulating over this disgusting display, this pathetic showing on the part of a pledge class that wasn't worthy of the name, and hands took hold of Benny and Chris, people shouting and jostling, the whinny of laughter, cries of "Gross!" and "Don't get any of that shit on me, man," the hands finding purchase at armpit and knee. They laid Benny and Chris side by side on Chris' bed, then thundered back down the three flights of stairs to the game room. Half an hour went by and both bottles of Don José were drained by the time anyone thought to look in on them, and another ten minutes elapsed before Dagan Drava, a pre-med student, realized that Chris wasn't breathing.

"So he was drunk," Jimmy told me, the band into their opening number now—blues, they were doing a blues tune that seemed vaguely familiar—"and who hasn't been drunk? I've been drunk a thousand times in my life, you know what I mean? So I figure, all the way up there with Caroline hyperventilating and what-if-ing and driving me half crazy, that we're going to walk into the hospital and he'll be sitting up in bed with a sheepish grin on his face, one hell of a headache, maybe, and a lesson learned, but no harm done."

Jimmy was wrong. His son had choked on his own vomit, inhaled it, compromising his lungs. No one knew how long he'd been lying there in the bed next to Benny Chung without drawing a breath before the E.R. team restarted his heart, and no one was sure of how much damage had been done to his brain functions. A CT scan showed edema of the brain tissue. He was in a coma. A machine was breathing for him. Caroline went after the doctors like an inquisitor, relentless, terrifying in her grief. She stalked the halls, chased them to their cars, harangued them on the phone, demanded—and got—the top neurologist in New England. Chris' eyes never opened. Beneath the lids, like a dirty secret, his pupils dilated to full and fixed there, focused on nothing. Two days later he was dead.

I bought Jimmy a drink, watched myself in the mirror behind the bar. I didn't look like anybody I knew, but there I was, slouched over my elbows and a fresh drink, taking in air and letting it seep back out again. The woman with the deep-dredged laugh was gone. A couple in their twenties had settled into the vacant spot on the other side of Jimmy, oblivious to the drama that had just played out here, the woman perched on the barstool while the man stood in place, rocking in her arms to the beat of the music. The band featured a harp player, and he moved round the confines of the stage like a caged animal, riffling the notes till he went all the way from despair to disbelief and back again, the bass player leaning in as if to brace himself, the guitar rising up slow and mournful out of the stew of the backbeat.

"Hey, don't feel sorry for me," Jimmy said. "I'm out here in California having the time of my life." He pointed a finger at the rain-streaked window. "All this sun really cheers me up."

I don't know why I asked—I was drunk, I guess, feeling maudlin, who knows?—but I said, "You got a place to stay tonight?"

He looked into the shot glass as if he might discover a motel key at the bottom of it. "I'm on sabbatical," he said. "Or on leave, actually. I was staying with my brother—up on Olive Mill?—but he got to be a pain in the ass. Caroline couldn't take it. She's back in New York. At least, I think she is."

"Hard luck," I said, just to say something.

"Oh, yeah," he said, "sure, and that's the long and the short of it. But I tell you, I clean up real nice, and what I plan to do is pick up one of these spare women here, like that one over there—the dye job looks like she just crawled out of a coffin? She'll take me home with her, what you want to bet? And what you want to bet she's got a shower, maybe even a Jacuzzi?"

I didn't want to bet anything. I wanted another drink, that was all. And after that, I wanted to have maybe one more, at this place up the street I'd been to a couple of times, just to see what was happening, because it was Saturday night and you never knew.

A WEEK LATER—it was the next Friday, actually—I went into a place down at the marina for cocktails with a woman I'd almost picked up after I left Jimmy at the steakhouse the previous Saturday. Her name was Steena, she was five-ten, blond, and just getting over a major breakup with a guy named Steve whose name dropped from her lips with the frequency of a speech impediment. She'd agreed to "have a drink" with me, and though I'd hoped for more, I had to assume, after we'd had two glasses each of Piper-Heidsieck at twelve and a half dollars per and a plate of oysters, that I wasn't *her* type either. The whole time she kept glancing at her watch, and finally her cell phone rang and she got up from the table and went out into the anteroom to take the call. It was Steve. She was sorry, but he wanted to meet her later, for dinner, and he sounded so sad and heartbroken and shot through with misery and contrition she couldn't refuse. I had nothing to say. I just stared at her, the plate of desecrated oysters between us. "So," she said, hovering over the table as if she were afraid to sit back down, "I guess I'm going to have to say goodbye. It's been nice, though. Really."

I paid the waitress and moved up to the bar, idly watching the Lakers go through their paces with the sound muted and gazing out the window on the pale bleached forest of the ships' masts gathered there against the night. I was drinking brandy and water, picking through a bowl of artificial snack food and waiting for something to happen, when I ran into the other man I wanted to tell you about. Shaq's monumental head loomed up on the screen and then faded away again, and I turned around and there he was, just settling into the seat beside me. For a minute I thought he was Jimmy—he had the same hangdog look, the rangy height, the air of an athlete gone to seed—and it gave me a start, because the last thing I needed the way I was feeling was another bout of one-way commiseration. He nodded a greeting, then looked up at the screen. "What's the score?"

"The Lakers are killing them," I said. "I think. I'm pretty sure, anyway." But this *was* Jimmy, had to be, Jimmy all dressed up and with his hair combed and looking satisfied with himself. It was then that I remembered the brother. "You wouldn't be Jimmy's brother, would you?" I said. "By any chance?"

"*Whose* brother?"

I felt foolish then. Obviously Jimmy hadn't given me his real name, and why would he? The alcohol bloomed in my brain, petals unfolding like a rosebud in time-lapse photography. "It's nothing," I said, "I just thought . . ." and let it die. I went back to watching the game. Helped myself to the artificial snacks. Had another brandy and water. After a while the man beside me ordered dinner at the bar, and I got into a conversation about recycling and the crime of waste with a startled-looking woman and her martini-fueled husband. Gradually, the bar filled up. The startled-looking woman and her husband went in to dinner and somebody else took their place. Nothing was happening. Absolutely nothing. I was thinking I should move on, pick up a pizza, some take-out, make it an early night, and I could envision myself standing at the supercharged counter of Paniagua's Pizza Palace, where you could get two slices with chorizo and jalapeños for three dollars and fifty cents, but instead I found myself turning to the man on my left. "You do have a brother, though, right?" I said.

He gave me a long, slow, deliberate look, then shrugged. "What, does he owe you money?"

So we talked about Jimmy, Jimmy's tragedy, Jimmy's refusal to accept facts and the way Jimmy was running hard up against the sharp edges of the world and was sure to wind up in a coffin just like his father before him and his son too if he didn't get himself into rehab as his number one priority. Then we talked about me, but I didn't reveal much, and then it was general subjects, the look of the people on TV as opposed to the look of the flesh-and-blood people sitting at the tables at our feet like an undiscovered tribe, and then, inevitably, we came back to alcohol. I told him of some of my escapades, he told me of his. I was probably on my sixth or seventh brandy and water when we got back as far as our mutual childhoods lived mutually under the shadow of booze, though on opposite coasts. The brother was in an expansive mood, his wife and six-year-old daughter gone for the weekend to a Little Miss pageant in Sacramento, and the four walls of his house—or eight or sixteen or however many there were—inadequate to contain him. I took a sip of my drink and let him fly.

He was three years older than Jimmy, and they had two other brothers and a sister, all younger. They moved around a lot as kids, but one winter they were living out in the country in Dutchess County, at the junction of two blacktop roads where there were a handful of summer cabins that had been converted to cheap year-round housing, a two-pump gas station where you could get milk, bread and Coke in the eight-ounce bottle, and a five-stool roadhouse with a jukebox and a griddle called the Pine-Top Tavern. The weather turned nasty, their father was out of work and about a month from bailing out for good, and neither of their parents left the tavern for more than a shower or a shave or to put a couple cans of chicken broth in a saucepan and dump a handful of rice and sliced wieners in on top of it so the kids would have something to eat. Jimmy's brother had a cough that wouldn't go away. Their little sister had burned her arm on the stove trying to make herself a can of tomato soup and the brother had to change her bandage twice a day and rub ointment into the exfoliated skin. Jimmy spent his time out in the weed-blistered lot behind the house, kicking a football as close to vertical as he could, over and over again, then slanting off to retrieve it before it could hit the ground. Their dog—Gomer, named after the TV character—had been killed crossing the road on Christmas Eve, and their father blamed one of the drunks leaving the tavern, but nobody did anything about it.

It was just after Christmas—or maybe after New Year's, because school had started up again—when a cold front came down out of Hudson Bay and froze everything so thoroughly nobody could stand to be out of doors more than five minutes at a time. The birds huddled under the eaves of the tavern, looking distressed; the squirrels hung like ornaments in the stripped trees. Everybody in the family drank hot tea thick with honey and the oily residue of the bitter lemon juice that came out of the plastic squeeze bottle, and that was the only time their hands seemed to warm up. When they went outside, the bare ground crackled underfoot as if it were crusted with snow, and for a few days there none of the converted cabins had water because the lines from the well had frozen underground. Jimmy's brother, though he had a cough that wouldn't go away, had to take a pail across the road to the pond and break the ice to get water for the stove.

He remembered his father, wizened forearms propped up on the bar in a stained khaki parka he'd worn in Korea, a sheaf of hair canted the wrong way because it hadn't seen a comb in days, the smoke of his cigarette fuming in the dark forge of the bar. And his mother, happiest woman in the world, laughing at anything, laughing till all the glasses were drained and the lights went out and the big-bellied bartender with the caved-in face shooed them out the door and locked the place up for the night. It was cold. The space heater did nothing, less than nothing, and Jimmy's brother could have earned his merit badge as a fire-starter that winter because all he did was comb the skeletal forest for fallen branches, rotten stumps and fence posts, anything that would burn, managing to keep at least a continuous smolder going day and night. And then he got up for school one morning and there was an old woman—or a woman his mother's age, anyway—laid out snoring on the couch in front of the fireplace where the dog used to sleep. He went into his parents' room and shook his mother awake. "There's somebody sleeping out there on the couch," he told her, and watched her gather her features together and assess the day. He had to repeat himself twice, the smell of her, of her warmth and the warmth of his father beside her, rising up to him with a sweet-sick odor of sex and infirmity, and then she murmured through her cracked lips, "Oh, that's only Grace. You know Grace—from the tavern? Her car won't start, that's all. Be a good boy, huh, and don't wake her?"

He didn't wake her. He got his brothers and sister out of bed, then huddled with them at the bus stop in the dark, jumping from foot to foot to keep warm and imagining himself on a polar expedition with Amundsen, sled dogs howling at the stars and the ice plates shifting like dominoes beneath their worn and bleeding paws. There was a pot on the stove when he got home from school, some sort of incarnadine stew with a smell of the exotic spices his mother never used—mace, cloves, fennel—and he thought of Grace, with her scraggle of gray-black hair and her face that was like a dried-up field plowed in both directions. He tasted it—they all sampled it, just to see if it was going to be worth eating—and somehow it even managed to taste of Grace, though how could anybody know what Grace tasted like unless they were a cannibal?

His parents weren't at home. They were three hundred feet away, in the tavern, with Grace and the rest of their good-time buddies. A few dispirited snowflakes sifted down out of the sky. He made himself a sandwich of peanut butter and sliced banana, then went into the tavern to see if his parents or anybody else there was in that phase of rhapsodic drunkenness where they gave up their loose change as if they were philanthropists rolling down Park Avenue in an open Rolls-Royce. One guy, hearty, younger than the rest, in a pair of galoshes with the buckles torn off, gave him a fifty-cent piece, and then his father told him to get the hell out of the bar and stay out till he was of legal age or he'd kick his ass for him but good.

The next morning was even colder, and Jimmy's brother was up early, shivering despite the rancid warmth generated by his three brothers and the cheap sleeping bag advertised for comfort even at five below zero, which might as well have been made of shredded newspaper for all the good it did. He put the kettle on to boil so they could have hot tea and instant oatmeal to fortify them out there in the wind while they were waiting for the school bus to come shunting down the hill with its headlights reduced to vestigial eyes and the driver propped up behind the black windshield like a blind cavefish given human form. The house was dark but for the overhead light in the kitchen. There was no sound anywhere, nothing from his parents or his brothers and sister, everybody locked in a sleep that was like a spell in a fairy tale, and he missed the dog then, if only to see it stretch and yawn and nose around in its dish. The kettle came to a boil and he'd actually put three tea bags in the pot and begun pouring the water before he realized that something was wrong. What was it? He strained his ears but there was nothing to hear. Not even the tick of the stove or the creak and whine of the house settling into the cold, no sound of stirring birds or tires revolving on the blacktop road. It was then that he thought to check the time.

There was a clock built into the stove, foreshortened hands painted gold behind a greased-over plastic lens. It read 3:35 A.M. Jimmy's brother could have kicked himself. He sat in the kitchen, shivering, and had a cup of tea, wishing it would snow so they'd call off school and he could sleep all day. After a while he decided to build up the fire in the living room and sit there on the couch and terrify himself with *Dracula*—he was halfway through, though he'd started it at Halloween—and then maybe he'd drift off for a while till it was time to get up. He shrugged into his coat and went to the kitchen door, thinking of the punky wood he and Jimmy had stacked in the shed over the weekend.

But then—and I was ahead of him here, because you'd have to be as blind as a cavefish yourself not to see where this was going—the storm door wouldn't give. There was something there, an immovable shadow stretched long and dark across the doorstep, and it took everything the brother had to wedge the door open enough to squeeze out into the night. And when he did pull himself out into the cold, and the killing, antipathetic breath of it hit him full in the face, he willed the shadow at his feet to take shape until he could distinguish the human form there, with her dried-out skin and fixed eyes and the dirty scraggle of gray-black hair.

"Grace?" I said.

Jimmy's brother nodded.

"Jesus," I said. "And your brother—did he see her there?"

He shrugged. "I don't know. I don't remember. She was a drunk, that was all, just another drunk."

WE SAT FOR A MOMENT, looking past our drinks to the marina and the black unbroken plane of the sea beyond it. I had an impulse to open up to him, to tell him my story, or one of my stories, as if we were clasping hands at an AA meeting, but I didn't. I made a clucking sound, meant to signify sympathy and understanding, threw some money on the bar and went out the door, feeling for my keys. What I didn't tell him, though he might have known it himself, was that Jimmy had put his son in a crematory box at the hospital and he put the box in the back of his Suburban and drove it home and into the garage, and all night, while his wife lay stiff and sedated in the big queen-sized bed upstairs, Jimmy hugged the coffin to him. I didn't tell him that life is a struggle against weakness, fought not in the brain or in the will but in the cells, in the enzymes, in the key the

DNA inserts into the tumbler of our personalities. And I didn't tell him that I had a son myself, just like Jimmy, though I didn't see him as much as I would have wanted to, not anymore.

The fact was that I hadn't wanted a son, hadn't planned on it or asked or prayed or hoped for or even imagined it. I was twenty-four. My wife was pregnant and I raged at her, *Get rid of it, you're ruining my life, we can't afford it, you're crazy, get rid of it, get rid of it.* She was complete in herself, sweet-faced and hard-willed, and mine was a voice she couldn't hear. She went to Lamaze classes, quit drinking, quit smoking, did her exercises, read all the books. My son was born in the Kaiser hospital in Panorama City, eight pounds, six ounces, as healthy as a rat and beautiful in his own way, and I was his father, though I wasn't ready to be. He was nine months old when one of my drinking buddies—call him Chris, why not?—came for the weekend and we went on a tear. My wife put up with it, even joined in a bit, and on Monday morning, when she had to go in early to work, Chris and I took her out for breakfast.

The day beat down like a hammer and everything in the visible world shone as if it had been lit from within. We'd been up till four, and now it was seven, and while we were waiting for a table Chris and I ducked into the men's room and alternated hits from a pint of Smirnoff we were planning to doctor our fresh-squeezed orange juice with. So we were feeling fine as we chased the waffles around our plates and my wife smiled and joked and the baby unfurled his arms and grabbed at things in high baby spirits. Then my wife touched up her makeup and left, and right away the mood changed—here was this baby, my son, with his multiplicity of needs, his diapers and his stroller and all the rest of it, and I was in charge.

We finally hit upon the plan of taking him to the beach, to get a little sun, throw a Frisbee, let the sand mold itself to us through the long, slow-simmering morning and into the afternoon and the barbecue I was planning for Chris' send-off. The beach was deserted, a board-stretched canvas for gulls and pelicans and snapping blue waves, and as soon as we stepped out of the car I felt everything was all right again. My son was wearing nothing but his diaper, and Chris and I were laughing over something, and I tossed my son up in the air, a game we played, and he loved it, squealing and crying out in baby ecstasy. I tossed him again, and then I tossed him to Chris and Chris tossed him back, and that was when I lost my balance and the black sea-honed beak of a half-buried rock loomed up on me and I saw my future in that instant: I was going to drop my son, let him slip through my fingers in a moment of aberration, and he was going to be damaged in a way that nobody could repair.

It didn't happen. I caught him, and held on, and I never let go.

Swept Away

PEOPLE CAN TALK, they can gossip and cavil and run down this one or the other, and certainly we have our faults, our black funks and suicides and crofters' wives running off with the first man who'll have them and a winter's night that stretches on through the days and weeks like a foretaste of the grave, but in the end the only real story here is the wind. The puff and blow of it. The ceaselessness. The squelched keening of air in movement, running with its currents like a new sea clamped atop the old, winnowing, harrowing, pinching everything down to nothing. It rakes the islands day and night, without respect to season, though if you polled the denizens of Yell, Funzie and Papa Stour, to a man, woman, lamb and pony they would account winter the worst for the bite of it and the sheer frenzy of its coming. One January within living memory the wind blew at gale force for twenty-nine days without remit, and on New Year's Eve back in '92 the gusts were estimated at 201 mph at the Muckle Flugga lighthouse here on the northernmost tip of the Isle of Unst. But that was only an estimate: the weather service's wind gauge was torn from its moorings and launched into eternity that day, along with a host of other things, stony and animate alike.

Junie Ooley should have known better. She was an American woman—*the American ornithological woman* is the way people around town came to refer to her, or sometimes just *the bird woman*—and she hadn't just barely alighted from the ferry when she was blindsided by Robbie Baikie's old one-eyed tom, which had been trying to inveigle

itself across the roof tiles of the kirk after an imaginary pigeon. Or perhaps the pigeon wasn't imaginary, but by the time the cat blinked his
eyes whatever he had seen was gone with the wind. At any rate, Junie
Ooley, who was at this juncture a stranger to us all, came banking up
the high street in a store-bought tartan skirt and a pair of black tights
climbing her queenly legs, a rucksack flailing at the small of her back
and both hands clamped firmly to her knit hat, and she never saw the
cat coming, for all her visual acuity and the fine-ground photographic
lenses she trucked with her everywhere. The cat—his name was Tiger
and he must have carried a good ten or twelve pounds of pigeon-fed
flesh on his bones—caught a gust and flew off the kirk tiles like a heat-
seeking missile locked in on Junie Ooley's hunched and flapping form.

The impact was dramatic, as you would have had reason to tes-
tify had you been meditating over a pint of bitter at the rattling window of Magnuson's Pub that day, and the bird woman, before she'd
had a chance even to discover the whereabouts of her lodgings or offer up a "good day" or "how do you do?" to a single soul, was laid out
flat on the flagstones, her lips quivering unconsciously over the lyrics
to a tune by the Artist Formerly Known as Prince. At least that was
what Robbie claimed afterward, and he's always been dead keen on
the Artist, ever since he came by the CD of *Purple Rain* in the used-
disc bin of a record shop in Aberdeen and got it for less than half of
what it would have cost new. We had to take his word for it. He was
the first one out the door and come to her aid.

There she was, flung down on the stones like a wilted flower
amidst the crumpled stalks of her limbs, the rucksack stuffed full of
spare black tights and her bird-watching paraphernalia, her kit and
dental floss and all the rest, and Tiger just pulling himself up into a
ball to blink his eyes and lick at his spanned paws in a distracted way,
when Duncan Stout, ninety-two years on this planet and in possession of the first Morris automobile ever manufactured, came down
the street in that very vehicle at twice his normal speed of five and a
half miles per hour, and if he discerned Junie Ooley lying there it was
anybody's guess. Robbie Baikie flailed his arms to head off Duncan's
car, but Duncan was the last man in these islands to be expecting

anything unexpected out there in the middle of the high street designed and reserved exclusively for the traffic of automobiles and lorries and the occasional dithering bicycle. He kept coming. His jaw was set, the cap pulled down to the orbits of his milk-white eyes. Robbie Baikie was not known for thinking on his feet—like many of us, he was a deliberative type—and by the time he thought to scoop Junie Ooley up in his arms the car was on them. Or just about.

People were shouting from the open door of the pub. Magnus Magnuson himself was in the street now, windmilling his arms and flinging out his feet in alarm, the bar rag still clutched in one hand like a flag of surrender. The car came on. Robbie stood there. Hopeless was the way it looked. But then we hadn't taken the wind into account, and how could any of us have forgotten its caprices, even for a minute? At that crucial instant, a gust came up the canyon of the high street and bowled Robbie Baikie over atop the bird woman even as it lifted the front end of Duncan's car and flung it into the near streetlamp, which never yielded.

The wind skreeled off down the street, carrying bits of paper, cans, bottles, old bones and rags and other refuse along with it. The bird woman's eyes blinked open. Robbie Baikie, all fifteen stone of him, lay pressed atop her in a defensive posture, anticipating the impact of the car, and he hadn't even thought to prop himself on his elbows to take some of the crush off her. Junie Ooley smelled the beer on him and the dulcet smoke of his pipe tobacco and the sweetness of the peat fire at Magnuson's and maybe even something of the sheep he kept, and she couldn't begin to imagine who this man was or what he was doing on top of her in the middle of the public street. "Get off me," she said in a voice so flat and calm Robbie wasn't sure he'd heard it at all, and because she was an American woman and didn't commonly make use of the term "clod," she added, "you big doof."

Robbie was shy with women—we all were, except for the women themselves, and they were shy with the men, at least for the first five years after the wedding—and he was still fumbling with the notion of what had happened to him and to her and to Duncan Stout's automobile and couldn't have said one word even if he'd wanted to.

"Get off," she repeated, and she'd begun to add physical empha-

sis to the imperative, writhing beneath him and bracing her up-
turned palms against the great unmoving slabs of his shoulders.

Robbie went to one knee, then pushed himself up even as the
bird woman rolled out from under him. In the next moment she was
on her feet, angrily shifting the straps of her rucksack where they bit
into the flesh, cursing him softly but emphatically and with a kind
of fluid improvisatory genius that made his face light up in wonder.
Twenty paces away, Duncan was trying to extricate himself from his
car, but the wind wouldn't let him. Howith Clarke, the greengrocer,
was out in the street now, surveying the damage with a sour face, and
Magnus was right there in the middle of things, his voice gone hoarse
with excitement. He was inquiring after Junie Ooley's condition—
"Are you all right, lass?"—when a gust lifted all four of them off their
feet and sent them tumbling like ninepins. That was enough for
Robbie. He picked himself up, took hold of the bird woman's arm
and frog-marched her into the pub.

In they came, and the wind with them, packets of crisps and beer
coasters sailing across the polished surface of the bar, and all of us instinctively grabbing for our hats. Robbie's head was bowed and his
hair blown straight up off his crown as if it had been done up in
a perm by some mad cosmetologist, and Junie Ooley heaving and
thrashing against him till he released her to spin away from him and
down the length of the bar. No one could see how pretty she was at
first, her face all deformed with surprise and rage and the petulant
crease stamped between her eyes. She didn't even so much as look in
our direction, but just threw herself back at Robbie and gave him a
shove as if they were children at war on the playground.

"What the hell do you think you're doing?" she demanded, her
voice piping high with her agitation. And then, glancing round at
the rest of us: "Did you see what this big *idiot* did to me out there?"

No one said a word. The smoke of the peat fire hung round us
like a thin curtain. Tim Maconochie's Airedale lifted his head from
the floor and laid it back down again.

The bird woman clenched her teeth, set her shoulders. "Well,
isn't anybody going to do anything?"

Magnus was the one to break the silence. He'd slipped back in behind the bar, unmindful of the chaff and bits of this and that that the wind had deposited in his hair. "The man saved your life, that's about all."

Robbie ducked his head out of modesty. His ears went crimson.

"Saved—?" A species of comprehension settled into her eyes. "I was . . . something hit me, something the wind blew . . ."

Tim Maconochie, though he wasn't any less tightfisted than the rest of us, cleared his throat and offered to buy the girl a drop of whisky to clear her head, and her face opened up then like the sun coming through the clouds so that we all had a good look at the beauty of her, and it was a beauty that made us glad to be alive in that moment to witness it. Whiskies went round. A blast of wind rattled the panes till we thought they would burst. Someone led Duncan in and sat him down in the corner with his pipe and a pint of ale. And then there was another round, and another, and all the while Junie Ooley was perched on a stool at the bar talking Robbie Baikie's big glowing ears right off him.

THAT WAS THE BEGINNING of a romance that stood the whole island on its head. Nobody had seen anything like it, at least since the two maundering teens from Cullivoe had drowned themselves in a suicide pact in the Ness of Houlland, and it was the more surprising because no one had ever suspected such depths of passion in a poor slug like Robbie Baikie. Robbie wasn't past thirty, but it was lassitude and the brick wall of introspection that made him sit at the bar till he carried the weight of a man twice his age, and none of us could remember him in the company of a woman, not since his mother died, anyway. He was the sort to let his sheep feed on the blighted tops of the heather and the wrack that blew up out of the sea and he kept his heart closed up like a lockbox. And now, all of a sudden, right before our eyes, he was a man transformed. That first night he led Junie Ooley up the street to her lodgings like a gallant out of the picture films, the two of them holding hands and leaning into the wind while cats and flowerpots and small children flew past them, and it seemed he was never away from her for five minutes consecutive after that.

He drove her all the wind-blasted way out to the bird sanctuary at Herma Ness and helped her set up her equipment in an abandoned crofter's cottage of such ancient provenance that not even Duncan Stout could say who the landlord might once have been. The cottage had a thatched roof, and though it was rotted through in half a dozen places and perfervid with the little lives of crawling things and rodents, she didn't seem particular. It was in the right place, on a broad barren moor that fell off into the sea amongst the cliffs where the birds made their nests, and that was all that mattered.

There was no fuss about Junie Ooley. She was her own woman, and no doubt about it. She'd come to see and study the flocks that gathered there in the spring—the kittiwakes, the puffins, terns and northern fulmars nesting the high ledges and spreading wide their wings to cruise out over the sea—and she had her array of cameras and telephoto lenses with her to take her photographs for the pricey high-grade magazines. If she had to rough it, she was prepared. There were the cynical amongst us who thought she was just making use of Robbie Baikie for the convenience of his Toyota minivan and the all-purpose, wraparound warmth of him, and there was no end to the gossip of the biddies and the potboilers and the kind who wouldn't know a good thing if it fell down out of Heaven and conked them on the head, but there were those who saw it for what it was: love, pure and simple.

IF ROBBIE NEVER much bothered about the moorits and Cheviots his poor dead and buried father had bred up over the years, now he positively neglected them. If he lost six Blackface ewes stranded by the tide or a Leicester tup caught on a bit of wire in his own yard, he never knew it. He was too busy elsewhere. The two of them—he and the bird woman—would be gone for a week at a time, scrabbling over the rock faces that dropped down to the sea, she with her cameras, he with the rucksack and lenses and the black bottles of stout and smoked-tongue sandwiches, and when we did see them in town they were either taking tea at the hotel or holding hands in the back nook of the pub. They scandalized Mrs. Dunwoodie, who let her rooms over the butcher's shop to Junie Ooley on a monthly basis, because she'd seen Robbie coming down the stairs with the girl on more than one occasion and once in the night heard what could only have been the chirps and muffled cries of coital transport drifting down from above. And a Haroldswick man—we won't name him here, for decency's sake—even claims that he saw the two of them cavorting in the altogether outside the stone cottage at Herma Ness.

One night when the wind was up they lingered in Magnuson's past the dinner hour, murmuring to each other in a soft indistinguishable fusion of voices, and Robbie drinking steadily, pints and whiskies both. We watched him rise for another round, then weave his way back to the table where she awaited him, a pint clutched in each of his big red hands. "You know what we say this time of year when the kittiwakes first return to us?" he asked her, his voice booming out suddenly and his face aflame with the drink and the very joy of her presence.

Conversations died. People looked up. He handed her the beer and she gave him a sweet inquisitive smile and we all wished the smile was for us and maybe we begrudged him it just the smallest bit. He spread his arms and recited a little poem for her, a poem we all knew as well as we knew our own names, the heart stirrings of an anonymous bird lover lost now to the architecture of time:

> Peerie mootie! Peerie mootie!
> O, du love, du joy, du Beauty!
> Whaar is du came frae? Whaar is du been?
> Wi di swittlin feet and di glitterin een?

It was startling to hear these sentiments from Robbie Baikie, a man's man who was hard even where he was soft, a man not given to maundering, and we all knew then just how far overboard he'd gone. Love was one thing—a rose blooming atop a prickly stem risen up out of the poor soil of these windswept islands, and it was a necessary thing, to be nourished, surely—but this was something else altogether. This was a kind of fealty, a slavery, a doom—he'd given her *our* poem, and in public no less—and we all shuddered to look on it.

"Robbie," Magnus cried out in a desperation that spoke for us all, "Robbie, let me stand you a drop of whisky, lad," but if Robbie heard him, he gave no sign of it. He took the bird woman's hand, a little bunch of chapped and wind-blistered knuckles, and brought it to his lips. "That's the way I feel about you," he said, and we all heard it.

IT WOULD BE USELESS to deny that we were all just waiting for the other shoe to drop. There was something inhuman in a passion so intense as that—it was a rabbity love, a tup's love, and it was bound to come crashing down to earth, just as the Artist lamented so memorably in "When Doves Cry." There were some of us who wondered if Robbie even listened to his own CDs anymore. Or heeded them.

And then, on a gloomy gray dour day with the wind sitting in the north and the temperatures threatening to take us all the way back to the doorstep of winter again, Robbie came thundering through the front door of the pub in a hurricane of flailing leaves, thistles, matchbooks and fish-and-chips papers and went straight to the bar for a double whisky. It was the first time since the ornithological woman had appeared amongst us that anyone had seen him alone, and if that wasn't sign enough, there were those who could divine by the way he held himself and the particular roseate hue of his ears that the end had come. He drank steadily for an hour or two, deflecting any and all comments—even the most innocuous observations about the weather—with a grunt or even a snarl. We gave him his space and sat at the window to watch the world tumble by.

Late in the day, the light of the westering sun slanted through the glass, picking out the shadow of the mullions, and for a moment it laid the glowing cross of our Saviour in the precise spot where Robbie's shoulder blades conjoined. He heaved a sigh then—a roaring, single-malt, tobacco-inflected groan it was, actually—and finally those massive shoulders began to quake and heave. The barmaid (Rose Ellen MacGooch, Donal MacGooch's youngest) laid a hand on his forearm and asked him what the matter was, though we all knew. People made their voices heard so he wouldn't think we were holding our breath; Magnus made a show of lighting his pipe at the far end of the bar; Tim Maconochie's dog let out an audible fart. A calm settled over the pub, and Robbie Baikie exhaled and delivered up the news in a voice that was like a scouring pad.

He'd asked her to marry him. Up there, in the crofter's hut, the wind keening and the kittiwakes sailing through the air like great overblown flakes of snow. They'd been out all morning, scaling the cliffs with numb hands, fighting the wind, and now they were sharing a sandwich and the stout over a turf fire. Robbie had kissed her, a long, lingering lover's kiss, and then, overcome by the emotion of the moment, he'd popped the question. Junie Ooley had drawn herself up, the eyes shining in her heaven-sent face, and told him she was flattered by the proposal, flattered and moved, deeply moved, but that she just wasn't ready to commit to something like that, like marriage, that is, what with him being a Shetland sheepman and she an American woman with a college degree and a rover at that. Would he come with her to Patagonia to photograph the *chimango* and the *ñandú*? Or to the Okefenokee Swamp in search of the elusive ivory bill? To Singapore? São Paolo? Even Edinburgh? He said he would. She called him a liar. And then they were shouting and she was out in the wind, her knit cap torn from her head in a blink and her hair beating mad at her green eyes, and he tried to pull her to him, to snatch her arm and hold her, but she was already at the brink of the cliff, already edging her way down amidst the fecal reek and the raucous avian cries. "Junie!" he shouted. "Junie, take my hand, you'll lose your balance in this wind, you know you will! Take my hand!"

And what did she say then? "I don't need any man to cling to." That was it. All she said and all she wrote. And he stood in the blast, watching her work her way from one handhold to another out over the yawning sea as the birds careened round her and her hair strangled her face, and then he strode back to the minivan, fired up the engine, and drove back into town.

THAT NIGHT THE WIND soughed and keened and rattled like a set of pipes through the canyon of the high street on till midnight or so, and then it came at us with a new sound, a sound people hadn't heard in these parts since '92. It was blowing a gale. Shingles fled before the gusts, shrubs gave up their grip on the earth, the sheep in the fields were snatched up and flung across the countryside like so many puffs of lint. Garages collapsed, bicycles raced down the street with no more than a ghost at the pedals. Robbie was unconscious in the sitting room of his cottage at the time, sad victim of drink and sorrow. He'd come home from the pub before the wind rose up in its fury, boiled himself a plate of liver muggies, then conked out in front of the telly before he could so much as lift a fork to them.

It was something striking the side of the house that brought him to his senses. He woke to darkness, the electric gone with the first furious gusts, and at first he didn't know where he was. Then the house shuddered again and the startled bellow of the Ayrshire cow he kept for her milk and butter roused him up out of the easy chair and he went to the door and stuck his head out into that wild night. Immediately the door was torn from his grasp, straining back on its hinges with a shriek even as the pale form of the cow shot past and rose up to tear away like a cloud over the shingles of the roof. He had one thought then, and one thought only: *Junie. Junie needs me.*

It was his luck that he carried five hundred pounds of coal in the back of his minivan as ballast, as so many of us do, because without it he'd never have kept the thing to the road. As it was, he had to dodge the hurtling sheep, rabbits that flew out of the shadows like nightjars, posts torn from their moorings, the odd roof or wall, even a boat or two lashed up out of the heaving seas. He could barely see the road for the blowing trash, the wind slammed at him like a fist and he had to fight the wheel to keep the car from flipping end over end. If he was half-looped still when he climbed into the car, now he was as sober as a foude, all the alcohol burned away in his veins with the terrible anxiety that drove him. He put his foot to the floor. He could only pray that he wouldn't be too late.

Then he was there, fighting his way out of the car, and he had to hold to the door to keep from being blown away himself. The moor was as black as the hide of an Angus bull. The wind shrieked in every passage, scouring the heather till it lay flat and cried out its agony. He could hear the sea battering the cliffs below. It was then that the door of the minivan gave way and in the next instant he was coasting out over the scrub like a tobogganer hurtling down Burrafirth Hill, and there'll be men to tell you it was a tree saved him from going over, but what tree could grow on an island as stingy as this? It was a thornbush is what it was, a toughened black unforgiving snarl of woody pith combed down to the ground with fifty years of buffeting, but it was enough. The shining white door of the minivan ran out to sea as if it would run forever, an awkward big plate of steel that might as well have been a Frisbee sailing out over the waves, but Robbie Baikie was saved, though the thorns dug into his hands and the wind took the hair off his head and flailed the beard from his cheeks. He squinted against it, against the airborne dirt and the darkness, and there it was, two hundred yards away and off behind him to the left: the crofter's cottage, and with her in it. "Junie!" he cried, but the wind beat at the sound of his voice and carried it away till it was no voice at all. "Junie!"

As for her, the bird woman, the American girl with the legs that took the breath out of you and the face and figure that were as near perfection as any man here had ever dreamed of on the best night of his life, she never knew Robbie had come for her. What she did know was that the wind was bad. Very bad. She must have struggled against it and realized how futile it was to do anything more than to succumb to it, to huddle and cling and wait it out. Where were the birds? she wondered. How would they weather this—on their wings? Out at sea? She was cold, shivering, the fire long since consumed by the gusts that tore at the chimney. And then the chimney went, with a sound of claws raking at a windowpane. There was a crack, and the roof beams gave way, and then it was the night staring down at her from above. She clung to the andirons, but the andirons blew away, and then she clung to the stones of the hearth but the stones were swept away as if they were nothing more than motes of dust, and what was she supposed to cling to then?

We never found her. Nobody did. There are some who'll say she was swept all the way to the coast of Norway and came ashore speaking Norse like a native or that a ship's captain, battened down in a storm-sea, found her curled round the pocked safety glass of the bridge like a living figurehead, but no one really believes it. Robbie

Baikie survived the night and he survived the mourning of her too. He sits even now over his pint and his drop of whisky in the back nook at Magnuson's, and if anybody should ask him about the only love of his life, the bird woman from America, he'll tell you he's heard her voice in the cries of the kittiwakes that swarm the skies in spring, and seen her face there too, hanging over the black crashing sea on the stiff white wings of a bird. Poor Robbie.

Dogology

IT WAS THE SEASON of mud, drainpipes drooling, the gutters clogged with debris, a battered and penitential robin fixed like a statue on every lawn. Julian was up early, a Saturday morning, beating eggs with a whisk and gazing idly out the kitchen window and into the colorless hide of the day, expecting nothing, when all at once the scrim of rain parted to reveal a dark, crouching presence in the far corner of the yard. At first glance, he took it to be a dog—a town ordinance he particularly detested disallowed fences higher than three feet, and so the contiguous lawns and flowerbeds of the neighborhood had become a sort of open savanna for roaming packs of dogs—but before the wind shifted and the needling rain closed in again, he saw that he was wrong. This figure, partially obscured by the resurgent forsythia bush, seemed out of proportion, all limbs, as if a dog had been mated with a monkey. And what was it, then? Raccoons had been at the trash lately, and he'd seen a opossum wavering down the street like a pale ghost one late night after a dreary overwrought movie Cara had insisted upon, but this was no opossum. Or raccoon either. It was dark in color, whatever it was—a bear, maybe, a yearling strayed down from the high ridges along the river, and hadn't Ben Ober told him somebody on F Street had found a bear in their swimming pool? He put down the whisk and went to fetch his glasses.

A sudden eruption of thunder set the dishes rattling on the drain-board, followed by an uncertain flicker of light that illuminated the dark room as if the bulb in the overhead fixture had gone loose in the socket. He wondered how Cara could sleep through all this, but the wonder was short-lived, because he really didn't give a damn one way or the other if she slept all day, all night, all week. Better she should sleep and give him some peace. He was in the living room now, the gloom ladled over everything, shadows leeching into black holes behind the leather couch and matching armchairs, the rubber plant a dark ladder in the corner and the shadowy fingers of the pot-ted palms reaching out for nothing. The thunder rolled again, the lightning flashed. His glasses were atop the TV, where he'd left them the night before while watching a sorry documentary about the chil-dren purportedly raised by wolves in India back in the nineteen twenties, two stringy girls in sepia photographs that revealed little and could have been faked in any case. He put his glasses on and padded back into the kitchen in his stocking feet, already having for-gotten why he'd gone to get them in the first place. Then he saw the whisk in a puddle of beaten egg on the counter, remembered, and peered out the window again.

The sight of the three dogs there—a pair of clownish chows and what looked to be a shepherd mix—did nothing but irritate him. He recognized this trio—they were the advance guard of the dog army that dropped their excrement all over the lawn, dug up his flower-beds, and, when he tried to shoo them, looked right through him as if he didn't exist. It wasn't that he had anything against dogs per se—it was their destructiveness he objected to, their arrogance, as if they owned the whole world and it was their privilege to do as they liked with it. He was about to step to the back door and chase them off, when the figure he'd first seen—the shadow beneath the for-sythia bush—suddenly emerged. It was no animal, he realized with a shock, but a woman, a young woman dressed all in black, with her black hair hanging wet in her face and the clothes stuck to her like a second skin, down on all fours like a dog herself, sniffing. He was dumbfounded. As stunned and amazed as if someone had just stepped into the kitchen and slapped him till his head rolled back on his shoulders.

He'd been aware of the rumors—there was a new couple in the neighborhood, over on F Street, and the woman was a little strange, dashing through people's yards at any hour of the day or night, baying at the moon and showing her teeth to anyone who got in her way—but he'd dismissed them as some sort of suburban legend. Yet here she was, in his yard, violating his privacy, in the company of a pack of dogs he'd like to see shot—and their owners too. He didn't know what to do. He was frozen there in his own kitchen, shadows undermining the flicker of the fluorescent tubes he'd installed over the counters, the omelet pan sending up a metallic stink of incineration. And then the three dogs lifted their heads as if they'd heard something in the distance, the thunder boomed overhead, and suddenly they leapt the fence in tandem and were gone. The woman rose up out of the mud at this point—she was wearing a sodden turtleneck, jeans, a watch cap—locked eyes with him across the expanse of the rain-screened yard for just an instant, or maybe he was imagining this part of it, and then she turned and took the fence in a single bound, vanishing into the rain.

CYNOMORPH

WHATEVER IT WAS they'd heard, it wasn't available to her, though she'd been trying to train her hearing away from the ceaseless clatter of the mechanical and tune it to the finer things, the wind stirring in the grass, the alarm call of a fallen nestling, the faintest sliver of a whimper from the dog three houses over, begging to be let out. And her nose. She'd made a point of sticking it in anything the dogs did, breathing deep of it, rebooting the olfactory receptors of a brain that had been deadened by perfume and underarm deodorant and all the other stifling odors of civilization. Every smell was a discovery, and every dog discovered more of the world in ten minutes running loose than a human being would discover in ten years of sitting behind the wheel of a car or standing at the lunch counter in a deli or even hiking the Alps. What she was doing, or attempting to do, was nothing short of reordering her senses so that she could think like a dog and interpret the whole world—not just the human world—as dogs did.

Why? Because no one had ever done it before. Whole hordes wanted to be primatologists or climb into speedboats and study whales and dolphins or cruise the veldt in a Land Rover to watch the lions suckle their young beneath the baobabs, but none of them gave a second thought to dogs. Dogs were beneath them. Dogs were common, pedestrian, no more exotic than the housefly or the Norway rat. Well, she was going to change all that. Or at least that was what she'd told herself after the graduate committee rejected her thesis, but that was a long time ago now—two years and more—and the door was rapidly closing on it.

But here she was moving again, and movement was good, it was her essence: up over the fence and into the next yard, dodging a clothesline, a cooking grill, a plastic trike, a sandbox, reminding herself always to keep her head down and go quadrupedal whenever possible, because how else was she going to hear, smell and see as the dogs did? Another fence, and there, at the far end of the yard, a shed, and the dense rust-colored tails of the chows wagging. The rain spat in her face, relentless. It had been coming down steadily most of the night, and now it seemed even heavier, as if it meant to drive her back indoors where she belonged. Lightning forked overhead. There was a rumble of thunder. She was shivering—had been shivering for the past hour, shivering so hard she thought her teeth were coming loose—and as she ran, doubled over in a crouch, she pumped her knees and flapped her arms in an attempt to generate some heat.

And what were the dogs onto now? She saw the one she called Barely disappear behind the shed and snake back out again, her tail rigid, sniffing now, barking, and suddenly they were all barking— the two chows and the semi-shepherd she'd named Factitious because he was such a sham, pretending he was a rover when he never strayed more than five blocks from his house on E Street. There was a smell of freshly turned earth, of compost and wood ash, of the half-drowned worms Snout the Afghan loved to gobble up off the pavement. She glanced toward the locked gray vault of the house, concerned that the noise would alert whoever lived here, but it was early yet, no lights on, no sign of activity. The dogs' bodies moiled. The barking went up a notch. She ran, hunched at the waist, hurrying.

And then, out of the corner of her eye, she caught a glimpse of A.1., the big-shouldered husky who'd earned his name by consuming half a bottle of steak sauce beside an overturned trash can one bright January morning. He was running—but where had he come from? She hadn't seen him all night and assumed he'd been wandering out at the limits of his range, over in Bethel or Georgetown. She watched him streak across the yard, ears pinned back, head low, her path converging on his until he disappeared behind the shed. Angling round the back of the thing—it was aluminum, one of those prefab articles they sell in the big warehouse stores—she found the compost pile her nose had alerted her to (good, good: she was improving) and a tower of old wicker chairs stacked up six feet high. A.1. never hesitated. He surged in at the base of the tower, his jaws snapping, and the second chow, the one she called Decidedly, was right behind him—and then she saw: there was something under there, a face with incendiary eyes, and it was growling for its life in a thin continuous whine that might have been the drone of a model airplane buzzing overhead.

What was it? She crouched low, came in close. A straggler appeared suddenly, a fluid sifting from the blind side of the back fence to the yard—it was Snout, gangly, goofy, the fastest dog in the neighborhood and the widest ranger, A.1.'s wife and the mother of his dispersed pups. And then all five of the dogs went in for the kill.

The thunder rolled again, concentrating the moment, and she got her first clear look: cream-colored fur, naked pink toes, a flash of teeth and burdened gums. It was a opossum, unlucky, doomed, caught out while creeping back to its nest on soft marsupial feet after a night of foraging among the trash cans. There was a roil of dogs, no barking now, just the persistent unraveling growls that were like curses, and the first splintering crunch of bone. The tower of wicker came down with a clatter, chairs upended and scattered, and the dogs hardly noticed. She glanced around her in alarm, but there was nobody to be seen, nothing moving but the million silver drill bits of the rain boring into the ground. Just as the next flash of lightning lit the sky, A.1. backed out from under the tumble of chairs with the carcass clenched in his jaws, furiously shaking it to snap a neck that was already two or three times broken, and she was startled to see how big the thing was—twenty pounds of meat, gristle, bone and hair, twenty pounds at least. He shook it again, then dropped it at his wife's feet as an offering. It lay still, the other dogs extending their snouts to sniff at it dispassionately, and they were scientists themselves, studying and measuring, remembering. And when the hairless pink young emerged from the pouch, she tried not to feel anything as the dogs snapped them up one by one.

CARA

"You MEAN you didn't confront her?"

Cara was in her royal purple robe—her "wrapper," as she insisted on calling it, as if they were at a country manor in the Cotswolds entertaining Lord and Lady Muckbright instead of in a tract house in suburban Connecticut—and she'd paused with a forkful of mushroom omelet halfway to her mouth. She was on her third cup of coffee and wearing her combative look.

"Confront her? I barely had time to recognize she was human." He was at the sink, scrubbing the omelet pan, and he paused to look bitterly out into the gray vacancy of the yard. "What did you expect me to do, chase her down? Make a citizen's arrest? What?"

The sound of Cara buttering her toast—she might have been flaying the flesh from a bone—set his teeth on edge. "I don't know," she said, "but we can't just have strangers lurking around any time they feel like it, can we? I mean, there are *laws*—"

"The way you talk you'd think I invited her. You think I like mental cases peeping in the window so I can't even have a moment's peace in my own house? On a Saturday morning, no less?"

"So do something."

"What? You tell me."

"Call the police, why don't you? That should be obvious, shouldn't it? And that's another thing—"

"I thought she was a bear."

"A bear? What, are you out of your mind? Are you drunk or something? A bear? I've never heard anything so asinine."

That was when the telephone rang. It was Ben Ober, his voice scraping through the wires like a set of hard chitinous claws scrabbling against the side of the house. "Julian?" he shouted. "Julian?"

Julian reassured him. "Yeah," he said, "it's me. I'm here."

"Can you hear me?"

"I can hear you."

"Listen, she's out in my yard right now, out behind the shed with a, I don't know, some kind of wolf it looks like, and that Afghan nobody seems to know who's the owner of—"

"Who?" he said, but even as he said it he knew. "Who're you talking about?"

"The dog woman." There was a pause, and Julian could hear him breathing into the mouthpiece as if he were deep underwater. "She seems to be—I think she's killing something out there."

THE WOLF CHILDREN OF MAYURBHANJ

IT WAS HIGH SUMMER, just before the rains set in, and the bush had shriveled back under the sun till you could see up the skirts of the sal trees, and all that had been hidden was revealed. People began to talk of a disturbing presence in the jungle outside of the tiny village of Godamuri in Mayurbhanj district, of a *bhut*, or spirit, sent to punish them for their refusal to honor the authority of the maharaja. This thing had been twice seen in the company of a wolf, a vague pale slash of movement in the incrassating twilight, and it was no wolf itself, of that the eyewitnesses were certain. Then came the rumor that there were two of them, quick, nasty, bloodless things of the night, and that their eyes flamed with an infernal heat that incinerated anyone who looked into them, and panic gripped the countryside. Mothers kept their children close, fires burned in the night. Then, finally, came the news that these things were concrete and actual and no mere figments of the imagination: their den—the demons' den itself—had been found in an abandoned termitarium in the dense jungle seven miles south of the village.

The rumors reached the Reverend J. A. L. Singh, of the Anglican mission and orphanage at Midnapore, and in September, after the monsoon clouds had peeled back from the skies and the rivers had receded, he made the long journey to Godamuri by bullock cart. One of his converts, a Kora tribesman by the name of Chunarem, who was prominent in the area, led him to the site. There, the Reverend, an astute and observant man and an amateur hunter acquainted with the habits of beasts, saw evidence of canine occupation of the termite mound—droppings, bones, tunnels of ingress and egress—and instructed that a *machan* be built in an overspreading tree nearby. Armed with his dependable twenty-bore Westley Richards rifle, the Reverend sat breathlessly in the *machan* and concentrated his field glasses on the main entrance to the den. The Reverend Singh was not one to believe in ghosts, other than the Holy Spirit, perhaps, and he expected nothing more remarkable than an albino wolf or perhaps a sloth bear gone white with age or dietary deficiency.

Dusk filtered up from the forest floor. Shadows pooled in the undergrowth, and then an early moon rose up pregnant from the horizon to soften them. Langurs whooped in the near distance, cicadas buzzed, a hundred species of beetles, moths and biting insects flapped round the Reverend's ears, but he held rigid and silent, his binoculars fixed on the entrance to the mound. And then suddenly a shape emerged, the triangular head of a wolf, followed by a smaller canine head and then something else altogether, with a neatly rounded cranium and foreshortened face. The wolf—the dam—stretched herself and slunk off into the undergrowth, followed by a pair of wolf cubs and the two other creatures, which were too long-legged and rangy to be canids; that was clear at a glance. Monkeys, the Reverend thought at first, or apes of some sort. But then, even though they were moving swiftly on all fours, the Reverend could see, to his amazement, that these weren't monkeys at all, or wolves or ghosts either.

DENNING

SHE NO LONGER BOTHERED with a notepad or the pocket tape recorder she'd once used to document the telling yip or strident howl. These were the accoutrements of civilization, and civilization got in the way of the kind of freedom she required if she was ever going to break loose of the constraints that had shackled field biologists from the beginning. Even her clothes seemed to get in the way, but she was sensible enough of the laws of the community to understand that they were necessary, at least for now. Still, she made a point of wearing the same things continuously for weeks on end—sans underwear or socks—in the expectation that her scent would invest them, and the scent of the pack too. How could she hope to gain their confidence if she smelled like the prize inside a box of detergent?

One afternoon toward the end of March, as she lay stretched out beneath a weak pale disc of a sun, trying to ignore the cold breeze and concentrate on the doings of the pack—they were excavating a den in the vacant quadrangle of former dairy pasture that was soon to become the J and K blocks of the ever-expanding development— she heard a car slow on the street a hundred yards distant and lifted her head lazily, as the dogs did, to investigate. It had been a quiet morning and a quieter afternoon, A.1. and Snout, as the alpha couple, looking on placidly as Decidedly, Barely and Factitious alternated the digging and a bulldog from B Street she hadn't yet named lay drooling in the dark wet earth that flew from the lip of the burrow. Snout had been chasing cars off and on all morning—to the dogs, automobiles were animate and ungovernable, big unruly ungulates that needed to be curtailed—and she guessed that the fortyish man climbing out of the sedan and working his tentative way across the lot had come to complain, because that was all her neighbors ever did: complain.

And that was a shame. She really didn't feel like getting into all that right now—explaining herself, defending the dogs, justifying, forever justifying—because for once she'd gotten into the rhythm of dogdom, found her way to the sacred place where to lie flat in the sun and breathe in the scents of fresh earth, dung, sprouting grass, was enough of an accomplishment for an entire day. Children were in school, adults at work. Peace reigned over the neighborhood. For the dogs—and for her too—this was bliss. Hominids had to keep busy, make a buck, put two sticks together, order and structure and *complain,* but canids could know contentment—and so could she if she could only penetrate deep enough.

Two shoes had arrived now. Loafers, buffed to brilliance and decorated with matching tassels of stripped hide. They'd come to rest on a trampled mound of fresh earth no more than twenty-four inches from her nose. She tried to ignore them, but there was a bright smear of mud or excrement gleaming on the toe of the left one; it *was* excrement, dog—the merest sniff told her that—and she was intrigued despite herself, though she refused to lift her eyes. And then a man's voice was speaking from somewhere high above the shoes, so high up and resonant with authority it might have been the voice of the alpha dog of all alpha dogs—God Himself.

The tone of the voice, but not the sense of it, appealed to the dogs, and the bulldog, who was present and accounted for because Snout was in heat, hence the den, ambled over to gaze up at the trousered legs in lovesick awe. "You know," the voice was saying, "you've really got the neighborhood in an uproar, and I'm sure you have your reasons, and I know these dogs aren't yours—" The voice faltered. "But Ben Ober—you know Ben Ober? Over on C Street?—well, he's claiming you're killing rabbits or something. Or you were. Last Saturday. Out on his lawn?" Another pause. "Remember, it was raining?"

A month back—two weeks ago, even—she would have felt obligated to explain herself, would have soothed and mollified and dredged up a battery of behavioral terms—proximate causation, copulation solicitation, naturalistic fallacy—to cow him, but today, under the pale sun, in the company of the pack, she just couldn't seem to muster the energy. She might have grunted—or maybe that was only the sound of her stomach rumbling. She couldn't remember when she'd eaten last.

The cuffs of the man's trousers were stiffly pressed into jutting cotton prows, perfectly aligned. The bulldog began to lick at first one, then the other. There was the faintest creak of tendon and patella, and two knees presented themselves, and then a fist, pressed to the earth for balance. She saw a crisp white strip of shirt cuff, the gold flash of watch and wedding band.

"Listen," he said, "I don't mean to stick my nose in where it's not wanted, and I'm sure you have your reasons for, for"—the knuckles retrenched to balance the movement of his upper body, a swing of the arm perhaps, or a jerk of the head—"all this. I'd just say live and let live, but I can't. And you know why not?"

She didn't answer, though she was on the verge—there was something about his voice that was magnetic, as if it could adhere to her and pull her to her feet again—but the bulldog distracted her. He'd gone up on his hind legs with a look of unfocused joy and begun humping the near leg of the man who belonged to the loafers, and her flash of epiphany deafened her to what he was saying. The bulldog had revealed his name to her: from now on she would know him as Humper.

"Because you upset my wife. You were out in our yard and I, she— Oh, Christ," he said, "I'm going about this all wrong. Look, let me introduce myself—I'm Julian Fox. We live on B Street, 2236? We never got to meet your husband and you when you moved in, I mean, the development's got so big—and impersonal, I guess—we never got the chance. But if you ever want to stop by, maybe for tea, a drink— the two of you, I mean—that would be, well, that would be great."

A DRINK ON B STREET

SHE WAS UPRIGHT and smiling, though her posture was terrible and she carried her own smell with her into the sterile sanctum of the house. He caught it immediately, unmistakably, and so did Cara, judging from the look on her face as she took the girl's hand. It was as if a breeze had wafted up from the bog they were draining over on G Street to make way for the tennis courts; the door stood open, and here was a raw infusion of the wild. Or the kennel. That was Cara's take on it, delivered in a stage whisper on the far side of the swing-ing doors to the kitchen as she fussed with the hors d'oeuvres and he poured vodka for the husband and tap water for the girl: *She smells like she's been sleeping in a kennel.* When he handed her the glass, he saw that there was dirt under her nails. Her hair shone with grease and there were bits of fluff or lint or something flecking the coils of it where it lay massed on her shoulders. Cara tried to draw her into small talk, but she wouldn't draw—she just kept nodding and smil-ing till the smile had nothing of greeting or joy left in it.

Cara had got their number from Bea Chiavone, who knew more about the business of her neighbors than a confessor, and one night last week she'd got through to the husband, who said his wife was out—which came as no surprise—but Cara had kept him on the line for a good ten minutes, digging for all she was worth, until he finally accepted the invitation to their "little cocktail party." Julian was doubt-ful, but before he'd had a chance to comb his hair or get his jacket on, the bell was ringing and there they were, the two of them, arm in arm on the doormat, half an hour early.

The husband, Don, was acceptable enough. Early thirties, bit of a paunch, his hair gone in a tonsure. He was a computer engineer. Worked for IBM. "Really?" Julian said. "Well, you must know Char-lie Hsiu, then—he's at the Yorktown office?"

Don gave him a blank look.

"He lives just up the street. I mean, I could give him a call, if, if—" He never finished the thought. Cara had gone to the door to greet Ben and Julie Ober, and the girl, left alone, had migrated to the corner by the rubber plant, where she seemed to be bent over now, sniffing at the potting soil. He tried not to stare—tried to hold the husband's eye and absorb what the husband was saying about interoffice poli-tics and his own role on the research end of things ("I guess I'm what you'd call the ultimate computer geek, never really get away from the monitor long enough to put a name to a face")—but he couldn't help stealing a glance under cover of the Obers' entrance. Ben was glad-handing, his voice booming, Cara was cooing something to Julie, and the girl (the husband had introduced her as Cynthia, but she'd murmured, "Call me C.f., capital C, lowercase f") had gone down on her knees beside the plant. He saw her wet a finger, dip it into the soil and bring it to her mouth.

While the La Portes—Cara's friends, dull as woodchips—came smirking through the door, expecting a freak show, Julian tipped back his glass and crossed the room to the girl. She was intent on the plant, rotating the terra-cotta pot to examine the saucer beneath it, on all fours now, her face close to the carpet. He cleared his throat, but she didn't respond. He watched the back of her head a moment, struck by the way her hair curtained her face and spilled down the rigid struts of her arms. She was dressed all in black, in a ribbed turtleneck, grass-stained jeans and a pair of canvas sneakers that were worn through at the heels. She wasn't wearing socks, or, as far as he could see, a brassiere either. But she'd clean up nicely, that was what he was thinking—she had a shape to her, anybody could see that, and eyes that could burn holes right through you. "So," he heard himself say, even as Ben's voice rose to a crescendo at the other end of the room, "you, uh, like houseplants?"

She made no effort to hide what she was doing, whatever it may have been—studying the weave of the carpet, looking to the alignment of the baseboard, inspecting for termites, who could say?—but instead turned to gaze up at him for the first time. "I hope you don't mind my asking," she said in her hush of a voice, "but did you ever have a dog here?"

He stood looking down at her, gripping his drink, feeling awkward and foolish in his own house. He was thinking of Seymour (or "See More," because as a pup he was always running off after things in the distance), picturing him now for the first time in how many years? Something passed through him then, a pang of regret carried in his blood, in his neurons: Seymour. He'd almost succeeded in forgetting him. "Yes," he said. "How did you know?"

She smiled. She was leaning back against the wall now, cradling her knees in the net of her interwoven fingers. "I've been training myself. My senses, I mean." She paused, still smiling up at him. "Did you know that when the Ninemile wolves came down into Montana from Alberta they were following scent trails laid down years before?

Think about it. All that weather, the seasons, trees falling and decaying. Can you imagine that?"

"Cara's allergic," he said. "I mean, that's why we had to get rid of him. Seymour. His name was Seymour."

There was a long braying burst of laughter from Ben Ober, who had an arm round the husband's shoulder and was painting something in the air with a stiffened forefinger. Cara stood just beyond him, with the La Portes, her face glowing as if it had been basted. Celia La Porte looked from him to the girl and back again, then arched her eyebrows wittily and raised her long-stemmed glass of Viognier, as if toasting him. All three of them burst into laughter. Julian turned his back.

"You didn't take him to the pound—did you?" The girl's eyes went flat. "Because that's a death sentence, I hope you realize that."

"Cara found a home for him."

They both looked to Cara then, her shining face, her anchorwoman's hair. "I'm sure," the girl said.

"No, really. She did."

The girl shrugged, looked away from him. "It doesn't matter," she said with a flare of anger, "dogs are just slaves anyway."

KAMALA AND AMALA

The Reverend Singh had wanted to return to the site the following afternoon and excavate the den, convinced that these furtive night creatures were in fact human children, children abducted from their cradles and living under the dominion of beasts—unbaptized and unsaved, their eternal souls at risk—but urgent business called him away to the south. When he returned, late in the evening, ten days later, he sat over a dinner of cooked vegetables, rice and *dal,* and listened as Chunarem told him of the wolf bitch that had haunted the village two years back after her pups had been removed from a den in the forest and sold for a few *annas* apiece at the Khuar market. She could be seen as dusk fell, her dugs swollen and glistening with extruded milk, her eyes shining with an unearthly blue light against the backdrop of the forest. People threw stones, but she never flinched. Everywhere she left diggings in the earth for farmers to step into on their way out to the fields, attempting, some said, to memorialize that den that had been robbed—or to avenge it. And she howled all night from the fringes of the village, howled so that it seemed she was inside the walls of every hut simultaneously, crooning her sorrow into the ears of each sleeping villager. The village dogs kept hard by, and those that didn't were found in the morning, their throats torn out. "It was she," the Reverend exclaimed, setting down his plate as the candles guttered and moths beat at the netting. "She was the abductress—it's as plain as morning."

A few days later he got up a party that included several railway men and returned to the termite mound, bent on rescue. In place of the rifle he carried a stout cudgel cut from a *mahua* branch, and he'd thought to bring a weighted net along as well. The sun hung overhead. All was still. And then the hired beaters started in, the noise of them racketing though the trees, coming closer and closer until they converged on the site, driving hares and bandicoots and the occasional gaur before them. The railway men tensed in the *machan,* their rifles trained on the entrance to the burrow, while Reverend Singh stood by with a party of diggers to effect the rescue when the time came. It was unlikely that the wolves would have been abroad in daylight, and so it was no surprise to the Reverend that no large animal was seen to run before the beaters and seek the shelter of the den. "Very well," he said, giving the signal. "I am satisfied. Commence the digging."

As soon as the blades of the first shovels struck the mound, a protracted snarling could be heard emanating from the depths of the burrow. After a few minutes of the tribesmen's digging, the she-wolf sprang out at them, ears flattened to her head, teeth flashing. One of the diggers went for her with his spear just as the railway men opened fire from the *machan* and turned her, snapping, on her own wounds; a moment later she lay stretched out dead in the dust of the laterite clay. In a trice the burrow was uncovered, and there they were, the spirits made flesh, huddled in a defensive posture with the two wolf cubs, snarling and panicked, scrabbling at the clay with their broken nails to dig themselves deeper. The tribesmen dropped their shovels and ran, panicked themselves, even as the Reverend Singh eased himself down into the hole and tried to separate child from wolf.

The larger of the wolf children, her hair a feral cap that masked her features, came at him biting and scratching, and finally he had no recourse but to throw the net over the pullulating bodies and restrain each of the creatures separately in one of the long, winding *gelaps* the local tribesmen use for winter wear. On inspection it was determined that the children were females, aged approximately three and six, of native stock, and apparently, judging from the dissimilarity of their features, unrelated. And this puzzled the Reverend, so far as he was concerned with the she-wolf's motives and behavior—she'd abducted the children on separate occasions, perhaps even from separate locales, and over the course of some time. Was this the bereaved bitch Chunarem had reported? Was she acting out of revenge? Or merely trying, in her own unknowable way, to replace what had been taken from her and ease the burden of her heart?

In any case, he had the children confined to a pen so that he could observe them, before caging them in the back of the bullock cart for the trip to Midnapore and the orphanage, where he planned to baptize and civilize them. He spent three full days studying them and taking notes in a leatherbound book he kept always at his side. He saw that they persisted in going on all fours, as if they didn't know any other way, and fled from the sunlight as if it were an instrument of torture. They thrust forward to lap water like the beasts of the forest and took nothing in their mouths but bits of twig and stone. At night they came to life and stalked the enclosure with shining eyes like the *bhuts* half the villagers still believed them to be. They did not know any of the languages of the human species, but communicated with each other—and with their sibling wolves—with a series of grunts, snarls and whimpers. When the moon rose, they sat on their haunches and howled.

It was Mrs. Singh who named them, some weeks later. They were pitiful, filthy, soiled with their own urine and excrement, undernourished and undersized. They had to be caged to keep them from harming the other children, and Mrs. Singh, though it broke her heart to do it, ordered them put in restraints so that the filth and the animal smell could be washed from them, even as their heads were shaved to defeat the ticks and fleas they'd inherited from the only mother they'd ever known. "They need delicate names," Mrs. Singh told her husband, "names to reflect the beauty and propriety they will grow into." She named the younger sister Amala, after a bright yellow flower native to Bengal, and she named the elder Kamala, after the lotus that blossoms deep in the jungle pools.

RUNNING WITH THE PACK

THE SUN STROKED HER like a hand, penetrated and massaged the dark yellowing contusion that had sprouted on the left side of her rib cage. Her bones felt as if they were about to crack open and deliver their marrow and her heart was still pounding, but she was here, among the dogs, at rest, and all that was winding down now. It was June, the season of pollen, the air supercharged with the scents of flowering, seeding, fruiting, and there were rabbits and squirrels everywhere. She lay prone at the lip of the den and watched the pups— long-muzzled like their mother and brindled Afghan peach and husky silver—as they worried a flap of skin and fur that Snout had peeled off the hot black glistening surface of the road and dropped at their feet. She was trying to focus on the dogs—on A.1., curled up nose to tail in the trampled weeds after regurgitating a mash of kibble for the pups, on Decidedly, his eyes half-closed as currents of air brought him messages from afar, on Humper and Factitious—but she couldn't let go of the pain in her ribs and what that pain foreshadowed from the human side of things.

Don had kicked her. Don had climbed out of the car, crossed the field and stood over her in his suede computer-engineer's ankle boots with the waffle bottoms and reinforced toes and lectured her while the dogs slunk low and rumbled deep in their throats. And, as his voice had grown louder, so too had the dogs' voices, till they were a chorus commenting on the ebb and flow of the action. When was she going to get her ass up out of the dirt and act like a normal human being? That was what he wanted to know. When was she going to cook a meal, run the vacuum, do the wash—his underwear, for Christ's sake? He was wearing dirty underwear, did she know that?

She had been lying stretched out flat on the mound, just as she was now. She glanced up at him as the dogs did, taking in a piece of him at a time, no direct stares, no challenges. She was in no mood. "All I want," she said, over the chorus of growls and low, warning barks, "is to be left alone."

"Left alone?" His voice tightened in a little yelp. "Left alone? You need help, that's what you need. You need a shrink, you know that?"

She didn't reply. She let the pack speak for her. The rumble of their response, the flattened ears and stiffened tails, the sharp, savage gleam of their eyes should have been enough, but Don wasn't attuned. The sun seeped into her. A grasshopper she'd been idly watching as it bent a dandelion under its weight suddenly took flight, right past her face, and it seemed the most natural thing in the world to snap at it and break it between her teeth.

Don let out some sort of exclamation—"My God, what are you doing? Get up out of that, get up out of that now!"—and it didn't help matters. The dogs closed in. They were fierce now, barking in savage recusancy, their emotions twisted in a single cord. But this was Don, she kept telling herself, Don from grad school, bright and buoyant Don, her mate, her husband, and what harm was there in that? He wanted her back home, back in the den, and that was his right. The only thing was, she wasn't going.

"This isn't research. This is bullshit. Look at you!"

"No," she said, giving him a lazy, sidelong look, though her heart was racing, "it's dog shit. It's on your shoes, Don. It's in your face. In your precious computer—"

That was when he'd kicked her. Twice, three times maybe. Kicked her in the ribs as if he were driving a ball over an imaginary set of up-rights in the distance, kicked and kicked again—before the dogs went for him. A.1. came in first, tearing at a spot just above his right knee, and then Humper, the bulldog who belonged to the feathery old lady up the block, got hold of his pantleg while Barely went for the crotch. Don screamed and thrashed all right—he was a big animal, two hundred and ten pounds, heavier by far than any of the dogs—and he threatened in his big-animal voice and fought back with all the violence of his big-animal limbs, but he backed off quickly enough, threatening still, as he made his way across the field and into the car. She heard the door slam, heard the motor scream, and then there was the last thing she heard: Snout barking at the wheels as the wheels revolved and took Don down the street and out of her life.

SURVIVAL OF THE FITTEST

"You know he's locked her out, don't you?"

"Who?" Though he knew perfectly well.

"Don. I'm talking about Don and the dog lady?"

There was the table, made of walnut varnished a century before, the crystal vase full of flowers, the speckless china, the meat, the vegetables, the pasta. Softly, so softly he could barely hear it, there was Bach too, piano pieces—partitas—and the smell of the fresh-cut flowers.

"Nobody knows where she's staying, unless it's out in the trash or the weeds or wherever. She's like a bag lady or something. And what she's eating. Bea said Jerrilyn Hunter said she saw her going through the trash at dawn one morning. Do you hear me? Are you even listening?"

"I don't know. Yeah. Yeah, I am." He'd been reading lately. About dogs. Half a shelf of books from the library in their plastic covers—behavior, breeds, courting, mating, whelping. He excised a piece of steak and lifted it to his lips. "Did you hear the Leibowitzes' Afghan had puppies?"

"*Puppies?* What in God's name are you talking about?" Her face was like a burr under the waistband, an irritant, something that needed to be removed and crushed.

"Only the alpha couple gets to breed, you know that, right? And so that would be the husky and the Leibowitzes' Afghan, and I don't know who the husky belongs to—but they're cute, real cute."

"You haven't been—? Don't tell me. Julian, use your sense: she's out of her mind. You want to know what else Bea said?"

"The alpha bitch," he said, and he didn't know why he was telling her this, "she'll actually hunt down and kill the pups of any other female in the pack who might have got pregnant, a survival of the fittest kind of thing—"

"She's crazy, bonkers, out of her *fucking* mind, Julian. They're going to have her committed, you know that? If this keeps up. And it will keep up, won't it, Julian? Won't it?"

THE COMMON ROOM AT MIDNAPORE

AT FIRST they would take nothing but water. The wolf pups, from which they'd been separated for reasons both of sanitation and acculturation, eagerly fed on milk-and-rice pap in their kennel in one of the outbuildings, but neither of the girls would touch the pan-warmed milk or rice or the stewed vegetables Mrs. Singh provided for them—even at night, when they were most active and their eyes spoke a language of desire all their own. Each morning and each evening before retiring, she would place a bowl on the floor in front of them, trying to tempt them with biscuits, confections, even a bit of boiled meat, though the Singhs were vegetarians themselves and repudiated the slaughter of animals for any purpose. The girls drew back into the recesses of the pen the Reverend had constructed in the orphanage's common room, showing their teeth. Days passed. They grew weaker. He tried to force-feed them balls of rice, but they scratched and tore at him with their nails and their teeth, setting up such a furious caterwauling of hisses, barks and snarls as to give rise to rumors among the servants that he was torturing them—or trying to exorcise the forest demons that inhabited them, as if he, an educated man, had given in to the superstitions of the tribesmen. Finally, in resignation, and though it was a risk to the security of the entire orphanage, he left the door to the pen standing open in the hope that the girls, on seeing the other small children at play and at dinner, would soften.

In the meanwhile, though the girls grew increasingly lethargic—or perhaps because of it—the Reverend was able to make a close and telling examination of their physiology and habits. Their means of locomotion had transformed their bodies in a peculiar way. For one thing, they had developed thick pads of callus at their elbows and knees, and toes that were of abnormal strength and inflexibility—indeed, when their feet were placed flat on the ground, all five toes stood up at a sharp angle. Their waists were narrow and extraordinarily supple, like a dog's, and their necks dense with the muscle that had accrued there as a result of leading with their heads. And they were fast, preternaturally fast, and stronger by far than any other child of their respective ages the Reverend and his wife had ever seen. In his diary, for the sake of posterity, the Reverend noted it all down.

Still, all the notes in the world wouldn't matter a whit if the wolf children didn't end their hunger strike, if that was what this was, and the Reverend and his wife had begun to lose hope for them, when the larger one—the one who would become known as Kamala—finally asserted herself. It was early in the evening, the day after the Reverend had ordered the door to the pen left open, and the children were eating their evening meal while Mrs. Singh and one of the servants looked on and the Reverend settled in with his pipe on the veranda. The weather was typical for Bengal in that season, the evening heavy and close, every living thing locked in the grip of the heat, nothing moving, not even the birds, and all the mission's doors and windows stood open to receive even the faintest breath of a breeze. Suddenly, without warning, Kamala bolted out of the pen, through the door and across the courtyard to where the orphanage dogs were being fed scraps of uncooked meat, gristle and bone left over from the preparation of the servants' meal, and before anyone could stop her she was down among them, slashing with her teeth, fighting off even the biggest and most aggressive of them until she'd bolted the red meat and carried off the long, hoofed shinbone of a gaur to gnaw in the farthest corner of her pen.

And so the Singhs, though it revolted them, fed the girls on raw meat until the crisis had passed, and then they gave them broth, which the girls lapped from their bowls, and finally meat that had been at least partially cooked. As for clothing—clothing for decency's sake—the girls rejected it as unnatural and confining, tearing any garment from their backs and limbs with their teeth, until Mrs. Singh hit on the idea of fashioning each of them a single tight-fitting strip of cloth they wore knotted round the waist and drawn up over their privates, a kind of diaper or loincloth they were forever soiling with their waste. It wasn't an ideal solution, but the Singhs were patient—the girls had suffered a kind of deprivation no other humans had ever suffered—and they understood that the ascent to civilization and light would be steep and long.

When Amala died, shortly after the wolf pups succumbed to what the Reverend presumed was distemper communicated through the orphanage dogs, her sister wouldn't let anyone approach the body. Looking back on it, the Reverend would see this as Kamala's most human moment—she was grieving, grieving because she had a soul, because she'd been baptized before the Lord and was no wolfling or jungle *bhut* but a human child after all, and here was the proof of it. But poor Amala. Her, they hadn't been able to save. Both girls had been dosed with sulfur powder, which caused them to expel a knot of roundworms up to six inches in length and as thick as the Reverend's little finger, but the treatment was perhaps too harsh for the three-year-old, who was suffering from fever and dysentery at the same time. She'd seemed all right, feverish but calm, and Mrs. Singh had tended her through the afternoon and evening. But when the Reverend's wife came into the pen in the morning, Kamala flew at her, raking her arms and legs and driving her back from the straw in which the cold body of her sister lay stretched out like a figure carved of wood. They restrained the girl and removed the corpse while Mrs. Singh retired to bandage her wounds and the Reverend locked the door of the pen to prevent any further violence. All that day Kamala lay immobile in the shadows at the back of the pen, wrapped in her own limbs. And then night fell, and she sat back on her haunches behind the rigid geometry of the bars and began to howl, softly at first, and then with increasing force and plangency until it was the very sound of desolation itself, rising up out of the compound to chase through the streets of the village and into the jungle beyond.

GOING TO THE DOGS

THE SKY WAS CLEAR all the way to the top of everything, the sun so thick in the trees he thought it would catch there and congeal among the motionless leaves. He didn't know what prompted him to do it exactly, but as he came across the field he balanced first on one leg, and then the other, to remove his shoes and socks. The grass—the weeds, wildflowers, puffs of mushroom, clover, swaths of moss—felt clean and cool against the lazy progress of his bare feet. Butterflies shifted and flapped, grasshoppers shone gold, the false bees hung suspended from invisible wires. Things rose up to greet him, things and smells he'd forgotten all about, and he took his time among them, moving forward only to be distracted again and again. He found her finally in the tall nodding weeds that concealed the entrance of the den, playing with the puppies. He didn't say hello, didn't say anything—just settled in on the mound beside her and let the pups surge into his arms. The pack barely raised its collective head.

Her eyes came to him and went away again. She was smiling, a loose, private smile that curled the corners of her mouth and lifted up into the smooth soft terrain of the silken skin under her eyes. Her clothes barely covered her anymore, the turtleneck torn at the throat and sagging across one clavicle, the black jeans hacked off crudely—or maybe chewed off—at the peaks of her thighs. The sneakers were gone altogether, and he saw that the pale yellow soles of her feet were hard with callus, and her hair—her hair was struck with sun and shining with the natural oil of her scalp.

He'd come with the vague idea—or no, the very specific idea—of asking her for one of the pups, but now he didn't know if that would do exactly. She would tell him that the pups weren't hers to give, that they belonged to the pack, and though each of the pack's members had a bed and a bowl of kibble awaiting it in one of the equitable houses of the alphabetical grid of the development springing up around them, they were free here, and the pups, at least, were slaves to no one. He felt the thrusting wet snouts of the creatures in his lap, the surge of their animacy, the softness of the stroked ears and the prick of the milk teeth, and he smelled them too, an authentic smell compounded of dirt, urine, saliva and something else also: the un-alloyed sweetness of life. After a while, he removed his shirt, and so what if the pups carried it off like a prize? The sun blessed him. He loosened his belt, gave himself some breathing room. He looked at her, stretched out beside him, at the lean, tanned, running length of her, and he heard himself say, finally, "Nice day, isn't it?"

"Don't talk," she said. "You'll spoil it."

"Right," he said. "Right. You're right."

And then she rolled over, bare flesh from the worried waistband of her cutoffs to the dimple of her breastbone and her breasts caught somewhere in between, under the yielding fabric. She was warm, warm as a fresh-drawn bath, the touch of her communicating every-thing to him, and the smell of her too—he let his hand go up under the flap of material and roam over her breasts, and then he bent closer, sniffing.

Her eyes were fixed on his. She didn't say anything, but a low throaty rumble escaped her throat.

WAITING FOR THE RAINS

THE REVEREND SINGH sat there on the veranda, waiting for the rains. He'd set his notebook aside, and now he leaned back in the wicker chair and pulled meditatively at his pipe. The children were at play in the courtyard, an array of flashing limbs and animated faces attended by their high, bright catcalls and shouts. The heat had loosened its grip ever so perceptibly, and they were all of them better for it. Except Kamala. She was indifferent. The chill of winter, the damp of the rains, the full merciless sway of the sun—it was all the same to her. His eyes came to rest on her where she lay across the courtyard in a stripe of sunlight, curled in the dirt with her knees drawn up beneath her and her chin resting atop the cradle of her crossed wrists. He watched her for a long while as she lay motionless there, no more aware of what she was than a dog or an ass, and he felt defeated, defeated and depressed. But then one of the children called out in a voice fluid with joy, a moment of triumph in a game among them, and the Reverend couldn't help but shift his eyes and look.

The Kind Assassin

What you hope for
Is that at some point of the pointless journey . . .
The kind assassin Sleep will draw a bead
And blow your brains out.

—RICHARD WILBUR

I WAS HAVING TROUBLE getting to sleep. Nothing serious, just the usual tossing and turning, the pillow converted to stone, every whisper of the night amplified to a shriek. I heard the refrigerator click on in the kitchen, the soft respiration of the dust-clogged motor that kept half a six-pack, last week's take-out Chinese and the crusted jar of capers at a safe and comfortable temperature, and then I heard it click off. Every seven and a half minutes—I timed it by the glowing green face of the deep-sea diver's watch my ex-wife gave me for Christmas last year—the neighbors' dog let out a single startled yelp, and twenty seconds later I heard the car of some drunk or shift worker laboring up the hill with an intermittent wheeze and blast of exhaust (and couldn't *anybody* in this neighborhood afford a new car—or at least a trip to the muffler shop?). It was three o'clock in the morning. Then it was four. I tried juggling invisible balls, repeating the names of my elementary school teachers, Mrs. Gold, Mrs. Cochrane, Miss Mandia, Miss Slivovitz, summoned their faces, the faces of as many of my classmates as I could remember, the faces of everybody in the neighborhood where I grew up, of everybody in New York, California, China, but it didn't do any good. I fell asleep ten minutes before the alarm hammered me back to consciousness.

By the time I got both legs into a pair of jeans and both arms through the armholes of my favorite Hawaiian shirt, I was running late for work. I didn't bother with gelling my hair or even looking at it, just grabbed a stocking cap and pulled it down to my eyebrows. Some sort of integument seemed to have been interposed between me and the outside world, some thick dullish skin that made every movement an ordeal, as if I were swimming in a medium ten times denser than water—and how the scalding twelve-ounce container of Starbuck's triple latte wound up clenched between my legs as I gripped the steering wheel of the car that didn't even feel like my own car— that felt borrowed or stolen—I'll never know.

All this by way of saying I was late getting to the studio. Fifteen minutes late, to be exact. The first face I saw, right there, stationed at the battered back door with the call letters KFUN pasted at eye level in strips of peeling black electrical tape, seemed to belong to Cuttler Ames, the program director. Seemed to, that is, because the studio was filled to the ceiling with this new element I had to fight my way through, at least until the caffeine began to take hold and the integument fell away like so much sloughed skin. Cuttler made his lemon-sucking face. "Don't tell me you overslept," he said. "Not today of all days. Tell me I'm wrong. Tell me your car threw a rod, tell me you got a speeding ticket, tell me your house burned down."

Cuttler was a Brit. He wore his hair long and his face baggy. His voice was like Karo syrup poured through an echo box. He'd limped through the noon-hour "Blast from the Past" show for six months before he was elevated to program director over the backs of a whole troop of more deserving men (and women). I didn't like him. Nobody liked him. "My house burned down," I said.

"Why don't you pull your head up out of your ass, will you? For once? Would that be too much to ask?" He turned to wheel away, resplendent in his black leather bell bottoms with the silver medallions sewed into the seams, then stopped to add, "Anthony's already in there, going it alone, which makes me wonder what we're paying *you* for, but let's not develop a sense of urgency here or anything—let's just linger in the corridor and make small talk, shall we?" A pause. The man was in a time warp. The leather pants, the wide-collared shirt, the pointy-toed boots: it was 1978 and Pink Floyd was ascendant. His eyes flamed briefly. "How did you sleep?"

Anthony was Tony, my morning-show partner. Sometimes, depending on his mood, Cuttler called him "Tony" like everybody else, except that he pronounced it "Tunny." The question of how I'd slept was of vital import on this particular morning, because I'd been in training for the past week under the direction of Dr. Laurie Pepper of the Sleep Institute, who was getting some high-profile publicity for her efforts, not to mention a reduced rate on her thirty-second spots. "You need to build up your sleep account," she told me, perched on the edge of the couch in my living room, and she prescribed long hot baths and sipping tepid milk before bed. "White noise helps," she said. "One of my clients, a guitarist in an A-list band whose name I can't reveal because of confidentiality issues, and I hope you'll understand, used to make a tape loop of the toilet flushing and play it back all night." She was in her mid-thirties and she had a pair of dramatic legs she showed off beneath short skirts and Morning Mist stockings, and in case anybody failed to take note she wore a gold anklet that spelled out *Somnus* in linked letters. "Roman god of sleep," she said when she saw where my eyes had wandered. She had a notepad in her lap. She consulted it and uncrossed her legs. "Sex helps," she said, coming back to the point she was pursuing. I told her I wasn't seeing anybody just then. She shrugged, an elegant little shift of the shoulders. "Masturbation, then."

There was a coffeepot and a tray of two-days'-stale doughnuts set up on a table against the wall just behind Cuttler, the remnants of a promotion for the local Krazy Kreme franchise. I went for them like a zombie, pausing only to reference his question. "Like shit," I said.

"Oh, smashing. Super. Our champion, our hero. I suppose you'll be drooling on the table ten minutes into the marathon."

I wanted a cigarette, though it was an urge I had to fight. Since Cuttler's accession we'd become a strictly tobacco-free workplace and I had to hide my Larks out of sight and blow smoke into a screw-top bottle when Tony and I were on the air. I could feel the caffeine working its way up the steep grades and inclines of my circulatory system like a train of linked locomotives, chugging away. In a burst of exhilaration I actually drew the pack from my pocket and shook out a cigarette, just to watch Cuttler's face go into isolation. I made as if to stick the cigarette between my lips, but then thought better of it and tucked it behind my ear. "No way," I said. "You want me to go twelve days, I'll go twelve days. Fourteen, fifteen, whatever you want. Jesus, I don't sleep anyway." And then I was in the booth with Tony, ad-libbing, doing routines, cueing up records and going to commercials I'd heard so many times I could have reprised them in my sleep—if I ever slept, that is.

IN THE MID-SIXTIES, Dr. Allan Rechtschaffen of the University of Chicago devised an experiment in sleep deprivation, using rats as his subject animals. He wired their rodent brains to an EEG machine and every time their brain waves showed them drifting off he ducked them in cold water. The rats didn't like this. They were in a lab, with plenty to eat and drink, a nice equitable temperature, no predators, no danger, nothing amiss but for the small inconvenience of the wires glued to the patches shaved into their skulls, but whenever they started dreaming they got wet. Normally, a rat will sleep thirteen hours a day on average, midway on the mammalian scale between the dolphin (at seven) and the bat (at twenty). These rats didn't sleep at all. A week went by. Though they ate twice as much as normal, they began to lose weight. Their fur thinned, their energy diminished. The first died after thirteen days. Within three weeks all of them were gone.

I mention it here because I want to emphasize that I went into all this with my eyes wide open. I was informed. I knew that the Chinese Communists had used sleep deprivation as a torture device and that the physiological and psychological effects of continual wakefulness can be debilitating, if not fatal. Like the rats, sleep-deprived people tend to eat more, and like the rats, to lose weight nonetheless. Their immune systems become compromised. Body temperatures drop. Disorientation occurs. Hallucinations are common. Beyond that, it was anybody's guess what would happen, though the fate of the rats was a pretty fair indication as far as I was concerned. And yet still, when Cuttler and Nguyen Tranh, the station's owner and manager, came up with the idea of a marathon—a "Wake-A-Thon," Tony was calling it—to boost ratings and coincidentally raise money for the National Narcolepsy Association, I was the first to volunteer. Why not?, was what I was thinking. At least it would be something different.

Thus, Dr. Laurie. If I was going to challenge the world record for continuous hours without sleep, I would need to be coached and monitored, and before I stepped into that glass booth at the intersection of Chapala and Oak in downtown San Roque at the conclusion of today's edition of "The Gooner & Boomer Morning-Drive Show" I would have built up my sleep account, replete with overdraft protection, to ease me on my way. Call it nerves, butterflies, anticipatory anxiety—whatever it was, I'd never slept worse in my life than during the past week, and my sleep account was bankrupt. Even before the last puerile sexual-innuendo-laden half-witted joke of the show was out of my mouth, I could picture myself out cold in the glass booth five minutes into the marathon, derisive faces pressed up against the transparent walls, all the bright liquid hopes and aspirations of what was once a career unstoppered and leaching off into the pipes. I cued up the new Weezer single and backed out of the booth.

There was a photographer from the local paper leaning up against the shoulder-greased wall in the corridor, the telltale traces of doughnut confection caught in the corners of his mouth. He glanced up at me with dead eyes, tugged at the camera strap as if it had grown into his flesh. "You ready for this, man?" Tony crowed, slipping out of the booth like a knife pulled from a corpse, and he threw an arm round my shoulder, grinning for the photographer. Tony's job was to represent the control group. Every morning, after our show, which we'd be broadcasting live from the glassed-in booth, he would go home to bed, then pop in at odd hours to sign autographs, hand out swag and keep me going with ever newer jokes and routines, which we would then work into the next morning's show. He'd spent the past week trying to twist Polish jokes to fit the insomnia envelope, as in how many insomniacs does it take to screw in a lightbulb and what did the insomniac say to the bartender? Tony squeezed my shoulder. "How you feeling?"

I just nodded in response. I felt all right, actually. Not rested, not calm, not confident, but all right. The sun slanted in through one of the grimy skylights and hit me in the face and it was like throwing cold water on a drunk. Plus I'd had two more cups of coffee and a Diet Coke while we were on the air, and the assault of the caffeine made me feel almost human. When Dr. Laurie, Nguyen and Cuttler stepped out of the shadows and locked arms with me and Tony to pose for the photographer, I braved the flash and showed every tooth I had.

THE FIRST MASOCHIST to subject himself to sleep withdrawal for the sake of ratings was a DJ named Peter Tripp, who had a daily show on WMGM in New York back in 1959. His glassed-in booth was in Times Square, and he made it through the two hundred hours of sleeplessness his program director had projected for him, though not without experiencing his share of delusions and waking nightmares. Toward the end of his trial, he somehow mistook the physician monitoring him for an undertaker come to pump him full of formaldehyde and they had to read him the riot act to get him back into the glass booth and finish out his sentence. Two hundred hours is just over eight days, but what Cuttler was shooting for here was twelve days, two hundred eighty-eight hours—a full twenty-four hours longer than the mark set by the *Guinness Book of World Records* champ, a high school senior from San Diego named Randy Gardner who'd employed himself as the test subject in a science project to monitor the effects of sleep deprivation. He was seventeen at the time, gifted with all the recuperative powers of the young, and he came out of it without any lasting adverse effects.

As I stood in the back hallway at KFUN, simulating insouciance for the photographer, I was thirty-three years old, sapped of enthusiasm after twelve years on the air, sleep-deprived and vulnerable, with the recuperative powers of a corpse. I was loveless, broke, bored to the point of rage, so fed up with KFUN, microphones, recording engineers and my drive-time partner I sometimes thought I'd choke him to death on the air the next time he opened his asinine mouth to spout one more asinine crack, to which I, an ass myself, would be obligated to respond. My career was a joke. The downmarket slide had begun. I didn't have a chance.

Outside, in the parking lot, there was a random aggregation of sixth-grade girls in KFUN T-shirts, flanked by their slack-jawed, work-worn mothers. When Tony, Dr. Laurie and I stepped out the door and made for the classic KFUN-yellow Eldorado convertible that would take us downtown to the glass booth, they let out a series of halfhearted shrieks and waved their complimentary KFUN bumper stickers like confetti. I slipped into the embrace of my wraparound shades and treated them to a grand wave in return, and then we were out in traffic, and people who may or may not have been KFUN listeners looked at us as if we were prisoners on the way to the gallows.

It was early yet, just before nine, but there were four or five bums already camped against the walls of the glass cubicle—it was Plexiglas, actually—and a pair of retirees in golf hats gaping at the thing as if it had been manufactured by aliens. The sun, softened by a trace of lingering fog, made a featherbed of the sidewalk, the parked cars shone dully and the palms stood watch in silhouette up and down both sides of the street. The photographer got a shot of me in conference with the more emaciated of the retirees, who informed me that he'd once stayed up forty-six hours straight, hunting Japs on Iwo Jima, then Dr. Laurie, whose function had now abruptly switched from sleep induction to prevention, led me into the booth where Tony had already stowed my satchel stuffed with clean underwear, shaving kit, two fresh shirts, a burlap bag of gravel (to sit on when I felt drowsy: Cuttler's idea) and eighteen thrillers plucked at random from the shelves of Wal-Mart. The format was simple: every fifteen minutes I would go live to the studio and update the time and remind everybody out there in KFUN land just how many consecutive waking hours I'd racked up. Every other hour I was allowed a five-minute break to visit the toilet facilities across the street at the Soul Shack Dance Club, which was co-sponsoring the event, but aside from that I was to remain on full public display, upright and attentive, and no matter what happened, my eyelids were never to close, even for an instant.

IT MAY SEEM HARD to believe—especially now, looking at it in retrospect—but those first few hours were the worst. Once the excitement of setting up in the booth (and cutting into Armageddon Annie's mid-morning show for a sixty-second exchange of canned jocularities—"How're you hanging, Boomer? Still awake after fifteen minutes?"), the effect of the last few sleepless nights hit me like an avalanche. I was sitting there at the console they'd set up for me, staring off down the avenue and thinking of Dr. Laurie's legs and what she could do for me in a strictly therapeutic way when all this was over and I really did have to get back to sleep, and I think I may have drifted for a minute. I wasn't asleep. I know that. But it was close, my eyelids listing, the image of Dr. Laurie slipping off her undies replaced by a cold sweeping wall of gray as if someone had suddenly flipped channels on me, and then I was no longer staring down the avenue but into the eyes, the deep sea–green startled eyes, of a girl of twenty or so in what looked to be a homemade knit cap with long trailing ear flaps. At first I thought I'd gone over the edge, already dreaming and not thirty minutes into the deal, because why would anyone be wearing a knit cap with earflaps in downtown San Roque where the sun was shining and the temperature stuck at seventy-two, day and night, as if there were a thermostat in the sky? But then she waved, touched two fingers to her lips and pressed them to the glass, and I knew I was awake.

I gave her my best radio-personality smile, ran a hand through my hair (now combed and gelled, just as my cheeks were smooth-shaven and my Hawaiian shirt wrinkle-free, because this was a performance above all else and I was representing KFUN to the public here, as Cuttler had reminded me sixteen times already that morning, lest I forget). She smiled back, and I noticed then that a crowd had begun to gather, maybe twenty people or so—shoppers, delivery truck drivers, mothers and babes, granddads, slope-shouldered truants from San Roque High, and even a solitary cop perched over his motionless bicycle—all drawn to the image of this woman pressed against the glass in a place on the sidewalk where no glass had been just a day ago. They saw her there, people who might have just strolled on obliviously by, and then they saw me, in my glass cage. I watched their faces, the private looks of absorption metamorphosing to surprise and then amusement, and something else too—recognition, and maybe even admiration. *Oh, yeah, they were thinking, I heard about this—that's Boomer in there, from KFUN, and he's setting the world record for staying awake. It's been almost an hour now. Cool.*

At least that's what I imagined, and I wasn't delusional yet, not by a long shot. That girl standing there had turned things around for me, and for the first time I felt a surge of pride, a sense of accomplishment and worth—enthusiasm, real enthusiasm—but of course, I was tired to the marrow already and experiencing a kind of hypnotic giddiness that could have been the precursor to any level of mental instability. In my exuberance I waved to the assembled crowd, mothers, bums and truants alike, and that seemed to break the spell—their eyes shifted away from me, they began to move off, and the new people who might have been their reinforcements just kept on walking past the glass booth as if it didn't exist. The girl tore a sheet from a loose-leaf notebook then and bent over it in concentration. I watched her write out a message in block letters as the pigeons dodged and ducked round her feet and the seagulls cut white flaps out of the sky overhead, and then she looked up, held my eyes, and pressed the paper to the glass. The message was simple, terse, to the point: YOU ARE MY GOD.

I FOUGHT SLEEP through the morning and into the early afternoon, so wired on caffeine my knees were sore from knocking together under the table. There are two low points in our circadian cycle, one to four in the morning, which seems self-evident, and, more surprisingly, the same hours in the afternoon. Or maybe it's not so surprising when you take into account the number of cultures that indulge the post-prandial nap or afternoon siesta. At any rate, on a normal day at this hour I'd be doing voice-overs on ads or dozing off in one of the endless meetings Cuttler and Nguyen seemed to call every other day to remind us of the cost of postage, long-distance phone calls and the paper towels in the restroom. The afternoon lull hit me. My head lolled on my shoulders like a bowling ball. I thought if I ate something it would help, so when Tony stopped in to glad-hand the bums and the half-dozen lingerers and gawkers gathered round the booth, I asked him to get me some Chinese takeout. I did the one forty-five spot ("Hey, out there in KFUN land, this is the Boomer, and yes, I'm still awake after three hours and forty-five minutes, and when you hear the tone it will be exactly—"), then bent to the still-warm cartons of kung pao chicken, scallops in black bean sauce and mu shu pork.

I couldn't eat. I lifted the first dripping forkful to my mouth and a dozen pairs of eyes locked on mine. The bums had been stretched out in comfort all morning, passing a short dog of Gallo white port, cadging change and hawking gobs of mucus onto the pavement, making merry at my expense, and now they just turned their heads to stare as if they somehow expected me to provide for them too. A trio of middle-aged women with Macy's bags looped over their wrists took one look at me and pulled up short as if they'd forgotten something (lunch, most likely). And one of the old men from the morning reappeared suddenly, licking his lips. I tried to smile and chew at the same time, but it wasn't working. I toyed with the food awhile, even picked up one of the thrillers and tried to block them out, but finally I set down the fork and pushed the cartons away. That was when the girl in the earflaps popped up out of nowhere—she must have been lurking in the bushes along the median or watching from the window of the Soul Shack—to painstakingly indite a second message. She pressed it to the glass. EAT, it read, YOU'RE GOING TO NEED YOUR STRENGTH.

THE GIRL'S NAME WAS Hezza Moore. She was of medium height, medium weight, medium coloring and medium attractiveness. We met formally just after the sun went down the evening of that first day. I'd got my second wind around seven or so (the second period of alertness in our circadian cycle, by the way, corresponding to the one we experience in the morning), and by the time the sun went down I felt as energized as Nosferatu climbing out of his coffin. I paced round the glass box, spanked off my quarter-hour spots with the rumbling monitory gusto that had won me my on-air moniker ten years back when I was an apprentice jock at KSOT in San Luis Obispo, did a few sets of jumping jacks, flossed my teeth and un-latched the glass door at the rear of the booth to embrace the night air.

I was thinking this is a lark, this is nothing, thinking I could go a month, a year, and who needed sleep anyway, when she materialized at the open door. She was still in the knit cap, but she seemed to be wearing mittens now too, and an old Salvation Army overcoat that dropped to the toes of her Doc Martens. "Hey," she said.

"Hey."

"You remember that Dishwalla promo you guys did six years ago?"

I gave her a blank look. The temperature reading on the display over the Bank of America down the street was 71°.

She'd edged partway into the booth, one foot on the plywood floor, her shoulders bridging the Plexiglas doorframe. "You know, the new CD and dinner for two at the Star of India? I was the four-teenth caller."

"Really?"

She beamed at me now, two dimples sucked down into her smile. The knit hat cut a slash just above her eyes, and her eyes jumped and settled, then jumped again. "Yeah," she went on, "but I was only fif-teen and I didn't have anybody to go with. I wound up going with my mom, and that was a drag. You should have been the prize, though. I mean, it was you telling us all that the fourteenth caller would win the free chapatis and the lime pickle and all the rest of it, and if it'd been you going to dinner with the fourteenth caller I would've died. Really, I would have. You know, I've never missed your show, not even once, ever since you went on the air? I even used to listen in school, in homeroom and first period, with headphones."

I held out my hand. "It's a real pleasure," I said, just to say it, and that was when she gave me her name. "You want an autograph? Or some of this swag?" I gestured to the heap of KFUN T-shirts, beanies,

CDs and concert tickets we were giving away as part of the Wake-A-Thon, teen treasure mounded in the corner of the glass booth just above the spot on the pavement outside where one of the bums—the one with the empty pantleg where his left foot should have been—was stretched out in bum nirvana, snoring lustily.

Her eyes changed. She looked down and then away. "Oh, no," she breathed finally. "No, I didn't come for any of that. Don't you realize what I'm saying?"

I didn't. A wave of exhaustion crashed inside of me and pulled back from the naked shingle with a long slow suck and moan.

"I came for you. I'm here for you. For as long as it takes." She lifted her eyes and gave me a searching look. "I'm your *angel,*" she said, and then she backed away and vanished into the night.

I MADE IT THROUGH the first week without closing my eyes once, not even in the privacy of the Soul Shack's unisex restroom, resorting to the Freon horn and the safety pin whenever I felt myself giving way. My body temperature dropped to 94.2 degrees at one point, but Dr. Laurie wrapped me in one of those thermal survival blankets and brought it back up to normal. Like the rats, I ate. Over-ate, actually, and by the second day I couldn't have cared if Mother Teresa and all the starving bald-headed waifs of Calcutta were camped outside the glass cube, I was eating and there were no two ways about it. Whereas before I'd made do like any other bachelor fending for himself, skipping breakfast most days and going to the deli for a meatball wedge in the afternoon and one fast-food venue or another in the evening, now I found myself gorging almost constantly. Tony and Dr. Laurie were bringing me pizza, sushi, tandoori chicken and super-sizer burritos around the clock. I was thirsty too. Couldn't get enough of the power drinks, of Red Bull, Jolt and Starbucks. The caffeine made me sizzle and it hollowed out its own place in the lining of my stomach, a low gastrointestinal burning that made me know I was alive. For the first few nights I felt a bit shaky during the down hours, from one to maybe five or so, but I never faltered, and there was always somebody there to monitor me, whether it was Dr. Laurie or one of our interns at the station. As the hours fell away, I felt stronger, more alive and awake, though the integument was back, draped over the world like a transparent screen, and everything—the way Hezza's mouth moved when she spoke, Tony's animated thrusts and jabs as he sat emoting beside me from six to nine each morning, even the way people and cars moved along the street—seemed to be happening at the bottom of the sea.

Cuttler made himself scarce the first week, chary of associating himself with failure, I suppose, but on the eighth day, when I was a mere seventy-three hours from the record, he showed up just after Tony and I had signed off and the blitzkrieg of ads leading into Annie's slot had begun cannonading over the airwaves. I was experiencing a little difficulty in recognizing people at this juncture—my eyes couldn't seem to focus and the pages of the thrillers were just an indecipherable blur—and I guess I didn't place him at first. He was standing there at the open door of the booth, a vaguely familiar figure in a canary-yellow long-sleeved shirt and trailing cerulean scarf, threads of graying blond hair hanging in his eyes—his small, pig-like eyes—and two mugs of piping hot coffee in his hands. Or maybe he was wearing a pullover that day, done up in psychedelic blots of color, or nothing at all. Maybe he was standing there naked, pale as a dead fish, loose and puffy and without definition beyond the compact swell of his gut and the shriveled little British package of his male equipment. Who was I to say? I was hallucinating at this point, experiencing as reality what Dr. Laurie called "hypnogogic reveries," the sort of images you summon up just before nodding off to Dreamland.

"Boomer, you astonish me, you really do," Cuttler might have said, and I think, in reconstructing events, he did. His figure loomed there in the doorway, the two coffee mugs emblazoned with the KFUN logo outstretched to Tony and me. "We all took bets, and I tell you, really, I've been on the losing end all week. Not that I didn't have faith, but knowing you, knowing your performance, that is, and the level of your attachment to, uh, *procedure* down at KFUN, I just didn't think—well, as I say, you do astonish me. Bravo. And keep it up, old chip."

My focus was wavering. I couldn't really feel the cup in my hands, couldn't tell if it was cold or hot, ceramic or Styrofoam (I was suffering from astereognosis, the inability to identify objects through the sense of touch, the very same condition that had afflicted Randy Gardner from the second day on). I felt irritated suddenly. Hot. Outraged. The feeling came up in me like a brush fire, and I couldn't have put the two proper nouns "Cuttler" and "Ames" together if they were the key to taking home the million-dollar prize on a quiz show. "Who the fuck are *you*?" I snarled, and the coffee seemed to snake out of the cup of its own accord.

Cuttler's canary-yellow shirt was canary no longer, if, in fact, that was what he was wearing that day. He snarled something back at me, something offensive and threatening, something about my status at the station, but then Tony, glad-faced, big-headed, cliché-spouting moron that he was, stepped in on my side. "Lay off him, Cutt," he might have said. "Can't you see the strain he's under here? Give us a break, will you?"

And now I felt warm to the bottom of my heart. Tony, good old reliable witty Tony, my partner and my fortress, was coming to my aid. "Tony," I said. "Tony." And left it at that.

Then somehow it was night and my mood shifted to the valedictory because I knew I was going to die just like the rats. My quarter-hour spots lacked vitality, or that was my sense of them ("Helloooo, you ladies and baboons out there in K-whatever land, do you know what the time is? Do you care? Because the Boomer doesn't"). The street outside the booth wasn't a street anymore but a portal to the underworld and the bums weren't bums either, but dark agents of death and decay. I saw my wife and her second husband rise up out of the fog, sprout fangs and wings and flap off into the night. My dead mother appeared briefly, rattling the ice cubes in her cocktail glass till the sound exploded around me like a train derailment. I shoved a gyro into my face, fascinated by the pooling orange grease on the console that seemed to have risen up out of the floor beneath me just to receive it. When Dr. Laurie, who might have been dressed that night like a streetwalker or maybe a nun, came in to monitor me, I may have grabbed for her breasts and hung on like a pair of human calipers until she slapped me back to my senses. And Hezza. My angel in earflaps. Hezza was there, always there, as sleepless as I, sometimes crouched in the bushes, sometimes manifesting herself in the booth with me, rubbing my shoulders and the small of my back with her medium-sized mittened hands and talking nonstop of bands, swag and the undying glamour of FM radio. Christ was in the desert. I was in the booth. My fingers couldn't feel and my eyes couldn't see.

ON THE TENTH DAY, I achieved clarity. Suddenly the ever-thickening skin of irreality was gone. I saw the street transformed, the fog dissipating that seemed to have been there all week pushing up against the glass walls like the halitosis of defeat, each wisp and tendril burnished by the sun till it glowed. I went live to the studio for my quarter-hour update and let my voice ooze out over the airwaves with such plasticity and oleaginous joy you would have thought I was applying for the job. When I got up to visit the facilities at the Soul Shack, a whole crowd of starry-eyed fans thumped and patted me and held out their hands in supplication even as the chant *Boomer, Boomer, Boomer* rose up like a careening wave to engulf us all in triumph and ecstasy. One more day to set the record, and then we'd see about the day beyond that—the twelfth day, the magic one, the day no other DJ or high school science nerd or speed freak would ever see or match, not as long as the Guinness Brewing Company kept its records into the burgeoning and glorious future.

I was running both taps, trying to make out the graffiti over the toilet and staring into my cratered eyes as if I might tumble into them and never emerge again, when there came a soft insistent rapping at the door. Clear-headed though I was, I felt a surge of irritation. Who in hell could this be? Didn't everybody in town, from the people in their aluminum rockers at the nursing home to the Soul Shack's ham-fisted bouncers, know that I had to have my five minutes of privacy here? Five minutes. Was that too much to ask? Sixty stinking minutes a day? Did they have to see me squatting over the toilet? Unzipping my fly? What did they want, blood? "Who is it?" I boomed.

The smallest voice: "It's me, Hezza."

I opened the door. Hezza's face was drawn and white, pale as a gutter leaf bleached by the winter rains. Beyond her I could see Rudy, our prissiest intern, studying the stopwatch that kept me strictly to my five minutes and not a second more. "Nazi!" I shouted at him, then pulled Hezza into the bathroom with me and shut the door.

She was shivering. Her eyes were red-rimmed, the irises faded till you couldn't tell what color they were anymore. She'd been keeping vigil. She was as tranced as I was. "Take your clothes off," I told her.

How much hesitation was there—half a second?

"Hurry!" I barked.

She was wearing blue jeans, a blouse under the long coat, nothing under that. The coat fell to the floor, the blouse parted, the jeans grabbed at her thighs, and her panties—yellow and gold butterflies and hovering bees, the panties of a child—slid to her knees. Hypnogogic reverie indeed. I tore the buttons off my third-favorite Hawaiian shirt, yanked at my belt, but it was too late, too far gone and lost, because Rudy was pounding on the door like the Gestapo with instructions from Cuttler to knock it off its hinges and snap an amyl nitrate cap under my nostrils if I lingered even a heartbeat too long.

I don't know. I can't remember. But I don't think I even touched her.

DAY ELEVEN WAS a circus. A zoo. I was in the cage, hallucinating, suffering from dissociated thinking, ataxia, blurred vision and homicidal rage, and the KFUN fans—a hundred of them at least, maybe two hundred—blocked the street, pressed up against the glass walls, gyrated and danced and shouted. Tony was with me full-time now, counting down to the moment of Randy Gardner's annihilation, the KFUN sound truck blasting up-to-the-minute KFUN hits to the masses, the police, the city council and the mayor getting in on the act—taking credit, even, though at a safe distance. The stores up and down the block were doing a brisk business in everything from T-shirts to birdcages to engagement rings, and the fast-food outlets were putting on extra shifts.

Hezza was in the booth with us, the booth that had grown crowded now because Dr. Laurie and Nguyen were hovering over the console like groupies, milking every moment for all it was worth, and nobody wanted Hezza there but me. I insisted. Got angry. Maybe even violent. So, though Cuttler and Rudy the intern bit their lips and looked as sour as spoiled milk, Hezza was right there in a plastic chair between me and Tony, her medium-sized mittened hand clutched in my own. And why not? I was the star here, I was the anchorite, I was the one nailed to the cross and hung out to dry for the public's amusement and edification and maybe even redemption. I was feeling grandiose. Above everybody and everything. Transcendent, I guess you'd call it. I wanted Hezza in the booth. Hezza was in the booth.

Tony and I stumbled our way through the show, the Boomer anything but, my wit dried up, my voice a freeze-dried rasp, a whisper. We played more music than usual, cueing up one insomnia tune after another, the Talking Heads' "Stay Up Late," the Beastie Boys' "No Sleep Till Brooklyn," a Cuttler Ames' blast from the past "Wake Me, Shake Me." The ads came fast and furious. Tony counted down the minutes in a voice that got increasingly hysterical. The record was in sight. I was going to make it—and what's more I was ready to shoot for the whole banana, the twelfth day, the immortal day, and I'd already told Cuttler as much. "It's in the bag," I told him, waving my arms over my head like an exercise guru. "No fears."

And then the final countdown, live on the air, 5-4-3-2-1, and a shout went up from the crowd, all those delirious bobbing heads, Hezza grinning up at me out of her parchment face and squeezing my hand as if she were milking it, Dr. Laurie beaming, Cuttler, Tony and the mayor jostling for position with Nick Nixon from the local TV station and a smattering of crews from as far away as Fresno and Bakersfield. "Speech!" somebody shouted, and they all took it up: "Speech, speech, speech!"

I rose from the chair, bits of pea stone gravel stuck to the backside of my sweaty trousers, Hezza rising with me. Tony was chanting along with the crowd now—or no, he was leading the chant, his voice booming out through the big speakers of the sound truck. It was my moment of glory. My first in a whole long dry spell that stretched all the way back to high school and a lead role in the Thespian Club's production of *The Music Man*. I lifted the mike to my lips, took a deep breath. "I just want to say"—my voice was thunderous, god-like—"I just want to say, Goodbye, Randy Gardner, R.I.P.!"

THEN I WAS ALONE again and it was dark. The morning had bled into afternoon and afternoon into evening, the world battened on the fading light, and with every sleepless minute a new record was being forged. Dr. Laurie begged me to quit at noon, three hours into the new record (actually six, if you consider that I'd been awake and alive for the show that first day before sequestering myself in the glass box). She reminded me of the rats—"They had hemorrhages in their brain tissue, Boomer; enough is enough"—but I ignored her. Cuttler wanted me to go twelve full days, and though I knew on some level he didn't care if I lived or died, I had to show him—show everybody—what I was made of. It was only sleep. I could sleep for a week when I was done. A month. But to stay awake just one more minute was to make history, and the next minute would make history all over again, and the next after that.

Hezza had melted away with the crowd. Dr. Laurie had gone home to sleep. Tony had a date. Cuttler was cuddled up at home with his snaggle-toothed British wife, listening to Deep Purple or some such crap. Even the bums had deserted me, taking their movable feast down the avenue to a less strenuous venue. The funny thing was, I felt fine. I didn't think sleep, not for a minute. What I saw and what I thought I saw were one and the same and I no longer cared to differentiate. I was living inside a dream and the dream was real life, and what was wrong with that?

I watched the KFUN fans line up outside the Soul Shack, watched the line swell and shrink, and fixated on the taillights of the cars moving silently down the boulevard. I couldn't read, couldn't watch the portable TV Tony had set up for me, couldn't even listen to the chatter of it. Everything seemed so inconsequential. I would say that my mind wandered, but the phrase doesn't begin to do justice to the state I was in—I no longer inhabited my body, no longer had a mind or a being. I felt a great peace descend on me, and I just sat there in silence, studying the red LED display on the console as it chopped and diced the hours, moving only to lift a listless hand to acknowledge the thumbs-up from one or another of the baggy-pantsed teens drifting by on the sidewalk. The club emptied, the streets went silent. I didn't even bother to take my restroom breaks.

In the morning, the light climbed down from the tops of the buildings, a light full of pigeons and hope, and Tony appeared, as usual, at quarter of six, with two cups of coffee. There was something wrong with him, I could see that right away. His face lacked dimension. It wasn't a face at all, but a flat screen painted with Tony-features. He looked worried. "Listen, Boom," he said, "you've got to give this up. No offense, but it's like having a dead man here doing the show with me. You know what you said yesterday, on the air, when I asked you how it felt to set the record? You remember that?"

I didn't. I gave him a numb look.

"You said, 'Fuck you, Dog Face.'"

"I said 'fuck'? On the air?"

Tony didn't respond. He handed me a coffee, sat down and put his headphones on. A moment fluttered by. I couldn't feel the paper cup in my hand. I studied Tony in profile, hoping to see how he was Tony, *if* he was Tony. "Just keep out of my way today, will you?" he said, turning on me abruptly. "And when the show's over, when you've got your twelve days in, you go home to bed. You hear me? Rudy's going to take over for you the next two days, so you get a little vacation here to get your head straight." And then, as if he felt he'd been too harsh, he put a hand on my shoulder and leaned into me. "You deserve it, man."

I don't remember anything of the show that day, except that Tony—Gooner, as the KFUN audience knew him—kept ringing down the curtain on my record, reminding everybody in KFUN land that the Boomer would be going on home to bed at the conclusion of the show, and what would the Boomer like? A foot massage? A naked blonde? A teddy bear? Couple of brewskies? Ha-ha, ha-ha. One more day, one more show, one more routine. But what Tony didn't know, or Cuttler Ames or Dr. Laurie either, was that I had no intention of giving up the microphone: I was shooting for thirteen days now, and after that it would be fourteen, maybe fifteen. Who could say?

A handful of people were milling around outside the glass booth as we closed out the show, but there was none of the ceremony of the preceding day. The record had been broken, the ratings boosted, and the stunt was over as far as anybody was concerned. The mayor certainly didn't show. Nor did Dr. Laurie. Tony let out a long trailing sigh after we signed off ("This is the Gooner—and the Boomer—saying *adiós, amigos,* and keep the faith, baby—at least till tomorrow morning, same time, same place") and made as if to help me out of the chair, but I shoved him away. He was standing, I was sitting. I was trembling all over, trembling as if I'd just been hosed down on an ice floe in the middle of the Arctic Ocean. *Don't touch me,* I muttered to myself. *Don't even think about it.* He dropped his face to mine, his big bloated moronic moon face that I wanted to smash till it shattered. "Come on, man," he said, "it's over. Beddy-bye. Time to crash."

I didn't move. Wouldn't look at him.

"Don't get psychotic on me now," he said, and he took hold of my left arm, but I shrugged him off. The people on the street stopped what they were doing. Heads turned, eyes zeroed in. He gave them a lame smile, as if it was all part of the act. "You're tired," he said, "that's all," but there was no conviction in his voice. "Boomer?" he said, as if I were floating away from him. "Boomer?" A minute later I heard the glass door at the back of the booth swing open and then shut.

At quarter past nine I went to do my update, but the mike was dead: they'd cut the power on me. I flicked the on/off button a couple of times, then shifted in my seat to glare at the engineer in the sound truck, but the engineer wasn't there—nobody was. So that was it. They were going to isolate me, the sons of bitches. Cut me off. Use me and discard me. I got up from my seat, and who was watching? Nobody. Or no, there was a six-year-old kid standing there gawking at me while his mother jawed with some other mother in front of the Burger King outlet across the street, and I locked eyes with him for an instant before I jerked the mike out of the socket. What came next I don't remember too clearly, or maybe I've repressed it, but it seems I began to pound the mike against the Plexiglas walls, whipping it like a lariat, and when that was in fragments, I went for the console.

When they finally got me out of there, I'm told, it was past noon and I was well into my thirteenth day—a record that has yet to be surpassed, incidentally, though I'm told there's a fakir in India who claims he hasn't slept in three months, but of course that's unofficial. Not to mention impossible. At any rate, Dr. Laurie had to come down and reason with me in a rigorous way, a squad car began circling the block, and Cuttler ordered Rudy and the sound engineer to cover up the glass walls with black plastic sheeting from the Home Depot up the street. We were getting publicity now, all right, but it wasn't exactly the touchy-feely sort of publicity our august program director had in mind. I'd latched the door from the inside and forced the remains of the console up against it as a makeshift barricade. Rudy was on the roof of the glass cage, unscrolling sheets of black plastic as if it were bunting. I watched Dr. Laurie's face on the other side of the transparent door, watched her mouth work professionally, noted and discarded each of her patent phrases, her false pleas and admonitions. Anything could have happened, because I wasn't going anywhere. And if it wasn't for Hezza I might still be in that glass box—or in the Violent Ward down at the County Hospital. It was that close.

I wasn't aware of how or when it occurred, but at some point I realized that Hezza's face had been transposed over Dr. Laurie's, and that Hezza was smiling at me out of the screwholes of her dimples. I don't know what it was—psychosis, terminal exhaustion or the simple joy of being alive—but I'd never seen anything more beautiful than the earflaps of her knit hat and the way they tucked into her cheeks and made her face into the face of a cut-out doll in a children's book. I smiled back. Then she bent her head, scribbled a moment, and pressed a sheet of paper to the glass. I LOVE YOU, it read.

OF COURSE, this is the sort of resolution we all hope for, even the sleep-deprived, but it wasn't as easy as all that. When we got to my place, when we got to the bed I hadn't seen in thirteen days, the skin of irreality was so thick I couldn't be sure who it was at my side— Hezza, Dr. Laurie, my ex-wife, one of the lean shopping machines

I'd watched striding down the avenue from the confines of my glass cage. There was a stripe of sun on the carpet. I pulled the curtains. It vanished. "Who are you?" I said, though the earflaps were a dead giveaway. Something began buzzing from the depths of the house. Outside in the alley the neighbor's dog barked sharply, once, twice, three times. She looked puzzled, looked hurt. "Hezza," she said. "I'm Hezza, don't you remember?"

This time I didn't have to shout, didn't have to do anything really except fall into her where she lay naked on the bed, the blissful bed, the place of sex and sleep. I made love to her through the sheath of exhaustion and afterward watched her eyes slip toward closure and listened to her breathing deepen into sleep. I was tired. Had never been so tired in my life. No one on this earth—no one, ever, not even Randy Gardner—had been so tired. I closed my eyes. Nothing happened. My eyes blinked open as if they'd been trip-wired. For a moment I lay there staring at the ceiling, then I closed them again and by force of will kept them closed. Still nothing. Hezza stirred in her sleep, kicked out at an imaginary something. And then a figure stepped out of the mist and I didn't see him. He had a gun, and I didn't see that either. Swiftly, a shadow moving over open ground, he came up behind me and fired, hitting the gap between the parietal plates.

Boom: I was gone.

The Swift Passage of the Animals

SHE WAS TRYING to tell him something about eels, how it had rained eels one night on a town in South America—in Colombia, she thought it was—but he was only half-listening. He was willing himself to focus on the road, the weather getting worse by the minute, and he had to keep one hand on the tuner because the radio was fading in and out as they looped higher into the mountains. "It was a water spout," she said, her face a soft pale shell floating on the undersea glow of the dash lights, "or that's what they think, anyway. I mean, that's the rational explanation—the eels congregating to feed or mate and then this eruption that flings them into the air. But imagine the people. Imagine them."

He could feel the rear wheels slipping away from him each time he steered into a curve, and there were nothing but curves, one switchback after another all the way up the flank of the mountain. The night was absolute, no lights, no habitation, nothing—they'd passed the last ranch house ten miles back and were deep into the national forest now, at fifty-five hundred feet and making for the Big Timber Lodge at seventy-two. There was a winter storm watch out for the Southern Sierras, he knew that, and he knew that the back road would be closed as soon as the first snow hit, but the alternative route—up the front of the mountain—was even more serpentine than this one, and a good half hour longer too. His feeling was that they'd make it before the rain turned to snow—or before anything accumulated, anyway. Was he a risk taker? Sure he was. And he was always in a hurry. Especially tonight. Especially with her.

"Zach—you listening to me?"

The radio caught a surging throb of chords and a wicked guitar lead burning over the top of them as if the guitarist's fingers had suddenly burst into flame, but before he could enjoy it or even recognize the tune, a wall of static shut it out and was suddenly replaced by a snatch of mariachi and a superslick DJ booming something in Spanish—used cars probably, judging from the tone of it. Or Viagra. *Estimados Señores! ¿Tienen Vds. problemas con su vigor?* His fingers tweaked the dial as delicately as a recording engineer's. But the static came back and persisted. "Shit," he muttered, and punched the thing off.

Now there was nothing but the wet slash of the wheels and the rise and fall of the engine—gun it here, lay off there, gun it, lay off—and the mnemonic echo of the question he'd yet to answer: *You listening to me?* "Yeah," he said, reaching for his buoyant tone—he *was* listening and there was nothing or no one he'd rather listen to because he was in love and the way she bit off her words, the dynamics of her voice, the whisper, the intonation, the soft sexy scratch of it shot from his eardrums right to his crotch, but this was sleet they were looking at now and the road was dark and he was pressing to get there. "The eels. And the people. They must've been surprised, huh?"

She feasted on that a moment and he snatched a glimpse at her, the slow satisfied smile floating on her uplifted face, and the wheels grabbed and slipped and grabbed again. "That's the thing," she said, her voice rich with the telling, "that's the whole point, to imagine that. They're in their huts, frame houses, whatever—tin roofs, maybe just thatch. But the tin roofs are cooler. Way cooler. Think of the tin roofs. It's like, 'Daddy! Mommy!' the kids call out, 'it's *really* raining!'"

This was hilarious—the picture of it, the way she framed it for him, carrying it into falsetto for the kids' voices—and they both broke up, laughing like kids themselves, kids set free in the back of the bus on a school trip. But then there was the road and a black tree-thick turn he nearly didn't make and the last spasm of laughter died in his throat.

A minute fled by, the wipers beating, sleet trapped in the headlights. She readjusted herself in the seat and he saw her hand—a white furtive ghost in the dark of the cab—reach down to check the seatbelt. "The tires are okay, aren't they?" she asked, trying—and failing—to keep the concern out of her voice.

"Oh, yeah," he said, "yeah, plenty of tread," though he'd begun to think he should have sprung for chains. The last sign he'd seen, way back, had said *Cars Required With Chains,* and that stabbed him with the first prick of worry, but chains were something like seventy-five bucks a set and you didn't need chains to get to work in Santa Monica. It seemed excessive to him. If he could have *rented* them, maybe—

And there went the back wheels again, fishtailing this time, a broad staggered Z inscribing itself across both sides of the road and thank God there was nobody else out here tonight, no chance of running into a vehicle coming down the opposite way, not with a winter storm watch and a road closure that was all but certain to go into effect at some point in the night . . .

"You're really skidding," she observed. He glanced at her a moment—sweet and compact in her black leggings and the sweater with the two reindeer prancing across her breasts—and then his eyes shot back to the road. Which was whitening before them, as if some cosmic hand had swept on ahead with a two-lane paintbrush.

"You know my theory?" he said, accelerating out of a turn and leaning into the pitch of the road—up and up, always up.

"No, what?"

"If you go fast enough"—he gave her a quick glance, straight-faced—"I mean really fast . . ."

"Yeah, uh-huh?"

"Well, it's obvious, isn't it? You won't have time to skid."

There was the briefest hesitation—one beat, and he loved that about her, that moment of process—and then they were laughing again, laughing so hard he thought he'd have to pull over to keep from collapsing.

HE'D MET HER three weeks ago, just before Thanksgiving, at a party in Silver Lake. Friends of friends. A Craftsman house, restored down to the last lick of varnish, good wines, hors d'oeuvres from the caterer, a roomful of studiously hip people who if they weren't rockers or filmmakers or poets had to be training to swim the Java Strait or climb solo up the South Col of Mount Diablo. He figured he'd tank up on the hors d'oeuvres, get smashed on somebody else's thirty-two-dollars-a-bottle Cabernet, then duck home and watch a movie on DVD, because he wasn't really interested in much more than that. Not yet. He'd been with Christine for two and a half years and then she met somebody at work, and that had shaved him right on down to the root.

Ontario was standing by the fire with his best friend Jared's sister, Mindy, and when he came to think of it later, he saw that there might have been more than a little matchmaking going on here from Mindy's perspective—she knew Ontario from her book club, and she knew that Ontario, sweet and shy and reposing on a raft of arcane information about meteorological events and the swift passage of the various animal species from this sore and wounded planet, was six months divorced and in need of diversion. As he was himself, at least in Mindy's eyes. The wine sang in his veins. He made his way over to the fire.

"So I suppose you must hear this all the time," he said, trying to be clever, trying to impress her after Mindy had embraced him and made the introductions, "but are your parents Canadian?"

"You guessed it."

"So your brother must be Saskatchewan, right? Or B.C., how about B.C.?"

Her hair shone. She was dressed all in black. Her eyes assessed him a moment—from behind the narrow plastic-frame glasses that were like a provocation, as if at any moment she would throw them off and dazzle the room with her unfettered beauty—and she very deliberately shifted the wineglass from one hand to the other. "Unfortunately, I don't have a brother," she said. "Or a sister either." Then she smiled, fully radiant. "If I did, though, I'd think my parents would have gone for Alberta if it was a girl—"

"And what, let me guess—*Newfoundland* if it was a boy."

She looked pleased. Her lips parted and she bit the tip of her tongue in anticipation of the punch line. "Right," she said, "and we'd call him Newf for short."

He'd phoned her the next night and taken her to dinner, and then to a concert two nights later, all the correspondences in alignment. She had a three-year-old daughter. Her ex paid alimony. She worked part-time as a receptionist and was taking courses at UCLA toward an advanced degree in environmental studies. One entire wall in her apartment, floor to ceiling, was dedicated to nature books, from Thoreau to Leopold to Wilson, Garrett, Quammen and Gould.

He fell. And fell hard.

EACH TURN WAS A duplicate of the one he'd just negotiated, hairpin to the right, hairpin to the left, more trees, more snow, more distance. The road was gone now altogether, replaced by a broad white featureless plain without discernible limits. He used the trunks of the trees as guideposts, trying to keep the car equidistant from those on the left and the ones that clipped by on the right like so many slats in a fence. It really wouldn't do to skid into any of these trees— they were yellow pines, sugar pines, Jeffreys and ponderosas, as wide around as the pillars of the Lincoln Memorial—but the gaps between them were what caught his attention. Go off the road there and no one could say how far you would drop. Guardrails? Not out here.

They were silent a moment, so he took up the eels again—just to hear his own voice by way of distraction. "So I suppose there's an upside—the villagers must have enjoyed a little fried eel and plantains. Or maybe they smoked them."

"You'd get awfully sick of eel after a couple days, don't you think?" She wasn't staring out the windshield into the white fury of the headlights, but watching him as if they were cruising down the Coast Highway under a ripe and delicate sun. "No, I think they went ahead and buried them—the ones that were too injured to crawl off."

"The stink, huh?"

"Or slither off. Did you know that eels—the American eel, which is what these were—can crawl overland? Like a snake?"

He squinted into the sleet, reached out to flick the radio back on, but thought better of it. "No, I don't think so. Or maybe. Maybe I did. I remember they used to be in every creek when I was a kid— you'd fish for trout and catch this big slick whipping thing that always seemed to swallow the hook and then you couldn't do anything but cut it loose. Because of the slime factor."

"They're all born in the Sargasso Sea, you know that, right? And that it's the females that migrate inland?"

He did. Because he was something of a nature buff himself, hiking up the canyons on weekends, poking under rocks and in the willows along the streambeds, trying to learn the lore, and his own bookshelves featured many of the same titles he'd found on hers. Which was one of the reasons they were going to Big Timber for the weekend—so he could show her the trails he'd discovered the past summer, take her on the Trail of a Hundred Giants and then down the Freeman Creek Trail to the Freeman Grove. She was from Boston and she'd never seen the redwoods and sequoias except in photographs. When she'd told him that, over a plate of mussels marinara at a semi-hip, over-priced place on Wilshire with red banquette seats and votive candles on the tables, he began to rhapsodize Big Timber till he'd made it out to be the earthly paradise itself. Which it was, for all he knew. He'd only been there twice, both times with Jared, on their mountain bikes, but it was as wild and beautiful as it must have been in Muir's time—sure it was—and he'd convinced her to have her sister babysit for the weekend so they could hike the trails and cross-country ski if there was enough snow, and then sit at the bar at the lodge till it was time to go to bed.

And that was the other reason for the trip, the unspoken promise percolating beneath the simple monosyllable of her assent—going to bed. On their first date she'd told him she was feeling fragile still—her word, not his—and wanted to take things slowly. All right. He respected that. But three weeks had gone by and when she'd agreed to come with him—for two days and two nights—he felt something pull loose inside of him.

"Right," he said, "and then they all return to the Sargasso Sea to mate."

"Amazing, isn't it?"

"All those eels," he said. "Eels from Ohio, Pennsylvania, Texas"—he gave her a look—"Ontario even."

That was when the wheels got away from him and the car spun across the road to glance off a white-capped boulder and into a glistening white ditch that undulated gracefully away from the hidden surface of the road, which was where he really and truly wanted to be.

THAT THEY WERE STUCK was a given. The passenger's side wheels were in the ditch, canting the car at an unfortunate angle, and beneath the furiously accumulating snow there was a glaze of ice that gave no purchase. He cursed under his breath—"Shit, shit, shit"—and slammed the wheel with his fist, and she said, "Are we stuck?" For a long moment he didn't respond, the wipers stupidly beating, the snow glossy in the headlights and driving down like a hard white rain. "Are you all right?" he said finally. "Because I—I mean, it just got away from me there. The road—it's like a skating rink or something." Her face was ghost-lit. He couldn't see her eyes. "Yeah," she said softly, "I'm fine."

When he cracked the door to get out and have a look, the snow stung his eyes and drove the breath from his lips. He caught a quick glimpse of her, huddled there in the passenger's seat—and there was the smell of her perfume too, of the heat of her body and the sleepy warmth of the car's interior—and then he slammed the door and walked round the car to assess the damage. The front fender on the passenger's side had been staved in where it had hit the boulder, but it didn't seem to be interfering with the wheel at all—and that was the good news. For the rest of it, the rear tires had dug themselves a pair of craters in the ice beneath the snow and the axle was resting on a scraped-bald patch of dirt just beneath the tailpipe. And the snow. The snow was coming down and the road was certain to be closed—till spring maybe—and he wasn't sure how many miles yet it was to the lodge. Five? Ten? Twenty? He couldn't begin to guess, and as he looked up into the thin streaming avenue of illumination the car's headlights afforded him, he realized he didn't recognize a thing. There were just trees. Trees and more trees.

Then the car door slammed and she was standing there beside him, the hood of her parka drawn tight over the oval of her face.

"You know, I grew up in snow, so this is nothing to me." She was grinning, actually grinning, the glow of the taillights giving her features a weird pinkish cast. "I'll tell you what we have to do, we have to jack up this back wheel here and put something under it."

"Like what?" The engine coughed softly, twice, three times, and then settled into its own rhythm. There was the smell of the exhaust and the sound of the miniature ice pellets in all their trillion permutations hissing off the hood of his jacket, off the trunk of the car, off her hood and the boughs of the trees. He looked round him bleakly—there was nothing, absolutely nothing, to see but for the hummocks of the snow, white fading to gray and then to a drifting pale nullity beyond the range of the headlights.

"I don't know," she said, "a log or something. You have a shovel in the trunk?"

He didn't have a shovel in the trunk—no shovel and no chains. He began to feel less a risk taker and more a fool, callow, rash, without foresight or calculation, the sort of blighted individual whose genetic infirmities get swallowed up in the food chain before he can reproduce and pass them on to vitiate the species. That was the way an evolutionist would see it—that was the way *she* would see it. "No, uh-uh, no shovel," he breathed, and then he was slogging round the car to reach in the driver's door, cut the engine and retrieve the keys—the jack was in the trunk, anyway. Or at least it had been, the last time he'd looked, but who obsessed over the contents of the trunk of their car? It was a place to put groceries, luggage, the big purchase at the mall.

Without the rumble of the engine, the night seemed to close in, the ceaseless hiss of the snow the only sound in the universe. He left the lights on, though the buzzer warned him against it, and then he was back with her, flinging open the trunk of the car, the interior of which immediately began to whiten with the descending snow. There were their bags—his black, hers pink—and there was the jack laid in against the inner panel where he'd flung it after changing a flat last summer. Or was it summer before last?

"Okay, great," she said, the pale puff of her breath clinging at her lips, "why don't you jack it up and I'll look for something to—pine boughs, we could use pine boughs. Do you have a knife with you? A hatchet? Anything to cut with?"

He was standing there, two feet from her, staring into the whitening trunk. There were two plastic quarts of motor oil in the back, a grease-stained T-shirt, half a dozen CDs he was afraid the valet at the Italian restaurant might have wanted to appropriate for himself, but no knives, no tools of any kind, other than the jack handle. "No, I don't think so."

She gave him a look then—the dark slits of her glasses, the pursed lips—but all she said was, "We could use the carpet. I mean, look"— and she was reaching in, experimentally lifting the fitted square of it from the mottled steel beneath.

The car was two years old and he was making monthly payments on it. It was the first car he'd ever bought new in his life and he'd picked it out over Christine's objections. He liked the sportiness of it, the power—he could blow by most cars on the freeway without really pushing it—and the color, a magnetic red that stood out a hundred yards away. He didn't want to tear out the carpeting—that was not an option, because they'd get out of this and laugh about it over drinks at the lodge, and there was no sense in getting panicky, no sense in destroying things unnecessarily—but she already had hold of it with one hand and was shoving the bags back away from it with the other, and he had no choice but to pitch in and help.

INSIDE THE CAR with the engine running, he was in a dream, a trance, as if he'd plunged to the bottom of the sea with Cousteau in his bathyscaphe and all the world had been reduced to this dim cab with the faint green glow of the dash lights and the hum of the heater. Ontario was there beside him, a dark presence in the passenger's seat, her head nestled in the crook of his arm. They'd agreed to run the car every fifteen minutes or so—and then only briefly—in order to conserve gas and still keep the engine warm enough to deliver up heat. And that was all right, though he kept waking from his dream to a kind of frantic beating in his chest because they were in trouble here, deep trouble, he knew that no matter how much he told himself the storm would tail off and they could wade through the snow to the lodge. And what of the car? With this heavy a snowfall the road would be closed till spring and the car would be abandoned until the snow melted away and revealed it there at the side of the road, in the ditch, and he'd have to beg a ride to work or squeeze onto one of those noxious buses with all the dregs of humanity. Still, it could be worse— at least he'd filled the gas tank before they'd started up the hill.

"Zach?" Her voice was murmurous with sleep.

"Yeah?"

"There's nothing to worry about, you know. I've got two strong legs. We can walk out in the morning and get somebody to help— snowmobilers. There's sure to be snowmobilers out—"

"Yeah," he said, "yeah, I'm sure," and he wanted to add, gloomily, that this wasn't suburban Massachusetts, that this was the wild, or at least as wild as it got in Southern California. There were mountain lions here, bears, pine martens, the ring-tailed cat. Last summer, with Jared, he'd seen a bear cub—a yearling, he guessed, a pretty substantial animal—out on the highway, this very highway, scraping the carcass of a crushed squirrel off the pavement with its teeth. They averaged twenty-plus feet of snow per season at this altitude and as much as forty during an El Niño year, and with his luck this would turn out to be an El Niño, no doubt about it, because it was coming down as if it wasn't going to stop till May. *Snowmobilers.* Fat chance. Still, there was the lodge, and if they could get there—when they got there—they'd be all right. And the car would keep—he felt sick about it and he'd need a new battery maybe, but that was something he could live with. The cold he didn't think about. Or the killing effort of slogging through knee-deep snow. That was for tomorrow. That was for daylight.

They'd spent a good hour or more trying to get the car out, the carpets expendable, his Thomas Guide, even his spare jacket and two back issues of *Nature* she'd brought along to pore over by the fire, but the best they'd been able to do was give the rear wheels a moment's purchase in order to shove the front end in deeper. By the time they gave up, he'd lost all sensation in his toes and fingertips, and that was when she thought of her cell phone—and he let her take it out and dial 911 because he didn't have the heart to tell her that cell phones were useless up here, out of range, just like the radio.

"Tell me a story," she said now. "Talk to me."

He cut the engine. The snow had long since turned to powder and it fell silently, the only sound the creak and groan of the automobile shutting down. The dark was all-embracing and the humps of the gathering snow clung to it. "I don't know," he said. "I don't know any stories."

"Tell me about the animals. Tell me about the bears."

He shrugged in the darkness, drew her to him. "They're all asleep now. But last summer—at the lodge?—there was one out back, a big cinnamon sow they said that must have weighed three hundred pounds or more. Jared and I were playing eight ball—there's a nice table there, by the way, and I'm challenging you to the world championship tomorrow afternoon, so you better limber up your fingers— and somebody said, *The bear's out there again,* and we must have watched the thing for half an hour before it lumbered off, and lumber it did. I mean, now I can understand the meaning of that word in a whole new way."

She was silent a moment, then she said, "The California grizzly's extinct, but you knew that, right?"

"Oh, yeah, yeah, I meant this was a black bear."

"They shot the last grizzly in Fresno, probably sniffing around somebody's sheep ranch, in 1922. Boom. And it was gone forever." There was a hitch in her voice, a sort of downbeat, as she settled into the arena of certainty, of what is and what was. The snow sifted down around them, a white sea in fragments—the dandruff of God, as his father used to call it when they went skiing at Mammoth over Christmas break each year. She paused a beat, then her voice came to him, soft as a prayer. "Did I ever tell you about the Carolina parakeet?"

IT WAS STILL SNOWING at first light and the wind had come up in the night and sculpted a drift that rose as high as the driver's side window, though he didn't know that yet. He woke from a dream that dissolved as soon as he opened his eyes, replaced by a sudden

sharp apprehension of loss: his car to be abandoned, the indeterminate walk ahead of them, the promise of the weekend crushed like a
bag full of nothing. All because he was an idiot. Because he'd taken
a chance and the chance had failed him. He thought back to yesterday afternoon, the unalloyed pleasure in her face as she tucked her
bag into the trunk and settled in beside him, the palms nodding in
a breeze off the ocean, the traffic light—lighter than he'd ever seen
it—one great tune after another on the radio, all beat and attitude,
his fingertips drumming on the steering wheel and how was work
and did the boss say anything about ducking out early? He wished
he could go back there, back to that moment when she slid in beside
him and the precipitation hadn't started in yet and he could have
chosen the main road, the one he knew would get them there, snow
or no snow. He wished he'd sprung for chains too. He wished a lot
of things. Wished he was at the lodge, waking up beside her in bed.
Or lingering over breakfast by the fire, big white oval plates of eggs
and ham and home fries, mimosas, Bloody Marys, the snow hanging
in the windows like a wraparound mural . . .

The car was cold—he could see the breath trailing from his
lips—and the windshield was opaque with the accumulation of snow
and the intricate frozen swirls of condensation that clung to the inner surface of the glass. Ontario was asleep, the hood framing her
face, her lips parted to expose the neat arc of her upper teeth, and for
a long moment he just stared at her, afraid to wake her, afraid to start
whatever was to come. What had she told him the night before? That
the wild was shrinking away and the major species of the earth were
headed for oblivion and there was nothing anyone could do about it.
He tried to dissuade her, pointing to the reintroduction of the wolf
in Yellowstone, the resilience of the puma and black bear popula-
tions in these woods, the urban invasion of deer, opossums and raccoons, but she wouldn't listen. This was her obsession, everything
dead or dying, the oceans depleted, the skies bereft, the plains and
the forests gone preternaturally silent, and she fell asleep in his arms
reciting the names of the creatures gone down as if she were saying
her prayers.

He listened to her breathing, the soft rattle of the air circulating through her nostrils and lifting and deflating her chest in a slow regular rhythm, and he watched her face, composed around dreams of the animals deserting their niches one by one. He didn't want to wake her. But he was cold and he had to relieve himself and then formulate some sort of plan or at least figure out where they were and how far they were going to have to walk, and so he turned over the engine to get some heat and cracked his door to discover the drift and the chill blue light trapped within it.

She sat up with a start, even as he put his shoulder to the door and the breath of the storm rode in on a cold whip of wind-flung snow. "Where are we?" she murmured, as if they could have been anyplace else, and then, vaguely pushing at the hood of her parka as if to run her fingers through her hair, "Is it still snowing?"

They relieved themselves privately, he on his side of the car—after planing off the drift with the dull knife-edge of the door—and she on hers. He stood there, the snow in his face, whiteness unrelieved, and drilled a steaming cavity into the drift while she squatted out of sight and the road revealed itself as a featureless river flowing away between the cleft banks of the trees. It took them a while to divide up their things—anything left behind, extra clothes, toiletry articles, makeup, jewelry, would go into the trunk, where they'd recover it next spring as if they were digging up a time capsule—and they shared one of the two power bars she'd brought along in her purse and a stick each of the beef jerky he found in his backpack. They ate in the car, talking softly, warming their fingers in the blast of the heater, the gas gauge run nearly all the way down now, but he'd worry about that later. Much later. He brooded as he worked his jaws over a plug of dried meat, kicking himself all over again, but she was unfazed. In fact, given the circumstances, given how miserable he was, she seemed inordinately cheerful, as if this was a big adventure—but then it wasn't her car, was it?

"Oh, come on, Zach," she said, her eyes startled and wide behind the constricting lenses, a faint trace of chocolate defining her upper lip, "we'll make the most of it. We were going to hike anyway, weren't we? And when we get to the lodge we'll see if maybe somebody can tow the car out—all right? And then we can play that game of pool you promised me."

His voice dropped to a croak. He was feeling sorry for himself and the more upbeat she was the more sorry he felt. "They can't," he said. "It's miles from the lodge and they don't plow here, there's no point in it. I mean, how would they get a tow truck in?"

The smile still clung to her lips, a patient smile, serene, beautiful. "Maybe you can get them to just plow one lane or something—or somebody with a snowplow on his pickup, something like that."

He turned his head, stared at the frosted-over side window. "Forget it," he said. "The car's here till May. Unless the yahoos come out and strip it."

"All right, then. Have it your way. But we'd better get walking or we'll be here till May ourselves, right?"

He didn't answer.

"It's that way, I assume," she said, pointing a gloved finger at the windshield.

He just looked at her, then shoved open the door and stepped out into the snow.

HE WAS TWENTY-EIGHT years old, in reasonably good shape—he worked out once or twice a week at the gym, made a point of walking the eight blocks to the grocery store every other day and went mountain biking in season—but the major part of his waking life was spent motionless in front of the computer screen, and that was what afflicted him now. The snow was thigh-deep, the air thin, and they hadn't gone half a mile before his clothes were damp with sweat and his legs felt like dead things grafted on at the hip. She followed three steps behind in the narrow gauge of the trail he broke for her, her eyes sharp and attuned, the pink bag thrown over one shoulder, thrusting out her arms for balance every so often as if she were walking a tightrope. Nothing moved ahead of them, not a bird or squirrel even. The silence pinned them in, as if they were in an infinite bed under a blanket as big as the sky.

"You look like a snowman," she said. "A walking snowman."

He took this as a signal to stop, and he planted his feet and ro-tated to face her. She seemed reduced somehow, as small as a child sent out to play with her sled on a day when the superintendent had closed down the schools, and he wanted to hug her to him protec-tively, wanted to make amends for his mood and the mess he'd gotten them into, but he didn't. The snow drove down, burying everything. There was a crown of it atop her hood, individual flakes caught like drift in her eyelashes and softening the frames of her glasses. "You too," he said, pulling for air as if he were drowning. "Both of us," he gasped. "Snowmen. Or snow man and snow woman."

Later on—and maybe they'd gone another mile—he made a dis-covery that caused his heart to leap up and then almost simultane-ously closed it down again. They'd come to a place he recognized even through the blowing snow and the shifting, subversive con-tours of the landscape—an intersection, with a half-buried stop sign. Straight ahead the road pushed deeper into the wilderness; to the left, it led to the Big Timber Lodge, and at least he knew where they were now, even if it wasn't nearly as close as he'd imagined. He'd been fooling himself, he knew that, but all along he'd been hoping they'd passed here in the disorientation of the night. "I know this place," he said. "The lodge is this way."

She was panting now too, though not ten minutes ago she'd been telling him how she never missed a day on the Stairmaster—or al-most never. "Fantastic," she said. "See, it wasn't so bad." She stamped in place, shook the snow from her shoulders. "How far from here?"

His voice sank. "Pretty far," he said.

"How far?"

He shrugged. Looked away from her even as a gust flung a fist of snow in his face. "Thirteen miles."

THERE CAME A POINT—it might have been half an hour later, forty-five minutes, he couldn't say—when he gave in and let her break trail ahead of him. He was wiped. He could barely lift his legs. And when he wasn't moving—if he paused even for a minute to catch his breath—the wind dug into him and he felt the sweat go cold under his arms and across his back. He couldn't believe how fast the snow was accumulating—it was up to his crotch now and even deeper in the drifts, the wind raking the trees till the needles whipped and sang, the temperature falling as if it were night already, though it was just past one. He watched her move ahead of him, head bobbing, arms churning, six steps and then a recuperative pause, her lower body sheared off at the waist as if she were wading across a river. She'd slipped a pair of jeans on over her leggings in the fastness of the car but she must have been cold, whether she'd grown up in the snow or not. He was thinking he'd have to catch her by the arm and reverse positions with her—he was the one who'd gotten her into this and he was going to lead her out of it—when suddenly she stopped and swung round on him, heaving for breath.

"Wow," she said, "this is something, huh?" Her face was chapped, blazing, the cord of the hood gone hard with a knot of ice; her nose was running and her mouth was set.

"Let me," he said, "it's my turn."

Her eyes gave him permission. Slowly, with the wind in his face and his feet shuffling like a drunk's, he waded on ahead of her.

"I wish we had snowshoes," she said at his back.

"Yeah, me too."

"Or skis."

"How about a snowmobile? Wouldn't that be nice?"

"Hot coffee," she said. "I'd settle for that."

"With a shot of brandy—or Kahlúa. How does Kahlúa sound?"

The wind came up. She didn't answer. After a while she asked him if he thought it was much farther and he halted and swung round on her. His fingers throbbed, his feet were dead. "I don't know—it can't be that much farther."

"How far do you think we've come? I mean, from where the road forked?"

He shrugged. "A couple miles, I guess, right?"

Her eyes narrowed against the wind. She ran a mittened hand under her nose. "You know what killed off the glyptodont?"

He hugged his arms to his chest and watched her, the wind-blown snow riding up his legs.

"Stupidity," she said, and then they moved on.

NEAR THE END, when the sky shaded perceptibly toward night and the ravens began to call from their hidden perches, she complained of numbness in her fingers and toes. Neither of them had spoken for a long while—speech was superfluous, a waste of energy in the face of what was turning out to be more of a trial than either of them could have imagined—and all he could say was that he was sorry for getting her into this and reassure her that they'd be there soon. The snow hadn't slackened all day—if anything, perversely, it seemed to be coming down even harder now—and the going was ever slower as the drifts mounted ahead of them. Earlier, they'd stopped to share the remaining power bar and she'd been sufficiently energetic still to regale him with stories of the last passenger pigeon dying on its perch in the Cincinnati Zoo and the last wolf shot in these mountains, of the aurochs and the giant sloth and half a dozen other poor doomed creatures winging by on their way to extinction even as he silently calculated their own chances. People froze to death out here, that much he knew. Hikers forever lost in the echoing canyons, snowmobilers awaiting rescue by their disabled machines, the unlucky and unprepared. But they weren't lost, he kept telling himself—they were on the road and it was just a matter of time and effort before they got to the lodge. Nothing to worry about. Nothing at all.

She was ahead of him, breaking trail, the snow up to her waist. "It's not just numb," she said, her breath trailing behind her. "It stings. It stings so bad."

The gloom deepened. He went on another five steps and pulled up short. "Maybe we should stop," he said, breathing so hard he felt as if his lungs had been turned inside out. "Just for a couple minutes. I have a tarp in my pack and we could make a little shelter. If we get out of the wind we can—"

"What?" she swung round on him, her face savage. "We can what—freeze to death? Is that what you want, huh?"

The snow absorbed them. Everything, even the trunks of the trees, faded to colorlessness. He didn't know what to do. He was the one at fault here and there was no way to make that right, but still, couldn't she see he was doing his best?

"No," he said, "that's not what I mean. I mean we could recoup our energy—it can't be much farther—and I could warm your feet. I mean, on my chest, under my parka—isn't that what you're supposed to do? Flesh to flesh?"

She snatched off her glasses and all her beauty flashed out, but it was a disengaged beauty, a bedraggled and fractious beauty. Her lips clenched, her eyes penetrated him. "Are you crazy? I'm going to take off my boots in this? Are you out of your mind?"

"Ontario," he whispered, "listen, come on, please," and he was shuffling forward to take her in his arms and press her to him, to have that at least, human warmth and comfort and all the trailing sorrowful release that comes with it, when the air suddenly bloomed with sound and they both turned to see the single Cyclopean eye of a snowmobile bounding toward them through the drifts.

A moment, and it was over. The engine screamed and then the driver saw them and let off on the throttle, the machine skidding to a halt just in front of them. The driver peeled back his goggles. There was a rime of ice in his beard. The exhaust took hold of the air and paralyzed it. "Jesus," he said, his eyes shying away from them, "I damn near run you down. You people lost or what?"

HE COULD HAVE STAYED where he was, could have waited while the man in the goggles sped Ontario back to the lodge and then returned for him, but he trudged on anyway, a matter of pride now, the man's incredulous laugh still echoing in his ears. *You mean you come up the back road? In this? Oh, man, you are really in the shits.* He was less than a mile from the lodge when the noise of the machine tore open the night and the headlight pinned him where he was. Then it was the wind and the exhaust and the bright running flash of the meaningless snow.

She was propped up by the fire with her boots off and a mug of coffee wrapped in her hands when he dragged himself in the door, shivering violently from that last wind-whipped run through the drifts. Her wet parka was flung over the chair beside her and one of her mittens lay curled on the floor beneath the chair. A group of men in plaid shirts and down vests were gathered at the bar, roaring over the weather and their tall drinks, and a subsidiary group hovered around Ontario, plying her with their insights as to the advisability of bringing a vehicle up the back road in winter and allowing as how you should never go anywhere this time of year without snowshoes, a GPS beacon and the means of setting up a shelter and building yourself a fire in the event you had to hole up. She was lucky, they were telling her, not to mention crazy. In fact, this was the craziest thing any of them had ever heard of. And they all—every man in the place—turned their heads to give him a look as he clumped toward the fire.

Someone shoved a hot drink in his hands and he tried to be a sport about it, tried to be grateful and humble as they crowded around him and offered up their mocking congratulations on his having made it— "You're a snow marathoner, isn't that a fact?" one of them shouted in his face—but humility had never been his strong suit and the longer it went on the angrier he felt. And it did go on, he and Ontario the entertainment for the night, the drinks circulating and the fire snapping, a woman at the bar now, heavyset and hearty and louder than any of the men, until finally the owner of the place came in the door, snow to his eyes, to get a look at this marvel. He was a big man, bearded like the rest of them, his face lit with amusement, proprietor of the Big Timber Lodge and king of all he surveyed. "Hello and welcome," he called in a hoarse, too-loud voice, gliding across the room to the fireplace, where Zach sat slumped and shivering beside Ontario. He took a minute, bending forward to poke solicitously at the coals. "So I hear you two took a little hike out there today."

Zach reddened. The laughter rose and ebbed. Ontario sat hunched over her coffee as the fire stirred and settled. Beyond the windows it was dark now, the snow reduced to a collision of particles beating across the cone of light cast by a single lamp nailed to the trunk of one of the massive trees that presided over the parking lot. "Yeah," Zach said, looking up into the man's face and allowing him half a smile, "a little stroll."

"But you're okay, right—both of you? You need anything—dinner? We can make you dinner, full menu tonight."

For the first time, Ontario spoke up. "Dinner would be nice," she murmured. Her hair was tangled and wet, her face bleached of color. "We haven't really eaten since lunch yesterday, I guess."

"Except for some beef jerky," Zach put in, just for the record. "And two power bars."

The big man straightened up. He was beaming at them, his eyes jumping from Zach to Ontario and back again. "Good," he said, rubbing his hands as if he'd just stepped away from the grill, as if the steaks had already been flipped and the potatoes were browning in the pan, "fine. Well, listen, you make yourselves comfortable, and if there's anything else, you just holler." He paused. "By the way," he added, leaning in to brace himself on the back of the chair, "you have a place to stay for the night?"

The fire snapped and spat. It was all winding down now. Zach put the mug to his lips and felt the hot jolt of the coffee like a bullet in the back of his throat. He didn't look at Ontario, didn't pat her hand or slip an arm round her shoulders. "We're going to need a room," he said, gazing up at the man, and in the space of that instant he could hear the faint hum of the wings and the beat of the paws and the long doomed drumming of the hooves before Ontario corrected him.

"No," she said. "Two rooms."

Jubilation

I'VE BEEN LIVING in Jubilation for almost two years now. There's been a lot of change in that time, both for the better and the worse, as you might expect in any real and authentic town composed of real and authentic people with their iron-clad personalities and various personal agendas, but overall I'd say I'm happy I chose the Contash Corp's vision of community living. I've got friends here, neighbors, people who care about me the way I care about them. We've had our crises, no question about it—Mother Nature has been pretty erratic these past two years—and there isn't a man, woman or child in Jubilation who isn't worried about maintaining property values in the face of all the naysaying and criticism that's come our way. Still, it's the *people* this whole thing is about, and the people I know are as determined and forward-looking a bunch as any you'd ever hope to find. We've built something here, something I think we can all be proud of.

It wasn't easy. From the beginning, everybody laughed behind my back. Everybody said, "Oh, sure, Jackson, you get divorced and the first thing you do is fly down to Florida and live in some theme park with Gulpy Gator and whoever—Chowchy the Lizard, right?—and you defend it with some tripe about community and the New Urbanists and we're supposed to say you're behaving rationally?" My ex-wife was the worst. Lauren. She made it sound as if I was personally going to drive the Sky Lift or slip into a Gulpy suit and greet people at the gates of Contash World, but the truth is I was a pioneer, I had a chance to get into something on the ground floor and make it work—*sacrifice* to make it work—and all the cynics I used to call friends just snickered in their apple martinis as if my post-divorce life was some opera bouffe staged for their amusement.

Take the lottery. They all thought I was crazy, but I booked my ticket, flew down to Orlando and took my place in line with six thousand strangers while the sun peeled the skin off the tip of my nose and baked through the soles of my shoes. There was sleet on the runway at LaGuardia when the plane took off, a foot and a half of snow expected in the suburbs, and it meant nothing to me, not any-more. The palms were nodding in a languid tropical breeze, the chiggers, no-see-ums and mosquitoes were all on vacation some-where, children scampered across the emerald grass and vigorous lit-tle birds darted in and out of the jasmine and hibiscus. It was early yet, not quite eight. People shuffled their feet, tapped their watches, gazed hopefully off into the distance while a hundred Contash greeters moved up and down the line with crullers and Styrofoam cups of coffee.

The excitement was contagious, and yet it was inseparable from a certain element of competitive anxiety—this was a random draw-ing, after all, and there would necessarily have to be winners and losers. Still, people were outgoing and friendly, chatting amongst themselves as if they'd known one another all their lives, sharing around cold cuts and homemade potato salad, swapping stories. Everybody knew the rules—there was no favoritism here. Charles Contash was founding a town, a prêt-à-porter community set down in the middle of the vacation wonderland itself, with Contash World on one side and Game Park U.S.A. on the other, and if you wanted in—no matter who you were or who you knew—you had to stand in line like anybody else.

Directly in front of me was a single mother in a powder-blue hal-ter top designed to show off her assets, which were considerable, and in front of her were two men holding hands; immediately behind me, silently masticating crullers, was a family of four, mom, pop, sis and junior, their faces haggard and interchangeable, and behind them, a black couple burying their heads in a glossy brochure. The single mother—she'd identified herself only as Vicki—had one fat ripe cream puff of a baby slung over her left shoulder, where it (he? she?)

was playing with the thin band of her spaghetti strap, while the other child, a boy of three or so decked out in a striped polo shirt and a pair of shorts he could grow into, clung to her knee as if he'd been fastened there with a strip of Velcro. "So what did you say your name was?" she asked, swinging round on me for what must have been the hundredth time in the past hour. The baby, in this view, was a pair of blinding white diapers and two swollen, rooting legs.

I told her my name was Jackson, and that I was pleased to meet her, and before she could say *Is that your first name or last?* I clarified the issue for her: "Jackson Peters Reilly. That's my mother's maiden name. Jackson. And her mother's maiden name was Peters."

She seemed to consider this a moment, her eyes drifting in and out of focus. She patted the baby's bottom for no good reason. "Wish I'd thought of that," she said. "This one's Ashley, and my son's Ethan— Say hello, Ethan. Ethan?" And then she laughed, a hearty, hopeful laugh that had nothing to do with rejection, abandonment or a night spent on the pavement with two exhausted children while holding a place something like four hundred deep in the lottery line. "Of course, my maiden name's Silinski, so it wouldn't exactly sound too feminine for little baby Ashley, now would it?"

She was flirting with me, and that was okay, that was fine, because wasn't that what I'd come down here for in the first place—to upgrade my social life? I was tired of New York. Tired of L.A. Tired of the anonymity, the hassle, the grab and squeeze and the hostility snarling just beneath the surface of every transaction, no matter how small or insignificant. "I don't know," I said, "sounds kind of chic to me. The doorbell rings and there's all these neighborhood kids chanting, 'Can Silinski come out to play?' Or the modeling agency calls. 'So what about Silinski,' they say, 'is she available?'"

I was doing fine, grinning and smooth-talking and sailing right along, though my back felt misaligned and my right hip throbbed where the pavement had bitten into it during a mostly sleepless night under the amber glow of the newly installed Contash streetlamps. I took a swig from my Evian bottle, tugged the plastic brim of my visor down to keep the sun from irradiating the creases at the corners of my eyes. There was one more Silinski trope on my tongue, the one that would bring her to her knees in adoration of my wit and charm, but I never got to utter it because at that moment the rolling blast of a Civil War cannon announced the official opening of the lottery, and everybody in line crowded closer as ten thousand balloons, in the powder-blue and sun-kissed orange of the Contash Corp, rose up like a mad flock into the sky.

"Welcome, all you friends and neighbors," boomed an amplified voice, and all eyes went to the head of the line. There, atop the four-story tower of the sales preview center, a tiny figure in the Contash colors held out his arms in benediction. "And all you little ones too— and remember, Gulpy Gator and Chowchy love you one and all, and so does our founder, Charles Contash, whose vision of community, of health and vigor and good schools and good neighbors, has never shone more brightly than it does today in Jubilation! No need to crowd, no need to fret. We've got two thousand Village Homes, Cottage Homes, Little Adobes and Mercado Street mini–luxury apartments available today, and three thousand more to come. So welcome, folks, and just step up and draw your lucky number from the hopper."

The press moved forward in all its human inevitability, and I had to brace myself to avoid trampling the young woman in front of me. As it was, the family of four gouged their angles into my flesh and I found myself making a nest of my arms for her, for Vicki, who in turn was shoved up against the hand-holding men in front of her. I could smell her, her breath sweet with the mints she'd been sucking all morning and the odor of her sweat and perfume rising up out of the confinement of her halter top. "Oh, God," she whispered, "God, I just pray—"

Her hair was in my mouth, caught in the bristles of my mustache. It was as if we were dancing, doing the Macarena or forming up a conga line, back to front. "Pray what?"

Her breath caught and then released in a respiratory tumult that was almost a sob: "That there's just one Mercado Street mini–luxury apartment left, just one, that's all I ask." And then she paused, the shining new moon of her face rising over her shoulder to gaze up into mine. "And you," she breathed, "I pray you get what you want too."

What I wanted was a detached home in the North Village section of town, on the near side of the artificial lake, a cool four hundred fifty thousand dollars for a ninety-by-thirty-foot lot and a wraparound porch that leered promiscuously at the wraparound porches of my neighbors, ten feet away on either side—one of the Casual Contempos or even one of the Little Adobes—and I wanted it so badly I would have taken Charles Contash himself hostage to get it. "A Casual Contempo," I said, and the family of four strained against me.

She was fighting for position. The child underfoot clung like a remora to the long tapered muscle of her leg. The baby began to fuss. She was put out, overwrought, not at all at her best, I could see that, but still her eyebrows lifted and she let out a low whistle. "Wow," she said, "you must be rich."

I wasn't rich, not by the standards I'd set for myself, but I'd sold my company to a bigger company and bought off my ex-wife, and what was left was more than adequate to set me up in a new life in a new house—and no, I wasn't retiring to Florida to play golf till I dropped dead of boredom, but just looking for what was missing in my life, for the values I'd grown up with in the suburbs, where there were no fences, no walls, no gated communities and private security guards, where everybody knew everybody else and democracy wasn't just a tattered banner the politicians unfurled for their convenience every four years. That was what the Jubilation Company promised. That and a rock-solid property valuation, propped up by Charles Contash and all the fiscal might of his entertainment and merchandising empire. The only catch was that you had to occupy your property a minimum of nine months out of the year and nobody could sell within two years of purchase, so as to discourage speculators, but to my way of thinking that wasn't a catch at all, if you were committed. And if you weren't, you had no business taking up space in line to begin with. "Not really," I said, enjoying the look on her face, the unconscious widening of her eyes, the way her lips parted in expectation. "Comfortable, I guess you'd say."

Then the line jerked again and we all revised our footing. "Mercado Street!" somebody shouted. "Penny Lane!" countered another, and there was a flicker of nervous laughter.

From where I was standing, I could barely see over the crush. A girl in a short blue skirt and orange heels stood on a platform at the head of the line, churning a gleaming stainless-steel hopper emblazoned with the Contash logo, and an LED display stood ready to flash the numbers as people extracted the little digitized cards from the depths of it. There was a ripple of excitement as the first man in line, a phys ed teacher from Las Vegas, New Mexico, climbed the steps of the platform. Rumor had it he'd been camped on the unforgiving concrete for over a month, eating his meals out of a microwave and doing calisthenics to keep in shape. I saw a running suit (blue with orange piping, what else?) surmounted by yard-wide shoulders and a head like a wrecking ball. The man bent to the hopper, straightened up again and handed a white plastic card to the girl, who in turn ran it under a scanner. The display flickered, and then flashed the number: 3,347. "Oh, God," Vicki muttered under her breath. My pulse was racing. I couldn't seem to swallow. The sun hung overhead like an over-ripe orange on a limb just out of reach as the crowd released a long slow withering exhalation. So what if the phys ed teacher had camped out for a month? He was a loser, and he was going to have to wait for Phase II construction to begin before he could even hope to become part of this.

None of the next five people managed to draw under 1,000, but at least they were in, at least there was that. "They look like they want houses, don't they?" Vicki said, a flutter of nerves undermining her voice. "I don't mean Casual Contempos," she said, "I wouldn't want to jinx that for you, but maybe the Little Adobes or the Courteous Coastals. But not apartments. No way."

Then a couple who looked as if they belonged on one of the Contash Corp's billboards drew number 5 and the crowd let out a collective groan before people recovered themselves and a spatter of applause went up. I shut my eyes. I hadn't eaten since the previous afternoon on the plane and I felt dizzy suddenly. *Get lucky,* I told myself. *Just get lucky, that's all.*

A breeze came up. The line moved forward step by step, slab by slab. As each number was displayed, a thrill ran through the crowd, and they were all neighbors, or potential neighbors, but that didn't mean they weren't betting against you. It took nearly an hour before the men in front of Vicki—Mark and his partner, Leonard, nicest guys in the world—mounted the steps to the platform and drew number 222. I watched in silence as they fell into each other's arms and improvised a little four-legged jig around the stage, and then Vicki was up there with the sun bringing out the highlights in her hair and drawing the color from her eyes as if they'd been inked in. The boy fidgeted. The baby squalled. She bent forward to draw her number, and when the display flashed 17 she flew down the steps and collapsed for sheer joy in the arms of the only man she knew in that whole astonished crowd—me—and everybody must have assumed I was the father of those creamy pale children until I climbed the steps myself and thrust my own arm into the hopper.

The stage seemed to go quiet suddenly, all that tumult of voices reduced to a whisper, tongues arrested, lips frozen in mid-sentence. I was going to get what I wanted. I was sure of it. My fingers closed on a card, one of thousands, and I fished it out and handed it to the girl; an instant later the number flashed on the board—4,971—and Vicki, poised at the foot of the steps with a glazed smile, looked right through me.

THERE ARE PEOPLE in this world who are content with the lot they're given, content to bow their heads and accept what comes, to wait, sacrifice and look to the future. I'm not one of them. Within an hour of the drawing, I'd traded number 4,971 and $10,000 cash for Mark and Leonard's number 222, and within a month of that I was reclining in a new white wicker chaise longue on the wraparound porch of my Casual Contempo discussing interior decoration with a very determined—and attractive—young woman from Coastal Design. The young woman's name was Felicia, and she wore her hair in a French braid that exposed the long cool nape of her neck. She was looking into my eyes and telling me in her soft breathy reconstructed tones what I needed vis-à-vis the eclectic neo-traditional aesthetic of the Jubilation Community—"Really, Mr. Reilly, you can mix and match to your heart's content, a Stickley sofa to go with your Craftsman windows set right next to a Chinese end table of lacquered rosewood with an ormolu inlay"—when I interrupted her. I listened to the ice cubes clink in my glass a moment, then asked her if she wouldn't prefer discussing my needs over a nice étoufée on the deck of the Cajun Kitchen overlooking lovely Lake Allagash. "Oh, I would love that, Mr. Reilly," she said, "more than practically anything I can think of, but Jeffrey—my sweet little husband of six months?—might just voice an objection." She crossed her legs, let one heel dangle strategically. "No, I think we'd better confine ourselves to the business at hand, don't you?"

I wrote her a check, and within forty-eight hours I was inhabiting a color plate torn out of one of the Jubilation brochures, replete with throw rugs, armoires, sideboards, a set of kitchen chairs designed by a Swedish sadist and a pair of antique brass water pitchers—or were they spittoons?—stuffed with the Concours d'Elegance mix of dried coastal wildflowers. It hadn't come cheap, but I wasn't complaining. This was what I'd wanted since the breath had gone out of my marriage and I'd begun living the nomadic life of the motor court, the high-rise hotel and the inn round the corner. I was home. For the first time in as long as I could remember, I felt oriented and secure.

I laid in provisions, rode my Exercycle, got into a couple of books I'd always meant to read (*Crime and Punishment, Judgment at Nuremberg, The Naked and the Dead*), took a divorcée named Cecily to the Chowchy Grill for dinner and afterward to a movie at the art deco palace designed by Cesar Pelli as the centerpiece of the Mercado Street pedestrian mall, and enjoyed the relatively bugless spring weather in a rented kayak out on Lake Allagash. By the end of the second month I'd lost eight pounds, my arms felt firmer and my face was as tan as a tennis pro's. I wished my wife could see me now, but even as I wished it, the image of her—the heavy, pouting lips and irascible lines etched into the corners of her mouth, the flaring eyes and belligerent stab of her chin—rose up to engulf me in sorrow. Raymond, that was the name of the man she was dating—Raymond, who owned his own restaurant and had a boat out on Long Island Sound.

At any rate, I was standing over the vegetable display at the Jubilation Market one afternoon watching my ex-wife's face superimpose itself on the gleaming epidermis of an oversized zucchini, when a familiar voice called out my name. It was Vicki. She was wearing a transparent blouse over a bikini top and she'd had her hair done up in a spill of tinted ringlets. A plastic shopping basket dangled from one hand. There were no children in sight. "I heard you got your Casual Contempo," she said. "How're you liking it?"

"A dream come true. And you?"

Her smile widened. "I got a job. At the company office? I'm assistant facilitator for tour groups."

"Tour groups? You mean here? Or over at Contash World?"

"You haven't noticed all the people in the streets?" she asked, holding her smile. "The ones with the cameras and the straw hats coming down to check us out and see what a model city looks like, works like? Look right there, right out the window there on the sidewalk in front of the Chowchy Grill. See that flock of Hawaiian shirts? And those women with the legs that look like they've just been pulled out of the deep freeze?"

I followed her gaze and there they were, tourists, milling around as if on a stage set. How had I failed to notice them? Even now one of them was backing away from the front of the grocery with a movie camera. "Tourists?" I murmured.

She nodded.

Maybe I was a little sour that morning, maybe I needed love and affection, not to mention sex, and maybe I was lonely and frustrated and beginning to feel the first stab of disappointment with my new life, but before I could think, I said, "They're worse than the ants. Do you have ants, by the way—in your apartment, I mean? The little minuscule ones that make ant freeways all over the floor, the kitchen counter, the walls?"

Her face fell, but then the smile came back, because she was determined to be chirpy and positive. "I wouldn't say they were worse than the ants—at least the ants clean up after themselves."

"And cockroaches. Or palmetto bugs—isn't that what we call them down here? I saw one the size of a frog the other day, right out on Penny Lane."

She had nothing to say to this, so I changed the subject and asked how her kids were doing.

"Oh, fine. Terrific. They're thriving." A pause. "My mother's down from Philadelphia—she's babysitting for me until I can find somebody permanent. While I'm at work, that is."

"Really," I said, reaching down to shift the offending zucchini to the bottom of the bin. "So are you free right now? For maybe a drink? Unless you have to rush home and cook or something."

She looked doubtful.

"What I mean is, don't you want to see what a neo-retro Casual Contempo looks like when it's fully furnished?"

THE FIRST REAL BUMP in the road came a week or two later. I'd been called away to consult with the transition team at my former company, and when I got back I found a notice in the mailbox from the Contash Corp's subsidiary, the Jubilation Company, or as we all knew it in short—and somewhat redundantly—the TJC. It seemed they were advising against our spending too much time on our wraparound porches, especially at sunrise and sunset, and to take all precautions while using the jogging trail round Lake Allagash or even window-shopping on Mercado Street. The problem was mosquitoes. Big, outsized Central Floridian mosquitoes that were found to be carrying encephalitis and dengue fever. The TJC was doing all it could vis-à-vis vector control, and they were contractually absolved from any responsibility—just read your Declaration of Covenants, Deeds and Restrictions—but in the interest of public safety they were advising everyone to stay indoors. Despite the heat. And the fact that staying in defeated the whole idea of the Casual Contempo, the wraparound porch and the free interplay between neighbors that lies at the core of what makes a real and actual town click.

I was brooding in the kitchen, idly scratching at the constellation of angry red welts on my right wrist and waiting for the meninges to start swelling in my brainpan, when a movement on the porch caught my eye. Two cloaked figures there, one large, one small, and a cloaked baby carriage. For a moment I didn't know what to make of it all, but the baby carriage was a dead giveaway: it was Vicki, dressed like a beekeeper, with little Ethan in his own miniature beekeeper's outfit beside her and baby Ashley imprisoned behind a wall of gauze in the depths of the carriage. "Christ," I said, ushering them in, "is this what we're going to have to start wearing now?"

She pulled back the veil to reveal that hopeful smile and the small shining miracle of her hair. "No, I don't think so," she said, bending to remove her son's impedimenta ("I don't want," he kept saying, "I don't want"). "There," she said, addressing the pale dwindling oval of his face, "there, it's all right now. And you can have a soda, if Jackson still has any left in the refrigerator—"

"Oh, yeah, sure," I said, and I was bending too. "Root beer? Or Seven-Up?"

We wound up sitting in the kitchen, drinking white wine and sharing a box of stale Triscuits while the baby slept and Ethan sucked at a can of Hires in front of the tube in the living room. Out back was the low fence that gave onto the nature preserve, with its bird-friendly marsh that also coincidentally happened to serve as a maternity ward for the mosquitoes, and beyond that was Lake Allagash. "At the office they're saying the mosquitoes are just seasonal," Vicki said, working a hand up under the tinted ringlets and giving them a shake, "and besides, they're pretty much spraying around the clock now, so I would think—well, I mean, they've had to close down some of the outdoor rides over at Contash World, and that means money lost, big money."

I wasn't a cynic, or I tried not to be, because a pioneer can't afford cynicism. Look on the bright side, that was what I maintained—there was no alternative. "Okay, fine, but have you seen my wrist? I mean, should I be concerned? Should I go to the doctor, do you think?"

She took my wrist in her cool grip, traced the bumps there with her index finger. She gave a little laugh. "Chigger bites, that's all. Nothing to worry about. And the mosquitoes'll just be a bad memory in a week or two, I guarantee it."

There was a moment of silence, during which we both gazed out the window on the marsh—or swamp, as I'd mistakenly called it before Vicki corrected me. We watched an egret rise up out of nowhere and sail off into the trees. Clouds massed on the horizon in a swell of pure, unadulterated white; the palmettos gathered and released the faintest trace of a breeze. Next door, the wraparound porch of my neighbors—the black couple, Sam and Ernesta Fills—was deserted. Ditto the porch of the house on the other side, into which Mark and Leonard, having traded $2,500 of the cash I'd given them for number 632 and a prime chance at a Casual Contempo, had recently moved. "No," she said finally, draining her wineglass and holding it out in one delicate hand so that I could refill it for her, "what I'd be concerned about if I was you is your neighbors across the street—the Weekses?"

I gave her a dumb stare.

"You know them—July and Fili Weeks and their three sons?"

"Yeah," I said, "sure." Everybody knew everybody else here. It was a rule.

From the TV in the other room came the sound of canned laughter, followed by Ethan's stuttering high whinny of an underdeveloped laugh. "What about the red curtains?" she said. "And that car? That whatever it is, that race car painted in the three ugliest shades of magenta they keep parked out there on the street where the whole world can see it? They're in violation of the code on something like eight counts already and they haven't been here a month yet."

I felt a prickle of alarm. We were all in this together, and if everybody didn't pitch in—if everybody didn't subscribe to the letter as far as the Covenants and Restrictions were concerned—what was going to happen to our property values? "Red curtains?" I said.

Her eyes were steely. "Just like in a whorehouse. And you know the rules—white, off-white, beige and taupe only."

"Has anybody talked to them? Can't anybody do anything?"

She set the glass down, drew her gaze away from the window and looked into my eyes. "You mean the Citizens' Committee?"

I shrugged. "Yeah. Sure. I guess."

She leaned in close. I could smell the rinse she used in her hair, and it was faintly intoxicating. I loved her eyes, loved the shape of her, loved the way she aspirated her *h*'s like an elocution teacher. "Don't you worry," she whispered. "We're already on it."

ONCE VICKI HAD MENTIONED the Weekses and the way they were flouting the code, I couldn't get them out of my head. July

Weeks was a salesman of some sort, aviation parts, I think it was—he worked for Cessna—and he seemed to spend most of his time, despite the mosquito scare, buried deep in his own white wicker chaise longue out on the wraparound porch of his Courteous Coastal directly across the street from me. He was a Southerner, and that was all right because this *was* the South, after all, but he had one of those accents that just went on clanging and jarring till you could barely understand a word he was saying. Not that I harbor any prejudices—he was my neighbor, and if he wanted to sound like an extra from *Deliverance,* that was his privilege. But I looked out the front window and saw that race car—*No excessive or unsightly vehicles, including campers, RVs, moving vans or trailers, shall be parked on the public streets for a period exceeding forty-eight continuous hours,* Section III, Article 12, Declaration of Covenants, Deeds and Restrictions—and the sight of it became an active irritation. Which was compounded by the fact that the eldest son, August, pulled up one afternoon in a pickup truck that sat about six feet up off its Bayou Crawler tires and deposited a boat trailer at the curb. The boat was painted puce with lime-green trim and it had a staved-in hull. Plus, there were those curtains.

A week went by. Two weeks. I got updates from Vicki—we were seeing each other just about every day now—and of course the Citizens' Committee, as an arm of the TJC, was threatening the Weekses with a lawsuit and the Weekses had hired an attorney and were threatening back, but nothing happened. I couldn't enjoy my wraparound porch or the view out my mullioned Craftsman windows. Every time I looked up, there was the boat, there was the car, and beyond them, the curtains. The situation began to weigh on me, so one night after dinner I strolled down the three broad inviting steps of my wraparound porch, waved a greeting to the Fills on my right and Mark and Leonard on my left, and crossed the street to mount the equally inviting steps of the Weekses' wraparound porch with the intention of setting Mr. Weeks straight on a few things. Or no, that sounds too harsh. I wanted to block out a couple issues with him and see if we couldn't resolve things amicably for all concerned.

He was sitting in the chaise longue, his wife in the wicker armchair beside him. An Atlanta Braves cap that looked as if it had just come off the shelf at Gulpy's Sports Emporium hid his brow and the crown of his head and he was wearing a pair of those squared-off black sunglasses for people with cataracts, and that reduced the sum of his expression to the sharp beak of his nose and an immobile mouth. The wife was a squat Korean woman whose name I could never remember. She was peeling the husk off of a dark pungent pod or tuber. It was a homey scene, and the moment couldn't have been more neighborly.

"Hi," I said (or maybe, prompted by the ambience, I might even have managed a "Howdy").

Neither of them said a word.

"Listen," I began, after standing there for an awkward moment (and what had I been expecting—mint juleps?). "Listen, about the curtains and the car and all that—the boat—I just wanted to say, well, I mean, it might seem like a small thing, it's ridiculous, really, but—"

He cut me off then. I don't know what he said, but it sounded something like "Rabid rabid gurtz."

The wife—her name came to me suddenly: Fili—translated. She carefully set aside the root or pod or whatever it was and gave me a flowering smile that revealed a set of the whitest and evenest teeth I'd ever seen. "He say you can blow it out you ass."

"No, no," I said, brushing right by it, "you misunderstand me. I'm not here to complain, or even to convince you of anything. It's just that, well, I'm your neighbor, and I thought if we—"

Here he spoke again, a low rumble of concatenated sounds that might have been expressive of digestive trouble, but the wife—Fili—seeing my blank expression, dutifully translated: "He say his gun—you know gun?—he say he keep gun loaded."

THINGS ARE NOT PERFECT. I never claimed they were. And if you're going to have a free and open town and not one of these gated neo-racist enclaves, you've got to be willing to accept that. The TJC sued the Weekses and the Weekses sued them back, and still the curtains flamed behind the windows and the garish race car and the unseaworthy boat sat at the curb across the street. So what I did to make myself feel better, was buy a dog. A Scottie. Lauren would never let me have a dog—she claimed to be allergic, but in fact she was pathologically averse to any intrusion on the rigid order she maintained around the house—and we never had any children either, which didn't affect me one way or the other, though I should say I was one of the few single men in Jubilation who didn't view Vicki's kids as a liability. I grew to like them, in fact—or Ethan, anyway; the baby was just a baby, practically inert if it wasn't shrieking as if it had just had the skin stripped from its limbs. But Ethan was something else. I liked the feel of his tiny bunched little sweating hand in mine as we strolled down to the Benny Tarpon Old Tyme Ice Cream Parlor in the evening or took a turn round Lake Allagash. He was always tugging me one way or the other, chattering, pointing like a tour director: "Look," he would say. "Look!"

I named the dog Bruce, after my grandfather on my mother's side. He was a year old and housetrained, and I loved the way the fur hid his paws so that he seemed to glide over the grass of the village green as if he had no means of locomotion beyond willpower and magic.

That was around the time we began to feel the effects of the three-year drought that none of the TJC salespeople had bothered to mention in their all-day seminars and living-color brochures. The wind came up out of the south carrying a freight of smoke (apparently the Everglades were on fire) and a fine brown dust that obliterated our lawns and flowerbeds and made a desert of the village green. The heat seemed to increase too, as if the fires had somehow turned up the thermostat, but the worst of it was the smell. Everywhere you went, whether you were standing on line at the bank, sunk into one of the magic-fingers lounge chairs at the movie theater or pulling your head up off the pillow in the morning, the stale smell of old smoke assaulted your nostrils.

I was walking Bruce up on Golfpark Drive one afternoon, where our select million-dollar-plus homes back up onto the golf course— and you have to realize that this is part of the Contash vision too, millionaires living cheek by jowl with single mothers like Vicki and all the others struggling to pay mortgages that were thirty-five percent higher than those in the surrounding area, not to mention special assessments and maintenance fees—when a man with a camera slung round his neck stopped me and asked if he could take my picture. The sky was marbled with smoke. Dust fled across the pavement. The birds were actually shrieking in the trees. "Me?" I said. "Why me?"

"I don't know," he said, snapping the picture. "I like your dog."

"You do?" I was flattered, I admit it, but I was on my guard too. Journalists from all over the world had descended on the town en masse, mainly to cook up dismissive articles about a legion of Stepford wives and robotic husbands living on a Contash movie set and doing daily obeisance to Gulpy Gator. None of them ever bothered to mention our equanimity, our openness and shared ideals. Why would they? Hard work and sacrifice never have made for good copy.

"Yeah, sure," he said, "and would you mind posing over there, by the gate to that gingerbread mansion? That's good. Nice." He took a series of shots, the camera whirring through its motions. He wore a buzz cut, a two-day growth of nearly translucent beard and a pair of tri-colored Nikes. "You do live here, don't you?" he asked finally. "I mean, you're an actual resident, right, and not a tourist?"

I felt a surge of pride. "That's right," I said. "I'm one of the originals."

He gave me an odd look, as if he were trying to sniff out an imposter. "Do they really pay you to walk the dog around the village green six times a day?"

"*Pay* me? Who?"

"You know, the town, the company. You can't have a town without people in it, right?" He looked down at Bruce, who was sniffing attentively at a dust-coated leaf. "Or dogs?" The camera clicked again, several times in succession. "I hear they pay that old lady on the moped too—and the guy that sets up his easel in front of the Gulpy monument every morning."

"Don't be ridiculous. You're out of your mind."

"And I'll tell you another thing—don't think just because you bought into the Contash lifestyle you're immune from all the shit that comes down in the real world, because you're not. In fact, I'd watch that dog if I were you—"

Somewhere the fires were burning. A rag of smoke flapped at my face and I began to cough. "You're one of those media types, aren't you?" I said, pounding at my breastbone. "You people disgust me. You don't even make a pretense of unbiased reporting—you just want to ridicule us and tear us down, isn't that right?" My dander was up. Who were these people to come in here and try to undermine everything we'd been working for? I shot him a look of impatience. "It wouldn't be jealousy, would it? By any chance?"

He shrugged, shifted the camera to one side and dug a cigarette out of his breast pocket. I watched him cup his hands against the breeze and light it. He flung the match in the bushes, a symbolic act, surely. "We used to have a Scottie when I was a kid," he said, exhaling. "So I'm just telling you—you'd be surprised what I know about this town, what goes on behind closed doors, the double-dealing, the payoffs, the flouting of the environmental regs, all the dirt the TJC and Charles Contash don't want you to know about. View me as a resource, your diligent representative of the fourth estate. Keep the dog away from the lake, that's all."

I was stubborn. I wasn't listening. "He can swim."

The man let out a short, unpleasant laugh. "I'm talking about alligators, my friend, and not the cuddly little cartoon kind. You might or might not know it because I'm sure it's not advertised in any of the TJC brochures, but when they built Contash World back in the sixties they evicted all the alligators, not to mention the coral snakes and cane rattlers and snapping turtles—and where do you think they put them?"

ALL RIGHT. I was forewarned. And what happened should never have happened, I know that, but there are hazards in any community, whether it be South Central L.A. or Scarsdale or Kuala Lumpur. I took Bruce around Lake Allagash—twice—and then went home and barbecued a platter of wings and ribs for Vicki and the kids and I thought no more about it. Alligators. They were there, sure they were, but so were the mosquitoes and the poison toads that looked like deflated kick balls and chased the dogs off their kibble. This was Florida. It was muggy. It was hot. We had our share of sand fleas and whatnot. But at least we didn't have to worry about bronchial pneumonia or snow tires.

The rains came in mid-September, a series of thunderstorms that rolled in off the Gulf and put out the fires. We had problems with snails and slugs for a while there, armadillos crawling up half-drowned on the lawn, snakes in the garage, walking catfish, that sort of thing— I even found an opossum curled up in the dryer one morning amidst my socks and boxer shorts. But the Citizens' Committee was active in picking up strays, nursing them back to health and restoring them to the ecosystem, so it wasn't as bad as you'd think. And after that, the sun came out and the earth just seemed to steam till every trace of mold and mud was erased and the flowers went mad with the glory of it. The smoke was gone, the snails had crawled back into their holes or dens or wherever they lived when they weren't smearing the windows with slime, and the air was scented so sweetly it was as if the Contash Corp had hired a fleet of crop dusters to spray air freshener over the town. Even the thermometer cooperated, the temperature holding at a nice equitable seventy-eight degrees for three days running. Tear the page out of the brochure: this was what we'd all come for.

I was sitting out on my wraparound porch, trying to ignore the decrepit boat and magenta car across the street, *Crime and Punishment* spread open in my lap (Raskolnikov was just climbing the steps to the old lady's place and I was waiting for the axe to fall), when Vicki called and proposed a picnic. She'd made up some sandwiches on the brown nut bread I like, asiago cheese, sweet onion and roasted red pepper, and she'd picked up a nice bottle of Chilean white at the Contash Liquor Mart. Was I ready for some sun? And maybe a little backrub afterward at her place?

Ethan wanted to go out on the water, but when we got to the Jubilation dock the sound of the ratcheting motors scared him, so we settled on an aluminum rowboat, and that was better—or would have been better—because we could hear ourselves think and didn't have to worry about all that spew of fumes, and that was a real concern for Vicki. We might have been raised in houses where our parents smoked two packs a day and sprayed Raid on the kitchen counter every time an ant or roach showed its face—or head or feelers or whatever—but there was no way any toxins were entering her children's systems, not if she could help it. So I rented the rowboat. "No problem," I told Vicki, who was looking terrific in a sunbonnet, her bikini top and a pair of skimpy shorts that showed off her smooth solid legs and the Gulpy tattoo on her ankle. The fact was I hadn't been kayaking since the rains started and the exercise was something I was looking forward to.

It took me a few strokes to reacquaint myself with the apparatus of oars and oarlocks, and we lurched away from the dock as if we'd been torpedoed, but I got into the rhythm of it soon enough and we glided cleanly out across the mirrored surface of the lake. Vicki didn't want me to go more than twenty or thirty feet from shore, and that was all right too, except that I found myself dredging up noxious-smelling clumps of pondweed that seemed to cast a powerful olfactory spell over Bruce. He kept snapping at the weed as I lifted first one oar and then the other to try to shake it off, and once or twice I had to drop the oars and discipline him because he was leaning so far out over the bow I thought we were going to lose him. Still, we saw birdlife everywhere we looked, herons, egrets, cormorants and anhingas, and Ethan got a real kick out of a clutch of painted turtles stacked up like dinner plates on a half-submerged log.

We'd gone half a mile or so, I guess, to the far side of the lake where the wake of the motorboats wouldn't interfere overmuch with the mustarding of the sandwiches and the delicate operation of pouring the wine into long-stemmed crystal glasses. The baby, wrapped up like a sausage in her life jacket—or life-cradle, might be more accurate—was asleep, a blissful baby smile painted on her lips. Bruce curled up at my feet in the brown swill at the bottom of the boat and Vicki sipped wine and gave me a look of contentment so deep and pure I was beginning to think I wouldn't mind seeing it across the breakfast table for the rest of my life. It was tranquil. Dragonflies hovering, fish rising, not a mosquito in sight. Even little Ethan, normally such a clingy kid, seemed to be enjoying himself tracing the pattern of his finger in the water as the boat rocked and drifted in a gentle airy dance.

About that water. The TJC assured us it was unpolluted by human waste and uncontaminated by farm runoff, and that its rusty color—it was nearly opaque and perpetually blooming with the microscopic creatures that comprise the bottom of the food chain in a healthy and thriving aquatic ecosystem—was perfectly natural. Though the lake had been dredged out of the swampland some forty years earlier, this was the way its waters had always looked, and the creatures that lived and throve here were grateful for it—like all of us in Jubilation, they had Charles Contash to thank for that too.

Well. We drifted, the dog and the baby snoozed, Vicki kept up a happy chatter on any number of topics, all of which seemed to have a subtext of sexual innuendo, and I just wasn't prepared for what came next, and I blame myself, I do. Maybe it was the wine or the influence of the sun and the faint sweet cleansing breeze, but I wasn't alert to the dangers inherent in the situation—I was an American, raised in a time of prosperity and peace, and I'd been spared the tumult and horror visited on so many of the less fortunate in this world. New York and L.A. might have been nasty places, and Lauren was certainly a plague in her own right, but nobody had ever bombed my village or shot down my family in the street, and when my parents died they died quietly, in their own beds.

I was in the act of extracting the wine bottle from its cradle of ice in the cooler when the boat gave a sudden lurch and I glanced up just in time to see the broad flat grinning reptilian head emerge from the water, pluck Ethan off the gunwale and vanish in the murk. It was like an illusion in a magic show, now he's here, now he isn't, and I wasn't able to respond until my brain replayed the scene and I felt the sudden horror knife at my heart. "Did you—?" I began, but Vicki was already screaming.

THE SEQUENCE OF EVENTS becomes a little confused for me at this juncture, but looking back on it, I'm fairly certain the funeral service preceded the thrashing we took from Hurricane Albert—I distinctly remember the volunteerism the community showed in dredging the lake, which would have been impossible after the hurricane hit. Sadly, no trace of little Ethan was ever found. No need to tell you how devastated I was—I was as hurt and wrung out as I've ever been in my life, and I'll never give up second-guessing myself—but even more, I was angry. Angry over the Contash Corp's failure to disclose the hazards lurking around us and furious over the way the press jumped on the story, as if the life of a child was worth no more than a crude joke or a wedge to drive between the citizens of the community and the rest of the so-called civilized world. *Alligator Mom.* That was what they called Vicki in headlines three inches high, and could anyone blame her for packing up and going back to her mother in Philadelphia? I took her place on the Citizens' Committee, though I'd never been involved in community affairs in my life to this point, and I was the one who pushed through the initiative to remove *all* the dangerous animals from the lake, no matter what their size or species (and that was a struggle too, the environmentalists crying foul in all their puritanical fervor, and one man—I won't name him here— even pushing to have the alligators' teeth capped as a compromise solution).

It wasn't all bad, though. The service at the Jubilation Non-Denominational Chapel, for all its solemnity, was a real inspiration to us all, a public demonstration of our solidarity and determination. Charles Contash himself flew in from a meeting with the Russian premier to give the eulogy, every man, woman and child in town turned out to pay their respects, and the cards and flowers poured in from all over the country. Even July Weeks turned up, despite his friction with the TJC, and we found common ground in our contempt for the reporters massed on the steps out front of the chapel. He stood tall that day, barring the door to anyone whose face he didn't recognize, and I forgave him his curtains, for the afternoon at least.

If anything, the hurricane brought us together even more than little Ethan's tragedy. I remember the sky taking on the deep purple-black hue of a bruise and the vanguard of the rain that lashed down in a fusillade of wind-whipped pellets and the winds that sucked the breath right out of your body. Sam and Ernesta Fills helped me board up the windows of my Casual Contempo, and together we helped Mark and Leonard and the Weekses with their places and then went looking to lend a hand wherever we could. And when the storm hit in all its intensity, just about everybody in town was bundled up safe and sound in the bastion of the movie palace, where the emergency generator allowed the TJC to lift the burden from our minds with a marathon showing of the Contash Corp's most-beloved family films. Of course, we emerged to the devastation of what the National Weather Service was calling the single most destructive storm of the past century, and a good proportion of Jubilation had been reduced to rubble or swept away altogether. I was luckier than most. I lost the back wall that gives onto the kitchen, which in turn was knee-deep in roiling brown water and packed to the ceiling with wind-blown debris, and my wraparound porch was wrapped around the Weekses' house, but on the plus side the offending race car and the boat were lifted right up into the sky and for all we know dropped somewhere over the Atlantic, and the Weekses' curtains aren't really an issue anymore.

As for myself, I've been rebuilding with the help of a low-interest loan secured through the Contash Corp, and I've begun, in a tentative way, to date Felicia, whose husband was one of the six fatalities we recorded once the storm had moved on. Beyond that, my committee work keeps me pretty busy, I've been keeping in touch with Vicki both by phone and e-mail, and every time I see Bruce chase a palmetto bug up the side of the new retaining wall, I just want to smile. And I do. I do smile. Sure, things could be better, but they could be worse too. I live in Jubilation. How bad can it be?

Rastrow's Island

A car radio bleats,
"Love, O careless Love. . . ."

—ROBERT LOWELL, "SKUNK HOUR"

SHE CALLED and he was ready if not eager to sell, because he'd had certain reverses, the market gone sour, Ruth in bed with something nobody was prepared to call cancer, and his daughter, Charlene, waiting for his check in her dorm room with her unpacked trunk full of last year's clothes and the grubby texts with the yellow scars of the USED stickers seared into their spines. "That's right," she said, her old lady's voice like the creak of oarlocks out on the bay in the first breath of dawn, "Mrs. Rastrow, Alice Rastrow, and I used to know your mother when she was alive." There was a sharp crackling jolt of static, as if an electrical storm were raging inside the wires, then her voice came back at him: "I never have put much confidence in realtors. Do you want to talk or not?"

"So go," Ruth said. Her face had taken on the shine and color of the elephant-ear fungus that grew out of the sodden logs in the ravine at the foot of the park. "Don't worry about me. Just go."

"You know what she's doing, don't you?"

"I know what she's doing."

"I never wanted to sell the place. I wanted it for Charlene, for Charlene's kids. To experience it the way I did, to have that, at least—" He saw the house then, a proud two-story assertion of will from the last century, four rooms down, four rooms up, the wood paintless now and worn to a weathered silver, the barn subsiding into its angles in a bed of lichen-smeared rock, the hedges gone to straw in the absence of human agency. And when was the last time—? Two summers ago? Three?

"It's just a summer house." She reached out a hand you could see right through and lifted the rimed water glass from the night table. He watched the hand tremble, fumble for the pills, and he looked away, out the window and down the row of townhouses and the slouching, copper-flagged maples. "Isn't that the first thing to go when you—?"

"Yeah," he said. "Yeah, I guess it is."

"I mean," and she paused to draw the water down, gulp the pills, "it's not as if we really need the place or anything."

THE WATER WAS CHOPPY, the wind cold, and he sat in his car with the engine running and the heater on full as the ferry slammed at the seething white roil of the waves and the island separated itself from the far shore and began to fan out across the horizon. When the rain came up, first as a spatter that might have been nothing more than the spray thrown up by the bow and then as a moving scrim that isolated him behind the wheel, he thought of switching on the windshield wipers, but he didn't. There was something about the opaque windows and the pitch of the deck tugging at the corners of the light that relaxed him—he could have been underwater, in a submarine, working his way along the bottom of the bay through the looming tangle of spars and timbers of the ships gone to wrack a hundred years ago. He laid his hand idly on the briefcase beside him. Inside were all the relevant papers he could think of: the deed, signed in his father's ecstatic rolling hand, termite, electrical, water rights. But what did she care about termites, about water or dry rot?—she wasn't going to live there. She wasn't going to live anywhere but the whitewashed stone cottage she was entombed in now, the one she'd been born in, and after that she had her place reserved in the cemetery beside her husband and two drowned children. She must have been eighty, he figured. Eighty, or close to it.

Ronald Rastrow—he was a violinist, or no, a violist—and his sister, Elyse. At night, in summer, above the thrum of the insects and the listless roll of the surf, you could hear his instrument tuned to some ancient sorrow and floating out across the water. He was twenty-two or -three, a student at Juilliard, and his sister must have been twenty or so. They went sailing under a full moon, rumors of a party onshore and Canadian whiskey and marijuana, the sea taut as a bedspread, a gentle breeze out of the east, and they never came back. He was twelve the summer it happened, and he used to thrill himself leaning out over the stern of the dingy till the shadow of his head and shoulders made the sea transparent and the dense architecture of the bottom rushed up at him in a revulsion of disordered secrets. He remembered the police divers gathered in a dark clump at the end of the pier. Volunteers. Adults, kids in sailboats, Curtis Mayhew's father in his fishing boat fitted out with a dragline, working up and down the bay as if he were plowing it for seed. It was a lobsterman who found them, both of them, tangled in his lines at the end of a long cold week that was like December in July.

He drove along the shore, past the saltbox cottages with their weathered shingles and the odd frame house that had acquired a new coat of paint, the trees stripped by the wind, nothing in the fields but pale dead stalks and the refulgent slabs of granite that bloomed in all seasons. There were a few new houses clustered around the village, leggy things, architecturally wise, but the gas station hadn't changed or the post office/general store or Dorcas' House of Clams (*Closed for the Season*). The woman behind the desk at The Seaside Rest (*Sep Units Avail by Day or Week*) took his money and handed him the key to the last cottage in a snaking string of them, though none of the intervening cottages seemed to be occupied. That struck him as a bit odd—she must have marked him down for a drug fiend or a prospective suicide—but it didn't bother him, not really. She didn't recognize him and he didn't recognize her, because people change and places change and what once was will never be again. He entered the cottage like an acolyte taking possession of his cell, a cold little box of a room with a bed, night table and chair, no TV. He spent half an hour down on his knees worshipping the AC/heater unit, but could raise no more than the faintest stale exhalation out of it. At quarter of one he got back in the car and drove out to Mrs. Rastrow's place.

There was a gate to be negotiated where the blacktop gave way to the dirt drive, and then there was the drive itself, unchanged in two hundred years, a pair of beaten parallel tracks with a yellow scruff of dead vegetation painted down the center of it. He parked beneath a denuded oak, went up the three stone steps and rang the bell. Standing there on the doorstep, the laden breeze in his face and the bay spread out before him in a graceful arc to Colson's Head, where the summer house stood amidst the fortress of trees like a chromatic miscalculation on a larger canvas, he felt the anxiety let go of him, eased by the simple step-by-step progress of his day, the business at hand, the feel of the island beneath his feet. She hadn't mentioned a price. But he had a figure in mind, a figure that would at least stanch his wounds, if not stop the bleeding altogether, and she had the kind of capital to take everything down to the essentials, everybody knew that—Mrs. Rastrow, Alice Rastrow, widow of Julius, the lumber baron. He'd prepared his opening words, and his smile, cool and at ease, because he wasn't going to be intimidated by her or let her see his need, and he listened to the bell ring through the house that was no mansion, no showplace, no testament to riches and self-aggrandizement but just what it was, and he pictured her moving through the dimness on her old lady's limbs like a deep-sea diver in his heavy, confining suit. A moment passed. Then another. He debated, then rang again.

His first surprise—the first in what would prove to be an unraveling skein of them—was the face at the door. The big pitted brown slab of oak pulled back and Mrs. Rastrow, ancient, crabbed, the whites of her eyes gone to yellow and her hair flown away in the white wisps of his recollection, was nowhere to be seen. A young Asian woman was standing there at the door, her eyes questioning, brow wrinkled, teeth bundled beneath the neat bow of her lips. Her hair shone as if it had been painted on. "I came to see Mrs. Rastrow," he said. "About the house?"

The woman—she looked to be in her late twenties, her body

squeezed into one of those luminous silk dresses the hostess in a Chinese restaurant might wear—showed no sign of recognition.

He gave her his name. "We had an appointment today," he said, "—for one?" Still nothing. He wondered if she spoke English. "I mean, me and Mrs. Rastrow? You know Mrs. Rastrow? Do you work for her?"

She pressed a hand to her lips in a flurry of painted nails and giggled through her fingers, and the curtain dropped. She was just a girl, pretty, casual, and she might have been standing in the middle of her own dorm room, sharing a joke with her friends. "It's just—you look like a potato peeler salesman or something standing there like that." Her smile opened up around even, white teeth. "I'm Rose," she said, and held out her hand.

There was a mudroom, flagstone underfoot, firewood stacked up like breastworks on both sides, and then the main room with its bare oak floors and plaster walls. A few museum pieces, tatted rug, a plush sofa with an orange cat curled up in the middle of it. Two lamps, their shades as thin as skin, glowed against the gray of the windows. Rose bent to the stove in the corner, opened the grate and laid two lengths of wood on the coals, and he stood there in the middle of the room watching the swell of her figure in the tight wrap of her dress and the silken flex and release of the muscles in her shoulders. The room was cold as a meat locker.

He was watching Rose, transfixed by the incongruity of her bent over the black stove in her golden Chinese restaurant dress that clung to her backside as if it had been sewn over her skin, and the old lady's voice startled him, for all the pep talk he'd given himself. "You came," she said, and there she was in the doorway, looking no different from the picture he'd held of her.

She waited for him to say something in response, and he complied, murmuring "Yes, sure, it's my pleasure," and then she was standing beside him and studying him out of her yellowed eyes. "Did you bring the papers?" she said.

He patted the briefcase. They were both standing, as if they'd just run into each other in a train station or the foyer at the theater, and

Rose was standing too, awaiting the moment of release. "Rose," she said then, her eyes snapping sharply to her, "fetch my reading glasses, will you?"

THE CAR HAD DEVELOPED a cough on the drive up from Boston, a consumptive wheeze that rattled the floorboards when he depressed the accelerator, and now, with the influence of the sea, it had gotten worse. He turned the key in the ignition and listened to the slow seep of strangulation, then put the car in gear, backed out from beneath the oak and made his hesitant way down the drive, wondering how much they were going to take him for this time when he brought it into the shop—if he made it to the shop, that is. There was no reward in any of this—he'd tried to keep the shock and disappointment from rising to his face when the old lady named her price—but at least, for now, there was the afternoon ahead and the rudimentary animal satisfaction of lunch, food to push into his maw and distract him, and he took the blacktop road back into the village and found a seat at the counter in the diner.

There were three other customers. The light through the windows was like concrete, like shale, the whole place hardened into its sediments. He didn't recognize anyone, and he ate his grilled cheese on white with his head down, gathering from the local newspaper that the creatures had deserted the sea en masse and left the lobstermen scrambling for government handouts and the cod fleet stranded at anchor. He'd countered the old lady's offer, but she'd held firm. At first he thought she hadn't even heard him. They'd moved to the sofa and she was looking through the papers, nodding her head like a battered old sea turtle fighting the pull of gravity, but she turned to him at last and said, "My offer is final. You might have known that." He fought himself, tried to get hold of his voice. He told her he'd think about it—sleep on it, he'd sleep on it—and have an answer for her in the morning.

It was raining again, a pulsing hard-driven rain that sheathed the car and ran slick over the pavement till the parking lot gleamed like the sea beyond it. He didn't want to go back to the cottage in the motor court, not yet anyway—the thought of it entered his mind like a closed box floating in the void, and he had to squeeze his eyes shut to make it disappear—and he wasn't much of a drinker, so there wasn't any solace in the lights of the bar across the street. Finally, he decided to do what he'd known he was going to do all along: drive out to the house and have a last look at it. Things would have to be sold, he told himself, things stored, winnowed, tossed into the trash.

As soon as he pulled into the dirt drive that dropped off the road and into the trees, he could see he'd been fooling himself. The place was an eyesore, vandalized and vandalized again, the paint gone, windows shattered, the porch skewed away from the foundation as if it had been shoved by the hand of a giant. He switched off the ignition and stepped out into the rain. Inside, there was nothing of value: graffiti on the walls, a stained mattress in the center of the living room, every stick of furniture broken down and fed to the fire, the toilet bowl smashed and something dead in the pit of it, rodent or bird, it didn't matter. He wandered through the rooms, stooping to pick things up and then drop them again. For a long while he stood at the kitchen sink, staring out into the rain.

The summer the Rastrows drowned, he'd lived primitive, out on the water all day every day, swimming, fishing, crabbing, racing from island to shore and back again under the belly of his sail. That was the year his parents had their friends from the city out to stay, the Morses—Mr. Morse, ventricose and roaring, with his head set tenuously atop the shaft of his neck, as if they'd given him the wrong size at birth, and Mrs. Morse, her face drawn to a point beneath the bleached bird fluff of her hair—and a woman who worked with his mother as a secretary, a divorcée with two shy pretty daughters his own age. And what was the woman's name? Jean. And the daughters? He could no longer remember, but they wore sunsuits that left their legs and midriffs bare, the field of their taut browned flesh a thrill and revelation to him. He couldn't look them in the face, couldn't even pretend. But they went off after a week to be with their father, and the Morses—and Jean—stayed on with his parents, sunning outside in the vinyl lawn chairs, drinking and playing cards so late in the night that their voices—murmurous, shrill suddenly, murmurous again—were like the disquisitions of the birds that wakened him at dawn to go down to the shore and the boat and the sun that burned the chill off the water.

There was something tumultuous going on amongst them—all five of them—but he didn't understand what it was till he looked back on it years later. It was something sexual, that much he knew, something forbidden and shameful and emotionally wrought. He lay in his bed upstairs, twelve years old and discovering his own body, and they shouted recriminations at each other a floor down. Mr. Morse took him and Jean out fishing for pollack one afternoon, the big man shirtless and rowing, Jean in the bow, an ice bucket sprouting a bristle of green-necked bottles between them. He fished. Baited his hook with squid and dropped the weighted line into the shifting gray deep. Behind him, Mr. Morse slipped his hand up under Jean's blouse and they kissed and wriggled against each other until they couldn't seem to catch their breath, even as he peered down into the water and pretended he didn't notice. He remembered a single voice raised in agony that night, a voice caught between a sob and a shriek, and in the morning Mrs. Morse was gone. A few days later, her husband got behind the wheel of Jean's car and the two of them pulled out of the drive. Nobody said a word. He sat with his parents at dinner—coleslaw, corn on the cob, hamburgers his father seared on the grill—and nobody said a word.

He was back at the motor court by five and he called Ruth just to hear the sound of her voice and to lie to her about the old lady's offer. Yes, he told her, yes, it was just what he'd expected and he'd close the deal tomorrow, no problem. Yes, he loved her. Yes, good night. Then, though he wasn't a drinker, he walked into the village and sat at the bar while the Celtics went through the motions up on the television screen and the six or seven patrons gathered there either cheered or groaned as the occasion demanded. He let two beers grow warm by the time he got to the bottom of them and he had a handful of saltines to steady his stomach. He was hoping someone would mention Mrs. Rastrow, offer up some information about her, some gossip about what she was doing to the island, about Rose, but nobody spoke to him, nobody even looked at him. By seven-thirty he was back in the cottage paging through half a dozen back issues of a news magazine the woman at the desk had given him with an apologetic thrust of her hand, and she was sorry they didn't have any TV for him to watch but maybe he'd be interested in these magazines?

He was reading of things that had happened five years ago—big stories, crises, and he couldn't for the life of him remember how any of them had turned out—when there was a knock at the door. It was Rose, dressed in a bulky sweater and blue jeans. The black patent-leather pumps she'd been wearing earlier had been replaced by tennis shoes. Her ankles were bare. "Hi," she said. "I thought I'd drop by to see how you were doing."

Everything in him seemed to seize up. How he was doing? He was doing poorly, feeling trapped and bereft, pressed for money, for luck, for hope, so worried about Ruth and her doctors and the tests and prescriptions and bills he didn't know how he was going to survive the night ahead, let alone the rest of the winter and the long unspooling year to come. Mrs. Rastrow—her employer, her *ally*—had cut the heart out of him. So how was he doing? He couldn't even open his mouth to tell her.

They were both standing at the open door. The night smelled like an old dishrag that had been frozen and defrosted again. "Because I felt bad this afternoon," she said, "I mean, not even offering you something to drink or a sandwich. Alice can be pretty abrupt, and I wanted to apologize."

"Okay," he said, "sure, I appreciate that." He was in his stocking feet, his shirt open at the collar to reveal the T-shirt beneath, and was it clean? His hair. Had he combed his hair? "Okay," he said again, not knowing what else to do.

"Do you have a minute?" She peered into the room as if it might conceal something she needed to be wary of. Her shoulders were bunched, her eyes gone wide. The night air leaked in around her, carrying a sour lingering odor now of panic and attrition—a skunk, somebody had surprised a skunk somewhere out on the road. Suddenly she was smiling. "I guess I'm the potato peeler salesman now, huh?"

"No," he said, "no," too forcefully, and he didn't know what he was up to—what *she* was up to, a young woman who lived with an old woman and wore tight silk Chinese dresses on an island that had no Chinese restaurants and no need of them—and then he was pulling the door back and inviting her in, their bodies pressed close in passing, and the door shutting behind them.

She took the chair, he the bed. "I'd offer you something," he said, "but—" and he threw up his hands and they both laughed. Was he drunk—two beers on an empty stomach? Was that it?

"I brought you something," she said, snapping open her purse to remove a brown paper bag and set it on the night table. There were oil stains on the bag, translucent continents, headlands, isthmuses painted across the surface in a random geography. "Tuna," she said. "Tuna on rye. I made them myself. And these"—lifting the sandwiches in their opaque paper from the bag and holding two cans of beer aloft. "I thought you'd be hungry. With the diner closing early, I mean." She pushed a beer across the table and handed him a sandwich. "I didn't know if you'd know that—that they close early this time of year?"

He told her he hadn't known, or he'd forgotten—or hadn't even thought of it, really—and he thanked her for thinking of him. They sipped their beers in silence a moment, the light on the night table the only illumination in the room, and then he said, "You know, that house belonged to my father. That's his signature on the deed. We spent summers here when I was a kid, best summers of my life. I was here when Mrs. Rastrow's—when Ronald and Elyse drowned. I was maybe twelve at the time, and I didn't really—I didn't understand you *could* die. Not if you were young. Up till that point it was old people who'd died, the lady next door—Mrs. Jennings—my grandmother, a great-aunt."

She just nodded, but he could see she was right there with him, the brightness in her eyes, the way she chewed, sipped. He felt the beer go to his head. He wanted to ask about her, how she'd come to the island—was it an ad in the paper, lumber heiress in need of a companion to wear silk Chinese dresses in a remote cottage, room and board and stipend and all the time in the world to paint, write, dream?—but he didn't want to be obvious. She was exotic. Chinese. The only Chinese person on the island, and it would be rude, maybe even faintly racist, to ask.

He watched her tuck the last corner of the sandwich in her mouth and tilt back the can to drain it. She wiped her lips with a paper napkin, then settled her hands over her knees and said, "You know, it's no use. She's never going to go any higher."

He was embarrassed suddenly—to bring all that into this?—and he just shrugged. It was a fait accompli. He was defeated and he knew it.

"She knows about your wife. And you know she could pay a fair price, even though the place is run-down, because it's not the money—she has all the money anybody could want—but she won't. I know her. She won't budge." She lifted her face so that the light cut it in two, the ridge of her nose and one eye shining, the rest in shadow. "She's just going to let it rot anyway. That's what she's doing with all of them."

"Spoils her view?"

She smiled. "Something like that."

Then the question he'd been swallowing since she'd appeared at the door, finally pried up off his tongue by the beer: "This isn't some kind of negotiation, is it? I mean, she didn't send you, did she?"

The question left a space for all the little sounds of the night to creep in: the cry of a shorebird, the wind scouring the beach, something ticking in the depths of the heater. She dropped her eyes. "No, that's not it at all," she murmured.

Well, what is it then? he wanted to say—almost said—but he felt a tightening across the surface of him, his flesh prickling and contracting as if all his defenses were going down at once, and the answer came to him. She was here for him, for a quick fix for loneliness and despair, here to listen to a voice besides Mrs. Rastrow's, to sleep in another bed, any bed, make contact where before there had been none. He got up from the bed, moved awkwardly toward her, and she got up too. They were as close as they'd been at the door. He could smell her, a sweet heat rising from the folds of the sweater, caught in the coils of her hair. "Did you want to maybe go over to the tavern?" she said. "For another beer, I mean? I only brought the two."

He didn't want another beer, hadn't wanted the first one. "No," he said in a whisper, and then he was holding her, pulling her to him as if she had no bones in her body, everything new and soft and started from scratch. Her cheek was pressed to his, scintillating, electric, *her cheek,* and she let him kiss her and her bones were gone and she was melting down away from the chair and into the bed. She didn't taste like Ruth. Didn't feel like her. Didn't conform to him the way Ruth had through all those years when she was well and alive and lit up like a meteor, and he had to say something, he didn't have any choice. "I don't think so," he said. "I'm sorry. I really don't."

She was beneath him on the bed, her hair in a sprawl. He pulled away from her—pushed himself up as if he were doing some sort of exercise, calisthenics of the will, the heaviest of heavy lifting—and before he knew what he was doing he was out the door and into the night. He thought he heard her call out his name, but the surf took it away. He was furious, raging, pounding his way down the dark strand as if every step was a murder—*That dried-up old bitch, and who does she think she is, anyway?*

A sudden wind came up off the shore to rake the trees, the branches rattling like claws, and the smell assaulted him again, the smell of rottenness and corruption, of animals and their glands. He kept walking, the wind in his face. Head down, shoulders pumping, he followed his legs till he got beyond the lights of the farthest house and the sky closed down and melded with the shore. There was something there ahead on the beach, a shape spawned from the shadows, and it took him a moment to see what it was: a trash can, let's all pitch in and keep the island clean, turned on its side in a spill of litter. And inside the can, the animal itself, coiled round the wedge of its head and the twin lights of its eyes. "Get out of that!" he shouted, looking for something to throw. "Get out!"

IN THE MORNING he made his way back up the long dirt drive and signed away the property. By noon, he was gone.

Chicxulub

MY DAUGHTER is walking along the roadside late at night—too late, really, for a seventeen-year-old to be out alone even in a town as safe as this—and it is raining, the first rain of the season, the streets slick with a fine immiscible glaze of water and petrochemicals so that even a driver in full possession of her faculties, a driver who hasn't consumed two apple martinis and three glasses of Hitching Post pinot noir before she gets behind the wheel of the car, will have trouble keeping the thing off the sidewalk and out of the gutters, the shrubbery, *the highway median,* for Christ's sake. . . . But that's not really what I want to talk about, or not yet, anyway.

Have you heard of Tunguska? In Russia?

This was the site of the last-known large-body impact on the Earth's surface, nearly a hundred years ago. Or that's not strictly accurate—the meteor, an estimated sixty yards across, never actually touched down. The force of its entry—the compression and super-heating of the air beneath it—caused it to explode some twenty-five thousand feet above the ground, but then the term "explode" hardly does justice to the event. There was a detonation—a flash, a thunder-clap—equal to the explosive power of eight hundred Hiroshima bombs. Thirty miles away, reindeer in their loping herds were struck dead by the blast wave, and the clothes of a hunter another thirty miles beyond that burst into flame even as he was poleaxed to the ground. Seven hundred square miles of Siberian forest were leveled in an instant. If the meteor had hit only four hours later it would have exploded over St. Petersburg and annihilated every living thing in that glorious and baroque city. And this was only a rock. And it was only sixty yards across.

My point? You'd better get down on your knees and pray to your gods, because each year this big spinning globe we ride intersects the orbits of some twenty million asteroids, at least a thousand of which are bigger than a mile in diameter.

But my daughter. She's out there in the dark and the rain, walking home. Maureen and I bought her a car, a Honda Civic, the safest thing on four wheels, but the car was used—pre-owned, in dealer-speak—and as it happens it's in the shop with transmission problems and, because she just had to see her friends and gossip and giggle and balance slick multicolored clumps of raw fish and pickled ginger on conjoined chopsticks at the mall, Kimberly picked her up and Kimberly will bring her home. Maddy has a cell phone and theoretically she could have called us, but she didn't—or that's how it appears. And so she's walking. In the rain. And Alice K. Petermann of 16 Briar Lane, white, divorced, a realtor with Hyperion who has picked at a salad and left her glasses on the bar, loses control of her car.

It is just past midnight. I am in bed with a book, naked, and hardly able to focus on the clustered words and rigid descending paragraphs, because Maureen is in the bathroom slipping into the sheer black negligee I bought her at Victoria's Secret for her birthday, and her every sound—the creak of the medicine cabinet on its hinges, the susurrus of the brush at her teeth, the tap running—electrifies me. I've lit a candle and am waiting for Maureen to step into the room so I can flick off the light. We had cocktails earlier, a bottle of wine with dinner, and we sat close on the couch and shared a joint in front of the fire because our daughter was out and we could do that and no one the wiser. I listen to the little sounds from the bathroom, seductive sounds, maddening. I am ready. More than ready. "Hey," I call, pitching my voice low, "are you coming or not? You don't expect me to wait all night, do you?"

Her face appears in the doorway, the pale lobes of her breasts and the dark nipples visible through the clinging black silk. "Oh, are you waiting for me?" she says, making a game of it. She hovers at the door, and I can see the smile creep across her lips, the pleasure of the moment, drawing it out. "Because I thought I might go down and work in the garden for a while—it won't take long, couple hours, maybe. You know, spread a little manure, bank up some of the mulch on the roses. You'll wait for me, won't you?"

Then the phone rings.

We stare blankly at each other through the first two rings and then Maureen says, "I better get it," and I say, "No, no, forget it— it's nothing. It's nobody."

But she's already moving.

"Forget it!" I shout, and her voice drifts back to me—"What if it's Maddy?"—and then I watch her put her lips to the receiver and whisper, "Hello?"

THE NIGHT of the Tunguska explosion the skies were unnaturally bright across Europe—as far away as London people strolled in the parks past midnight and read novels out of doors while the sheep kept right on grazing and the birds stirred uneasily in the trees. There were no stars visible, no moon—just a pale, quivering light, as if all the color had been bleached out of the sky. But of course that midnight glow and the fate of those unhappy Siberian reindeer were nothing at all compared to what would have happened if a larger object had invaded the Earth's atmosphere. On average, objects greater than a hundred yards in diameter strike the planet once every five thousand years and asteroids half a mile across thunder down at intervals of three hundred thousand years. Three hundred thousand years is a long time in anybody's book. But if—when—such a collision occurs, the explosion will be in the million megaton range and will cloak the atmosphere in dust, thrusting the entire planet into a deep freeze and effectively stifling all plant growth for a period of a year or more. There will be no crops. No forage. No sun.

THERE HAS BEEN an accident, that is what the voice on the other end of the line is telling my wife, and the victim is Madeline Biehn, of 1337 Laurel Drive, according to the I.D. the paramedics found in her purse. (The purse, with the silver clasp that has been driven half an inch into the flesh under her arm from the force of the impact, is a little thing, no bigger than a hardcover book, with a ribbon-thin strap, the same purse all the girls carry, as if it's part of a uniform.) Is this her parent or guardian speaking?

I hear my wife say, "This is her mother." And then, the bottom dropping out of her voice, "Is she—?"

Is she? They don't answer such questions, don't volunteer information, not over the phone. The next ten seconds are thunderous, cataclysmic, my wife standing there numbly with the phone in her hand as if it's some unidentifiable object she's found in the street while I fumble out of bed to snatch for my pants—and my shoes, where are my shoes? The car keys? My wallet? This is the true panic, the loss of faith and control, the nameless named, the punch in the heart and the struggle for breath. I say the only thing I can think to say, just to hear my own voice, just to get things straight, "She was in an accident. Is that what they said?"

"She was hit by a car. She's—they don't know. In surgery."

"What hospital? Did they say what hospital?"

My wife is in motion now too, the negligee ridiculous, unequal to the task, and she jerks it over her head and flings it to the floor even as she snatches up a blouse, shorts, flip-flops—anything, anything to cover her nakedness and get her out the door. The dog is whining in the kitchen. There is the sound of the rain on the roof, intensifying, hammering at the gutters. I don't bother with shoes— there are no shoes, shoes do not exist—and my shirt hangs limply from my shoulders, misbuttoned, sagging, tails hanging loose, and we're in the car now and the driver's side wiper is beating out of sync and the night closing on us like a fist.

AND THEN there's Chicxulub. Sixty-five million years ago, an asteroid (or perhaps a comet—no one is quite certain) collided with the Earth on what is now the Yucatán Peninsula. Judging from the impact crater, which is one hundred and twenty miles wide, the object—this big flaming ball—was some six miles across. When it came down, day became night and that night extended so far into the future that at least seventy-five percent of all known species were extinguished, including the dinosaurs in nearly all their forms and array and some ninety percent of the oceans' plankton, which in turn devastated the pelagic food chain. How fast was it traveling? The nearest estimates put it at 54,000 miles an hour, more than sixty times the speed of a bullet. Astrophysicists call such objects "civilization enders," and calculate the chances that a disaster of this magnitude will occur during any individual's lifetime at roughly one in ten thousand, the same odds as dying in an auto accident in the next ten months—or, more tellingly, living to be a hundred in the company of your spouse.

ALL I SEE is windows, an endless grid of lit windows climbing one atop the other into the night, as the car shoots through the *Emergency Vehicles Only* lane and slides in hard against the curb. Both doors fling open simultaneously. Maureen is already out on the sidewalk, already slamming the door behind her and breaking into a trot, and I'm right on her heels, the keys still in the ignition and the lights stabbing at the pale underbelly of a diagonally parked ambulance— and they can have the car, anybody can have it and keep it forever, if they'll just tell me my daughter is all right. *Just tell me,* I mutter, hurrying, out of breath, soaked through to the skin, *just tell me and it's yours,* and this is a prayer, the first of them in a long discontinuous string, addressed to whomever or whatever may be listening. Overhead, the sky is having a seizure, black above, quicksilver below, the rain coming down in windblown arcs, and I wouldn't even notice but for the fact that we are suddenly—instantly—wet, our hair knotted and clinging and our clothes stuck like flypaper to the slick tegument of our skin.

In we come, side by side, through the doors that jolt back from us in alarm, and all I can think is that the hospital is a death factory and that we have come to it like the walking dead, haggard, sallow, shoeless. "My daughter," I say to the nurse at the admittance desk, "she's—they called. You called. She's been in an accident."

Maureen is at my side, tugging at the fingers of one hand as if she's trying to remove an invisible glove, her shoulders slumped, mouth set, the wet blouse shrink-wrapping her. "A car. A car accident."

"Name?" the nurse asks. (About this nurse: she's young, Filipina, with opaque eyes and the bone structure of a cadaver; every day she sees death and it blinds her. She doesn't see us. She sees a computer screen, she sees the TV monitor mounted in the corner and the shadows that pass there, she sees the walls, the floor, the naked light of the fluorescent tube. But not us. Not us.)

For one resounding moment that thumps in my ears and then thumps again, I can't remember my daughter's name—I can picture her leaning into the mound of textbooks spread out on the dining room table, the glow of the overhead light making a nimbus of her hair as she glances up at me with a glum look and half a rueful smile, as if to say, *It's all in a day's work for a teenager, Dad, and you're lucky you're not in high school anymore,* but her name is gone.

"Maddy," my wife says. "Madeline Biehn."

I watch, mesmerized, as the nurse's fleshless fingers maneuver the mouse, her eyes fixed on the screen before her. A click. Another click. The eyes lift to take us in, even as they dodge away again. "She's still in surgery," she says.

"Where is it?" I demand. "What room? Where do we go?"

Maureen's voice cuts in then, elemental, chilling, and it's not a question she's posing, not a statement or demand, but a plea: "What's wrong with her?"

Another click, but this one is just for show, and the eyes never move from the screen. "There was an accident," the nurse says. "She was brought in by the paramedics. That's all I can tell you."

It is then that I become aware that we are not alone, that there are others milling around the room—other zombies like us, hurriedly dressed and streaming water till the beige carpet is black with it, shuffling, moaning, clutching at one another with eyes gone null and void—and why, I wonder, do I despise this nurse more than any human being I've ever encountered, this young woman not much older than my daughter, with her hair pulled back in a bun and the white cap like a party favor perched atop it, *who is just doing her job*? Why do I want to reach across the counter that separates us and awaken her to a swift sure knowledge of hate and fear and pain? Why?

"Ted," Maureen says, and I feel her grip at my elbow, and then we're moving again—hurrying, sweeping, practically running—out of this place, down a corridor under the glare of the lights that are a kind of death in themselves, and into a worse place, a far worse place.

THE THING THAT disturbs me about Chicxulub, aside from the fact that it erased the dinosaurs and wrought catastrophic and irreversible change, is the deeper implication that we, and all our works and worries and attachments, are so utterly inconsequential. Death cancels our individuality, we know that, yes, but ontogeny recapitulates phylogeny and the kind goes on, human life and culture succeed us—that, in the absence of God, is what allows us to accept the death of the individual. But when you throw Chicxulub into the mix—or the next Chicxulub, the Chicxulub that could come howling down to obliterate all and everything even as your eyes skim the lines of this page—where does that leave us?

"YOU'RE THE PARENTS?"

We are in another room, gone deeper now, the walls closing in, the loudspeakers murmuring their eternal incantations, *Dr. Chandrasoma to Emergency, Dr. Bell, paging Dr. Bell,* and here is another nurse, grimmer, older, with deader eyes and lines like the strings of a tobacco pouch pulled tight round her lips. She's addressing us, me and my wife, but I have nothing to say, either in denial or affirmation. I'm paralyzed, struck dumb. If I claim Maddy as my own—and I'm making deals again—then I'm sure to jinx her, because those powers that might or might not be, those gods of the infinite and the minute, will see how desperately I love her and they'll take her away just to spite me for refusing to believe in them. *Voodoo, Hoodoo, Santeria, Bless me, Father, for I have sinned.* I hear Maureen's voice, emerging from a locked vault, the single whispered monosyllable, and then: "Is she going to be all right?"

"I don't have that information," the nurse says, and her voice is neutral, robotic even. This is not her daughter. Her daughter's at home, asleep in a pile of teddy bears, pink sheets, fluffy pillows, the night light glowing like the all-seeing eye of a sentinel.

I can't help myself. It's that neutrality, that maddening clinical neutrality, and can't anybody take any responsibility for anything? "What information *do* you have?" I say, and maybe I'm too loud, maybe I am. "Isn't that your job, for Christ's sake, to know what's going on here? You call us up in the middle of the night—our daughter's hurt, she's been in an accident, and you tell me you don't have *any fucking information*?"

People turn their heads, eyes burn into us. They're slouched in orange plastic chairs, stretched out on the floor, praying, pacing, their lips moving in silence. They want information too. We all want information. We want news, good news: it was all a mistake, minor cuts and bruises—contusions, that's the word—and your daughter, son, husband, grandmother, first cousin twice removed will be walking through that door over there any minute . . .

The nurse drills me with a look, and then she's coming out from behind the desk, a short woman, dumpy—almost a dwarf—and striding briskly to the door, which swings open on another room, deeper yet. "If you'll just follow me, please," she says.

Sheepish suddenly, I duck my head and comply, two steps behind Maureen. This room is smaller, an examining room, with a set of scales and charts on the walls and its slab of a table covered with a sheet of antiseptic paper. "Wait here," the nurse tells us, already shifting her weight to make her escape. "The doctor'll be in in a minute."

"What doctor?" I want to know. "What for? What does he want?"

But the door is already closed.

I turn to Maureen. She's standing there in the middle of the room, afraid to touch anything or to sit down or even move for fear of breaking the spell. She's listening for footsteps, her eyes fixed on the other door, the one at the rear of the room. I hear myself murmur her name, and then she's in my arms, sobbing, and I know I should hold her, know that we both need it, the human contact, the love and support, but all I feel is the burden of her—there is nothing or no one that can make this better, can't she see that? I don't want to console or be consoled. I don't want to be touched. I just want my daughter back, that's all, nothing else.

Maureen's voice comes from so deep in her throat I can barely make out what she's saying. It takes a second to register, even as she pulls away from me, her face crumpled and red, and this is her prayer, whispered aloud: "She's going to be all right, isn't she?"

"Sure," I say, "sure she is. She'll be fine. She'll have some bruises, that's for sure, maybe a couple broken bones even . . ." and I trail off, trying to picture it, the crutches, the cast, Band-Aids, gauze: our daughter returned to us in a halo of shimmering light.

"It was a car," she says. "A car, Ted. A car hit her."

The room seems to tick and buzz with the fading energy of the larger edifice, and I can't help thinking of the congeries of wires strung inside the walls, the cables bringing power to the X-ray lab, the EKG and EEG machines, the life-support systems, and of the myriad pipes and the fluids they drain. A car. Three thousand pounds of steel, chrome, glass, iron.

"What was she even doing walking like that? She knows better than that."

My wife nods, the wet ropes of her hair beating at her shoulders like the flails of the penitents. "She probably had a fight with Kimberly, I'll bet that's it. I'll bet anything."

"Where is the son of a bitch?" I snarl. "This doctor—where is he?"

We are in that room, in that purgatory of a room, for a good hour or more. Twice I thrust my head out the door to give the nurse an annihilating look, but there is no news, no doctor, no nothing. And then, at quarter past two, the inner door swings open, and there he is, a man too young to be a doctor, an infant with a smooth bland face and hair that rides a wave up off his brow, and he doesn't have to say a thing, not a word, because I can see what he's bringing us and my heart seizes with the shock of it. He looks to Maureen, looks to me, then drops his eyes. "I'm sorry," he says.

WHEN IT COMES, the meteor will punch through the atmosphere and strike the Earth in the space of a single second, vaporizing on impact and creating a fireball several miles wide that will in that moment achieve temperatures of 60,000 degrees Kelvin, or ten times the surface reading of the sun. If it is Chicxulub-sized and it hits one of our landmasses, some two hundred thousand cubic kilometers of the Earth's surface will be thrust up into the atmosphere, even as the thermal radiation of the blast sets fire to the planet's cities and forests. This will be succeeded by seismic and volcanic activity on a scale unknown in human history, and then the dark night of cosmic winter. If it should land in the sea, as the Chicxulub meteor did, it would spew superheated water into the atmosphere instead, extinguishing the light of the sun and triggering the same scenario of seismic catastrophe and eternal winter, while simultaneously sending out a rippling ring of water three miles high to rock the continents as if they were saucers in a dishpan.

So what does it matter? What does anything matter? We are powerless. We are bereft. And the gods—all the gods of all the ages combined—are nothing but a rumor.

THE GURNEY IS the focal point in a room of gurneys, people laid out as if there's been a war, the beaked noses of the victims poking up out of the maze of sheets like a series of topographic blips on a glaciated plane. These people are alive still, fluids dripping into their veins, machines monitoring their vital signs, nurses hovering over them like ghouls, but they'll be dead soon, all of them. That much is clear. But *the* gurney, the one against the back wall with the sheet pulled up over the impossibly small and reduced form, this is all that matters. The doctor leads us across the room, talking in a low voice of internal injuries, a ruptured spleen, trauma to the brain stem, and I can barely control my feet. Maureen clings to me. The lights dim.

Can I tell you how hard it is to lift this sheet? Thin percale, and it might as well be made of lead, iron, iridium, might as well be the repository of all the dark matter in the universe. The doctor steps back, hands folded before him. The entire room or triage ward or whatever it is holds its breath. Maureen moves in beside me till our shoulders are touching, till I can feel the flesh and the heat of her pressing into me, and I think of this child we've made together, this thing under the sheet, and the hand clenches at the end of my arm, the fingers there, prehensile, taking hold. The sheet draws back millimeter by millimeter, the slow striptease of death—and I can't do this, I can't—until Maureen lunges forward and jerks the thing off in a single violent motion.

It takes us a moment—the shock of the bloated and discolored flesh, the crusted mat of blood at the temple and the rag of the hair, this obscene violation of everything we know and expect and love— before the surge of joy hits us. Maddy is a redhead, like her mother, and though she's seventeen, she's as rangy and thin as a child, with oversized hands and feet, and she never did pierce that smooth sweet run of flesh beneath her lower lip. I can't speak. I'm rushing still with the euphoria of this new mainline drug I've discovered, soaring over the room, the hospital, the whole planet. Maureen says it for me: "This is not our daughter."

OUR DAUGHTER IS not in the hospital. Our daughter is asleep in her room beneath the benevolent gaze of the posters on the wall, Britney and Brad and Justin, her things scattered around her as if laid out for a rummage sale. Our daughter has in fact gone to Hana Sushi at the mall, as planned, and Kimberly has driven her home. Our daughter has, unbeknownst to us or anyone else, fudged the rules a bit, the smallest thing in the world, nothing really, the sort of thing every teenager does without thinking twice, loaning her ID to her second-best friend, Kristi Cherwin, because Kristi is sixteen and Kristi wants to see—is dying to see—the movie at the Cineplex with Brad Pitt in it, the one rated NC17. Our daughter doesn't know that we've been to the hospital, doesn't know about Alice K. Petermann and the pinot noir and the glasses left on the bar, doesn't know that even now the phone is ringing at the Cherwins'.

I am sitting on the couch with a drink, staring into the ashes of the fire. Maureen is in the kitchen with a mug of Ovaltine, gazing va-cantly out the window where the first streaks of light have begun to limn the trunks of the trees. I try to picture the Cherwins—they've been to the house a few times, Ed and Lucinda—and I draw a blank until a backlit scene from the past presents itself, a cookout at their place, the adults gathered around the grill with gin and tonics, the radio playing some forgotten song, the children—our daughters—

riding their bikes up and down the cobbled drive, making a game of it, spinning, dodging, lifting the front wheels from the ground even as their hair fans out behind them and the sun crashes through the trees. Flip a coin ten times and it could turn up heads ten times in a row—or not once. The rock is coming, the new Chicxulub, hurtling through the dark and the cold to remake our fate. But not tonight. Not for me.

For the Cherwins, it's already here.

Here Comes

HE DIDN'T KNOW how it happened, exactly—lack of foresight on his part, lack of caring, planning, holding something back for a rainy day—but in rapid succession he lost his job, his girlfriend and the roof over his head, waking up one morning to find himself sprawled out on the sidewalk in front of the post office. The sun drilled him where he lay. Both knees were torn out of his jeans and the right sleeve of his jacket was gone altogether. People were skirting him, clopping by like a whole herd of self-righteous Republicans, though they were mostly Latino—and mostly illegal—in this part of town. He sat up, feeling around for his hat, which he seemed to be sitting on. The pavement glistened minutely.

What was motivating him at the moment was thirst, the kind of thirst that made him suspect everything and everybody, because somebody had to have done this to him, deprived him of fluids, dredged his throat with a swab, left him here stranded like a nomad in the desert. Just beyond his reach, and he noticed this in the way of a detective meditating on a crime scene, was a brown paper bag with the green neck of a Mogen David 20/20 bottle peeping out of it. The bag had been crushed, and the bottle with it; ants had gathered for the feast. In real time, the time dictated by the sun in the sky and the progressive seep of movement all around him, a woman who must have had three hundred pounds packed like mocha fudge into the sausage skin of her monumental blue-and-white-flecked top and matching toreador pants stepped daintily over the splayed impediment of his legs and shot him a look of disgust. Cars pulled up, engines ticking, then rattled away. Exhaust hovered in a poisonous cloud. Two gulls, perched atop the convenient drive-up mail depository, watched him out of their assayers' eyes, big birds, vagrant and opportunistic, half again as tall as the boombox he'd left behind at Dana's when she drilled him out the door.

It wasn't an alcoholic beverage he wanted, though he wouldn't turn down a beer, but water, just that, something to wet his mouth and dribble down his throat. He made a failed effort to rise, and then somehow his feet found their place beneath him and he shoved himself up and snatched his cap off the pavement in a single graceless lurch. He let the blood pound in his ears a minute, then scanned the street for a source of H_2O.

To be homeless, in July, in a tourist-infested city on the coast of Southern California, wasn't as bad maybe as being homeless in Cleveland or Bogotá, but it wasn't what he was used to. Even at his worst, even when he got going on the bottle and couldn't stop, he was used to four walls and a bed, and if not a kitchen, at least a hotplate. A chair. A table. A place to put his things, wash up, have a smoke and listen to music while dreaming over a paperback mystery—he loved mysteries and police procedurals, and horror, nothing better than horror when you're wrapped up in bed and the fog transfigures the streets and alleyways outside till anything could be lurking there. Except you. Because you're in bed, in your room, with the door shut and locked and the blankets pulled up to your chin, reading. And smoking. But Dana's face was like a cleaver, sharp and shining and merciless, and it cleaved and chopped till he had no choice but to get out the door or leave his limbs and digits behind. So now he was on the street, and everything he did, every last twitch and snort and furtive palpation of his scrotum, was a public performance, open to interpretation and subject to the judgment of strangers. Idiotic strangers. Strangers who were no better than him or anybody else, but who made way for him in a parting wave as if he was going to stick to the bottom of their shoes.

Across the street, kitty-corner to where he found himself at the moment, was a gas station—it floated there like a mirage, rippling gently in the convection waves rising up off the blacktop—and a gas station was a place where all sorts of fluids were dispensed, including water. Or so he reasoned. All right, then. He began to move, one scuffing sneaker following the other.

HE WAS RUNNING the hose over the back of his head when he became aware that someone was addressing him. He didn't look up right away—he knew what was coming—but he made sure to twist off the spigot without hesitation. Then he ran his fingers through his hair, because if there was one thing that made him feel the strain of his circumstances it was unwashed hair, knocked the hat twice on his thigh and clapped it on his head like a helmet. He wasn't presentable, he knew that. He looked like a bum—for all intents and purposes he *was* a bum, or at least making a pretty fair run at becoming one—and it just didn't pay to make eye contact. Raymond rose slowly to his feet.

A man was standing there in the alley amidst the debris of torn-up boxes and discarded oil cans, the sun cutting into his eyes. Five minutes from picking himself up off the burning sidewalk, Raymond was in no condition to make fine distinctions, but he could see that whatever he was the man was no outraged service station attendant or hostile mechanic, no cop or security guard. He had a dog with him, for one thing, a little buff and yellow mutt that seemed to be composed entirely of hacked-off whiskers, and for another, he was dressed all in blue jeans, including two blue-jean jackets but no shirt, and none of the ensemble looked as if it had been washed and tumble-dried in recent memory. Raymond relaxed. He was in the presence of a fellow loser.

"Nice hat," the man said. He looked to be in his thirties, long hair slicked back close to his scalp and tucked behind his ears, the beard neatly clipped, big hands dangling from his doubled-up sleeves. He was grinning. At least there was that.

"Oh, this?" Raymond's hand went reflexively to his head. "It's just . . . it's nothing. It used to belong to my girlfriend."

"Yeah, I guess so, because why would a guy wear a hat like that, right?"

The hat—it was a cheap baseball cap made of plastic mesh—

featured a black badge on the crown, and a legend, in a tiny, loop-
ing, gold script, that read: *You Can Pet My Cat, But Don't Touch
My Pussy.* To Dana's mind, this was the height of subversive humor
and she insisted on wearing the thing whenever they went out bar-
hopping, which was every night except when they gave up all pretense and got a bottle at Von's and drank at home in front of the TV.
He'd snatched it off her head the night she shoved him out the door
with nothing but the clothes on his back, and it served her right, because she had his boombox and his other pair of shoes and his books
and bedroll and shaving kit, and by the next afternoon the locks had
been changed and every time he went over to demand his things back
she just sat there in the window with her knifeblade of a face and
waited for one of the neighbors to call the cops.

Raymond was new to all this. He was shy, lonely, angry. It had
been something like five or six days now, and during that time he'd
kept away from the street people, bedding down wherever he could
(but not on the sidewalk, that was crazy, and he still didn't know
how that happened), eating when he felt like it and steadily drinking
up what was left of his last and final paycheck. He ducked his head.
"Right," he murmured.

The man introduced himself through his shining wet-toothed
grin, because he was just there to get a little drink of fresh H_2O
himself, and then he was thinking about maybe going into the convenience store on the corner and picking up a nice twelve-pack of
Keystone and maybe sitting down by the beach and watching the
A-types jog by with their dogs and their two-hundred-dollar running shoes. His name was Schuyler, Rudolph Schuyler, though everybody called him Sky for short, and his dog was Pal.

The light was like a scimitar, cutting the alley in two. Raymond
didn't think he'd ever seen a line so sharp, a shadow so deep, and that
was a kind of revelation, a paean to what man had built—a rectilin-
ear gas station and a neatly proportionate fence topped with a spray
of pink-tinged trumpet flowers—and how God had come to light it
like a photographer setting up the trickiest shot of his life. And there
was a shot just as tricky played out over and over throughout the city,
the country, the world even. He patted down his pockets, felt some-

thing there still, a few bucks, anyway. When he looked up at Sky, when he finally looked him in the eye, he heard his own voice crawling out of his throat as if there were somebody else in there speaking for him. "Am I hearing you right, or is that an invitation?"

AFTER THE FIRST twelve-pack, there was another—Raymond's treat—because the great and wise and all-knowing people who brewed the beer in their big vats and sealed it in the shining aluminum cans that were like little pills, little individual doses delivered up in the convenient twelve-ounce format, had foreseen the need and stocked the shelves to overflowing. "You know," Raymond said, easing back the flip-top on a fresh can, "I read in the paper a couple years ago about that time the mudslides put Big Sur out of business, I mean going both ways on Highway 1—did you hear about that? They had no beer, I mean—they ran out. You remember that?"

Sky was leaning back against one of the polished boulders the city had dumped along the beach as a seawall, both jackets spread out beneath him, his bare chest and arms exposed to the sun. He was tanned right down to the roots of his hair, tanned like a tennis pro or maybe a diving instructor, somebody vigorous and clean making a clean living under the sun. Out here, on the beach, he didn't look like a bum—or at least not one of the mental cases you saw on the streets, immured in the walking dungeon of their own stink. "Yeah," he said. "Maybe. I mean, I don't know—no beer?" He laughed. "How'd they survive?"

Raymond shrugged. He was looking out to sea, out to where the shimmer of the waves met the horizon in an explosion of light as if diamonds were being ground up in a thin band that stretched laterally as far as you could see. "They're all rich people up there. I guess they just dug the single-malt scotch and green Chartreuse out of their liquor cabinets and forgot about it. Or their wine cellars, or whatever. But the trucks couldn't get through, so there was no beer, no potato chips, no Slim Jims."

"What, no Pampers and underarm deodorant? What's a young mother to do?"

"No Kotex," Raymond said, tipping back his beer and reaching for another one. The cans were getting warm, though he'd stowed them in the shade, in a crevice between two boulders the size of Volkswagens, but he didn't mind: warm was better than nothing. He was enjoying himself. "No condoms. No Preparation-H."

"Yeah," Sky said, "but let me tell you, those people suck up there. Big-time. And I know from experience, because if you haven't got a motel key on you to show the cops—right there, show me a motel key, motherfucker—they put you in the car and drive you out to the city limits, period, no arguments. As if this wasn't America or something."

Raymond had nothing to say to that. He understood where the city fathers were coming from: who wanted an army of bums camped out on the streets? It turned off the tourists, and the tourists were what made a place like Big Sur click in the first place. Or this town. This town right here.

"So how long?" Sky asked, turning to him with eyes drawn down to slits against the sun.

Raymond took a pull at the fresh beer in his hands and felt warm all over, felt good, felt superior. "I don't know, a couple days. A week maybe. I had a place but my girlfriend—she's a bitch, a real queen bitch—kicked me out."

A rope of muscle flashed across Sky's shoulders as he reached for another beer and felt for the pop-top. "No," he said, "I mean how long were the roads closed down, like a week, two weeks, what?"

"Months. Months at least."

"Wow. Picture that. But if you had beer and jug wine—and maybe a little stash of canned food, Dinty Moore and the like, it must have been like paradise, if not for the cops, I mean. But even the cops. What are they going to do, kick you out of a place that's already closed off? Kick you out of nowhere? Like, I'm sorry, officer, I'd really like to accommodate you here, but where the fuck you expect me to go, huh, motherfucker? Like, suck on this."

Raymond took a moment to think about that, about the kind of paradise that must have been, or might have been—or could have been under the right conditions—and then, unaccountably, he found himself staring into the glazed brown eyes of a German shepherd with a foam-flecked muzzle and a red bandanna looped round its neck. One minute there'd been nothing there but the open vista of the sea, and now here was this big panting animal crowding his frame of reference and looking at him as if it expected him to get down on all fours and chase it round the beach. "Nice dog," Raymond said, giving the broad triangular head a pat. The dog panted, stray grains of sand glistening along the black seam of its lips. Pal, curled up at Sky's feet, never even so much as twitched a muscle. In the next moment two girls in tube tops and shorts jogged by on the compacted sand at the foot of the waves, beautiful girls with their hair and everything else bouncing in the shattered light, and they shouted for the dog and Raymond eased back and popped another beer, wondering why anybody would want to go to work nine-to-five and live in an apartment you had to kill yourself just to make the rent on when you could just kick back, like this, and let the dogs and the women present themselves to you as if you were a potentate on his throne.

THE NEXT THING HE KNEW, the sun was going down. It balanced there on the flat cobalt palm of the ocean, trembling like the flame of a gas stove, till the water took hold of it and spread it across the surface in even, rippling strokes. The palms turned pink overhead. Birds—or were they bats?—hurled themselves from one shadow to another. Raymond was drunk, deeply, blissfully drunk, the original pair of twelve-packs transubstantiated into short-necked pints of wine, then into liters of Black Cat and finally wine again, out of the gallon jug. Somewhere along the line there had been food—Stagg chili, cold, straight from the can—and there was an interlude during which he sat by the fountain at the foot of the pier while Pal, tricked out in a little blue crepe doll's dress Sky had dug out of the bottom of a Dumpster, danced and did backflips for the tourists. Now there was the beach, the deep-anchored palm against which he was resting his complicit spine, and the sun drowning itself in color.

The jug came to him, fat and heavy as a bowling ball, and he lifted it to his lips and drank, then passed it on to Sky, who lingered over it before passing it to a tall, mad-haired, slit-eyed guy named

Dougie—or was it Droogie? Droogie, yeah. That was it. Like in that old movie, the Kubrick one, and why couldn't he remember the name of it? Not that it mattered. Not really. Not anymore. All that—movies, books, the knowledge you could wield like a hammer—belonged to another world. Things were more immediate here, more elemental, like where you were going to relieve yourself without getting busted and where the next bottle was coming from.

During the afternoon, he'd spent a fruitful hour removing the left sleeve of his jacket, to give the thing proportion—to make it look as if it were a fashion statement instead of a disaster—but now, as the sun faded, he began to feel a chill at his back and wished he'd left it alone. There was still the problem of where he was going to sleep. It was one thing to sit around and pass a bottle in a circle of like-minded souls, the sun on your face and the sea breeze ruffling the hair at the back of your neck, and another thing altogether to wake up on the sidewalk like some terminal-stage loser with Swiss cheese for a brain.

Droogie—or maybe it *was* Dougie after all—was going on about the Chumash Casino, how he'd hit a thousand-dollar payoff on a slot machine there one night and booked himself into the bridal suite with a lady and a case of champagne and couldn't find so much as a nickel in his pocket come morning. Another guy—beard, tattoos, one lens gone from his glasses so it looked as if his eye had been staved in—said that was nothing, he'd scored five g's at Vegas one time, and then Sky cut in with a question for the group, which had grown to six now, including a woman about thirty who kept picking at the dirty yellow dress she wore over her jeans as if she were trying to break it down into its constituent fibers. Sky wanted to know if anybody felt like a nice pepperoni pizza—or maybe one of those thick-crust Hawaiian jobs, with the pineapple and ham?

Nobody said anything. The jug went round. Finally, from the echoing depths of his inner self, Raymond heard a voice saying, "Yeah, sure. I could go for it."

"All right, my man," Sky said, rising up from the cradle of his tree, "you are elected."

It was all coming from very far off. Raymond didn't know what was required, didn't have a clue.

"Come on, man, let's hump it. I said pizza. Didn't you hear me? Pizza!"

Then they were making their way through the deep sand above tide line and into the parking lot with its shrouded cars and drifting trash, Pal clicking along behind them. The last pay phone in the world stood at the far end of the lot. Sky dropped two coins into it and gave him his instructions: "Be forceful, be a man who knows what he wants, with his feet up on the padded stool in his condo—and don't slur. They'll want a call-back number, but they never call back. Make one up. Or your girlfriend. Use your girlfriend's number."

Later, much later, when the fog had settled in like an amphibious skin stretched over everything and the driftwood fire had burned down to coals, Sky pushed himself up from the sand and stretched his arms out in front of him. "Well," he said, "how about that pizza?" Raymond blinked up at him. The others had wandered off separately, ghosts dissolving in the mist, all except for the woman. At one point, Dougie had bent over her and tugged at her arm as if he were trying to tear a fistful of weeds up out of the ground, but she wasn't giving an inch and they'd hissed at each other for what seemed like a week before Sky said, "Why don't you just give it up already," and Dougie stalked off into the mist. She was sitting beside Raymond now, her lips wet on the neck of the bottle, nothing but dregs and saliva left at this point. "I don't know if I could eat," she said.

"Everybody's got to eat, right, Ray? Am I right?"

Raymond didn't have an opinion. He wanted to go get another bottle before the stores closed, but his money was gone.

"I don't know," the woman said doubtfully.

But Sky roused them, and a moment later they were all three stumbling through the sand to the sidewalk and along the sidewalk to the boulevard, Pal leading the way with his tail thrust up like a banner. It was unnaturally quiet, everything held fast in the grip of the fog. Cars drifted silently by as if towed on a wire, one pulled along after the other, their headlights barely visible. There was a faint music playing somewhere, saxophone and drums, and it came to them in snatches as they walked in the deep shadow of a bank of condos thrown up for the convenience of the tourists. Raymond didn't know what he was doing or where he was going, and he didn't care, because Sky was there and Sky was in command. His feet hit the pavement and he tried to keep from lurching into the shrubs that bristled along the high stucco walls of the condos. At one point the woman bumped up against him and he put his arm out to steady her, and in that moment of casual intimacy, he mumbled something along the lines of, "You know, I don't even know what to call you."

"Her name's Knitsy," Sky said over his shoulder. "Because her fingers are always knitting in the air—isn't that right, Knitsy? I mean, knitting nothing, right?"

Her voice was breathy and shallow, with a sharp rural twang to it. "Sure," she said, "that's right."

"And what's that rhyme with—ditzy, right?"

"Sure, whatever."

Raymond wanted to ask her about that, make a joke, but it would have been a cruel joke, and so he kept it to himself. *Knitsy.* Let her knit, and let the guy with the broken glasses stare out at the world like an ambassador with a pince-nez and let Sky lord it over everybody. What difference did it make? The world was nothing but cruelty and stupidity anyway. And he himself? He was drunk, very drunk. Too drunk to keep walking and too drunk to lie down.

They were away from the beach now, trailing down the alley behind Giulio's Pizza Kitchen and the One-Stop Travel Shop. Sky motioned for silence, and they hung back in the shadows, whispering—hide-and-seek, that's what it was, hide-and-seek—while Pal trotted across the pavement to reconnoiter the Dumpster. Reeling, watching the spots swell and explode before his eyes, Raymond felt Knitsy's cold rough hand snake out and take hold of his own. His heart was thrumming. The fog sifted through the alley, etherized and unreal. Lit by the dull yellow glow of the streetlight on the corner, the dog might have been onstage somewhere, on TV, in a video, going through the repertoire of his tricks, and they watched as he sniffed and squirmed, prancing back and forth, till he finally went up on his hind legs and began to paw at the belly of the Dumpster. And then Sky was there, lifting the metal lid and retrieving the two large pies, still snug in their boxes, one decorated with pepperoni, the other with pineapple and ham.

IN THE MORNING—the morning, that was the hurtful time—Raymond woke to a shifting light, the peeling tan upthrust trunks of a grove of eucalyptus, and the sky revealed in a frame of leaves. He was on his back, something underneath him—a plastic tarp—and a blanket, heavy with dew, thrown over the cage of his chest. Beside him, snoring lightly and twitching in her sleep, was a woman with dirty fanned-out blondish hair and the deep indigo tattoo of a scorpion crawling up her neck. But that was no surprise—nothing was a surprise, unless it was the sidewalk, and this wasn't the sidewalk. This was—he lifted his head to take in the half-collapsed teepee fashioned of blue tarps backed up against a chain-link fence, the scrub at his feet, the trash scattered over the leaf litter and the pregnant rise of the mound giving onto the railroad tracks—this was the woods. He saw Pal then, Pal poking his whiskered head out of the teepee to give him an unfathomable look, and beyond Pal, Sky's red Mongoose mountain bike, for which—and it was all coming back to him now—Sky had paid nearly a third of his monthly SSI disability check. So this was Knitsy, then, and that was Sky inside the collapsing teepee. Or wigwam. Call it a wigwam. Better sound to it.

His head slipped back to the tarp. He tried to close his eyes, to fight down the stirring in his lower abdomen that was like the first stab of stomach distress—what his mother used to call the runs—but the thirst wouldn't let him. It was there again, powerful, imperious, parching him all the way from his throat up into the recesses of his skull. *I've got to get out of here,* he was thinking, *got to get up and out of here, find money, find work, a toilet, a tap, four walls to hide myself in.* But he couldn't move. Not yet.

That first night, the night she locked the door on him, they'd been drinking bourbon with beer chasers, and all his muscles were sapped—or his bones, his bones seemed to have melted away so that all he wanted to do was seek the lowest point, like water—and the best he could do was hammer on the door and shout the sort of incoherent things you shout at times like that until the police came and she told them she paid the rent around here and she didn't know him anymore and didn't want to. He wound up sleeping in the back of the building, under the oleanders against the fence, which made his face and hands break out in shining welts that were like fresh burns. He was planning on using his key after she left for work, but she didn't leave for work, just sat there in the window drinking bourbon and waiting for the locksmith. That night he pounded on the door again, but he melted away when he saw the police cruiser coming up the street, and after that, he gave it up. First month, last month, security: where was he going to get that? He tried calling his brother collect in Tampa but his brother wouldn't take the call. The bars were open though, and the corner stores with the Coors signs flashing in the windows. He got loaded, got hammered, wound up on the sidewalk. Now he was here.

He dozed. Came to. Dozed. And then, out of some beaten fog of a dream, he heard footsteps crunching gravel, a yip from Pal, and a voice—Sky's voice—raised in song: "Here comes Santa Claus, here comes Santa Claus, right down Santa Claus Lane."

Knitsy stirred, and they both came up simultaneously into the bewilderment of the day. Her hair was bunched on one side, her dress torn at the collar to reveal a stained thermal T-shirt beneath it. A warm, brewing odor rose from her. She looked at Raymond and her eyes retreated into her head.

Sky was standing over them now, a silver twelve-pack of beer in each hand. "Hey, you two lovebirds, Christmas came early this year," he said, handing a can first to Raymond, then Knitsy. The can was cold; the top peeled back with a hiss. Raymond didn't want a beer— he wanted to clean up his act, go back to Dana and beg her to let him in, if only for a shower and a shave and a change of clothes so he could go back to his boss—his ex-boss, the smug, fat, self-satisfied son of a bitch who'd canned him because he had a couple of drinks and came back late from lunch once or twice—and grovel at his feet, at anybody's feet, because he was out of money and out of luck and this was no way to live. But he took that beer and he thanked Sky for it, and for the next one after that, and before long the sun got caught in the trees and every single thing, every little detail, seemed just as fine as fine could be.

When the beer was gone and he could taste nothing in his throat but the rinsed-out metallic sourness of it, he pushed himself up and stood unsteadily in the high weeds. Judging from the sun, it must have been past noon, not that it mattered, because Dana didn't get home from work till five and if he went over there and tried the door or the windows or even sat out back in the lawnchair, the old lady next door would have the cops on him in a heartbeat. She was his enemy, in collusion with Dana, and the two of them were out to destroy him, he saw that much now. And what had he done to deserve it? He'd got drunk a couple times, that was all, and when Dana came needling at him, he'd defended himself—with his hands, not his fists, his hands—and she'd gone running next door to Mrs. Ruiz and Mrs. Ruiz had called the cops for her. So he couldn't go there, not till Dana came home, and even then it was a stretch to think she'd open the door to him, but what choice did he have?

There was a smell of menthol on the air, and he couldn't place it at first, until he looked down and saw the litter of eucalyptus buds scattered underfoot, every one a perfectly formed little nugget awaiting a layer of dirt and a little rain. They were beautiful in their way, all these silver nuggets spread out before him like spare change, and he fumbled open his fly and gave them a little dose of salts and urea to help them along, a real altruist, a nature boy all the way. Was he laughing? Yes, sure he was, and why not? Nature boy. "There was a boy, a very strange and *something* boy," he sang, and then he was singing "Here Comes Santa Claus," because Sky had put it in his head and he couldn't get it out.

Beyond the railroad tracks was the freeway, and he could hear the continuous rush of tires like white noise in the background of the film that was his life, a confused film begun somewhere in the middle with a close-up of his dangling empty hands and pulling back for a shot of Knitsy passed out on the tarp, her head thrown back and her mouth hanging open so you could see that at least at some point in her life she'd been to the dentist. Pal wasn't in the frame. Or Sky either. Half an hour ago he'd slipped a couple of beers in his pockets, whistled for the dog, and headed up the tracks in the direction of the pier. Raymond looked off down the tracks a long moment, looked to Knitsy, sprawled there in the weeds as if she'd been flung off the back of the train as it roared by—*Lovebirds? What in Christ's name had Sky meant by that?*—then started up the slope to where the rails burned in the light.

He wasn't a bum and he wasn't a drunk, not the way these others were, and he kept telling himself that as he made his way along the tracks, lit up on Sky's beer under the noonday sun that was peeling the skin off the tip of his nose. He'd always had a place to stay, always fended for himself, and that was the way it was going to be this time too. All it was was a binge, and the binge was over—it was over now—even if he didn't want it to be. He was out of money, and that was that. He was going to walk into town, find the unemployment office, and put in an application, and then he was going to see if he could patch things up with Dana, at least until he could collect his first check and find himself a room someplace—and no sense kidding himself, Dana was nothing but a pain in the ass, dragging him down with her bourbon, bourbon, bourbon, and he was through with her. Finally and absolutely. He didn't even like bourbon. Please. Give him vodka any day.

The tracks swept around a bend ahead and followed a trestle over the boulevard that ran along the beach, and he was thinking he didn't want to risk the trestle—you were always reading about somebody getting hit by a train out here, the last time a deaf-mute who couldn't hear the whistle, and that was pathetic—when he saw a figure approaching him in the distance. It was Dougie—or Droogie—and he had something in his hand, a pole or a stick, that caught the sun in a metallic shimmer. When he got closer, Raymond saw that it was a length of pipe ripped out of one of the public restrooms in the park or lifted from a construction site, and Dougie kept swinging it out away from his body and clapping it back in again as if he were trying to tenderize the flesh of his leg. He stopped ten feet from Raymond, and Raymond stopped too. "You seen Knitsy? Because I'm going to kill the bitch."

Raymond didn't answer. The beer had made him slow.

"What are you, deaf, motherfucker? I said, you seen Knitsy?"

It took him a minute, staring into the slits of the man's eyes as if he could find the answer there. He was conflicted. He was. But the pipe focused his attention. "I don't know, I think she's"—he gestured with a jerk of his head—"back there, you know, in the trees back there."

The man took a step closer and swiped at the near rail with the pipe till it clanged and clanged again. "Son of a bitch. It's Sky, then, right? She's with Sky? Because I'm going to kill his ass too."

Raymond didn't have anything to say to this. He just shrugged and moved on, even as Dougie cursed at his back. "I won't forget you either, you sorry son of a bitch. Payback time, I'm telling you, *payback*," but Raymond just kept going, all the way down the tracks and across the trestle and into town. It was nothing to him. He was out of this. He was gone. Let them work it out among themselves, that's what he figured.

He waited till six, when he was sure she'd be there, and walked up the familiar street with its kids and dogs and beat-up cars and the men home from work and sitting out on the porch with a beer to take in the lingering sun, another day down, a job well done and a beer well deserved. Nobody waved to him, nobody said a word or even looked at him twice, and you would have thought he'd never lived here, never paid rent or electric bills or brought back a distillery's worth of bourbon in the plastic two-liter jug, night after night for a year and more. All right. Well, fuck them. He didn't need them or anybody else, except maybe Dana and a little sympathy. A shower, a shave, a couple of bucks to get him back on his feet again, that was all, because he'd had enough of sleeping in the bushes like some vagrant.

The only problem was, Dana wasn't home. He didn't hear the buzz of the TV she switched on the minute she came in the door and kept going till she passed out in front of it at midnight, or the canned diarrhea of the easy-listening crap she played on the radio in the kitchen all the time. He knocked. Rang the buzzer. Leaned out away from the porch to cup his hands over the shifting mirror of the front window and peer inside. But by this time Mrs. Ruiz was out on her own porch, twenty feet away, giving him an uncompromising look out of her flat black old-lady's eyes.

He thought of the Wildcat then—that's where she'd be, sitting at the bar with one of her hopeless, titanic, frizzy-haired friends from work with their dried-blood fingernails and greasy lipstick, knocking back bourbon and water as if they were afraid Prohibition was going to start up again at the stroke of the hour. It would be a walk—two miles, at least, but he was used to walking since his last DUI, and he had nothing better to do. The afternoon had been an exercise in futility, because by the time he got to the head of the line at the unemployment office he realized he was wearing the pussy hat (no choice, what with the state of his hair) and that they'd probably laugh him out of the place, so he just turned around and walked out the door. He was hungry—he hadn't put anything on his stomach since the pizza the night before—but he wouldn't go to the soup kitchen or the mission or whatever it was. That was were the bums went, and he was no bum, not yet anyway. Once the effects of the beer wore off, he wanted a drink, but without money or an ATM card or a bank account to go with it, he just couldn't see how he was going to get one. For a while there he'd lingered in the back of the liquor department at the grocery store, thinking to liberate something from the cooler, but they had television monitors mounted on the walls and a vigilant little smooth-skinned guy with a mustache and a tie who kept asking if he could help him find anything, and that was probably the low point of his day. Till now. Because now he just backed down off the porch, shot Mrs. Ruiz a look of burning hate, and started walking.

There was some coming and going at the Wildcat, people milling around the door in schools like fish, like barracuda—or no, like guppies, bloated and shining with all their trumped-up colors—but he peered in the window and didn't see Dana there at the bar. In the off chance she was in the ladies' or in the back room, he went in to have a look for himself. She wasn't there. It was crowded, though, the speakers were putting out music and there was a pervasive rising odor of rum and sour mix that brought him back to happier times, like the week before last. He took the opportunity to duck into the men's and wash some of the grit off his face and hands and smooth back the gray-flecked scrub of a beard that made him look about sixty years old, though he was only thirty-two—or no, thirty-three. Thirty-three, last birthday. He thought to reverse the hat, too, just for the sake of respectability, and then he stood at the bar awhile, hoping somebody would turn up and stand him a couple of drinks. Nobody did. Steve, the bartender, asked him if he wanted anything, and he asked Steve if he'd seen Dana. Yeah, she'd been in earlier. Did he want anything?

"Double vodka on the rocks."

"You going to pay for it this time?"

"When did I never pay?"

There was a song on he hated. Somebody jostled him, gave him a look. Steve didn't answer.

"Can I put it on Dana's tab?"

"Dana doesn't have a tab. It's cash only, my friend."

He got loud then, because he wanted that drink, and they knew him, didn't they? What did they think he was, some kind of deadbeat or something? But when Steve came out from behind the bar he felt it all go out of him in a long hissing rush of air. "All right," he said. "Okay, I hear you," and then he was back out on the street.

His feet hurt. He was at the tail end of a week-long drunk and he felt sick and debilitated, his stomach clenched around a hard little ball of nothing, his head full of beating wings, the rasp of feathers, a hiss that was no sound at all. Dana was out there somewhere—it wasn't that big a town, a grid of palmy streets configured around the tourist haven of the main drag, and a bar and T-shirt shop on every corner—and if he could only find her, go down on his knees to her, abase himself, beg and whine and lie and wheedle, she would relent, he knew she would. He was heading back up the street with the appealing idea of forcing a back window at the house, climbing in, making a sandwich and washing it down with bourbon and just crawling into bed and let come what will, when he spotted Dana's car in the lot behind the movie theater.

That was her car, no doubt about it, a ravaged brown Corolla with a rearranged front bumper and the dark slit at the top of the passenger's side window where it wouldn't roll up all the way. He

crossed the street, sidled through the lot like any other carefree movie-
goer and casually worked his arm through the crack of the window till
he caught the handle and popped open the door. There was change
in the glove compartment, maybe twelve or thirteen dollars' worth
of quarters, dimes and nickels—and one Sacajawea dollar—she kept
there against emergencies, and it took him no more than thirty seconds to scoop it up and weigh down his pockets. Then he relocked the
door, eased it shut and headed back down the block, looking for the
nearest liquor store.

IT WAS GETTING DARK when he made his way down to the beach,
hoping to find Sky there, singing one of his Christmas songs, singing
"Rudolph the Red-Nosed Reindeer" or "I Saw Mommy Kissing Santa
Claus," singing just for the sheer joy of it, because every day was
Christmas when you had your SSI check in your pocket and an ever-
changing cast of lubricated tourists to provide you with doggie bags of
veal piccata and a fistful of change. He had a pint of Popov in one
hand and a Big Mac in the other, and he was alternately taking a swig
from the bottle and a bite of the sandwich, feeling good all over again.
A police cruiser came down the street as he was crossing at the light,
but the bottle was clothed in its brown paper bag and the eyes of the
men behind the windshield passed over him as if he didn't exist.

The cool breath of a breeze rode up off the water. He could hear
the waves lifting and falling against the plane of the beach with a low
reverberant boom, could feel the concussion radiating through the
worn-out soles of his sneakers and up into his feet and ankles like a
new kind of friction. The parking lot was deserted, five cars exactly,
and the gulls had taken over as if he'd walked into that other movie,
the Hitchcock one, what was it called? With Tippi Hedren? They
were grouped at the edge of the pavement, a hundred of them or
more, pale and motionless as statues. "Tippi, Tippi, Tippi," he said
aloud. "The Tipster." There was a smell of iodine and whatever the
tide had brought in.

He went from fire to fire on the beach, shared a swig of vodka in
exchange for whatever the huddled groups were drinking, saw the
guy with the broken glasses—Herbert, his name was Herbert—and

a few other faces he vaguely recognized, but no Sky and no Pal. The night was clear, the stars alive and spread over the deepening sky all the way out to the Channel Islands and down as far as Rincón to the east. He shuffled through the still-warm sand in a kind of bliss, the second pint of vodka pressed to his lips, all the rough edges of things worn smooth, all his problems reduced to zero. He was going to find Sky, Sky his benefactor, the songbird, and see if he wanted a hit or two of vodka, and maybe they could sit around the fire and sing, order up another pizza, lie there and stare up at the stars as if they owned them all. It was early yet. The night was young.

The train gave him his first scare. He'd just come across the trestle and stepped to one side, careful of his footing in the loose stone, when the whistle sounded behind him. He was drunk and slow to react, sure, but it just about scared him out of his skin nonetheless. There was a rush of air and then the train—it was a freight, a thousand dark, clanking cars—went by like thunder, like war. He twisted his right ankle trying to lurch out of the way and went down hard in the bushes, but he held on to the bottle, that was the important thing, because the bottle—and most of it was left—was an offering for Sky, and maybe Knitsy too, if she was there. For a long while, as the sound of the train faded in the distance, he sat there in the dark, rubbing his ankle and laughing softly to himself—he could have been like the deaf-mute, somebody Dana would read about in the morning paper. *Raymond Leitner, cut down by the southbound. After a week-long illness. Currently—make that permanently—unemployed. Survived by his loving mother. Wherever she might be.*

When he got close enough to the camp to see the glow of candlelight suffusing the walls of the wigwam, he was startled by a sudden harsh shout and then Pal started barking, and there was movement there, framed against the drizzle of the light. "I said you ever touch her I'm going to kill your ass, because she's my soulmate, you motherfucker, my *soulmate,* and you know it!"

Sky's voice sang out, harsh and ragged, "Get off of me, get out of here, go on, get out!" And the barking. The barking rose to a frenzy, high-pitched, breathless, and then suddenly there was the dull wet thump of a blow, and the barking ceased, even as the movement shook the floating walls and the light snuffed out. "Here comes, you son of a bitch," Dougie's voice shouted out, "I'll give you here comes," and there was that wet sound again, the percussion of unyielding metal and yielding flesh, and again, and again.

Raymond froze. He took a step back in the dark, collided with something that shouldn't have been there, a solid immovable shape stretched out across the flat of the ground—and the tarp, the tarp he'd slept on—and the ankle gave way. He went down again, and the bottle with him, the sudden explosion of its shattering like gunfire in the night. His blood raced. He felt around him for a branch, a rock, anything, and that was when his hands told him what it was he'd tripped over. Her hair was the first thing, then the slick cotton of the dress, and everything wet and cold.

The night went silent. He couldn't see, all the shadings of uncommitted dark swelling and shrinking around him. A shadow rose up then out of the black pool of the ground no more than twenty feet away, rose to full height, and began to slash at the darkness where the wigwam would have been, and Dougie was cursing, raging, beating at everything in the night till the galvanized post rang out against the stones. Raymond was no longer drunk. He didn't move, didn't breathe. The post rose and fell till the shadows changed shape and the curses subsided into sobs and choked, half-formed phrases, to barks and whispers, and then there was another sound, the clangor of the post flung away against the stones of the railway bed and a new metallic sound, the whirring of gears, and suddenly the shadow was moving off down the deserted tracks on the dark skeleton of a mountain bike.

It took him nearly an hour, hobbled by the ankle that felt as if it had been snapped off the bone, sharpened to a point and jammed back in again, an hour treading along the railway ties, through the sand, up the sidewalks still full of safe, oblivious people passing from one appointment to another. He just kept walking, rotating up off the bad ankle, and they saw his face and stood aside for him. Dogs barked. Cars shot past. There were shouts and voices in the night. He had never been down there by the railroad tracks, never been to

any bum's encampment, never passed a bottle with a bunch of dere-
licts, and there'd never been any question in his mind about going to
Sky's aid or calling the police or anything else. He was just walking,
that was all, walking home. And when he got there, when he saw
Dana just getting out of her car, her face softened with drink and her
hair newly cut, cut short as an acolyte's, he got down on his knees
and crawled to her.

All the Wrecks I've Crawled Out Of

ALL I WANTED, really, was to attain mythic status. Along the lines, say, of James Dean, Brom Bones, Paul Bunyan, my father. My father was a giant among men, with good-sized trees for arms and fists like buckets of nails, and I was not a giant among men. I wasn't even a man, though I began to look like one as I grew into my shoulders and eventually found something to shave off my cheeks after a close and patient scrutiny, and I manfully flunked out of three colleges and worked at digging graves at the Beth-El cemetery and shoveling chicken shit at the Shepherd Hill Egg Farm till I got smart and started bartending. That was a kind of wreckage, I suppose—flunking out—but there was much more to come, wrecks both literal and figurative, replete with flames, blood, crushed metal and broken hearts, a whole swath of destruction and self-immolation, my own personal skid marks etched into the road of my life and maybe yours too.

So. Where to start? With Helen, I suppose, Helen Kreisler. She was a cocktail waitress at the restaurant where I was mixing drinks six and a half days a week, four years older than I when I met her— that is, twenty-seven—and with a face that wasn't exactly pretty in any conventional sense, but more a field for the play of psychodrama, martyrdom and high-level neurosis. It was an old face, much older than her cheerleader's body and her still relatively tender years, a face full of worry, with lines scored around her eyes and dug deep into the corners of her mouth. She wore her hair long and parted in the middle, after the fashion of the day, and her eyes—the exact color of aluminum foil—jumped out of her tanned face from a hundred feet away. They were alien eyes, that's what I called them. And her too. *Alien,* that was my pet name for her, and I used it to urge her on when she was on top of me and my hands were on her breasts and her mouth had gone slack with the feeling of what I was doing to her.

It was about a month after I started working at Brennan's Steakhouse that we decided to move in together. We found a two-bedroom house dropped down in a blizzard of trees by the side of a frozen lake. This was in suburban New York, by the way, in the farthest, darkest reaches of northern Westchester, where the nights were black-dark and close. The house was cheap, so far as rent was concerned, because it was a summer house, minimally insulated, but as we were soon to discover, two hundred dollars a month would go up the chimney or stovepipe or whatever it was that was connected to the fuel-evaporating furnace in the basement. Helen was charmed despite the water-stained exterior walls and the stink of frozen mouseshit and ancient congealed grease that hit you in the face like a two-by-four the minute you stepped in the door, and we lied to the landlady (a mustachioed widow with breasts the size of New Jersey and Connecticut respectively) about our marital status, got out our wallets and put down our first and last months' rent. It was a move up for me at any rate, because to this point I'd been living in a basement apartment at my parents' house, sleeping late as bartenders will do, and listening to the heavy stolid tread of my father's footsteps above me as he maneuvered around his coffee cup in the morning before leaving for work.

Helen fixed the place up with some cheap rugs and prints and a truckload of bric-a-brac from the local head shop—candles, incense burners, ceramic bongs, that sort of thing. We never cooked. We were very drunk and very stoned. Meals, in which we weren't especially interested, came to us out of a saucepan at the restaurant—except for breakfast, a fuzzy, woozy meal heavy on the sugars and starches and consumed languidly at the diner. Our sex was youthful, fueled by hormonal rushes, pot and amyl nitrate, and I was feeling pretty good about things—about myself, I mean—for the first time in my life.

But before I get into all that, I ought to tell you about the first of the wrecks, the one from which all the others seemed to spool out like fishing line that's been on the shelf too long. It was my first night at work, at Brennan's, that is. I'd done a little bartending weekends in college, but it was strictly beer, 7&7, rum and Coke, that sort of thing, and I was a little tentative about Brennan's, a big softly lit place that managed to be intimate and frenziedly public at the same time, and Ski Silinski, the other bartender, gave me two shots of 151 and a Tuinol to calm me before the crush started. Well, the crush started, and I was still about as hyper as you can get without strictly requiring a straitjacket, but way up on the high end of that barely controlled hysteria there was a calm plateau of rum, Tuinol and the beer I sipped steadily all night long—and this was a place I aspired to reach eventually, once the restaurant closed down and I could haul myself up there and fade into a warm, post-conscious glow. We did something like a hundred and ten dinners that night, I met and flirted with Helen and three other cocktail waitresses and half a dozen partially lit female customers, and, all things considered, acquitted myself well. Ski and I had the door locked, the glasses washed and to-morrow's fruit cut and stowed when Jimmy Brennan walked in.

Helen and one of the other waitresses—Adele-something—were sitting at the bar, the stereo was cranked and we were having a cele-bratory nightcap at the time. It didn't faze Jimmy. He was the owner, only thirty-two years old, and he'd really stepped in it with this place, the first West Coast-style steak-and-salad-bar restaurant in the area. He drove a new Triumph, British racing green, and he drank martinis, straight up with a twist. "How'd it go tonight, Lester?" he asked, settling his lean frame on a barstool even as Ski set a martini, new-born and gleaming with condensation, before him.

I gave the waitresses a look. They were in their skimpy waitress outfits, long bare perfect legs crossed at the knee, cigarettes propped between the elegantly bunched knuckles that in turn propped up their weary silken heads. I was a man among men—and women—and I feared no evil and felt no pain. "Fine," I said, but I was already amending what seemed a much-too-modest assessment. "No, better than fine: great. Stupendous. Magnificent."

Jimmy Brennan wore glasses, the thin silver-framed discs made popular two years earlier by John Lennon. His eyes were bright behind them and I attributed that brightness to the keenness of mind and Darwinian fortitude that had made him rich at thirty-two, but I was wrong. That gleam was the gleam of alcohol, nothing more. Jimmy Brennan was, as I would discover, an alcoholic, though at the time that seemed just fine to me—anything that altered your consciousness and heightened your perceptions was cool in the extreme, as far as I was concerned.

Jimmy Brennan bought us a round, and then another. Helen gave me a look out of her silver-foil eyes—a look of lust, complicity, warning?—picked up her bag and left with Adele. It was three-thirty in the morning. Ski, who at twenty-seven was married and a father, pleaded his wife. The door closed behind him and I remember vividly the sound of the latch clicking into place as he turned his key from the outside. "Well," Jimmy said, slapping my back, "I guess it's just us, huh?"

I don't remember much of the rest of it, except this: I was in my car when I woke up, there was a weak pale sun draped over everything like a crust of vomit, and it was very, very hot. And more: there was a stranger in a yellow slicker beating out the glass of the driver's side window and I was trying to fight him off till the flames licking away at my calves began to make their point more emphatically than he could ever have. As I later reconstructed it, or as it was reconstructed for me, I'd apparently left the bar in the cold glow of dawn, fired up the engine of my car and then passed out with my foot to the floor. But as Jimmy said when he saw me behind the bar the next night, "It could have been worse—think what would've happened if the thing had been in gear."

MY FATHER SEEMED TO THINK the whole affair was pretty idiotic, but he didn't deliver any lectures. It was idiotic, but by some convoluted way of thinking, it was manly too. And funny. Deeply, richly, skin-of-the-teeth and laughing-in-the-face-of-Mr.-D. funny. He rubbed his balding head with his nail-bucket hands and said he guessed I could take my mother's car to work until I could find myself another heap of bolts, but he hoped I'd show a little more restraint and maybe pour a drop or two of coffee into my brandy before trying to make it home on all that glare ice.

Helen—the new and exciting Helen with the silver-foil eyes—didn't seem particularly impressed with my first-night exploits, which had already entered the realm of legend by the time I got to work at four the following afternoon, but she didn't seem offended or put off in any way either. We worked together through the cocktail-hour rush and into the depths of a very busy evening, exchanging the thousand small quips and intimacies that pass between bartender and cocktail waitress in the course of an eight-hour shift, and then it was closing time and there was Jimmy Brennan, at the very hub of the same unfolding scenario that had played itself out so disastrously the night before. Had I learned my lesson? Had the two-paragraph story in the local paper crediting Fireman Samuel L. Calabrese with saving my sorry life had any effect? Or the loss of my car and the humiliation of having to drive my mother's? Not a whit. Jimmy Brennan bought and I poured, and he went off on a long soliloquy about beef suppliers and how they weren't competent to do a thing about the quality of the frozen lobster tails for Surf 'n' Turf, and I probably would have gone out and wrecked my mother's car if it wasn't for Helen.

She was sitting down at the end of the bar with Adele, Ski, another cocktail waitress and two waiters who'd stayed on to drink deep after we shut down the kitchen. What she was doing was smoking a cigarette and drinking a Black Russian and watching me out of those freakish eyes as if I were some kind of wonder of nature. I liked that look. I liked it a lot. And when she got up to whisper something in my ear, hot breath and expressive lips and an invitation that electrified me from my scalp to my groin, I cut Jimmy Brennan off in the middle of an aside about what he was paying per case for well-vodka and said, "Sorry, gotta go. Helen's having car trouble and she needs a ride, isn't that right, Helen?"

She already had her coat on, a complicated thing full of pleats and buckles that drove right down to the toes of her boots, and she shook out her hair with a sideways flip of her head before clapping a knit hat over it. "Yeah," she said. "That's right."

There were no wrecks that night. We left my mother's car in the lot out front of Brennan's and Helen drove me to the apartment she and Adele shared on the second floor of an old frame house in York-town. It was dark—intensely, preternaturally dark (or maybe it was just the crust of salt, sand and frozen slush on the windshield that made it seem that way)—and when we swung into a narrow drive hemmed in by long-legged pines, the house suddenly loomed up out of nowhere like the prow of a boat anchored in the night. "This is it?" I said, just to hear the sound of my own voice, and she said something like "Home sweet home" as she cut the engine and the lights died.

The next thing I knew we were on the porch, bathed in the dull yel-low glow of a superfluous bug light, locked out and freezing; she gave me a ghostly smile, dug through her purse, dropped her keys twice, then her gloves and compact, and finally announced that the house key was missing. In response, I drew her to me and kissed her, my mind skewed by vodka and the joint we'd shared in the car, our breath steam-ing, heavy winter coats keeping our bodies apart—and then, with a growing sense of urgency, I tried the door. It was locked, all right. But I was feeling heroic and reckless, and I put my shoulder to it—just once, but with real feeling—and the bolt gave and we were in.

Upstairs, at the end of the hallway, was Helen's superheated lair, a place that looked pretty much the way our mutual place would look, but which was a revelation to me at the time. There was order here, femininity, floors that gave back the light, books and records arranged alphabetically on brick-and-board shelves, prints on the walls, a clean sink and a clean toilet. And there was a smell connected to and interwoven with it all, sweet and astringent at the same time. It might have been patchouli, but I didn't know what patchouli was or how it was supposed to smell, just that it was exotic, and that was enough for me. There were cats—two of them, Siamese or some close approximation—but you can't have everything. I was hooked. "Nice place," I said, working at the buttons of my coat while the cats yowled for food or attention or both, and Helen fluttered around the living room, lighting candles and slipping a record on the stereo.

I didn't know what to do with myself, so I eased my haunches down on the floor in a pile of pillows—there was no furniture in the usual sense—and shrugged out of my coat. It was hot as a steam-bath, Helen had left the room through a set of bead curtains that were still clacking, and a beer had magically appeared in my hand. I tried to relax, but the image of what was to come and what was expected of me and how exactly to go about it without ruining everything weighed on me so heavily even the chugging of the beer had no effect. Then Helen returned in a white terrycloth robe, her hair freshly brushed and shining. "So," she said, settling into the pillows beside me and looking suddenly as vulnerable and uncertain as I, "you want to get high?"

We smoked hash. We listened to music, very loud music—Buffalo Springfield; Blood, Sweat and Tears; the Moody Blues—and that provided an excuse for not saying much of anything beyond the occasional murmur as the pipe was passed or the lighter sprang to life. The touch of her hand as we shared the pipe set me on fire though and the music invested me with every nuance and I thought for a while I was floating about three feet above the floor. I was thinking sex, she was thinking sex, but neither of us made a move.

And then, somehow, Adele was there, compact, full-breasted Adele, with her sheenless eyes and the dark slash of her bangs obliterating her eyebrows. She was wearing a pair of black pantihose and nothing else, and she settled into the pillows on my left, languidly reaching for the pipe. She didn't say anything for a long while—none of us did—and I don't know what she was thinking, so natural and naked and warm, but I was suffering from sensory overload. Two women, I was thinking, and the image of my father and my sad dumpy mother floated up in my brain just as one of the cats climbed into Adele's lap and settled itself between her breasts.

That was when I felt Helen's hand take hold of mine. She was standing, and she pulled me to my feet with surprising force, and then she led me through the bead curtains and down a hall and into her bedroom. And the first thing she did, before I could take hold of her and let all the rest unfold, was shut the door—and lock it.

AND SO WE MOVED in together, in the house that started off smelling of freeze-dried mouseshit and wound up taking on the scent of patchouli. I was content. For the first time I was off on my own, independent, an adult, a man. I had a woman. I had a house. Two cats. Heating bills. And I came home to all that pretty religiously for the first month or two, but then, on the nights when I was working and Helen wasn't, I started staying after closing with Jimmy Brennan and a few of the other employees. The term Quaalude speaks to me now when I think back on it, that very specific term that calls up the image of a little white pill that kicked your legs out from under you and made your voice run down like a wind-up motor in need of rewinding. Especially when you judiciously built your high around it with a selection of high-octane drinks, pot, hash, and anything else you could get your hands on.

There we were, sitting at the bar, the music on full, the lights down low, talking into the night, bullshitting, getting stoned and progressively more stoned, and Helen waiting for me in our little house at the end of the road by the frozen lake. That was the setting for the second wreck—or it wasn't a wreck in the fundamental, literal sense of the word, because Helen's VW bus was barely damaged, aside from some unexpected wear and tear on the left front fender and a barely noticeable little twist to the front bumper. It was four or five in the morning, the sky a big black puddle of nothing, three feet of dogshit-strewn snow piled up on either side of the road till it looked like a long snaking bobsled run. The bus fired up with a tinny rattle and I took off, but I was in a state of advanced confusion, I guess, and I went right by the turnoff for our road, the one that led to the little house by the frozen lake, and instead found myself out on the main highway, bouncing back and forth between the snow berms like a poolball that can't decide on a pocket.

There was something in the urgency of the lights flashing behind me that got me to pull over, and then there was a cop standing there in his jackboots and wide-brimmed hat, shining a flashlight in my face. "Out of the car," he said, and I complied, or tried to, but I missed my footing and pitched face-forward into the snow. And when I awoke this time, there were no firemen present and no flames, just an ugly pale-gray concrete-block room with graffiti scrawled over it and three or four hopeless-looking jerks sitting around on the floor.

I got shakily to my feet, glanced around me and went instinctively to the door, a heavy sliding affair with a little barred window set in the center of it at eye-level. My hands took hold of the handle and I gave the door a tug. Nothing. I tried again. Same lack of result. And then I turned round on my companions, these pathetic strangers with death masks for faces and seriously disarranged hair, and said, as if I was in a dream, "Hey, it's locked."

That was when one of the men on the floor stirred himself long enough to glance up at me out of blood-flecked eyes and a face that was exactly like a bucket of pus. "What the fuck you think, mother-fucker," he said. "Your ass is in jail."

THEN IT WAS SPRING and the ice receded from the shore of the lake to reveal a black band of dead water, the driveway turned to mud and the ditches along the blacktop road began to ululate with the orgasmic cries of the nondescript little toads known as spring peepers. The heating bill began to recede too, and to celebrate that minor miracle and the rebirth of all things green and good, I took my Alien—Helen, that is—out for dinner at Capelli's, where all the waiters faked an Italian accent, whether they were Puerto Ricans or Swedes, and you couldn't pick up a cigarette without one of them rushing over to light it for you. It was dark. It smelled good. Some-body's grandmother was out in the kitchen, cooking, and we ate the usual things—canneloni, baked ziti, pasta primavera—and paid about twice what we would have paid in the usual places. I was beginning to know a little about wine, so I ordered a bottle of the second-highest-priced red on the menu, and when we finished that, I ordered another. For dessert, my balled fist presented Helen with two little white Rorer Quaaludes.

She was looking good, silver-eyed and tanned from an early-spring ski trip to Vermont with Adele and one of the other waitresses. I watched the rings glitter on her fingers as she lifted her glass to wash down the pills, and then she set the glass down and eased back into her chair under the weight of all that food and wine. "I finally met Kurt," she said.

I was having a scotch and Drambuie as an after-dinner drink, no dessert thanks, and enjoying the scene, which was very formal and adult, old guys in suits slurping up linguine, busty wives with poodle hair and furs, people of forty and maybe beyond out here in the hinterlands living the good life. "Kurt who?" I said.

"Kurt Ramos? Adele's ex?" She leaned forward, her elbows splayed on the tabletop. "He was bartending at this place in Stowe—he's a Sagittarius, very creative. Funny too. He paints and writes poetry and had one of his poems almost published in the *Hudson Review,* and of course, Adele knew he was going to be there, I mean that was the whole point. He's thirty-four, I think. Or thirty-five. You think that's too much? Age-wise, I mean? Adele's only twenty-four."

"*Almost* published?" I said.

Helen shrugged. "I don't know the details. The editor wrote him a long letter or something."

"He is pretty old. But then so are you, and you don't mind having a baby like me around, do you?"

"Four years, kiddo," she said. "Three years and nine months, actually. I'm not an old lady yet. But what do you think—is he too old for her?"

I didn't think anything. Helen was always giving these speeches about so-and-so and their sex life, who was cheating on who, the I Ching, reincarnation, cat-breeding, UFOs and the way people's characters could be read like brownie recipes according to their astrological charts. I gave her a sly smile and put my hand on her leg. "Age is relative," I said. "Isn't it?"

And then the strangest thing happened, by way of coincidence, that is—there was a flurry of activity in the foyer, the bowing and scraping of waiters, the little tap dance of leather soles as coats were removed, and suddenly the maître d' was leading Adele and the very same Kurt Ramos past our table.

Helen saw them first. "Adele!" she chirped, already rising up out of the chair with a big stoned grin on her face, and then I glanced up and saw Adele there in a sweater so tight she must have been born in it (but no, no, I had vivid proof to the contrary). Beside her, loping along with an athletic stride, was Kurt Ramos, half-German, half–Puerto Rican, with crazily staring eyes and slick black hair that hung to his shoulders. He was wearing a tan trenchcoat, bell-bottoms and a pair of red bowling shoes he'd borrowed from a bowling alley one night. There were exclamations of surprise all around, the girls embraced as if they hadn't seen each other in twelve years and I found myself wrapping my hand round Kurt Ramos' in a complicated soul shake. "Good to meet you, man," I said in my best imitation of a very hip adult, but he just stared right through me.

IN MAY, Ski Silinski quit to move up to Maine and live among goats and liberated women on a commune, leaving his wife and kid behind, and I found myself elevated to head bartender at the ripe age of twenty-three. I was making good money, getting at least a modicum of exercise rowing Helen around the defrosted lake every afternoon, and aside from the minorest of scrapes, I hadn't really wrecked anything or anybody in a whole long string of weeks. Plus, I was ascending to the legendary status I'd sought all along, stoked by the Fireman Calabrese incident and the high drama of my unconscious dive into the hands of the state police. I'd begun dealing Quaaludes in a quiet way, I tripped and had revelatory visions and went to concerts with Helen, Adele and Kurt, and I pretty generally felt on top of things. The prevailing ethos was simple in those days—the more drugs you ingested, the hipper you were, and the hipper you were, the more people sought you out for praise, drugs and admiration. I even got to the point where I could match Jimmy Brennan drink for drink and still make it home alive—or at least partially so.

Anyway, Ski quit and on my recommendation we hired Kurt Ramos as second bartender, and the two of us made quite a pair behind the bar, he with his shower-curtain hair and staring eyes and me with my fixed grin that was impervious to anything life or the pharmaceutical industry could throw at it. We washed glasses, cut fruit, mixed drinks, talked about everything and nothing. He told me about Hawaii and Amsterdam, drugs, women he'd known, and he showed me his poetry, which seemed pretty banal to me, but who was I to judge? When work was over, he and Adele would come over to our place for long stoned discussions and gleeful drug abuse, or we'd go to a late movie or another bar. I liked him. He had heart and style and he never tried to pull rank on me by virtue of his greater age and wisdom, as Jimmy Brennan and his drinking cronies never failed to do.

It was a month or so after Kurt started working behind the bar that my parents came in for the first time. They'd been threatening to make an appearance ever since I'd got the job—my mother wanted to check the place out because she'd heard so much about it, everybody had, and my father seemed amused by the idea of his son officially making him a drink and pushing it across the bar to him on a little napkin. "You'd have to give me a discount," he kept saying. "Wouldn't you?" And then he'd laugh his high husky laugh till the laugh became a smoker's cough and he'd cross the kitchen to the sink and drop a ball of sputum in the drain.

I was shaking a martini for a middle-aged guy at the end of the bar when I glanced up and saw my father looming there in the doorway. The sun was setting, a fat red disc on the horizon, and my father extinguished it with the spread of his shoulders as he maneuvered my mother through the door. The hostess—a terminally pretty girl by the name of Jane Nardone—went up to him with a dripping smile and asked if he'd like a table for two. "Yeah, sure," I heard him say in his rasping voice, "but only after my son makes a me a vodka gimlet—or maybe two." He put his hands on his hips and looked down at the little painted doll that was Jane Nardone. "That okay with you?" Then he made his way across the room to where I stood behind the bar in white shirt and tie.

"Nice place," he grunted, helping my mother up onto a barstool and settling in beside her. My mother was heavily made-up and liquid-eyed, which meant she'd already had a couple of drinks, and she was clutching a black patent-leather purse the size of a refrigerator. "Hi, honey," she said, "working hard?"

For a minute I was frozen there at the bar, one hand on the shaker, the other on the glass. There went my cool, the legend dissolved,

Lester the ultra-wild one nothing more than a boy-faced boy—and with parents, no less. It was Kurt who saved the day. He was thirty-five years old after all, with hollow cheeks and the faintest weave of gray in his mustache, and he had nothing to prove. He was cool, genuinely cool, and I was an idiot. "Mr. Rifkin," he said, "Mrs. Rifkin. Lester's told me a lot about you"—a glowing, beautiful, scintillating lie. "What can I get you?"

"Yeah," I said, adjusting the edges of my fixed smile just a degree, "what'll it be?"

And that was fine. My father had three drinks at the bar and got very convivial with Kurt, and my mother, perched on the edge of the stool and drinking Manhattans, corralled anybody she could—Jane, Adele, Helen, random customers, even one of the busboys—and told them all about my potty training, my elementary school triumphs and the .417 batting average I carried one year in Little League. Jimmy Brennan came in and bought everybody a round. We were very busy. I was glowing. My father was glowing. Jane showed him and my mother to the best table in the house and they kept Helen and two waiters schmoozing over a long, lingering, three-course dinner with dessert, after-dinner drinks and coffee. Which I paid for. Happily.

THE SUMMER THAT YEAR was typical—heat, mosquitoes, fat green flies droning aimlessly round the kitchen, the air so dense with moisture even the frogs were sweating. Helen and I put off going to bed later and later each night, hoping it would cool off so we could actually sleep instead of sweating reservoirs on each other, and we saw dawn more times than I'd like to remember. Half the time I wound up passed out on the couch, and I would wake at one or two in the afternoon in a state of advanced dehydration. Iced coffee would help, especially with a shot or two of Kahlúa in it, and maybe a Seconal to kill some of the pain of the previous night's afflictions, but by the time we got around to the deli for a sandwich to go, it was four and we were on our way to work. That became a real grind, especially when I only got Monday nights off. But then, right in the middle of a heat wave, Jimmy Brennan's mother died and the restaurant closed down for three days. It was a tragedy for Jimmy, and worse for his mother, but for us—Helen, Kurt, Adele and me—it was like Christmas in July. Three whole days off. I couldn't believe it.

Jimmy flew back to California, somebody pinned a notice to the front door of the restaurant, and we took advantage of the fact that Kurt had recently come into twenty hits of blotter acid to plan a day around some pastoral activities. We filled a cooler with sangria and sandwiches and hiked into the back end of Wicopee Reservoir, deep in Fahnestock Park, a place where swimming was prohibited and trespassing forbidden. Our purpose? To swim. And trespass. We could have spent the day on our own muddy little lake, but there were houses, cabins, people, cars, boats and dogs everywhere, and we wanted privacy, not to mention adventure. What we wanted, specifically, was to be nude, because we were very hip and the puritanical mores of the false and decrepit society our parents had so totteringly constructed didn't apply to us.

We parked off the Taconic Parkway—far off, behind a thick screen of trees where the police wouldn't discover the car and become overly curious as to the whereabouts of its former occupants—shouldered our day packs, hefted the cooler, and started off through the woods. As soon as we were out of sight of the road, Kurt paused to strip off his T-shirt and shorts, and it was immediately evident that he'd done this before—and often—because he had no tan line whatever. Adele was next. She threw down her pack, dropped her shorts, and in a slow tease unbuttoned her shirt, watching me all the time. The woods were streaked with sun, deerflies nagged at us, I was sweating. I set down the cooler, and though I'd begun to put on weight and was feeling self-conscious about it, I tried to be casual as I rolled the sweaty T-shirt up over my gut and chest and then kicked free of my shorts. Helen was watching me too, and Kurt—all three of them were—and I clapped on my sunglasses to mask my eyes. Then it was Helen's turn. She gave me a look out of her silver-foil eyes, then laughed—a long musical girlish laugh—before pulling the shirt over her head and dropping her shorts and panties in a single motion. *"Voilà!"* she said, and laughed again.

And what was I thinking? "How about a hit of that acid, Kurt?" I said, locked away behind my shades.

He looked dubious. Lean, naked and suntanned and caught between two impulses. "Sure," he said, shrugging, the green mottled arena of the untrodden woods opening up around him, "why not? But the lake's maybe a mile off and I can still hear the parkway, for Christ's sake, but yeah, sure, it's going to take a while to kick in anyway."

It was a sacramental moment. We lined up naked under the trees and Kurt tore off a hit for each of us and laid it on our tongues, and then we hoisted our packs, I picked up the cooler, and we started off down the path. Kurt, who'd been here before, was in front, leading the way; the two girls were next, Adele and then Helen; and I brought up the rear, seeing nothing of the sky, the trees, the ferns or the myriad wonders of nature. No, I saw only the naked buttocks of the naked women as they eased themselves down the path or climbed over a downed tree or a spike of granite, and it was all I could do to keep cool in a vigilantly hip and matter-of-fact way, and fight down an erection.

After a while, the lake began to peek through the trees, a silver sheen cut up in segments, now shining in a gap over here, now over there. We came down to it like pilgrims, the acid already starting to kick in and alter the colors and texture ever so subtly, and the first thing we did was drop our packs and the cooler and cannonade into the water in an explosion of hoots and shouts that echoed out over the lake like rolling thunder. There was splashing and frolicking and plenty of incidental and not-so-incidental contact. We bobbed like seals. The sun hung fat in the sky. There was no finer moment. And then, at some point, we found ourselves sitting cross-legged on a blanket and passing round the bota bag of sangria and a joint, before falling to the sandwiches. After that, we lay back and stared up into the shifting shapes of the trees, letting the natural world sink slowly in.

I don't remember exactly what happened next—maybe I was seeing things, maybe I was dozing—but when I came back to the world, what I saw was no hallucination. Kurt was having sex with Helen, my Helen, my Alien, and Adele was deeply involved too, very busy with her hands and tongue. I was thoroughly stoned—tripping, and so were they—but I wasn't shocked or surprised or jealous, or not that I would admit to myself. I was hip. I was a man. And if Kurt could fuck Helen, then I could fuck Adele. A quid pro quo, right? That was only fair.

Helen was making certain small noises, whispery rasping intimate noises that I knew better than anyone in the world, and those noises provoked me to get up off the blanket and move over to where Adele was lying at the periphery of all that passionate action as if she were somehow controlling it. I put one hand on her shoulder and the other between her legs, and she turned to me with her black eyes and the black slash of her bangs caught in the depths of them, and she smiled and pulled me down.

WHAT HAPPENED NEXT, of course, is just another kind of wreckage. It wasn't as immediate maybe as turning over a car or driving it into the trees, but it cut just as wide a swath and it hurt, ultimately, beyond the capacity of any wound that can be closed with stitches. Bang up your head, it's no problem—you're a man, you'll grow another one. Broken leg, crushed ribs—you're impervious. But if there's one thing I've learned, it's that the emotional wrecks are the worst. You can't see the scars, but they're there, and they're a long time healing.

Anyway, later that day, sunburned and sated, we all came back to our house at the end of the lane on the muddy lake, showered—individually—and ordered up take-out Chinese, which we washed down with frozen margaritas while huddling on the floor and watching a truly hilarious old black-and-white horror film on the tube. Then there came a moment when we all looked at one another—consenting adults, armored in hip—and before we knew it we were reprising the afternoon's scenario. Finally, very late, I found my way to bed, and it was Adele, not Helen, who joined me there. To sleep.

I was stupid. I was inadequate. I was a boy playing at being a man. But the whole thing thrilled me—two women, two women at my disposal—and I never even heard Helen when she told me she wanted to break it off. "I don't trust myself," she said. "I don't love him, I love you. You're my man. This is our house." The aluminum eyes fell away into her head and she looked older than ever, older than the mummy's ghost, older than my mother. We were in the kitchen, staring into cups of coffee. It was a week after the restaurant had opened up again, four in the morning, impossibly hot, the night alive with the shriek of every disturbed and horny insect, and we'd just got done entertaining Kurt and Adele in the way that had become usual and I didn't want to hear her, not a word.

"Listen," I said, half-stoned and rubbed raw between the legs, "listen, Alien, it's okay, there's nothing wrong with it—you don't want to get yourself buried in all that bourgeois shit. I mean, that's what started the War. That's what our parents are like. We're above that. We are."

The house was still. Her voice was very quiet. "No," she said, shaking her head slowly and definitively, "no we're not."

A MONTH WENT BY, and nothing changed. Then another. The days began to grow shorter, the nights took on a chill and the monster in the basement clanked and rumbled into action, devouring fuel oil once again. I was tending bar one night at the end of September, maybe twenty customers sitting there staring at me, Jimmy Brennan and a few of his buddies at the end of the bar, couples lingering over the tables, when the phone rang. It had been a slow night—we'd only done maybe fifty dinners—but the bar had filled up after we shut the kitchen down, and everybody seemed unnaturally thirsty. Helen had gone home early, as had Adele and Kurt, and I was getting drinks at the bar and taking orders at the tables too. I picked the phone up on the second ring. "Brennan's," I said, "how can I help you?"

It was Helen. Her voice was thick, gritty, full of something I hadn't heard in it before. "That you, Les?" she said.

"Yeah, what's up?" I pinned the phone to one shoulder with my chin to keep my hands free, and began dipping glasses in the rinse water and stacking them to dry. I kept my eyes on the customers.

"I just wanted to tell you I'm moving out."

I watched Jimmy Brennan light a cigarette and lean out over the bar to fetch himself an ashtray. I caught his eye and signaled "just a minute," then turned my back to the bar. "What do you mean?" I said, and I had to whisper. "What are you saying?"

"What am I saying? You want to know what I'm saying, Les—do you really?" There it was, the grit in her voice, and more than that—anger, hostility. "What I'm saying is I'm moving in with Kurt and Adele because I'm in love with Kurt. You understand that? You understand what I'm saying? It's over. Totally. Adioski."

"Sure," I whispered, and I was numb, no more capable of thought or feeling than the empty beer mug I was turning over in my hands, "—if that's what you want. But when, I mean, when are you—?"

There was a pause, and I thought I heard her catch her breath, as if she were fighting back the kind of emotion I couldn't begin to express. "I won't be there when you get home," she said.

Somebody was calling me—"Hey, bartender!"—and I swung round on a big stupid-looking guy with a Fu Manchu mustache who came in every night for two or three drinks and never left more than a quarter tip. "Another round here, huh?"

"And, Les," she was saying through that cold aperture molded to my ear like a compress, "the rent's only paid through the thirtieth, so I don't know what you're going to do—"

"Hey, bartender!"

"—and you know what, Les? I don't care. I really don't."

I stayed late that night. The bar was alive, roaring, seething with camaraderie, chaos, every kind of possibility. My friends were there, my employer, customers I saw every night and wanted to embrace. I drank everything that came my way. I went out to the kitchen and smoked a joint with the busboys. Muddy Waters thumped through the speakers with his mojo workin' ("All you womens, stand in line, / I'll make love to you, babe, / In five minutes' time, / Ain't that a man?"). I talked a couple of people comatose, smoked a whole pack of cigarettes. Then came the moment I'd been dreading since I'd hung up the phone—Jimmy Brennan got up off his barstool and shut down the lights and it was time to go home.

Outside, the sky seemed to rise up out of itself and pull the stars taut like separate strands of hair till everything blurred and there was no more fire, just ice. It was cold. My breath steamed in the sick yellow glow of the streetlights. I must have stood in the empty parking lot for a full five minutes before I realized Helen had the van—her van—and I had no way to get home and nobody to call. But then I heard a noise behind me, the rattle of keys, a slurred curse, and there was Jimmy Brennan, locking up, and I shouted, "Jimmy, hey, Jimmy, how about a ride?" He looked puzzled, as if the pavement had begun to speak, but the light caught the discs of his glasses and something like recognition slowly transformed his face. "Sure," he said, unsteady on his feet, "sure, no problem."

He drove like a zombie, staring straight ahead, the radio tuned so low all I could hear was the dull muted snarl of the bass. We didn't say much, maybe nothing at all. He had his problems, and I had mine. He let me off at the end of the dark lane and I fumbled my way into the dark house and fled away to unconsciousness before I could think to turn the lights on.

Two days later I put down five hundred dollars on a used Dodge the color of dried blood and moved in with Phil Cherniske, one of the waiters at Brennan's, who by a cruel stroke of fate happened to live on the next street over from the one I'd just vacated, right on the shore of the same muddy lake. Phil's place stank of mouseshit too, and of course it lacked the feminine touches I'd grown accustomed to and cleanliness wasn't all that high on the list of priorities, but who was I to complain? It was a place in which to breathe, sleep, shit, brood and get stoned.

In the meanwhile, I tried to get hold of Helen. She'd quit Brennan's the day after our phone conversation, and when I called Kurt and Adele's, she refused to talk to me. Adele wouldn't say a word the next day at work and it was awkward in the extreme going through an eight-hour shift behind the bar with Kurt, no matter how hip and impervious I tried to be. We dodged round each other a hundred times, made the smallest of small talk, gave elaborate consideration to customers at the far end of the bar. I wanted to kill him, that's what I wanted to do, and I probably would have too, except that violence was so unhip and immature. Helen's name never passed my lips. I froze Kurt out. And Adele too. And to everybody else I was a combination of Mahatma Gandhi and Santa Claus, my frozen smile opening up into a big slobbering insincere grin. "Hey, man," I said to the cheapazoid with the mustache, "how you doin'?"

On my break and after work, I called Kurt and Adele's number over and over, but Helen wasn't answering. Twice I drove my Dodge down the street past their house, but nobody was home the first time and then all three of them were there the next, and I couldn't face going up those steps. For a while I entertained a fantasy of butting down the door, kicking Kurt in the crotch and dragging Helen out to the car by her hair, but it faded away in a pharmaceutical haze. I didn't run through a checklist of emotions, like one of those phony Ph.D.s in the women's magazines Helen stacked up on the coffee table like miniature Bibles and Korans—that wasn't my way at all. I didn't even tell my parents we weren't together anymore. I just got high. And higher.

That was what brought about the culminating wreck—of that series, anyway. I was feeling bad one day, bad in every sense of the word, and since it was my day off, I spent the afternoon chasing down drugs in every house and apartment I could think of in Westchester and Putnam Counties, hitting up friends, acquaintances and acquaintances of acquaintances. Phil Cherniske was with me for part of the time, but then he had to go to work, and I found myself driving around the back roads, stoned on a whole smorgasbord of things, a bottle of vodka propped between my legs. I was looking at leaves, flaming leaves, and I was holding a conversation with myself and letting the car take me wherever it wanted. I think I must have pulled over and nodded out for a while, because all of a sudden (I'd say "magically," but this was more like treachery) the leaves were gone and it was dark. There was nothing to do but head for the restaurant.

I came through the door in an envelope of refrigerated air and the place opened up to me, warm and frank and smelling of cigarettes, steak on the grill, fresh-cut lime. I wasn't hungry myself, not even close to it, so I settled in at the bar and watched people eat dinner.

Kurt was bartending, and at first he tried to be chummy and unctuous, as if nothing had happened, but the look on my face drove him to the far end of the bar, where he tried to keep himself urgently occupied. It was good sitting there with a cigarette and a pocketful of pills, lifting a finger to summon him when my drink needed refreshing—once I even made him light my cigarette, and all the while I stared hate into his eyes. Adele was waitressing, along with Jane Nardone, recently elevated from hostess. I never even looked at Adele, but at some point it seemed I tried to get overly friendly with Jane in the corner and Phil had to come out of the kitchen and put a hand on my arm. "Brennan'll be in soon, you know," Phil said, his hand like a clamp on the meat of my arm. "They'll eighty-six you. They will."

I gave him a leer and shook him off. "Hey, barkeep," I shouted so that the whole place heard me, all the Surf 'n' Turf gnashers and their dates and the idiots lined up at the bar, "give me another cocktail down here, will you? What, do you want me to die of thirst?"

Dinner was over and the kitchen closed by the time things got ugly. I was out of line and I knew it, and I deserved what was coming to me—that's not to say it didn't hurt, though, getting tossed out of my own restaurant, my sanctuary, my place of employ, recreation and release, the place where the flame was kept and the legend accruing. But tossed I was, cut off, eighty-sixed, banned. I don't know what precipitated it exactly, something with Kurt, something I said that he didn't like after a whole long night of things he didn't like, and it got physical. Next thing I knew, Phil, Kurt, Jimmy Brennan and two of the busboys had ten arms around me and we were all heaving and banging into the walls until the door flew open and I was out on the pavement where some bleached-out overweight woman and her two kids stepped over me as if I were a leper. I tried to get back in—uncool, unhip, raging with every kind of resentment and hurt—but they'd locked the door against me, and the last thing I remember seeing was Kurt Ramos' puffed-up face peering out at me through the little window in the door.

I climbed into my car and fired it up with a roar that gave testimony to a seriously compromised exhaust system. When the smoke cleared—and I hoped they were all watching—I hit the gas, jammed the lever into gear and shot out onto the highway on screaming tires. Where was I headed? I didn't know. Home, I guessed. There was no place else to go.

Now, to set this up properly, I should tell you that there was one wicked turn on the long dark blacktop road that led to that dark lane on the muddy lake, a ninety-degree hairpin turn the Alien had christened "Lester's Corner" because of the inevitability of the forces gathered there, and that was part of the legend too. I knew that corner was there, I was supremely conscious of it, and though I can't say I always coasted smoothly through it without some last-minute wheel-jerking and tire-squealing, it hadn't really been a problem. Up to this point.

At any rate, I wasn't really paying attention that night and my reaction time must have been somewhere in the range of the Alzheimer's patient on medication—in fact, for those few seconds I *was* an Alzheimer's patient on medication—and I didn't even know where I was until I felt the car slip out from under me. Or no, that isn't right. It was the road—the road slipped out from under me, and it felt just as if I were on a roller coaster, released from the pull of gravity. The car ricocheted off a tree that would have swatted me down like a fly if I'd hit it head-on, blasted down an embankment and wound up on its roof in a stew of skunk cabbage and muck. I wasn't wearing a seatbelt, of course—I don't even know if they'd been invented yet, and if they had, there wouldn't have been one in that car—and I found myself puddled up in the well of the roof like an egg inside a crushed shell.

There was no sense in staying there, underneath two tons of crumpled and drooling machinery—that wasn't the way things were supposed to be, even I could see that—so I poked my hands through the gap where the driver's side window had formerly been and felt them sink into the cold ooze. There was a smell of gasoline, but it was overpowered by the reek of deconstructed skunk cabbage, and I didn't give the situation any more thought or calculation than a groundhog does when he pulls himself out of his burrow, and the next thing I knew I was standing up to my ankles in cold muck, looking up in the direction of the road. There were lights there, and a shadowy figure in a long winter coat. "You all right?" a voice called down to me.

"Yeah, sure," I said, "no problem," and then I was lurching up the embankment on splayed feet, oozing muck. When I got to the top, a guy my age was standing there. He looked a little bit like Kurt—same hair, same slope to the shoulders—but he wasn't Kurt, and that was a good thing. "What happened?" he said. "You lose control?"

It was a ridiculous question, but I answered it. "Something like that," I said, my voice thick with alcohol and methaqualone.

"Sure you're not hurt? You want to go to the hospital or anything?"

I took a minute to pat myself down, the night air like the breath of some expiring beast. "No," I said, slowly shaking my head in the glare of the headlights, "I'm not hurt. Not that I know of, anyway."

We stood there in silence a moment, contemplating the overturned hulk of the car. One wheel, persistent to the point of absurdity, kept spinning at the center of a gulf of shadow. "Listen," I said finally, "can you give me a lift?"

"A lift? But what about—?"

"Tomorrow," I said, and I let one hand rise and then drop.

There was another silence, and he was thinking it over, I could see that. From his point of view, this was no happy occasion. I wasn't bleeding, but I stank like a corpse and I was leaving the scene of an accident and he was a witness and all the rest of it. But he was a good man, and he surprised me. "Yeah, sure," he said, after a minute. "Climb in."

That was when things got very strange. Because as I directed him to my house at the end of the lane by the side of the soon-to-be-refrozen lake, a curtain fell over my mind. It was a dense curtain, weighted at the ends, and it admitted no glimmer of light. "Here," I said, "stop here," and the curtain fell over that part of my life that played itself out at Phil Cherniske's house.

A moment later, I found myself alone in the night, the taillights of the good samaritan's car winking once at the corner and then vanishing. I walked down the dark lane thinking of Helen, Helen with her silver-foil eyes and smooth sweet smile, and I mounted the steps and turned the handle of the door thinking of her, but it wouldn't turn, because it was locked. I knocked then, knocked at my own door, knocked until my knuckles bled, but there was no one home.

Blinded by the Light

So the sky is falling. Or, to be more precise, the sky is emitting poisonous rays, rays that have sprinkled the stigmata of skin cancer across both of Manuel Banquedano's cheeks and the tip of his nose and sprouted the cataracts in Slobodan Abarca's rheumy old eyes. That is what the tireless Mr. John Longworth, of Long Beach, California, U.S.A., would have us believe. I have been to Long Beach, California, on two occasions, and I give no credence whatever to a man who would consciously assent to live in a place like that. He is, in fact, just what my neighbors say he is—an alarmist, like the chicken in the children's tale who thinks the sky is falling just because something hit him on the head. On *his* head. On his individual and prejudicial head. And so the barnyard goes into a panic—and to what end? Nothing. A big fat zero.

But let me tell you about him, about Mr. John Longworth, Ph.D., and how he came to us with his theories, and you can judge for yourself. First, though, introductions are in order. I am Bob Fernando Castillo and I own an *estancia* of 50,000 acres to the south of Punta Arenas, on which I graze some 9,000 sheep, for wool and mutton both. My father, God rest his soul, owned Estancia Castillo before me and his father before him, all the way back to the time Punta Arenas was a penal colony and then one of the great trading towns of the world—that is, until the Americans of the North broke through the Isthmus of Panama and the ships stopped rounding Cape Horn. In any case, that is a long and venerable ownership in anybody's book. I am fifty-three years old and in good health and vigor and I am married to the former Isabela Mackenzie, who has given me seven fine children, the eldest of whom, Bob Fernando Jr., is now twenty-two years old.

It was September last, when Don Pablo Antofagasta gave his annual three-day *fiesta primavera* to welcome in the spring, that Mr. John Longworth first appeared among us. We don't have much society out here, unless we take the long and killing drive into Punta Arenas, a city of 110,000 souls, and we look forward with keen anticipation to such entertainments—and not only the adults, but the children too. The landowners from several of the *estancias,* even the most far-flung, gather annually for Don Pablo's extravaganza and they bring their children and some of the house servants as well (and even, as in the case of Don Benedicto Braun, their dogs and horses). None of this presents a problem for Don Pablo, one of the wealthiest and most generous among us. As we say, the size of his purse is exceeded only by the size of his heart.

I arrived on the Thursday preceding the big weekend, flying over the *pampas* in the Piper Super Cub with my daughter, Paloma, to get a jump on the others and have a quiet night sitting by the fire with Don Pablo and his eighty-year-old Iberian *jerez.* Isabela, Bob Fernando Jr. and the rest of the family would be making the twelve-hour drive over washboard roads and tortured gullies the following morning, and frankly, my kidneys can no longer stand that sort of pounding. I still ride—horseback, that is—but I leave the Suburban and the Range Rover to Isabela and to Bob Fernando Jr. At any rate, the flight was a joy, soaring on the back of the implacable wind that rakes our country day and night, and I taxied right up to the big house on the airstrip Don Pablo scrupulously maintains.

Don Pablo emerged from the house to greet us even before the prop had stopped spinning, as eager for our company as we were for his. (Paloma has always been his favorite, and she's grown into a tall, straight-backed girl of eighteen with intelligent eyes and a mane of hair so thick and luxuriant it almost seems unnatural, and I don't mind saying how proud I am of her.) My old friend strode across the struggling lawn in boots and puttees and one of those plaid flannel shirts he mail-orders from Boston, Teresa and two of the children in tow. It took me half a moment to shut down the engine and stow away my aeronautical sunglasses for the return flight, and when I looked up again, a fourth figure had appeared at Don Pablo's side, matching him stride for stride.

"Cómo estás, mi amigo estimado?" Don Pablo cried, taking my hand and embracing me, and then he turned to Paloma to kiss her cheek and exclaim on her beauty and how she'd grown. Then it was my turn to embrace Teresa and the children and press some sweets into the little ones' hands. Finally, I looked up into an untethered North American face, red hair and a red mustache and six feet six inches of raw bone and sinew ending in a little bony afterthought of a head no bigger than a tropical coconut and weighted down by a nose to end all noses. This nose was an affliction and nothing less, a tool for probing and rooting, and I instinctively looked away from it as I took the man's knotty gangling hand in my own and heard Don Pablo pronounce, "Mr. John Longworth, a scientist from North America who has come to us to study our exemplary skies."

"Mucho gusto en conocerle," he said, and his Spanish was very good indeed, but for the North American twang and his maddening tendency to over-pronounce the consonants till you felt as if he were battering both sides of your head with a wet root. He was dressed in a fashion I can only call bizarre, all cultural differences aside, his hands gloved, his frame draped in an ankle-length London Fog trenchcoat and his disproportionately small head dwarfed by a pair of wraparound sunglasses and a deerstalker cap. His nose, cheeks and hard horny chin were nearly fluorescent with what I later learned was sunblock, applied in layers.

"A pleasure," I assured him, stretching the truth for the sake of politesse, after which he made his introductions to my daughter with a sort of slobbering formality, and we all went in to dinner.

THERE WAS, as I soon discovered, to be one topic of conversation and one topic only throughout the meal—indeed, throughout the entire three days of the *fiesta,* whenever and wherever Mr. John Longworth was able to insinuate himself, and he seemed to have an almost supernatural ability to appear everywhere at once, as ubiquitous as a cockroach. And what was this penetrating and all-devouring topic? The sky. Or rather the hole he perceived in the sky over Magallanes, Tierra del Fuego and the Antarctic, a hole that would admit all the poisons of the universe and ultimately lead to the destruction of man and nature. He talked of algae and krill, of acid rain and carbon dioxide and storms that would sweep the earth with a fury unknown since creation. I took him for an enthusiast at best, but deep down I wondered what asylum he'd escaped from and when they'd be coming to reclaim him.

He began over the soup course, addressing the table at large as if he were standing at a podium and interrupting Don Pablo and me in a reminiscence of a salmon-fishing excursion to the Penitente River undertaken in our youth. "None of you," he said, battering us with those consonants, "especially someone with such fair skin as Paloma here or Señora Antofagasta, should leave the house this time of year without the maximum of protection. We're talking ultraviolet-B, radiation that increases by as much as one thousand percent over Punta Arenas in the spring because of the hole in the ozone layer."

Paloma, a perspicacious girl educated by the nuns in Santiago and on her way to the university in the fall, gave him a deadpan look. "But, Mr. Longworth," she said, her voice as clear as a bell and without a trace of intimidation or awe, "if what you say is true, we'll have to give up our string bikinis."

I couldn't help myself—I laughed aloud and Don Pablo joined me. Tierra del Fuego is hardly the place for sunbathers—or bikinis either. But John Longworth didn't seem to appreciate my daughter's satiric intent, nor was he to be deterred. "If you were to go out there now, right outside this window, for one hour unprotected under the sun, that is, without clothing—or, er, in a bikini, I mean—I can guarantee you that your skin would blister and that those blisters could and would constitute the incipient stages of melanoma, not to mention the damage to your eyes and immune system."

"Such beautiful eyes," Don Pablo observed with his customary gallantry. "And is Paloma to incarcerate them behind dark glasses, and my wife too?"

"If you don't want to see them go blind," he retorted without pausing to draw breath.

The thought, as we say, brought my kettle to a boil: who was this insufferable person with his stabbing nose and deformed head to lecture us? And on what authority? "I'm sorry, señor," I said, "but I've heard some far-fetched pronouncements of doom in my time, and this one takes the cake. Millenarian hysteria is what I say it is. Proof, sir. What proof do you offer?"

I realized immediately that I'd made a serious miscalculation. I could see it in the man's pale leaping eyes, in the way his brow contracted and that ponderous instrument of his nose began to sniff at the air as if he were a bloodhound off after a scent. For the next hour and a half, or until I retreated to my room, begging indigestion, I was carpet-bombed with statistics, chemical analyses, papers, studies, obscure terms and obscurer texts, until all I could think was that the end of the planet would be a relief if only because it would put an end to the incessant, nagging, pontificating, consonant-battering voice of the first-class bore across the table from me.

AT THE TIME, I couldn't foresee what was coming, though if I'd had my wits about me it would have been a different story. Then I could have made plans, could have arranged to be in Paris, Rio or Long Beach, could have been in the hospital, for that matter, having my trick knee repaired after all these years. Anything, even dental work, would have been preferable to what fell out. But before I go any further I should tell you that there are no hotels in the Magallanes region, once you leave the city, and that we have consequently developed among us a strong and enduring tradition of hospitality—no stranger, no matter how personally obnoxious or undeserving, is turned away from the door. This is open range, overflown by caracara and condor and haunted by *ñandú,* guanaco and puma, a waste of dwarf trees and merciless winds where the unfamiliar and the unfortunate collide in the face of the wanderer. This is to say that three weeks to the day from the conclusion of Don Pablo's *fiesta*, Mr. John Longworth arrived at the Estancia Castillo in all his long-nosed splendor, and he arrived to stay.

We were all just sitting down to a supper of mutton chops and new potatoes with a relish of chiles and onions in a white sauce I myself had instructed the cook to prepare, when Slobodan Abarca, my foreman and one of the most respected *huasos* in the province, came to the door with the news that he'd heard a plane approaching from the east and that it sounded like Don Pablo's Cessna. We hurried outside, all of us, even the servants, and scanned the iron slab of the sky. Don Pablo's plane appeared as a speck on the horizon, and I was astonished at the acuity of Slobodan Abarca's hearing, a sense he's developed since his eyes began to go bad on him, and before we knew it the plane was passing over the house and banking for the runway. We watched the little craft fight the winds that threatened to flip it over on its back at every maneuver, and suddenly it was on the ground, leaping and ratcheting over the greening turf. Don Pablo emerged from the cockpit, the lank raw form of John Longworth uncoiling itself behind him.

I was stunned. So stunned I was barely able to croak out a greeting as the wind beat the hair about my ears and the food went cold on the table, but Bob Fernando Jr., who'd apparently struck up a friendship with the North American during the *fiesta*, rushed to welcome him. I embraced Don Pablo and numbly took John Longworth's hand in my own as Isabela looked on with a serene smile and Paloma gave our guest a look that would have frozen my blood had I only suspected its meaning. "Welcome," I said, the words rattling in my throat.

Don Pablo, my old friend, wasn't himself, I could see that at a glance. He had the shamed and defeated look of Señora Whiskers, our black Labrador, when she does her business in the corner behind the stove instead of outside in the infinite grass. I asked him what was wrong, but he didn't answer—or perhaps he didn't hear, what with the wind. A few of the men helped unload Mr. John Longworth's baggage, which was wound so tightly inside the aircraft I was amazed it had been able to get off the ground, and I took Don Pablo by the arm to escort him into the house, but he shook me off. "I can't stay," he said, staring at his shoes.

"Can't stay?"

"Don Bob," he said, and still he wouldn't look me in the eye, "I hate to do this to you, but Teresa's expecting me and I can't—" He glanced up then at John Longworth, towering and skeletal in his huge flapping trenchcoat, and he repeated "I can't" once more, and turned his back on me.

Half an hour later I sat glumly at the head of the table, the departing whine of Don Pablo's engine humming in my ears, the desiccated remains of my reheated chops and reconstituted white sauce laid out like burnt offerings on my plate, while John Longworth addressed himself to the meal before him as if he'd spent the past three weeks lashed to a pole on the *pampas*. He had, I noticed, the rare ability to eat and talk at the same time, as if he were a ventriloquist, and with every bite of lamb and potatoes he tied off the strings of one breathless sentence and unleashed the next. The children were all ears as he and Bob Fernando Jr. spoke mysteriously of the sport of basketball, which my son had come to appreciate during his junior year abroad at the University of Akron, in Ohio, and even Isabela and Paloma leaned imperceptibly toward him as if to catch every precious twist and turn of his speech. This depressed me, not that I felt left out or that I wasn't pleased on their account to have the rare guest among us as a sort of linguistic treat, but I knew that it was only a matter of time before he switched from the esoterica of an obscure and I'm sure tedious game to his one and true subject—after all, what sense was there in discussing a mere sport when the sky itself was corrupted?

I didn't have long to wait. There was a pause just after my son had expressed his exact agreement with something John Longworth had said regarding the "three-point shot," whatever that might be, and John Longworth took advantage of the caesura to abruptly change the subject. "I found an entire population of blind rabbits on Don Pablo's ranch," he said, apropos of nothing and without visibly pausing to chew or swallow.

I shifted uneasily in my chair. Serafina crept noiselessly into the room to clear away the plates and serve dessert, port wine and brandy. I could hear the wind at the panes. Paloma was the first to respond, and at the time I thought she was goading him on, but as I was to discover it was another thing altogether. "Inheritance?" she asked. "Or mutation?"

That was all the encouragement he needed, this windbag, this doomsayer, this howling bore with the pointed nose and coconut head, and the lecture it precipitated was to last through dessert, cocoa and *maté* in front of the fire and the first, second and third strokes of the *niñitos'* bedtime. "Neither," he said, "though if they were to survive blind through countless generations—not very likely, I'm afraid—they might well develop a genetic protection of some sort, just as the sub-Saharan Africans developed an increase of melanin in their skin to combat the sun. But, of course, we've so radically altered these creatures' environment that it's too late for that." He paused over an enormous forkful of cheesecake. "Don Bob," he said, looking me squarely in the eye over the clutter of the table and the dimpled faces of my little ones, "those rabbits were blinded by the sun's radiation, though you refuse to see it, and I could just stroll up to them and pluck them up by the ears, as many as you could count in a day, and they had no more defense than a stone."

The challenge was mine to accept, and though I'd heard rumors of blind salmon in the upper reaches of the rivers and birds blinded and game too, I wasn't about to let him have his way at my own table in my own house. "Yes," I observed drily, "and I suppose you'll be prescribing smoked lenses for all the creatures of the *pampas* now, am I right?"

He made no answer, which surprised me. Had he finally been stumped, bested, caught in his web of intrigue and hyperbole? But no: I'd been too sanguine. Calamities never end—they just go on spinning out disaster from their own imperturbable centers. "Maybe not for the rabbits," he said finally, "but certainly this creature here could do with a pair . . ."

I leaned out from my chair and looked down the length of the table to where Señora Whiskers, that apostate, sat with her head in the madman's lap. "What do you mean?" I demanded.

Paloma was watching, Isabela too; Bob Fernando Jr. and the little ones sat rigid in their chairs. "Call her to you," he said.

I called. And the dog, reluctant at first, came down the length of the table to her master. "Yes?" I said.

"Do you see the way she walks, head down, sniffing her way? Haven't you noticed her butting into the furniture, scraping the doorframes? Look into her eyes, Don Bob: she's going blind."

THE NEXT MORNING I awoke to a sound I'd never before heard, a ceaseless rapid thumping, as of a huge penitential heart caught up in the rhythm of its sorrows. Isabela awoke beside me and I peered through the blinds into the courtyard that was still heavy with shadow under a rare crystalline sky. Figures moved there in the courtyard as if in a dream—my children, all of them, even Paloma—and they fought over the swollen globe of a thumping orange ball and flung it high against an orange hoop shrouded in mesh. They were shouting, crying out in a kind of naked joy that approached the ecstatic, and the trenchcoat and the nose and the shrunken bulb of the bobbing head presided over all: *basketball.*

Was I disturbed? Yes. Happy for them, happy for their fluid grace and their joy, but struck deep in my bowels with the insidiousness of it: first basketball and then the scripture of doom. Indeed, they were already dressed like the man's disciples, in hats with earmuffs and the swirling greatcoats we'd long since put away for winter, and the exposed flesh of their hands and faces glistened with his sunblock. Worse: their eyes were visored behind pairs of identical black sunglasses, Mr. John Longworth's gift to them, along with the gift of hopelessness and terror. The sky was falling, and now they knew it too.

I stood there dumbfounded at the window. I didn't have the heart to break up their game or to forbid the practice of it—that would have played into his hands, that would have made me the voice of sanity and restraint (and clearly, with this basketball, sanity and restraint were about as welcome as an explosion at *siesta* time). Nor could I, as *dueño* of one of the most venerable *estancias* in the country, attempt to interdict my guest from speaking of certain worrisome and fantastical subjects, no matter how distasteful I found them personally. But what could I do? He was clearly deluded, if not downright dangerous, but he had the ready weight of his texts and studies to counterbalance any arguments I might make.

The dog wasn't blind, any fool could see that. Perhaps her eyes were a bit cloudy, but that was to be expected in a dog of her age, and what if she was losing her sight, what did that prove? I'd had any number of dogs go blind, deaf, lame and senile over the years. That was the way of dogs, and of men too. It was sad, it was regrettable, but it was part of the grand design and there was no sense in running round the barnyard crowing your head off about it. I decided in that moment to go away for a few days, to let the basketball and the novelty of Mr. John Longworth dissipate like the atmospheric gases of which he spoke so endlessly.

"Isabela," I said, still standing at the window, still recoiling from that subversive thump, thump, thump, "I'm thinking of going out to the upper range for a few days to look into the health of Manuel Banquedano's flock—pack up my things for me, will you?"

THIS WAS LAMBING SEASON, and most of the *huasos* were in the fields with the flocks to discourage eagle and puma alike. It is a time that never fails to move me, to strengthen my ties to the earth and its rejuvenant cycles, as it must have strengthened those ties for my father and his father before him. There were the lambs, appeared from nowhere on tottering legs, suckling and frolicking in the waste, and they were money in my pocket and the pockets of my children, they were provender and clothing, riches on the hoof. I camped with the men, roasted a haunch of lamb over the open fire, passed a bottle of *aguardiente*. But this time was different, this time I found myself studying the pattern of moles, pimples, warts and freckles spread across Manuel Banquedano's face and thinking the worst, this time I gazed out over the craggy *cerros* and open plains and saw the gaunt flapping figure of Mr. John Longworth like some apparition out of Apocalypse. I lasted four days only, and then, like Christ trudging up the hill to the place of skulls, I came back home to my fate.

Our guest had been busy in my absence. I'd asked Slobodan Abarca to keep an eye on him, and the first thing I did after greeting Isabela and the children was to amble out to the bunkhouse and have a private conference with the old *huaso.* The day was gloomy and cold, the wind in an uproar over something. I stepped in the door of the long low-frame building, the very floorboards of which gave off a complicated essence of tobacco, sweat and boot leather, and found it deserted but for the figure of Slobodan Abarca, bent over a chessboard by the window in the rear. I recognized the familiar sun-bleached *poncho* and *manta,* the spade-like wedge of the back of his head with its patches of parti-colored hair and oversized ears, and then he turned to me and I saw with a shock that he was wearing dark glasses. Inside. Over a chessboard. I was speechless.

"Don Bob," Slobodan Abarca said then in his creaking, unoiled tones, "I want to go back out on the range with the others and I don't care how old and feeble you think I am, anything is better than this. One more day with that devil from hell and I swear I slit my throat."

It seemed that when John Longworth wasn't out "taking measurements" or inspecting the teeth, eyes, pelt and tongue of every creature he could trap, coerce or pin down, he was lecturing the ranch hands, the smith and the household help on the grisly fate that awaited them. They were doomed, he told them—all of mankind was doomed and the drop of that doom was imminent—and if they valued the little time left to them they would pack up and move north, north to Puerto Montt or Concepción, anywhere away from the poisonous hole in the sky. And those spots on their hands, their throats, between their shoulderblades and caught fast in the cleavage of their breasts, those spots were cancerous or at the very least pre-cancerous. They needed a doctor, a dermatologist, an oncologist. They needed to stay out of the sun. They needed laser surgery. Sunblock. Dark glasses. (The latter he provided, out of a seemingly endless supply, and the credulous fools, believers in the voodoo of science, dutifully clamped them to their faces.) The kitchen staff was threatening a strike and Crispín Mansilla, who looks after the automobiles, had been so terrified of an open sore on his nose that he'd taken his bicycle and set out on the road for Punta Arenas two days previous and no one had heard from him since.

But worse, far worse. Slobodan Abarca confided something to me that made the blood boil in my veins, made me think of the braided bullhide whip hanging over the fireplace and the pearl-handled dueling pistols my grandfather had once used to settle a dispute over waterfowl rights on the south shore of Lake Castillo: Mr. John Longworth had been paying his special attentions to my daughter. Whisperings were overheard, tête-à-têtes observed, banter and tomfoolery taken note of. They were discovered walking along the lakeshore with their shoulders touching and perhaps even their hands intertwined (Slobodan Abarca couldn't be sure, what with his failing eyes), they sought each other out at meals, solemnly bounced the basketball in the courtyard and then passed it between them as if it were some rare prize. He was thirty if he was a day, this usurper, this snout, this Mr. John Longworth, and my Paloma was just out of the care of the nuns, an infant still and with her whole life ahead of her. I was incensed. Killing off the natural world was one thing, terrifying honest people, gibbering like a lunatic day and night till the whole *estancia* was in revolt, but insinuating himself in my daughter's affections—well, this was, quite simply, the end.

I stalked up the hill and across the yard, blind to everything, such a storm raging inside me I thought I would explode. The wind howled. It shrieked blood and vengeance and flung black grains of dirt in my face, grains of the unforgiving *pampas* on which I was nurtured and hardened, and I ground them between my teeth. I raged through the house and the servants quailed and the children cried, but Mr. John Longworth was nowhere to be found. Pausing only to snatch up one of my grandfather's pistols from its velvet cradle in the great hall, I flung myself out the back door and searched the stables, the smokehouse, the generator room. And then, rounding the corner by the hogpen, I detected a movement out of the corner of my eye, and there he was.

Ungainly as a carrion bird, the coat ends tenting round him in the wind, he was bent over one of the hogs, peering into the cramped universe of its malicious little eyes as if he could see all the evil of the world at work there. I confronted him with a shout and he looked up from beneath the brim of his hat and the fastness of his wraparound glasses, but he didn't flinch, even as I closed the ground be-

tween us with the pistol held out before me like a homing device. "I
hate to be the bringer of bad news all the time," he called out, already
lecturing as I approached, "but this pig is in need of veterinary care.
It's not just the eyes, I'm afraid, but the skin too—you see here?"

I'd stopped ten paces from him, the pistol trained on the nugget
of his head. The pig looked up at me hopefully. Its companions
grunted, rolled in the dust, united their backsides against the wind.

"Melanoma," he said sadly, shaking his visored head. "Most of
the others have got it too."

"We're going for a ride," I said.

His jaw dropped beneath the screen of the glasses and I could see
the intricate work of his front teeth. He tried for a smile. "A ride?"

"Your time is up here, *señor*," I said, and the wind peeled back the
sleeve of my jacket against the naked thrust of the gun. "I'm deliver-
ing you to Estancia Braun. Now. Without your things, without even
so much as a bag, and without any goodbyes either. You'll have to
live without your basketball hoop and sunblock for a few days, I'm
afraid—at least until I have your baggage delivered. Now get to your
feet—the plane is fueled and ready."

He gathered himself up then and rose from the ground, the wind
beating at his garments and lifting the hair round his glistening ears.
"It'll do no good to deny it, Don Bob," he said, talking over his
shoulder as he moved off toward the shed where the Super Cub stood
out of the wind. "It's criminal to keep animals out in the open in
conditions like these, it's irresponsible, mad—think of your children, your wife. The land is no good anymore—it's dead, or it will
be. And it's we who've killed it, the so-called civilized nations, with
our air conditioners and underarm deodorant. It'll be decades before
the CFCs are eliminated from the atmosphere, if ever, and by then
there will be nothing left here but blind rabbits and birds that fly
into the sides of rotting buildings. It's over, Don Bob—your life here
is finished."

I didn't believe a word of it—naysaying and bitterness, that's all it
was. I wanted to shoot him right then and there, on the spot, and
have done with it—how could I in good conscience deliver him to
Don Benedicto Braun, or to anyone, for that matter? He was the

poison, he was the plague, he was the ecological disaster. We walked grimly into the wind and he never stopped talking. Snatches of the litany came back to me—ultraviolet, ozone, a hole in the sky bigger than the United States—but I only snarled out directions in reply: "To the left, over there, take hold of the doors and push them inward."

In the end, he didn't fight me. He folded up his limbs and squeezed into the passenger seat and I set aside the pistol and started up the engine. The familiar throb and roar calmed me somewhat, and it had the added virtue of rendering Mr. John Longworth's jeremiad inaudible. The wind assailed us as we taxied out to the grassy runway—I shouldn't have been flying that afternoon at all, but as you can no doubt appreciate, I was a desperate man. After a rocky take-off we climbed into a sky that opened above us in all its infinite glory but which must have seemed woefully sad and depleted to my passenger's degraded eyes. We coasted high over the wind-whipped trees, the naked rock, the flocks whitening the pastures like distant snow, and he never shut up, not for a second. I tuned him out, let my mind go blank, and watched the horizon for the first weathered outbuildings of Estancia Braun.

They say that courtesy is merely the veneer of civilization, the first thing sacrificed in a crisis, and I don't doubt the truth of it. I wonder what became of my manners on that punishing wind-torn afternoon—you would have thought I'd been raised among the Indians, so eager was I to dump my unholy cargo and flee. Like Don Pablo, I didn't linger, and I could read the surprise and disappointment and perhaps even hurt in Don Benedicto's face when I pressed his hand and climbed back into the plane. "Weather!" I shouted, and pointed to the sky, where a wall of cloud was already sealing us in. I looked back as he receded on the ground beneath me, the inhuman form of Mr. John Longworth at his side, long arms gesticulating, the lecture already begun. It wasn't until I reached the verges of my own property, Estancia Castillo stretched out beneath me like a worn carpet and the dead black clouds moving in to strangle the sky, that I had my moment of doubt. What if he was right? I thought. What if Manuel Banquedano truly was riddled with cancer, what if the dog had been blinded by the light, what if my children were at risk? What then?

The limitless turf unraveled beneath me and I reached up a hand to rub at my eyes, weary suddenly, a man wearing the crown of defeat. A hellish vision came to me then, a vision of 9,000 sheep bleating on the range, their fleece stained and blackened, and every one of them, every one of those inestimable and beloved animals, my inheritance, my life, imprisoned behind a glistening new pair of wraparound sunglasses. So powerful was the vision I could almost hear them baa-ing out their distress. My heart seized. Tears started up in my eyes. Why go on? I was thinking. What hope is there?

But then the sun broke through the gloom in two pillars of fire, the visible world come to life with a suddenness that took away my breath, color bursting out everywhere, the range green all the way to the horizon, trees nodding in the wind, the very rock faces of the *cerros* set aflame, and the vision was gone. I listened to the drone of the engine, tipped the wings toward home, and never gave it another thought.

Tooth and Claw

THE WEATHER had absolutely nothing to do with it—though the rain had been falling off and on throughout the day and the way the gutters were dripping made me feel as if despair was the mildest term in the dictionary—because I would have gone down to Daggett's that afternoon even if the sun was shining and all the fronds of the palm trees were gilded with light. The problem was work. Or, more specifically, the lack of it. The boss had called at six-thirty A.M. to tell me not to come in, because the guy I'd been replacing had recovered sufficiently from his wrenched back to feel up to working, and no, he wasn't firing me, because they'd be onto a new job next week and he could use all the hands he could get. "So take a couple days off and enjoy yourself," he'd rumbled into the phone in his low hoarse uneven voice that always seemed on the verge of morphing into something else altogether—squawks and bleats or maybe just static. "You're young, right? Go out and get yourself some tail. Get drunk. Go to the library. Help old ladies across the street. You know what I mean?"

It had been a long day: breakfast out of a cardboard box while cartoon images flickered and faded and reconstituted themselves on the TV screen, and then some desultory reading, starting with the newspaper and a couple of *National Geographic*s I'd picked up at a yard sale, lunch at the deli where I had ham and cheese in a tortilla wrap and exchanged exactly eleven words with the girl behind the counter (*Number 7, please, no mayo; Have a nice day; You too*), and a walk to the beach that left my sneakers sodden. And after all that it was only three o'clock in the afternoon and I had to force myself to stay away from the bar till five, five at least.

I wasn't stupid. And I had no intention of becoming a drunk like all the hard-assed old men in the shopping mall–blighted town I grew up in, silent men with hate in their eyes and complaint eating away at their insides—like my own dead father, for that matter—but I was new here, or relatively new (nine weeks now and counting) and Daggett's was the only place where I felt comfortable. And why? Precisely because it was filled with old men drinking themselves into oblivion. It made me think of home. Or feel at home, anyway.

The irony wasn't lost on me. The whole reason I'd moved out to the Coast to live, first with my Aunt Kim and her husband, Waverley, and then in my own one-bedroom apartment with kitchenette and a three-by-six-foot balcony with a partially obscured view of the Pacific, half a mile off, was so that I could inject a little excitement into my life and mingle with all the college students in the bars that lined State Street cheek to jowl, but here I was hanging out in an old man's bar that smelled of death and vomit and felt as closed-in as a submarine, when just outside the door were all the exotic sun-struck glories of California. Where it never rained. Except in winter. And it was winter now.

I nodded self-consciously at the six or seven regulars lined up at the bar, then ordered a Jack-and-Coke, the only drink besides beer I liked the taste of, and I didn't really like the taste of beer. There were sports on the three TVs hanging from the ceiling—this was a sports bar—but the volume was down and the speakers were blaring the same tired hits of the sixties I could have heard back home. Ad nauseam. When the bartender—*he* was young at least, as were the waitresses, thankfully—set down my drink, I made a comment about the weather, "Nice day for sunbathing, isn't it?" and the two regulars nearest me glanced up with something like interest in their eyes. "Or maybe bird-watching," I added, feeling encouraged, and they swung their heads back to the familiar triangulation of their splayed elbows and cocktail glasses and that was the end of that.

It must have been seven or so, the rain still coming down and people briefly enlivened by the novelty of it as they came and went in spasms of umbrella furling and unfurling, when a guy about my own age—or no, he must have been thirty, or close to it—came in and took the seat beside me. He was wearing a baseball cap, a jeans jacket and a T-shirt that said *Obligatory Death,* which I took to be the name of a band, though I'd never heard of them. His hair was blond, cut short around the ears, and he wore a soul beard that was like a pale stripe painted under his lip by a very unsteady hand. We exchanged the standard greeting—*What's up?*—and then he flagged down the bartender and ordered a draft beer, a shot of tomato juice and two raw eggs.

"Raw eggs?" the bartender echoed, as if he hadn't heard him right.

"Yeah. Two raw eggs, in the shell."

The bartender—his name was Chris, or maybe it was Matt—gave a smile and scratched the back of his head. "We can do them over-easy or sunny-side up or poached even, but *raw,* I don't know. I mean, nobody's ever requested raw before—"

"Ask the chef, why don't you?"

The bartender shrugged. "Sure," he said, "no problem." He started off in the direction of the kitchen, then pulled up short. "You want toast with that, home fries, or what?"

"Just the eggs."

Everybody was watching now, any little drama worth the price of admission, especially on a night like this, but the bartender—Chris, his name was definitely Chris—just went down to the other end of the bar and communicated the order to the waitress, who made a notation in her pad and disappeared into the kitchen. A moment went by, and then the man turned to me and said in a voice loud enough for everybody to hear, "Jesus, this music sucks. Are we caught in a time warp here, or what?"

The old men—the regulars—glanced up from their drinks and gave him a look, but they were gray-haired and slack in the belly and they knew their limits. One of them said something about the game on the TV and one of the others chimed in and the conversation started back up in an exclusionary way.

"Yeah," I heard myself say, "it really sucks," and before I knew it

I was talking passionately about the bands that meant the most to me even as the new guy poured tomato juice in his beer and sipped the foam off the top, while the music rumbled defiantly on and people came in the door with wet shoes and dripping umbrellas to crowd in behind us. The eggs, brown-shelled and naked in the middle of a standard dinner plate, were delivered by Daria, a waitress I'd had my eye on, though I hadn't yet worked up the nerve to say more than hello and goodbye to her. "Your order, sir," she said, easing the plate down on the bar. "You need anything with that? Ketchup? Tabasco?"

"No," he said, "no, that's fine," and everyone was waiting for him to crack the eggs over his beer, but he didn't even look at them. He was looking at Daria, holding her with his eyes. "So what's your name?" he asked, grinning.

She told him, and she was grinning too.

"Nice to meet you," he said, taking her hand. "I'm Ludwig."

"Ludwig," she repeated, pronouncing it with a hard *v*, as he had, though as far as I could tell—from his clothes and accent, which was pure Southern California—he wasn't German. Or if he was, he sure had his English down.

"Are you German?" Daria was flirting with him, and the realization of it began to harden me against him in the most rudimentary way.

"No," he said, "I'm from Hermosa Beach, born and raised. It's the name, right?"

"I had this German teacher last year? His name was Ludwig, that's all."

"You're in college?"

She told him she was, which was news to me. Working her way through. Majoring in business. She wanted to own her own restaurant someday.

"It was my mother's idea," he said, as if he'd been mulling it over. "She was listening to the 'Eroica' Symphony the night I was born." He shrugged. "It's been my curse ever since."

"I don't know," she said, "I think it's kind of cute. You don't get many Ludwigs, you know?"

"Yeah, tell me about it," he said, sipping at his beer.

She lingered, though there were other things she could have been

doing. The sound of the rain intensified so that for a moment it overcame the drone of the speakers. "So what about the eggs," she said,
"you going to need utensils, or—"

"Or what? Am I going to suck them out of the shell?"

"Yeah," she said, "something like that."

He reached out a hand cluttered with silver to embrace the eggs
and gently roll them back and forth across the gleaming expanse of
the plate. "No, I'm just going to fondle them," he said, and he got
the expected response: she laughed. "But does anybody still play dice
around here?" he called down the bar as the eyes of the regulars slid
in our direction and then away again.

In those days—and this was ten years ago or more—the game of
Horse was popular in certain California bars, as were smoking, unprotected sex and various other adult pleasures that may or may not
have been hazardous to your health. There were five dice, shaken in
a cup, and you slammed that cup down on the bar, trying for the
highest cumulative score, which was thirty. Anything could be bet
on, from the next round of drinks to ponying up for the jukebox.

The rain hissed at the door and it opened briefly to admit a
stamping, umbrella-less couple. Ludwig's question hung unanswered
on the air. "No? How about you, Daria?"

"I'm working, actually."

He turned to me. I had no work in the morning or the next
morning either—maybe no work at all. My apartment wasn't what
I'd thought it would be, not without anybody to share it with, and
I'd already vowed to myself that I'd rather sleep on the streets than go
back to my aunt's because going back there would represent the
worst kind of defeat. *Take good care of my baby, Kim,* my mother had
said when she'd dropped me off. *He's the only one I've got.*

"Sure," I said, "I guess. What're we playing for—for drinks,
right?" I began fumbling in my pockets, awkward, shoulders dipping—
I was drunk, I could feel it. "Because I don't have, well, maybe ten
bucks—"

"No," he said, "no," already rising from his seat, "you just wait
here, just one minute, you'll see," and then he was out the door and
into the grip of the rain.

Daria hadn't moved. She was dressed in the standard outfit for Daggett's employees, shorts, white ankle socks and a T-shirt with the name of the establishment blazoned across the chest, her legs pale and silken in the flickering light of the fake fireplace in the corner. She gave me a sympathetic look and I shrugged to show her I was ready for anything, a real man of the world.

There was a noise at the door—a scraping and shifting—and we all looked up to see Ludwig struggling with something against the backdrop of the rain. His hat had been knocked askew and water dripped from his nose and chin. It took a moment, one shoulder pinning the door open, and then he lifted a cage—a substantial cage, two and a half feet high and maybe four long—through the doorway and set it down against the wall. No one moved. No one said a word. There was something in the cage, the apprehension of it as sharp and sudden as the smell it brought with it, something wild and alien and very definitely out of the ordinary on what to this point had been a painfully ordinary night.

Ludwig wiped the moisture from his face with a swipe of his sleeve, straightened out his hat and came back to the bar, looking jaunty and refreshed. "All right," he said, "don't be shy—go have a look. It won't bite. Or it will, it definitely will, but just don't get your fingers near it, that's all—"

I saw coiled limbs, claws, yellow eyes. Whatever it was, the thing hadn't moved, not even to blink. I was going to ask what it was, when Daria, still at my side, said, "It's a cat, some kind of wild cat. Right? A what—a lynx or something?"

"You can't have that thing in here," one of the regulars said, but already he was getting up out of his seat to have a look at it—everyone was getting up now, shoving back chairs and rising from the tables, crowding around.

"It's a serval," Ludwig was saying. "From Africa. Thirty-five pounds of muscle and quicker than a snake."

And where had he gotten it? He'd won it, in a bar in Arizona, on a roll of the dice.

How long had he had it? Two years.

What was its name? Cat. Just Cat. And yes, it was a male, and no, he didn't want to get rid of it but he was moving overseas on a new job and there was just no way he could take it with him, so he felt it was apropos—that was the word he used, *apropos*—to give it up in the way he'd gotten it.

He turned to me. "What was your name again?"

"Junior," I said. "James Jr. Turner, I mean. James Turner Jr. But everybody calls me Junior." I wanted to add, "Because of my father, so people wouldn't confuse us," but I left it at that, because it got even more complicated considering that my father was six months dead and I could be anybody I wanted.

"Okay, Junior, here's the deal," Ludwig said. "Your ten bucks against the cat, one roll, what do you say?"

I wanted to say that I had no place for the thing, that I didn't want a cat of any kind or even a guinea pig or a fish in a bowl and that the ten dollars was meaningless, but everyone was watching me and I couldn't back out without feeling the shame rise to my face— and there was Daria to consider, because she was watching me too. "Yeah," I said. "Yeah, okay, sure."

Sixty seconds later I was still solvent and richer by one cat and one cage. I'd gotten lucky—or unlucky, depending on how you want to look at it—and rolled three fives and two fours; Ludwig rolled a combined eleven. He finished his beer in a gulp, took my hand to seal the deal and offer his congratulations, and then started toward the door. "But what do I feed it?" I called. "I mean, what does it eat?"

"Eggs," he said, "it loves eggs. And meat. Raw. No kibble, forget kibble. This is the real deal, this animal, and you need to treat it right." He was at the door, looking down at the thing with what might have been wistfulness or satisfaction, I couldn't tell which, then he reached down behind the cage to unfasten something there—a gleam of black leather—and toss it to me: it was a glove, or a gauntlet actually, as long as my arm. "You'll want to wear this when you feed him," he said, and then he was gone.

FOR A LONG MOMENT I stared at the door, trying to work out what had happened, and then I looked at the regulars—the expressions on their faces—and at the other customers, locals or maybe even tourists who'd come in for a beer or burger or the catch of the day and had all this strangeness thrust on them, and finally at the cage. Daria was bent beside it, cooing to the animal inside, Ludwig's eggs cradled in one hand. She was short and compact, conventionally pretty, with the round eyes and symmetrical features of an anime heroine, her running shoes no bigger than a child's, her blond hair pulled back in a ponytail, and I'd noticed all that before, over the course of weeks of study, but now it came back to me with the force of revelation. She was beautiful, a beautiful girl propped on one knee while her shorts rode up in back and the T-shirt bunched beneath her breasts, offering this cat—my cat—the smallest comfort, as if it were a kitten she'd found abandoned on the street.

"Jesus, what are you going to do with the thing?" Chris had come out from behind the bar and he was standing beside me now, looking awed.

I told him I didn't know. That I hadn't planned on owning a wild cat, hadn't even known they existed—servals, that is—until five minutes ago.

"You live around here?"

"Bayview Apartments."

"They accept pets?"

I'd never really given it much thought, but they did, they must have—the guy next door to me had a pair of yapping little dogs with bows in their hair and the woman down the hall had a Doberman that was forever scrabbling its nails on the linoleum when she came in and out with it, which she seemed to do about a hundred times a day. But this was something different. This was something that might push at the parameters of the standard lease. "Yeah," I said, "I think so."

There was a single slot where the door of the cage fastened that was big enough to receive an egg without crushing its shell, and Daria, still cooing, rolled first one egg, then the other, through the aperture. For a moment, nothing happened. Then the cat, hunched against the mesh, shifted position ever so slightly and took the first egg in its mouth—two teeth like hypodermics, a crunch, and then the soft frictive scrape of its tongue.

Daria rose and came to me with a look of wonder. "Don't do a thing till I get off, okay?" she said, and in her fervor she took hold of my arm. "I get off at nine, so you wait, okay?"

"Yeah," I said. "Sure."

"We can put him in the back of the storage room for now, and then, well, I guess we can use my pickup—"

I didn't have the leisure to reflect on how complex things had become all of a sudden, and even if I had I don't think I would have behaved any differently. I just nodded at her, stared into her plenary eyes and nodded.

"He's going to be all right," she said, and added, "He will," as if I'd been disagreeing with her. "I've got to get back to work, but you wait, okay? You wait right here." Chris was watching. The manager was watching. The regulars had all craned their necks and half the dinner customers too. Daria patted down her apron, smoothed back her hair. "What did you say your name was again?"

So I HAD A CAT. And a girl. We put the thing in the back of her red Toyota pickup, threw a tarp over it to keep the rain off, and drove to Von's, where I watched Daria march up and down the aisles seeking out kitty litter and the biggest cat pan they had (we settled for a dishpan, hard blue plastic that looked all but indestructible), and then it was on to the meat counter. "I've only got ten bucks," I said.

She gave me a withering look. "This animal's got to eat," she informed me, and she reached back to slip the band from her ponytail so that her hair fell glistening across her shoulders, a storm of hair, fluid and loose, the ends trailing down her back like liquid in motion. She tossed her head impatiently. "You do have a credit card, don't you?"

Ten minutes later I was directing her back to my building, where I had her park next to the Mustang I'd inherited when my father died, and then we went up the outside stairs and along the walkway to my apartment on the second floor. "I'm sorry," I said, swinging open the door and hitting the light switch, "but I'm afraid I'm not much of a housekeeper." I was going to add that I hadn't expected company either, or I would have straightened up, but Daria just strode right in, cleared a spot on the counter and set down the groceries. I watched her shoulders as she reached into the depths of one bag after another and extracted the forty-odd dollars' worth of chicken parts and ribeye steak (marked down for quick sale) we'd selected in the meat department.

"Okay," she said, turning to me as soon as she'd made space in the refrigerator for it all, "now where are we going to put the cat, because I don't think we should leave it out there in the truck any longer than we have to, do you? Cats don't like the rain, I know that—I have two of them. Or one's a kitten really." She was on the other side of the kitchen counter, a clutter of crusted dishes and glasses sprouting various colonies of mold separating us. "You have a bedroom, right?"

I did. But if I was embarrassed by the state of the kitchen and living room—this was my first venture at living alone, and the need for order hadn't really seemed paramount to me—then the thought of the bedroom, with its funk of dirty clothes and unwashed sheets, the reeking workboots and the duffel bag out of which I'd been living, gave me pause. Here was this beautiful apparition in my kitchen, the only person besides my aunt who'd ever stepped through the door of my apartment, and now she was about to discover the sad lonely disorder at the heart of my life. "Yeah," I said, "that door there, to the left of the bathroom," but she was already in the room, pushing things aside, a frown of concentration pressed between her eyes.

"You're going to have to clear this out," she said. "The bed, everything. All your clothes."

I was standing in the doorway, watching her. "What do you mean 'clear it out'?"

She lifted her face. "You don't think that animal can stay caged up like that, do you? There's hardly room for it to turn around. And that's just cruel." She drilled me with that look again, then put her hands on her hips. "I'll help you," she said. "It shouldn't take ten minutes—"

Then it was up the stairs with the cat, the two of us fighting the awkwardness of the cage. We kept the tarp knotted tightly in place, both to keep the rain off the cat and disguise it from any of my neighbors who might happen by, and though we shifted the angle of the thing coming up the stairs, the animal didn't make a sound. We had a little trouble getting the cage through the doorway—the cat seemed to concentrate its weight as if in silent protest—but we managed, and then we maneuvered it into the bedroom and set it down in the middle of the rug. Daria had already arranged the litter box in the corner, atop several sheets of newspaper, and she'd taken my biggest stewpot, filled it with water and placed it just inside the door, where I could get to it easily. "Okay," she said, glancing up at me with a satisfied look, "it's time for the unveiling," and she bent to unfasten the tarp.

The overhead light glared, the tarp slid from the cage and puddled on the floor, and there was the cat, pressed to the mesh in a compression of limbs, the yellow eyes seizing on us. "Nice kitty," Daria cooed. "Does he want out of that awful cage? Hmm? Does he? And meat—does he want meat?"

So far, I'd gone along with everything in a kind of daze, but this was problematic. Who knew what the thing would do, what its habits were, its needs? "How are we going to—?" I began, and left the rest unspoken. The overhead light glared down on me and the alcohol whispered in my blood. "You remember what that guy said about feeding him, right?" In the back of my head, there was the smallest glimmer of a further complication: once he was out of the cage, how would we—how would I—ever get him back into it?

For the first time, Daria looked doubtful. "We'll have to be quick," she said.

And so we were. Daria stood at the bedroom door, ready to slam it shut, while I leaned forward, my heart pounding, and slipped the release bolt on the cage. I was nimble in those days—twenty-three years old and with excellent reflexes despite the four or five Jack-and-Cokes I'd downed through the course of the evening—and I sprang for the door the instant the bolt was released. Exhilaration burned in me. And it burned in the cat too, because at the first click of the bolt it came to life as if it had been hot-wired. A screech tore through the room, the cage flew open and the thing was an airborne blur slamming against the cheap plywood panel of the bedroom door, even as Daria and I fought to force it shut.

IN THE MORNING (she'd slept on the couch, curled up in the fetal position, faintly snoring; I was stretched out on the mattress we'd removed from the bedroom and tucked against the wall under the TV) I was faced with a number of problems. I'd awakened before her, jolted out of a dreamless sleep by a flash of awareness, and for a long while I just lay there watching her. I could have gone on watching her all morning, thrilled by her presence, her hair, the repose of her face, if it weren't for the cat. It hadn't made a sound, and it didn't stink, not yet, but its existence was communicated to me nonetheless—it was there, and I could feel it. I would have to feed it, and after the previous night's episode, that was going to require some thought and preparation, and I would have to offer Daria something too, if only to hold her here a little longer. Eggs, I could scramble some eggs, but there was no bread for toast, no milk, no sugar for the coffee. And she would want to freshen up in the bathroom—women always freshened up in the morning, I was pretty sure of that. I thought of the neatly folded little matching towels in the guest bathroom at my aunt's and contrasted that image with the corrugated rag wadded up on the floor somewhere in my own bathroom. Maybe I should go out for muffins or bagels or something, I thought—and a new towel. But did they sell towels at the 7-Eleven? I didn't have a clue.

We'd stayed up late, sharing the last of the hot cocoa out of the foil packet and talking in a specific way about the cat that had brought us to that moment on my greasy couch in my semi-darkened living room and then more generally about our own lives and thoughts and hopes and ambitions. I'd heard about her mother, her two sisters, the courses she was taking at the university. Heard about Daggett's, the regulars, the tips—or lack of them. And her restaurant fantasy. It was amazingly detailed, right down to the number of tables she was planning on, the dinnerware, the cutlery and the paintings on the walls, as well as the decor and the clientele—"Late twenties, early thirties, career people, no kids"—and a dozen or more of the dishes she would specialize in. My ambitions were more modest. I told her how I'd finished community college without any particular aim or interest, and how I was working setting tile for a friend of my aunt and uncle; beyond that, I was hoping to maybe travel up the coast and see Oregon. I'd heard a lot about Oregon, I told her. Very clean. Very natural up there. Had she ever been to Oregon? No, but she'd like to go. I remembered telling her that she ought to open her restaurant up there, someplace by the water, where people could look out and take in the view. "Yeah," she said, "yeah, that would be cool," and then she'd yawned and dropped her head to the pillow.

I was just getting up to go to the bathroom and to see what I could do about the towel in there, thinking vaguely of splashing some aftershave on it to fight down any offensive odors it might have picked up, when her eyes flashed open. She didn't say my name or wonder where she was or ask for breakfast or where the bathroom was. She just said, "We have to feed that cat."

"Don't you want coffee or anything—breakfast? I can make breakfast."

She threw back the blanket and I saw that her legs were bare—she was wearing the Daggett's T-shirt over a pair of shiny black panties; her running shoes, socks and shorts were balled up on the rug beneath her. "Sure," she said, "coffee sounds nice," and she pushed her fingers through her hair on both sides of her head and then let it all fall forward to obscure her face. She sat there a moment before leaning forward to dig a hair clip out of her purse, arch her back and pull the hair tight in a ponytail. "But I am worried about the cat, in new surroundings and all. The poor thing—we should have fed him last night."

Perhaps so. And certainly I didn't want to contradict her—I wanted to be amicable and charming, wanted to ingratiate myself in any way I could—but we'd both been so terrified of the animal's power in that moment when we'd released it from the cage that neither of us had felt up to the challenge of attempting to feed it. Attempting to feed it would mean opening that door again and that was going to take some thought and commitment. "Yeah," I said. "We should have. And we will, we will, but coffee, coffee first—you want a cup? I can make you a cup?"

So we drank coffee and ate the strawberry Pop-Tarts I found in the cupboard above the sink and made small talk as if we'd awakened together a hundred mornings running and it was so tranquil and so domestic and so right I never wanted it to end. We were talking about work and about what time she had to be in that afternoon, when her brow furrowed and her eyes sharpened and she said, "I wish I could see it. When we feed it, I mean. Couldn't you like cut a peephole in the door or something?"

I was glad for the distraction, damage deposit notwithstanding. And the idea appealed to me: now we could see what the thing—my pet—was up to, and if we could see it, then it wouldn't seem so unapproachable and mysterious. I'd have to get to know it eventually, have to name it and tame it, maybe even walk it on a leash. I had a brief vision of myself sauntering down the sidewalk, this id with claws at my side, turning heads and cowing the weight lifters with their Dobermans and Rottweilers, and then I fished my power drill out from under the sink and cut a neat hole, half an inch in diameter, in the bedroom door. As soon as it was finished, Daria put her eye to it.

"Well?"

"The poor thing. He's pacing back and forth like an animal in a zoo."

She moved to the side and took my arm as I pressed my eye to the hole. The cat flowed like molten ore from one corner of the room to the other, its yellow eyes fixed on the door, the dun, faintly spotted skin stretched like spandex over its seething muscles. I saw that the kitty litter had been upended and the hard blue plastic pan reduced to chewed-over pellets, and wondered about that, about where the thing would do its business if not in the pan. "It turned over the kitty pan," I said.

She was still holding to my arm. "I know."

"It chewed it to shreds."

"Metal. We'll have to get a metal one, like a trough or something."

I took my eye from the peephole and turned to her. "But how am I going to change it—don't you have to change it?"

Her eyes were shining. "Oh, it'll settle down. It's just a big kitty, that's all"—and then for the cat, in a syrupy coo—"Isn't that right, kittums?" Next, she went to the refrigerator and extracted one of the steaks, a good pound and a half of meat. "Put on the glove," she said, "and I'll hold on to the doorknob while you feed him."

"What about the blood—won't the blood get on the carpet?" The gauntlet smelled of saddle soap and it was gouged and pitted down the length of it; it fit me as if it had been custom-made.

"I'll press the blood out with a paper towel—here, look," she said, dabbing at the meat in the bottom of the sink and then lifting it on the end of a fork. I took the fork from her and together we went to the bedroom door.

I don't know if the cat scented the blood or whether it heard us at the door, but the instant I turned the knob it was there. I counted three, then jerked the door back just enough to get my arm and the dangle of meat into the room even as the cat exploded against the doorframe and the meat vanished. We pulled the door to—Daria's face was flushed and she seemed to be giggling or gasping for air—and then we took turns watching the thing drag the steak back and forth across the rug as if it still needed killing. By the time it was done, there was blood everywhere, even on the ceiling.

AFTER DARIA LEFT for work I didn't know what to do with myself. The cat was ominously silent and when I pressed my eye to the peephole I saw that it had dragged its cage into the far corner and was slumped behind it, apparently asleep. I flicked on the TV and sat through the usual idiocy, which was briefly enlivened by a nature show on the Serengeti that gave a cursory glimpse of a cat like mine—*The serval lives in rocky kopjes where it keeps a wary eye on its enemies, the lion and hyena, feeding principally on small prey, rabbits, birds, even snakes and lizards,* the narrator informed me in a hushed voice—and then I went to the sandwich shop and ordered the Number 7 special, no mayo, and took it down to the beach. It was a clear day, all the haze and particulate matter washed clean of the air by the previous day's deluge, and I sat there with the sun on my face and watched the waves ride in on top of one another while I ate and considered the altered condition of my life. Daria's face had gotten serious as she stood at the door, her T-shirt rumpled, her hair pulled back so tightly from her scalp I could make out each individual strand. "Take care of our cat now, okay?" she said. "I'll be back as soon as I get off." I shrugged in a helpless, submissive way, the pain of her leaving as acute as anything I'd ever felt. "Sure," I said, and then she reached for my shoulders and pulled me to her for a kiss—on the lips. "You're sweet," she said.

So I was sweet. No one had ever called me sweet before, not since childhood anyway, and I have to admit the designation thrilled me, bloomed inside me like the promise of things to come. I began to see her as a prime mover in my life, her naked legs stretched out on the couch, the hair falling across her shoulders at the kitchen table, her lips locked on mine. But as I sat there eating my ham-and-cheese wrap, a conflicting thought came to me: there had to be someone in her life already, a girl that beautiful, working in a bar, and I was de-luding myself to think I had a chance with her. She had to have a boyfriend—she could even be engaged, for all I knew. I tried to fo-cus on the previous night, on her hands and fingers—had she been wearing a ring? And if she had, then where was the fiancé, the boy-friend, whoever he was? I hated him already, and I didn't know if he even existed.

The upshot of all this was that I found myself in the cool subter-ranean glow of Daggett's at three-thirty in the afternoon, nursing a Jack-and-Coke like one of the regulars while Daria, the ring finger of her left hand as unencumbered as mine, went round clearing up af-ter the lunch crowd and setting the tables for the dinner rush. Chris came on at five, and he called me by my name and refreshed my drink before he even glanced at the regulars, and for the next hour or so, during the lulls, we conversed about any number of things, begin-ning with the most obvious—the cat—but veering into sports, mu-sic, books and films, and I found myself expanding into a new place altogether. At one point, Daria stopped by to ask if the cat was set-tling in—Was he still pacing around neurotically or what?—and I could tell her with some assurance that he was asleep. "He's probably nocturnal," I said, "or something like that." And then, with Chris looking on, I couldn't help adding, "You're still coming over, right? After work? To help me feed him, I mean."

She looked to Chris, then let her gaze wander out over the room. "Oh, yeah," she said, "yeah," and there was a catch of hesitation in her voice, "I'll be there."

I let that hang a moment, but I was insecure and the alcohol was having its effect and I couldn't leave it alone. "We can drive over together," I said, "because I didn't bring my car."

SHE WAS LOOKING tired by the end of her shift, the bounce gone out of her step, her hair a shade duller under the drab lights, and even as I switched to coffee I noticed Chris slipping her a shot of something down at the end of the bar. I'd had a sandwich around six, and then, so as not to seem overanxious, I'd taken a walk, which brought me into another bar down the street, where I had a Jack-and-Coke and didn't say a word to anyone, and then I'd returned at eight to drink coffee and watch her and hold her to her promise.

We didn't say much on the way over to my place. It was only a five-minute drive, and there was a song on we both liked. Plus, it seemed to me that when you were comfortable with someone you could respect the silences. I'd gone to the cash machine earlier and in a hopeful mood stocked up on breakfast things—eggs, English muffins, a quart each of no-fat and two-percent milk, an expensive Chinese tea that came in individual foil packets—and I'd picked up two bottles of a local Chardonnay that was supposed to be really superior, or at least that was what the guy in the liquor department had told me, as well as a bag of corn chips and a jar of salsa. There were two new bathroom towels hanging on the rack beside the medicine cabinet and I'd given the whole place a good vacuuming and left the dishes to soak in a sink of scalding water and the last few molecules of dish soap left in the plastic container I'd brought with me from my aunt's. The final touch was a pair of clean sheets and a light blanket folded suggestively over the arm of the couch.

Daria didn't seem to notice—she went straight to the bedroom door and affixed her eye to the peephole. "I can't see anything," she said, leaning into the door in her shorts, the muscles of her calves flexing as she went up on her toes. "It's too bad we didn't think of a night light or something—"

I was watching her out of the corner of my eye—admiring her, amazed all over again at her presence—while working the corkscrew in the bottle. I asked her if she'd like a glass of wine. "Chardonnay," I said. "It's a local one, really superior."

"I'd love a glass," she said, turning away from the door and crossing the room to me. I didn't have wineglasses, so we made do with the milky-looking water glasses my aunt had dug out of a box in her basement. "But I wonder if you could maybe slip your arm in the door and turn on the light in there," she said. "I'm worried about him. And plus, we've got to feed him again, right?"

"Sure," I said, "yeah, no problem," but I was in no hurry. I refilled our glasses and broke out the corn chips and salsa, which she seemed happy enough to see. For a long while we stood at the kitchen counter, dipping chips and savoring the wine, and then she went to the refrigerator, extracted a slab of meat, and began patting it down with paper towels. I took her cue, donned the gauntlet, braced myself and jerked the bedroom door open just enough to get my hand in and flick on the light. The cat, which of course had sterling night vision, nearly tore the glove from my arm, and yet the suddenness of the light seemed to confuse it just long enough for me to salvage the situation. The door slammed on a puzzled yowl.

Daria immediately put her eye to the peephole. "Oh my God," she murmured.

"What's he doing?"

"Pacing. But here, you have a look."

The carpeting—every last strip of it—had been torn out of the floor, leaving an expanse of dirty plywood studded with nails, and there seemed to be a hole in the plasterboard just to the left of the window. A substantial hole. Even through the closed door I could smell the reek of cat piss or spray or whatever it was. "There goes my deposit," I said.

She was right there beside me, her hand on my shoulder. "He'll settle down," she assured me, "once he gets used to the place. All cats are like that—they have to establish their territory, is all."

"You don't think he can get inside the walls, do you?"

"No," she said, "no way, he's too big—"

The only thing I could think to do, especially after an entire day of drinking, was to pour more wine, which I did. Then we repeated the ritual of the morning's feeding—the steak on the fork, the blur of the cat, the savage thump at the door—and took turns watching it eat. After a while, bored with the spectacle—or "sated," maybe that's a better word—we found ourselves on the couch and there was a movie on TV and we finished the wine and the chips and we never stopped talking, a comment on this movie leading to a discussion of movies in general, a reflection on the wine dredging up our mutual experiences of wine tastings and the horrors of Cribari red and Boone's Farm and all the rest. It was midnight before we knew it and she was yawning and stretching.

"I've really got to get home," she said, but she didn't move. "I'm wiped. Just wiped."

"You're welcome to stay over," I said, "I mean, if you don't want to drive, after all the wine and all—"

A moment drifted by, neither of us speaking, and then she made a sort of humming noise—"Mmmm"—and held out her arms to me even as she sank down into the couch.

I was up before her in the morning, careful not to wake her as I eased myself from the mattress where we'd wound up sleeping because the couch was too narrow for the two of us. My head ached—I wasn't used to so much alcohol—and the effigy of the cat lurked somewhere behind that ache, but I felt buoyant and optimistic. Daria was asleep on the mattress, the cat was hunkered down in his room, and all was right with the world. I brewed coffee, toasted muffins and fried eggs, and when she woke I was there to feed her. "What do you say to breakfast in bed?" I murmured, easing down beside her with a plate of eggs over-easy and a mug of coffee.

I was so intent on watching her eat I barely touched my own food. After a while, I got up and turned on the radio and there was that song again, the one we'd heard coming home the night before, and we both listened to it all the way through without saying a word. When the disc jockey came on with his gasping juvenile voice and lame jokes, she got up and went to the bathroom, passing right by the bedroom door without a thought for the cat. She was in the bathroom a long while, running water, flushing, showering, and I felt lost without her. I wanted to tell her I loved her, wanted to extend a whole list of invitations to her: she could move in with me, stay here indefinitely, bring her cats with her, no problem, and we could both look after the big cat together, see to its needs, tame it and make it happy in its new home—no more cages, and meat, plenty of meat. I was scrubbing the frying pan when she emerged, her hair wrapped in one of the new towels. She was wearing her makeup and she was dressed in her Daggett's outfit. "Hey," I said.

She didn't answer. She was bent over the couch now, stuffing things into her purse.

"You look terrific," I said.

There was a sound from the bedroom then, a low moan that might have been the expiring gasp of the cat's prey and I wondered if it had found something in there, a rat, a stray bird attracted to the window, an escaped hamster or lizard. "Listen, Junior," she said, ignoring the moaning, which grew higher and more attenuated now, "you're a nice guy, you really are."

I was behind the Formica counter. My hands were in the dishwater. Something pounded in my head and I knew what was coming, heard it in her voice, saw it in the way she ducked her head and averted her eyes.

"I can't—I have to tell you something, okay? Because you're sweet, you are, and I want to be honest with you."

She raised her face to me all of a sudden, let her eyes stab at mine and then dodge away again. "I have a boyfriend. He's away at school. And I don't know why . . . I mean, I just don't want to give you the wrong impression. It was nice. It was."

The moaning cut off abruptly on a rising note. I didn't know what to say—I was new at this, new and useless. Suddenly I was desperate, looking for anything, any stratagem, the magic words that would make it all right again. "The cat," I said. "What about the cat?"

Her voice was soft. "He'll be all right. Just feed him. Be nice to him." She was at the door, the purse slung over one shoulder. "Patience," she said, "that's all it takes. A little patience."

"Wait," I said. "Wait."

"I've got to go."

"Will I see you later?"

"No," she said. "No, I don't think so."

As soon as her pickup pulled out of the lot, I called my boss. He answered on the first ring, raising his voice to be heard over the ambient noise. I could hear the tile saw going in the background, the irregular banging of a hammer, the radio tuned to some jittery right-wing propagandist. "I want to come in," I said.

"Who is this?"

"Junior."

"Monday, Monday at the earliest."

I told him I was going crazy cooped up in my apartment, but he didn't seem to hear me. "What is it?" he said. "Money? Because I'll advance you on next week if you really need it, though it'll mean a trip to the bank I wasn't planning on. Which is a pain in the ass. But I'll do it. Just say the word."

"No, it's not the money, it's just—"

He cut me off. "Don't you ever listen to anything I say? Didn't I tell you to go out and get yourself laid? That's what you're supposed to be doing at your age. It's what I'd be doing."

"Can't I just, I don't know, help out?"

"Monday," he said.

I was angry suddenly and I slammed the phone down. My eyes went to the hole cut in the bedroom door and then to the breakfast plates, egg yolk congealing there in bright yellow stripes, the muffin, Daria's muffin, untouched but for a single neat bite cut out of the round. It was Friday. I hated my life. How could I have been so stupid?

There was no sound from the bedroom, and as I laced my sneakers I fought down the urge to go to the peephole and see what the cat had accomplished in the night—I just didn't want to think about it. Whether it had vanished like the bad odor of a bad dream or chewed through the wall and devoured the neighbor's yapping little dogs or broken loose and smuggled itself onto a boat back to Africa, it was all the same to me. The only thing I did know was that there was no way I was going to attempt to feed that thing on my own, not without Daria there. It could starve for all I cared, starve and rot.

Eventually, I fished a jean jacket out of a pile of clothes on the floor and went down to the beach. The day was overcast and a cold wind out of the east scoured the sand. I must have walked for hours and then, for lack of anything better to do, I went to a movie, after which I had a sandwich at a new place downtown where the college students were rumored to hang out. There were no students there as far as I could see, just old men who looked exactly like the regulars at Daggett's, and they had their square-shouldered old wives with them and their squalling unhappy children. By four I hit my first bar, and by six I was drunk.

I tried to stay away from Daggett's—*Give her a day or two,* I told myself, *don't nag, don't be a burden*—but at quarter of nine I found myself at the bar, ordering a Jack-and-Coke from Chris. Chris gave me a look, and everything had changed since yesterday. "You sure?" he said.

I asked him what he meant.

"You look like you've had enough, buddy."

I craned my neck to look for Daria, but all I saw were the regulars, hunched over their drinks. "Just pour," I said.

The music was there like a persistent annoyance, dead music, ancient, appreciated by no one, not even the regulars. It droned on. Chris set down my drink and I lifted it to my lips. "Where's Daria?" I asked.

"She got off early. Said she was tired. Slow night, you know?"

I felt a stab of disappointment, jealousy, hate. "You have a number for her?"

Chris gave me a wary look, because he knew something I didn't. "You mean she didn't give you her number?"

"No," I said, "we never—well, she was *at* my house . . ."

"We can't give out personal information."

"To me? I said she was at my house. Last night. I need to talk to her, and it's urgent—about the cat. She's really into the cat, you know?"

"Sorry."

I threw it back at him. "You're sorry? Well, fuck you—I'm sorry too."

"You know what, buddy—"

"Junior, the name's Junior."

He leaned into the bar, both arms propped before him, and in a very soft voice he said, "I think you better leave now."

IT HAD BEGUN to rain, a soft patter in the leaves that grew steadier and harder as I walked home. Cars went by on the boulevard with the sound of paper tearing, and they dragged whole worlds behind them. The streetlights were dim. There was nobody out. When I came up the hill to my apartment I saw the Mustang standing there under the carport, and though I'd always been averse to drinking and driving—a lesson I'd learned from my father's hapless example—I got behind the wheel and drove up to the jobsite with a crystalline clarity that would have scared me in any other state of mind. There was an aluminum ladder there, and I focused on that—the picture of it lying against the building—till I arrived and hauled it out of the mud and tied it to the roof of the car without a thought for the paint job or anything else.

When I got back, I fumbled in the rain with the overzealous knots I'd tied until I got the ladder free and then I hauled it around the back of the apartment. I was drunk, yes, but cautious too—if anyone had seen me, in the dark, propping a ladder against the wall of an apartment building, even my own apartment building, things could have gotten difficult in a hurry. I couldn't very well claim to be painting, could I? Not at night. Not in the rain. Luckily, though, no one was around. I made my way up the ladder, and when I got to the level of the bedroom the odor hit me, a rank fecal wind sifting out of the dark slit of the window. The cat. The cat was in there, watching me. I was sure of it. I must have waited there in the rain for fifteen minutes or more before I got up the nerve to fling the window open, and then I ducked my head and crouched reflexively against the wall. Nothing happened. After a moment, I made my way down the ladder.

I didn't want to go in the apartment, didn't want to think about it, didn't know if a cat of that size could climb down the rungs of a ladder or leap twenty feet into the air or unfurl its hidden wings and fly. I stood and watched the dense black hole of the window for a long while and then I went back to the car and sat listening to the radio in the dark till I fell asleep.

In the morning—there were no heraldic rays of sunshine, nothing like that, just more rain—I let myself into the apartment and crept across the room as stealthily as if I'd come to burgle it. When I reached the bedroom door, I put my eye to the peephole and saw a mound of carpet propped up against an empty cage—a den, a makeshift den—and only then did I begin to feel something for the cat, for its bewilderment, its fear and distrust of an alien environment: this was no rocky kopje, this was my bedroom on the second floor of a run-down apartment building in a seaside town a whole continent and a fathomless ocean away from its home. Nothing moved inside. Surely it must have been gone, one great leap and then the bounding limbs, grass beneath its feet, solid earth. It was gone. Sure it was. I steeled myself, pulled open the door and slipped inside. And then—and I don't know why—I pulled the door shut behind me.

The Doubtfulness of Water: Madam Knight's Journey to New York, 1702

BOSTON TO DEDHAM

THE ROAD WAS DARK, even at six in the evening, and if it held any wonders aside from the odd snug house or the stubble field, she couldn't have said because all that was visible was the white stripe of heaven overhead. Her horse was no more than a sound and a presence now, the heat of its internal engine rising round her in a miasma of sweat dried and reconstituted a hundred times over, even as she began to feel the repetition of its gait in the deep recesses of her seat and that appendage at the base of the spine her mother used to call the tailbone. Cousin Robert was some indeterminate distance ahead of her, the slow crepitating slap of his mount's hooves creating a new kind of silence that fed off the only sound in the world and then swallowed it up in a tower of vegetation as dense and continuous as the waves of the sea. Though it was only the second of October, there had been frost, and that was a small comfort in all of this hurt and upset, because it drew down the insects that a month earlier would have eaten her alive. The horse swayed, the stars staggered and flashed. She wanted to call out to Robert to ask if it was much farther yet, but she restrained herself. She'd talked till her throat went dry as they'd left town in the declining sun and he'd done his best to keep up though he wasn't naturally a talker, and eventually, as the shadows came down and the rhythmic movement of the animals dulled their senses, they'd fallen silent. She resigned herself. Rode on. And just as she'd given up hope, a light appeared ahead.

AT DEDHAM

ROBERT HER COUSIN leaving her to await the Post at the cottage of the Reverend and Madam Belcher before turning round for Boston with a dozen admonitions on his lips—She should have gone by sea as there was no telling what surprises lay ahead on the road in that savage country and she was to travel solely with trusted companions and the Post, et cetera—she settled in by the fire with a cup of tea and explained her business to Madam Belcher in her cap and the Reverend with his pipe. Yes, she felt responsible. And yes, it was she who'd introduced her boarder, a young widow, to her kinsman, Caleb Trowbridge, only to have him die four months after the wedding and leave the poor woman twice widowed. There were matters of the estate to be settled in both New Haven and New York, and it was her intention to act in the widow's behalf, being a widow herself and knowing how cruel such divisions of property can be.

An old dog lay on the rug. A tallow candle held a braided flame above it. There was a single ornament on the wall, a saying out of the Bible in needlepoint: *He shall come down like rain upon the mown grass: as showers that water the earth.* After a pause, the Reverend's wife asked if she would like another cup.

Sarah's eyes rose from the fire to the black square of the window. "You're very kind," she said, "but no thank you." She was concerned about the Post. Shouldn't he have been here by now? Had she somehow managed to miss him? Because if she had, there was no sense in going on—she might just as well admit defeat and find a guide back to Boston in the morning. "But where can the Post be?" she asked, turning to the Reverend.

The Reverend was a big block of a man with a nose to support the weight of his fine-ground spectacles. He cleared his throat. "Might be he's gone on to the Billingses, where he's used to lodge."

She listened to the hiss of the water trapped in a birch stick on the fire. Her whole body ached with the soreness of the saddle. "And how far would that be?"

"Twelve mile on."

AT DEDHAM TAVERN

SHE SAT in a corner in her riding clothes while the Reverend brought the hostess to her, the boards of the floor unswept, tobacco dragons putting their claws into the air and every man with a black cud of chew in his mouth. The woman came to her with her hair in a snarl and her hands patting at her hips, open-faced and wondering. The Reverend stood beside her with his nose and his spectacles, the crown of his hat poking into the timbers overhead. Could she be of assistance?

"Yes, I'd like some refreshment, if you please. And I'll need a guide to take me as far as the Billingses' to meet up with the Post."

"The Billingses? At this hour of night?"

The hostess had raised her voice so that every soul in the place could appreciate the clear and irrefragable reason of what she was saying, and she went on to point out that it was twelve miles in the dark and that there would be none there to take her, but that her son John, if the payment was requisite to his risking life and limb, might be induced to go. Even at this unholy hour.

And where was John?

"You never mind. Just state your price."

Madam Knight sat as still as if she were in her own parlor with her mother and daughter and Mrs. Trowbridge and her two boarders gathered round her. She was thirty-eight years old, with a face that had once been pretty, and though she was plump and her hands were soft, she was used to work and to hard-dealing and she was no barmaid in a country tavern. She gazed calmly on the hostess and said nothing.

"Two pieces of eight," the woman said. "And a dram."

A moment passed, every ear in the place attuned to the sequel. "I will not be accessory to such extortion," Sarah pronounced in an even voice, "not if I have to find my own way, alone and defenseless in the dark."

The hostess went on like a singing Quaker, mounting excuse atop argument, and the men stopped chewing and held the pewter mugs arrested in their hands, until finally an old long-nosed cadaver who looked to be twice the hostess's age rose up from the near table and asked how much she *would* pay him to show her the way.

Sarah was nonplussed. "Who are you?"

"John," he said, and jerked a finger toward the hostess. "'Er son."

DEDHAM TO THE BILLINGSES'

IF THE ROAD had been dark before, now it was as if she were blind and afflicted and the horse blind too. Clouds had rolled in to pull a shade over the stars and planets while she'd sat listening to the hostess at the tavern, and if it weren't for the sense of hearing and the feel of a damp breeze on her face, she might as well have been locked in a closet somewhere. John was just there ahead of her, as Cousin Robert had been earlier, but John was a talker and the strings of his sentences pulled her forward like a spare set of reins. Like his mother, he was a monologuist. His subject was himself and the myriad dangers of the road—savage Indians, catamounts, bears, wolves and common thieves—he'd managed to overthrow by his own cunning and heroism in the weeks and months just recently passed. "There was a man 'ere, on this very spot, murdered and drawn into four pieces by a Pequot with two brass rings in 'is ears," he told her. "Rum was the cause of it. If I'd passed by an hour before it would have been me." And: "The catamount's a wicked thing. Gets a horse by the nostrils and then rakes out the innards with 'is hinder claws. I've seen it myself." And again: "Then you've got your shades of the murdered. When the wind is down you hear them hollowin' at every crossroads."

She wasn't impressed. They'd hanged women for witches in her time, and every corner, even in town, seemed to be the haunt of one goblin or another. Stories and wives' tales, legends to titillate the children before bed. There were real dangers in the world, dangers here in the dark, but they were overhead and underfoot, the nagging branch and open gully, the horse misstepping and coming down hard on her, the invisible limb to brain her as she levitated by, but she tried not to think of them, tried to trust in her guide—John the living cadaver—and the horse beneath her. She gripped the saddle and tried to ease the ache in her seat, which had radiated out to her limbs now and her backbone, even her neck, and she let her mind go numb with the night and the sweet released odors of the leaves they crushed underfoot.

AT THE BILLINGSES'

SHE WOULD NEVER have known the house was there but for the sudden scent of wood smoke and the narrowest ribbon of light that hung in the void like the spare edge of something grander. "If you'll just alight, then, Missus," John was saying, and she could feel his hand at her elbow to help her down, "and take yourself right on through that door there."

"What door?"

"There. Right before your face."

He led her forward even as the horses stamped in their impatience to be rid of the saddle. She felt stone beneath her feet and focused on the ribbon of light till the door fell inward and she was in the room itself, low beams, plank floor, a single lantern and the fire dead in the hearth. In the next instant a young woman of fifteen or so rose up out of the inglenook with a contorted face and demanded to know who she was and what she was doing in her house at such an hour. The girl stood with her legs apart, as if ready to defend herself. Her voice was strained. "I never seen a woman on the road so dreadful late. Who are you? Where are you going? You scared me out of my wits."

"This *is* a lodging house, or am I mistaken?" Sarah drew herself up, sorer than she'd ever been in her life, the back of a horse—any horse—like the Devil's own rack, and all she wanted was a bed, not provender, not company, not even civility—just that: a bed.

"My ma's asleep," the girl said, standing her ground. "So's my pa. And William too."

"It's William I've come about. He's the Post, isn't he?"

"I suspect."

"Well, I'll be traveling west with him in the morning and I'll need a bed for the night. You *do* have a bed?" Even as she said it she entertained a vision of sleeping rough, stretched out on the cold ground amidst the dried-out husks of the fallen leaves, prey to anything that stalked or crept, and she felt all the strength go out of her. She never pleaded. It wasn't in her nature. But she was slipping fast when the door suddenly opened behind her and John stepped into the room.

The girl's eyes ran to him. "Lawful heart, John, is it you?" she cried, and then it was all right, and she offered a chair and a biscuit and darted away upstairs only to appear a moment later with three rings on her fingers and her hair brushed back from her brow. And then the chattering began, one topic flung down as quickly as the next was taken up, and all Sarah wanted was that bed, which finally she found in a little back lean-to that wasn't much bigger than the bedstead itself. As for comfort, the bed was like a mound of bricks, the shuck mattress even worse. No matter. Exhaustion overcame her. She undressed and slid in under the counterpane even as the bed lice stole out for the feast.

THE BILLINGSES' TO FOXVALE

She arose stiff in the morning, feeling as if she'd been pounded head to toe with the flat head of a mallet, and the girl was nowhere to be seen. But William was there, scooping porridge out of a bowl by the fire, and the mistress of the house. Sarah made her own introductions, paid for her bed, a mug of coffee that scalded her palate, and her own wooden bowl of porridge, and then she climbed back into the rack of the saddle and they were gone by eight in the morning.

The country they passed through rolled one way and the other, liberally partitioned by streams, creeks, freshets and swamps, the hooves of the horses eternally flinging up ovals of black muck that smelled of things dead and buried. There were birds in the trees still, though the summer flocks were gone, and every branch seemed to hold a squirrel or chipmunk. The leaves were in color, the dragonflies glazed and hovering over the shadows in the road ahead, and in the clearings goldenrod nodding bright on a thousand stalks. For the first time she found herself relaxing, settling into the slow-haunching rhythm of the horse as she followed the Post's back and the swishing tail of his mount through one glade after another. There were no houses, no people. She heard a gabbling in the forest and saw the dark-clothed shapes there—turkeys, in all their powers and dominions, turkeys enough to feed all of Boston—and she couldn't help thinking of the basted bird in a pan over the fire.

At first she'd tried to make conversation with William (a man in his twenties, kempt, lean as a pole, taciturn) just to be civil, but talk seemed superfluous out here in the wild and she let her thoughts wander as if she were at prayer or drifting through the mutating moments before sleep comes. *You should have gone by sea,* Cousin Robert had said, and he was right of course, except that the rollicking of the waters devastated her—she'd been once with her father in a dingy to Nantucket when she was a girl, and once was enough. She could still remember the way her stomach heaved and the fear she'd felt of the implacable depths where unseen things—leviathan, the shark, the crab and suckerfish—rolled in darkness. She'd never learned to swim. Why would she, living in town, and when even the water of the lakes and the river was like the breath of mid-winter, and the sea worse, far worse, with men falling overboard from the fishing boats and drowning from the shock of it? No, she would keep the solid earth under her feet. Or her horse's feet, at any rate.

Sure progress, the crown of the day: there was the sun, the solemn drapery of the forest, birdsong. She was lulled, half asleep, expecting nothing but more of the same, when suddenly a small thicket of trees detached itself from the wood and ambled out into the road so that her mount pulled up and flung its near eye back at her. It took two catapulting moments for the image to jell, and then she let out a scream that was the only human sound for twenty miles around.

The thing—the walking forest—was bearded and antlered and had eyes that shone like the Indian money they made of shells. It produced a sound of its own—a blunt bewildered bleat of alarm—and then it was gone and William, taciturn William, was there at her side. "It's nothing to worry yourself over," he said, and she saw that he was grinning as if he'd just heard a joke—or formulated one. He had a story to tell at the tavern that night, that's what it was, and she was the brunt of it, the widow from Boston who wouldn't recognize a—what was it, a moose?—if it came right up and grazed out of her hand.

AT FOXVALE

THE BOARD WAS primitive, to say the least, Sarah sitting at table with William while William discharged his letters to Nathan, the western Post, and the hostess bringing in a cheese that was like no cheese she'd ever seen. Eating was one of her small pleasures, and at home she always took care with the menu, serving up fish or viands in a savory sauce or peas boiled with a bit of salt meat, fresh roasted venison, Indian corn and squashes and pies—her speciality—made from the ripe fruit of the season, blueberry, raspberry, pumpkin, apple. But here the woods gathered close so that it was like night in the middle of a towering bright day, and there were none of the niceties of civilization, either in the serving or the quality. The cheese—harder than the bed she'd slept in the night before—barely took to the knife, and then it was a dish of pork and cabbage, which looked to be the remains of dinner. She found that she was hungry despite herself—ravenous, actually, with the exercise and air—and she took a larger portion than she would have liked.

"Tucking in there, Missus, eh?" William observed, giving her that same grin even as he nudged Nathan, and here was another story.

"We've been on the road since eight in the morning," she said, wondering for the life of her what was so amusing about sheltering in a hovel in the woods fit only for a band of naked savages, "and it's now past two in the afternoon. A woman has got to eat, if only to keep up her strength." She was throwing it back at them, and why not—that was how she felt. And she *was* hungry, nothing to be ashamed of there. But the sauce was the strangest color—a purple so deep it was nearly black—and the thought came to her that the hostess had stewed the meal in her dye kettle.

William was watching her. As was Nathan. The hostess had vanished in the back room and the sound of the fowl scratching in the dirt of the yard came to her as if she were standing there amongst them. Very slowly a branch outside the sole window dipped in the breeze and parted the dense shadow on the wall. She hesitated, the spoon hovering over the dish—they were both of them grinning like fools—and then she plunged in.

FOXVALE TO PROVIDENCE

THIS WAS THE LEG of the journey that wore on her most. The new man—Nathan—rode hard and she had to struggle to keep up with him, or at least keep him in sight. Though he'd seen her discharge William handsomely enough and pay for his refreshment too, he didn't seem in the least solicitous. He was a hat and a pair of shoulders and a back, receding, always receding. Her mount wasn't much taller than a pony and tended to lag no matter how much encouragement she gave him, running to his own head and not a pace faster. The clouds closed in. A light rain began to awaken the dust. Nathan was gone.

She'd never been out alone in the wilderness in her life. When she was younger she'd gone berrying on the outskirts of town or spent a warm afternoon sitting by a cool brook, but the wild was nothing she wanted or recognized. It was a waste, all of it, and the sooner it was civilized and cultivated, the sooner people could live as they did in England, with security and dignity—and cleanliness—the better. To her mind, aside from the dangers that seemed to multiply with every step they took—a moose, indeed—it was the dirt that damned the wild more than anything. She hadn't felt even remotely clean since she'd left town, though she'd done her best to beat the soil from her skirts, brush her shoes of mud and see to the demands of her hair. And now she was wet and the horse was wet and her baggage and the road before her, and every leaf on every tree shone and dripped.

She tried to concentrate her thoughts on easeful things, the tea set in her parlor and her daughter and Mrs. Trowbridge pouring out the tea and artfully arranging the pastries on the platter, because it was teatime now, and if it was raining there they'd have built up the fire to take the damp out of the air—but she couldn't hold the picture long. Her thoughts kept coming back to the present and the dangers of the road. Every stump seen at a distance seemed to transform itself into a bear or wolf, every copse was the haunt of Indians mad with rum and lust, the birds fallen silent now and the rain awakening the mosquitoes that dove at her hands and face where they'd coarsened in the sun. She'd thought she was going on an adventure, a respite from town and gossip and all the constraints of widowhood, something she could look back on and tell over and over again to her daughter and the grandchildren she saw as clearly as if they'd already come into existence—but she wasn't foolish, and she wasn't blindered. She'd expected a degree of hardship, an untenanted road, insects and the like, wild animals, and yet in her mind the road always ran between inns with reasonable beds and service and a rough but hardy and well-tendered fare. But this was impossible. This rain, these bugs, this throbbing ache in her seat that was like a hot poker applied to her backside by one of Satan's own fiends. She hated this. Hated it.

AT PROVIDENCE FERRY

IT GOT WORSE.

Nathan's silhouette presented itself to her at the top of a rise, unkempt now and dripping. Slowly, with the testudineous progress of something you might crush underfoot, she made her way up the hill to him, and when she got there he pointed down at the lashing dun waves of the Seekonk River and the distant figure of the ferryman. She didn't say a word, but when they got there, when the water was beating to and fro and the ferryman accepting her coin, she held back. "The water looks doubtful," she said, trying to keep her voice from deserting her.

"This?" Nathan looked puzzled. "I'd call this calm, Missus," he said. "And the quicker we're over it, the better, because there's worse to come."

She closed her eyes fast, drew in a single breath and held it till they were across and she knew she was alive still and climbing back into the saddle even as the rain quickened its pace and the road ahead turned to sludge.

PROVIDENCE FERRY TO THE HAVENSES'

THEY HADN'T GONE on a quarter of an hour when they came to a second river, the name of which she never did learn. It was dark as a brew with the runoff of the rain and ran in sheets over the submerged rocks and boiled up again round the visible ones. She felt herself seize at the sight of it, though Nathan assured her it wasn't what it seemed—"No depth to it at all and we're used to ride across it even at spring thaw"—and when they were there at the crossing and Nathan's mount already hock-deep in the surge, she just couldn't go on. He remonstrated with her—they were late on the road already, dusk was falling, there was another crossing after this one and fourteen miles more to the next stage—but she was adamant. There was no inducement in the world that would make her risk that torrent.

The rain had begun to let up now and a few late faltering streaks of sun shone through the clouds across the river. But wasn't that a house there on the far shore? A cabin, crudely made of logs with the bark peeled back and smoke rising palely from the stacked stone of the chimney? The current sang. Nathan swung his horse round on the shingle and gave her a look of hatred. "Does someone live there?" she asked. "In that cabin there?"

He didn't answer. Just thrust his horse into the current and floundered through it with a crashing like cymbals and she was so furious she would have shot him right through his pinched shoulder blades if only she'd had the means. He was deserting her. Leaving her to the wolves, the murderers and the haunts. "You come back here!" she shouted, but there were only his shoulders, receding.

That was her low point. She tried, at first, to screw up her courage and follow him—it wasn't so deep, after all, she could see that—but the way the water seemed to speak and hiss and mock her was enough to warn her off. She dismounted. There was a chill in the air, her clothes wet still, the night descending. She should have stayed home. Should have listened to Robert and her daughter and everyone else she talked to—women simply did not travel the Post Road, not without their husbands or brothers or kinsmen there to guide and protect them, and even then, it was a risk. Something settled in the back of her throat, a hard bolus of self-pity and despair. She couldn't swallow. One more minute of this, one more minute of this water and these trees, these endless trees, and she was going to break down and sob like a child. But then, out there on the naked back of the water, she saw the envelope of the birchbark canoe coming toward her and a boy in it and Nathan beckoning to her from the far shore.

What to say? That the crossing—eyes tight shut and her grip on the papery gunwales like the grip of death—was the single worst moment of her life, at least until the next crossing, through which they plunged in a pit of darkness so universal that it was only the tug of the reins, the murmur of the current and the sudden icy stab of the water at her calves to let her know she was in it and through it? Or that the fourteen miles remaining were so tedious she could scarcely stay awake and upright in the saddle despite the horripilating shivers that tossed her from one side to the other like a ball in a child's game? Say it. And say that she thought she was dreaming when the Post sounded his horn and the snug, well-lit house of the Havenses materialized out of the night.

AT THE HAVENSES'

AS WEARY AS SHE WAS, as worn and dispirited, she couldn't help feeling her soul rise up and shout when she stepped through the door. There was Mr. Havens, solicitous and stout, and Mrs. Havens beside him with a welcoming smile, the fire going hard in the hearth and a smell of beef broth to perfume the air. She saw immediately that these were people civil and clean, with a well-ordered house and every sign of a demanding mistress, a picture on one wall of the sitting room and a glass vase of dried flowers set atop an oiled sideboard on the other. Chairs were drawn up to the fire and a number of people cozily ensconced there with their mugs and pipes and they all had a greeting on their lips. Mrs. Havens helped her off with her riding clothes and hung them up to dry and then asked if she could get her anything by way of refreshment, Sarah answering that she had a portion of chocolate with her and wondered if she might have some milk heated in a pan. And then she was shown to her room—small but sufficient and tidy—and the door was shut and she felt as if she'd come through a storm and shipwreck and washed up safe.

She must have dozed, because she came back with a start when Mrs. Havens rapped at the door. "Yes?" Sarah called, and for a moment she didn't know where she was.

A murmur from the other side of the door: "Your chocolate, Missus."

The milk had been boiled with the chocolate in a clean brass kettle, and there was enough of it to give her three cups full. And there were corn cakes, still warm from the griddle. This was heaven, she was thinking, very heaven, dipping the cakes into the chocolate and warming her hands at the cup, but then the voices began to intrude. It seemed that her apartment, separated from the kitchen by a board partition, wasn't quite as private as she'd supposed. Next door to her—just beyond that thin rumor of a wall—were three, or was it four, of the town's topers, and all of them arguing a single point at once.

She listened, frozen on the starched white field of the bed, and she might as well have been right out there amongst them.

"No," a voice declared, "that's not it at all. Narragansett means 'briar' in the Indian language, and the patch of it was right out there on Peter Parker's place, twenty feet high and more—"

"I beg to differ, but it was a spring here—and that's where the country gets it name. Waters of a healing property, I'm told."

"Yes? And where is it, then? Why aren't you drinking the waters now—why aren't we all?"

A scuffle of mugs, the scrape of chair legs. "But we are—only it's been distilled out of cane." Laughter rang out, there was a dull booming as fists pounded the tabletop, and then someone followed it up with a foul remark, in foul language.

And so it went, for what seemed like hours. Exhausted as she was, there was no hope of sleep as long as the rum held out, and she began to pray the keg would run dry, though she was a practical soul who'd never had the calling and she never expected her prayers to be answered since there were so many worthier than she calling on the same power at the same moment. But the voices next door grew thicker, as if they'd started chewing maple sap boiled to gum, and the argument settled into a faintly disputatious murmur and then finally a pure drugged intake and outlay of breath that formed the respiratory foundation of her dreams.

THE HAVENSES' TO THE PAUKATAUG

THE NEXT KNOCK came at four in the morning, black as pitch and no breakfast but what was portable, and here they were, back out on the road in the dark and cold, deep in the Narragansett country now, which to Sarah's mind was just more of the same: the hard road, the shadowy trees and the reptatory murmur of the waters that were all running underfoot to gather in some terrible place ahead. "Narragansett," she whispered to herself, as if it were an incantation, but she had to be forgiven if she couldn't seem to muster much enthusiasm for the origins of the name.

They'd been joined at the Havenses' by a French doctor, a slight man with a limp and a disproportionate nose, whose name she couldn't pronounce and whose accent made him difficult to understand, so that they were a party of three now for this leg of the journey. Not that it made a particle of difference, except that Nathan and the doctor rode on at such a furious pace as to leave her a mile and more behind, alone with her thoughts and whatever frights the unbroken wood might harbor. From time to time she'd spy them on a hill up ahead of her, waiting to see that she was still on the road and not lying murdered in a ditch, and then they'd tug at the reins again and vanish over the rise.

The Post had warned her that there was no accommodation or refreshment on this stretch of the road—no human habitation at all—for a full twenty-two miles, but as the morning wore on it seemed as if they'd gone a hundred miles before she saw the two figures poised on a ridge up ahead, looking back at her and pointing to a tight tourniquet of smoke in the distance. She'd been down on foot and leading her mount at that point, just to ease the soreness of her seat and thighs, but now she remounted with some effort and found her way to the source of the smoke: an ordinary set down beside a brook in a clearing of the trees.

Painfully she dismounted and painfully accepted the refreshment the landlady had to offer—stewed meat and Indian bread, unleavened—and then sat over the journal she'd determined to keep while the landlady went on to the doctor about her physical complaints in a voice loud enough to be heard all the way to Kingston town and back. The woman spoke of her privates as if they were public, and perhaps they were, but just hearing it was enough to turn Sarah's stomach and she had to take her book and sit out in the courtyard amongst the flies, which were especially thick here, as if they'd gathered for some sort of convention. She sat on a stump and swatted and shooed and blotted her precious paper with the effort until the Frenchman and the Post, still chewing a cud of stewed meat, saddled up and moved on down the road, and she had no choice but to rouse herself and follow on in their wake.

The country was unremarkable, the road boggy, the sun an affliction. Her hands and face were burned where they were exposed and the pain of it was like being freshly slapped every ten seconds. She saw a pair of foxes and what might have been a wolf, loping and rangy, with something dangling from its jaws. The sight of it gave her a start, but the thing ignored her and went about its business, which was slipping into a ravine with its prey in order to feed in some dark den, and then she almost wished it would emerge round the next bend to attack her, if only to put an end to the ceaseless swaying and battering of the horse beneath her. Nothing of the sort happened, however, and at around one in the afternoon she found Post and doctor waiting for her on the shores of a broad tidal river she knew she would never get across, not in this lifetime.

AT THE PAUKATAUG

"WELL, THE ROAD ENDS here, then, Missus, because the doctor has his business in Kingston town and I've got the letters to deliver." The Post was leaning across his saddle, giving her a look of indifference. He was going to desert her and it didn't bother him a whit.

The doctor said something then about the ebbing tide, but she couldn't quite fathom what he was getting at until Nathan translated: "He says it's easier crossing at low tide—"

"Well, when is that, pray?"

"Three hour. Maybe more."

"And you won't wait?"

Neither man spoke. They were both of them like the boys she used to teach at school, caught out at something—doing wrong and knowing it—but unequal to admitting it. She felt her jaws clench. "You'd desert me, then?"

It took a moment, and then Nathan pointed an insolent finger at what at first she'd taken to be a heap of flood-run brush, but which she now saw was some sort of habitation. "Old Man Cotter lives there," he said, and at the sound of his voice a great gray-winged bird rose out of the shallows at river's edge and ascended like a kite on the currents of the air. "He'll take you in."

Stunned, she just sat there astride her horse and watched the Post and doctor slash into the current until the water was at their waists and all that was visible of their mounts were their heads and a flat sheen of pounding rump, and then she made her way to the ramshackle collection of weathered boards and knocked at the door. The old man who answered gave her a startled look, as if he'd never seen a woman before, or a lady at any rate, but she steeled herself, and trusting in human kindness, offered him a coin and asked if she might shelter with him until the tide drew off. Very slowly, as if it were coming from a long way off, the old man discovered a smile and then stood back and held the door open for her. She hesitated—the floor was bare earth and there were animal skins on the wall, the place as dank and cold as a cellar. She turned to look back at the river, but the Post and his companion were already gone and the day was blowing away to the east in a tatter of cloud. She stepped inside.

THE PAUKATAUG TO STONINGTOWN

THERE WAS A WIFE inside that hut and two children, both girls and ill-favored, and the whole miserable family dressed in rags and deerskin, and no furniture but for the rounds of logs cut for stools, a bed with a glass bottle hanging at the head of it for what purpose she could only imagine (decoration?), an earthen cup, a pewter basin and a board supported on rough-cut props to serve as a table. The hearth was a crude array of blackened stone, and as Sarah stepped through the door the wife was just setting a few knots of wood to the flame. "I don't mean to intrude," she said, all the family's starved blue eyes on her, "but I've been deserted here at the river and I don't know what else to do—"

The wife looked down at her feet and murmured that she was welcome and could make herself at home and that they were very honored to have her. "Here," she said, "you just sit here," and she indicated the bed. After that, no one said a word, the girls slipping out the door as soon as they could and the old man responding to Sarah's questions and observations ("It must be solitary out here" and "Do you get into Stoningtown much?") with a short sharp grunt of denial or affirmation. The dirt of the floor was pounded hard. The fire was meager. A draft flowed continuously through the gaps in the river-run boards that made the walls of the place. She was cold, hungry, tired, uncomfortable. She closed her eyes and endured.

When she opened them, there was a new person in the room. At first she took him to be a wild Indian because there was no stitch of civilized clothing about him, from his moccasins to his buck-skin shirt and crude hat tanned with the fur of some creature still on it, but she gathered from the conversation—what little of it there was—that he was the son-in-law of the old man and woman and living off in the deeper wild in a hovel of his own with their daughter, also named Sarah. No introductions were made, and the man all but ignored her, till finally Mr. Cotter rose to his feet and said, "Well, the river'll be down now and I expect it's time you wanted to go, Missus."

Sarah began to gather herself up, thanking them for their hospitality, such as it was, but then wondered aloud who was to escort her across the river? And beyond, on the road to Stoningtown?

The old man gestured toward his son-in-law, who looked up at her now from out of the depths of his own cold blue eyes. "If you'd give him something, Missus, I'm sure George here could be persuaded."

STONINGTOWN TO NEW LONDON FERRY

IT WAS PAST DARK when they limped into Stoningtown and her guide (no, he hadn't murdered her along the road or robbed her or even offered up an uncivil remark, and she reminded herself the whole way not to judge people by their appearances, though she could hardly help herself) showed her to the Saxtons', where she was to spend the night in the cleanest and most orderly house she'd yet seen since leaving Boston. Will Saxton was a kinsman on her mother's side and he and his wife had been expecting her, and they sat her before the fire and fed her till she could eat no more. Oysters, that was what she was to remember of Stoningtown, dripping from the sea and roasted over the coals till the shells popped open, and a lobster fish as long as her arm. And a featherbed she could sink into as if it were a snowdrift, if only the snow were a warm and comforting thing and not the particles of ice flung down out of the sky by a wrathful God.

She left at three the following afternoon—Thursday, her fourth day on the road—in the company of the Saxtons' neighbor, Mr. Polly, and his daughter, Jemima, who looked to be fourteen or so. The road here was clear and dry but for the dull brown puddles that spotted the surface like a geographical pox, but they were easy enough to avoid and the weather was cool and fair with scarcely the breath of a breeze. They looked out to the sea and moved along at a reasonable rate—Mr. Polly, a man her own age and cultivated, a farmer and schoolmaster, setting a pace to accommodate his daughter. All went well for the first hour or so, and then the daughter—Jemima—began to complain.

The saddle was too hard for her. The horse was lame and couldn't keep to a regular gait. She was bored. The countryside was ill-favored—or no, it wasn't just ill-favored but what you'd expect to see on the outskirts of hell. Could she get down and walk now? For just a hundred yards? Her backside was broken. Couldn't they stop? Couldn't they buy that man's farm over there and live in it for the rest of their lives?

Finally—and this when they were in sight of New London and the ferry itself—she got down from the horse in the middle of the road and refused to go a step farther.

Sarah was herself in a savage mood, wishing for the hundredth time that she'd stayed home in her parlor and let Mrs. Trowbridge worry over her own affairs, and each second she had to sit on that horse without moving forward was a goad to her temper. Mr. Polly gave her a look as if to say *What am I to do?* and before she could think she said that if it was her daughter she'd give her a whipping she'd never forget.

Jemima, big in the shoulder, with a broad red face beneath her bonnet, informed her that she wasn't her daughter and glad of it too. "You're an old hag from hell," she spat, her face twisted in a knot, "and I wouldn't live with you—or listen to you either—if I was an orphan and starving."

The trees stood still. In the near distance there was a farm and a pen and a smell of cattle. Then the father dismounted, took the daughter by the arm and marched into a thicket of the woods, where both their voices were raised in anger until the first blow descended. And then there were screams, raw, outraged, crescendoing, until you would have thought the savages had got hold of her to strip the skin from her limbs with their bloody knives. The blows stopped. Silence reigned. And Jemima, looking sullen and even redder in the face and probably elsewhere too, followed her father out of the thicket and climbed wearily back into the saddle. She didn't speak another word till they arrived at the ferry.

AT NEW LONDON

SHE WOULD JUST AS soon forget about that careening ride over the Thames on the ferry, with the wind coming up sudden and hard and the horses jerking one way and the other and Jemima screaming like a mud hen and roaring out at her father to save her because she was afraid of going overboard and Sarah's own stomach coming up on her till there was nothing left in it and the certainty that she would die stuck there in her throat like a criminal's dagger, because here she was handsomely lodged at the house of the Reverend Gordon Saltonstall, minister of the town, and he and the Reverend Mrs. Saltonstall entertained her with their high-minded conversation and a board fit for royalty. Her bed was hard, the room Spartan. But she was among civilized people now, in a real and actual town, and she slept as if she were stretched out in her own bed at home.

NEW LONDON TO SAYBROOK AND
ON TO KILLINGWORTH

FOR ALL THAT, she awoke early and anxious. She felt a lightness in her head, which was the surest sign she was catching cold, and she thought of those long hours in the rain on the road to the Havenses' and the unwholesome night airs she'd been compelled to breathe through the traverse of a hundred bogs and low places along the road, and all at once she saw herself dying there in the Reverend's bed and buried in his churchyard so many hard miles from home. She pictured her daughter then, pale, sickly, always her mother's child and afraid of her own shadow, having to make this grueling journey just to stand over her mother's grave in an alien place, and she got up out of the bed choking back a sob. Her nose dripped. Her limbs ached. She was a widow alone in the world and in a strange place and she'd never felt so sorry for herself in her life. Still, she managed to pull on her clothes and boots and find her way to the kitchen where the servant had got the fire going and she warmed herself and had a cup of the Reverend's Jamaica coffee and felt perceptibly better. As soon as the Reverend appeared, she begged him to find her a guide to New Haven, where she could go to her kinsmen and feel safe from all illness and accident.

The Reverend said he knew just the man and went out to fetch him, and by eight o'clock in the morning she was back in the saddle and enjoying the company of Mr. Joshua Wheeler, a young gentleman of the town who had business in New Haven. He was educated and had a fresh look about him, but was crippled in the right arm as the result of a riding accident when he was a boy. He talked of *The Pilgrim's Progress, Paradise Lost* and *The Holy Bible* as if he'd written them himself, and though her acquaintance with all three was not what it was once or should have been, she was able to quote him three lines of Milton—"And fast by, hanging in a golden chain, / This pendent world, in bigness as a star / Of smallest magnitude close by the moon"—and he rewarded her with a smile that made the wilderness melt away to nothing. He was like her own husband, the late, lamented Mr. Knight, when he was twenty and two, that was what she was thinking, and her nose stopped dripping and the miles fell away behind them without effort or pain.

Until they came to the bridge near Lyme. It was a doubtful affair at best, rickety and swaybacked, and it took everything she had in her to urge her mount out onto it. The horse stepped forward awkwardly, the bridge dipped, the river ran slick and hard beneath it. Her heart was in her mouth. "Get on," she told the horse, but she kept her voice low for fear of startling him, and the animal moved forward another five paces and froze there as if he'd been turned to stone. From the far side, where the trees framed him on his mount and the sun shone sick and pale off the naked rock, Mr. Wheeler called out encouragement. "Come ahead, Sarah," he urged. "It's as safe as anything." If she hadn't been so scared, suspended there over the river and at the mercy of a dumb beast that could decide to stagger sideways as easily as go forward, she might have reflected on how easy it was for him to say since he was already over on solid ground and didn't have her fear of water. Or bridges. She gave him a worried glance and saw from the look on his face that he could have dashed across the bridge time and again without a thought and that he knew how to swim like a champion and trusted his horse and was too young yet to know how the hurts of the world accumulate. A long moment passed. She leaned close to the horse's ear and made a clicking noise. Nothing happened. Finally, in exasperation, she resorted to the whip—just the merest flicker of it across the animal's hindquarters—and the horse bucked and the world spun as if it were indeed hanging from a pendant and she knew she was dead. Somehow, though, she'd got to the other side, and somehow she managed to fight down her nerves and forge on, even to Saybrook Ferry and beyond.

She must not have said two words to Mr. Wheeler the rest of the way, but when they disembarked from the ferry he suggested they stop at the ordinary there to bait the horses and take this opportunity of refreshment. It was two in the afternoon. Sarah had had nothing since breakfast, and that she couldn't keep down for worry over falling sick on the road, and so she agreed and they found themselves at a table with one respectable diner and three or four local idlers. The landlady—in a dirty apron, hair hanging loose and scratching at her scalp with both hands as if to dislodge some foreign thing clinging there—told them she'd broil some mutton if they'd like, but as good as that sounded, Sarah couldn't muster much enthusiasm. She kept thinking of the landlady's hands in her hair, and when the dish did come—the mutton pickled, with cabbage and a bit of turnip in a sauce that was so ancient it might have been scraped together from the moss grown on the skulls of the Christian martyrs—she found she had no appetite. Nor did Mr. Wheeler, who tried gamely to lift the spoon a second time to his lips, but wound up pushing the dish to the corner of the table while Sarah paid sixpence apiece for their dinners, or rather the smell of dinner.

They pressed on after that for Killingworth and arrived by seven at night. It was Friday now, the end of her fifth day on the road. She didn't care about the bed or the food—though the former was soft and the latter savory, roasted venison, in fact—but only the road ahead and the sanctuary of Thomas Trowbridge's house in New Haven. If she could have flown, if she could have mounted on the back of some great eagle or griffin, she would have done it without a second thought. *New Haven,* she told herself as she drifted off to sleep despite the noise and furor of the inn and the topers who seemed to have followed her all the way from Dedham Tavern, *New Haven tomorrow.*

KILLINGWORTH TO NEW HAVEN

THEY SET OUT early after a satisfactory breakfast, and though there were the Hammonasett, the East and West Rivers to cross and a dozen lesser waters, the fords were shallow and she barely hesitated. It was overcast and cool, the breeze running in off the sea to loosen her hair and beat it about her bonnet, Mr. Wheeler giving her a second day's course in literature, the way relatively easy. And what did she see in that country on the far side of the Connecticut River? Habitations few and far between, a clutch of small boats at sea, two Indians walking along the roadway in their tatters with scallop shells stuck in their ears and dragging the carcass of some dead half-skinned animal in the dirt behind them. She saw shorebirds, a spouting whale out to sea, a saltwater farm on a promontory swallowed up in mist, and, as they got closer to their destination, boys and dogs and rude houses and yards chopped out of the surrounding forest, stubble fields and pumpkins still fat on the vine and scattered like big glowing cannonballs across the landscape. And then they were arrived and she was so relieved to see her cousin Thomas Trowbridge standing there outside his considerable stone house with his wife, Hannah, and a sleek black dog that she nearly forgot to introduce Mr. Wheeler properly, but they were all in the parlor by then and tea was brewing and something in the pot so ambrosial she could have fainted for the very richness of the smell.

AT NEW HAVEN

SHE STAYED two months, or one day short of it, having arrived on Saturday, the seventh of October, and leaving for New York on the sixth of December in the company of Mr. Trowbridge. In the interim, she vanquished her cold, wrote in her journal and prosecuted her business, at the same time taking advantage of this period of quiet to learn something of the people and customs of the Connecticut Colony, which to her mind at least, seemed inferior in most respects to the Massachusetts. The leaves brightened and fell, the weather grew bitter. She spun wool. Sat by the fire and chatted with Mrs. Trowbridge while the servants made a show of being busy and the slaves skulked in the kitchen to escape the cold of the fields. There were savages here aplenty, more even than at home, and they were a particularly poor and poorly attired lot, living on their own lands but suffering from a lack of Christian charity on the part of the citizenry. And the people themselves could have benefited from even the most rudimentary education—there wasn't a man or woman walking the streets who was capable of engaging in a conversation that stretched beyond the limits of a sow's indigestion or the salting of pilchards for the barrel.

One afternoon she happened to be at a merchant's house, looking to acquire a few articles to give the Trowbridges in thanks for their hospitality, when in walked a rangy tall bumpkin dressed in skins and Indian shoes and with his cheeks distended by a black plug of tobacco. He stood in the middle of the room, barely glancing at the articles on display, spitting continuously into the dirt of the floor and then covering it over again with the sole of his shoe till he'd made his own personal wallow. The merchant looked inquiringly at him, but he wasn't able to raise his eyes from the floor. Finally, after what must have been five full minutes of silence, he blurted out, "Have you any ribbands and hatbands to sell, I pray?" The merchant avowed he did and then the bumpkin wanted to know the price and the ribbons were produced; at that very instant, in came his inamorata, dropping curtsies and telling him how pretty the ribbon was and what a gentleman he was to buy it for her and did they have any hood silk and thread silk to sew it with? Well, the merchant did, and they bartered over that for half the hour, the bumpkin all the while spitting and spitting again and his wife—if she was his wife—simpering at his arm.

That night, at supper, she remarked to Mrs. Trowbridge that some of her neighbors seemed to lack breeding and Mrs. Trowbridge threw her eyes to the ceiling and said she didn't have to tell *her*.

NEW HAVEN TO FAIRFIELD

THE SADDLE AGAIN. If she'd begun to harden herself to it on the long road from Boston to New Haven, now her layover with the Trowbridges had softened her and the pains that had lain dormant these two months began to reassert themselves. And it was bitter out of doors, a taut curtain of iron-gray cloud pinning them to the earth even as the wind stabbed at her bones and jerked loose every bit of chaff and ordure in the road and flung it in her face. The breath of the horse was palpable. Her fingers and toes lost all feeling and never regained them, not for two days running.

There was a brief contretemps at the Stratford Ferry—water, more water—and she froze upright with fear and at first wouldn't budge from the horse, Thomas Trowbridge's wide lunar face floating somewhere beneath her as he pleaded and reasoned and tried repeatedly to take hold of her hand, but in the end she mastered herself and the expedition went forward. The water beat at the flat bottom of the boat and she buried her face in her hands to keep herself from screaming, and then she thought she was screaming but it was only the gulls, white ghosts crying in the gloom. After that, she was only too glad to dismount at the ordinary two miles up the road and sit by the fire while the horses were baited and the hostess served up a hot punch and a pumpkin / Indian bread that proved, unfortunately, to be inedible.

By seven at night they came to Fairfield, and lodged there.

FAIRFIELD TO RYE

THEY SET OUT early, arriving just after noon at Norowalk, where the food, for once, was presentable and fresh, though the fried venison the landlady served up could have used more pepper in the seasoning and the tea was as weak as dishwater. The road from there to Rye was eight hours and more, a light snow swirling round them and the last four hours of the journey prosecuted in utter darkness, with only the faint tracks of a previous traveler to show them the way through the pale gauze of the night. And here she had a new sensation—her feet ached, aside from having gone numb with the cold, that is. For there was a prodigious high hill along the road, a mile or more in length, and they had to go afoot here, leading their horses behind them. Her legs took on all of her weight. They sank beneath her. She couldn't lift them. Couldn't breathe. And there was

Thomas Trowbridge plodding ahead of her like a spirit risen in his winding sheet and his horse white too and the snow still falling as if it had been coming down since the beginning of creation and every-thing else—the sun, the fields, high summer and green crops—had been an illusion. "Is it much farther yet?" she asked, gasping for breath, and she must have asked a thousand times. "Na much," came the reply, blown back in the wind.

A French family kept the ordinary at Rye, and this was a novelty to her. She sat by the fire, shivering till she thought she would split in two, and then, so famished from the ordeal of the road and the cold and the weather she could have eaten up every last scrap of food in the county, she asked for a fricassee, which the Frenchman claimed as his speciality. "Oh, Madame," he told her, all the while drawing at his pewter cup, "I can prepare a fricassee to fit a king, your king or mine." But when it came it was like no fricassee she'd ever seen or tasted, its sauce like gluten and spiced so even a starving dog would have spat it out. She was outraged and she told him so, even as Thomas Trowbridge shoveled a simple dinner of salt pork and fried eggs into his groaning maw and pronounced it as good as he'd ever tasted. "I won't eat this," Sarah said, piercing the Frenchman with a look. "You'll cook me eggs."

"I will cook you nothing," the Frenchman said. "I go to bed now. And so do you."

RYE TO SPUYTEN DUYVIL

THE NIGHT WAS SLEEPLESS and miserable, the bed an instrument of torture, Thomas Trowbridge and another gentleman making their beds in the same room and keeping her awake and furious with their blowing and snorting till she thought she'd have to get up and stuff rags down their throats, and they were away at first light, without breakfast. The previous day's snow had accumulated only to three or four inches but it had frozen hard during the night so that each step of her horse groaned and crackled underfoot. To say that she ached would be an understatement, and there was the cold—bitterer even than yesterday—and the scare her horse gave her every two minutes when its feet skewed away and it made a slow, heaving recovery that at any moment could have been its last. Did she picture herself down beneath the beast with her leg fractured so that the bone protruded and the unblemished snow ran red with her blood? She did. Repeatedly.

By seven in the morning they reached the French town of New Rochelle, and her previous experience of Frenchmen notwithstanding, had an excellent breakfast at an ordinary there. She was so frozen she could scarcely lift the fork to her mouth and found she had no desire to leave the fireside ever again, no matter that her family would never more lay eyes on her and the widowed Mrs. Trowbridge would die in penury and the life of Boston—and its gossip—would go on without Sarah Kemble Knight ever seeing or knowing of it. But within an hour of their alighting, they were back on the road even as she cursed Thomas Trowbridge under her breath and her horse stumbled and slid and made risk of her life and limb with every clumsy faltering step.

They rode all day, through an increasingly civilized country, from time to time meeting other people on the road, people on foot, on horseback, in wagons. Cold, sore and miserable as she was, she nonetheless couldn't help feeling her spirits lighten as they came closer to their destination—here was real progress, in a peopled country, the wilderness falling away to the axe on both sides of the road. She took it all in and thought to memorialize it in her journal when they were arrived at New York late that night. All well and good. But then came the final crisis, the one that nearly prevented her from laying eyes on that so nearly foreign city with its Dutchmen pulling at their clay pipes and playing at draughts in stifling taverns, the women in their peculiar dress and jeweled earrings—even the dogs that looked to be from another world—and the amenable society of the Governor Lord Cornbury from the Jerseys and the solid brick buildings built cheek to jowl all through the lower town and a hundred other things. The sleighing parties. The shops. The houses of entertainment in a place called the Bowery and the good drink—choice beer, metheglin and cider—and a standard board that consisted of five and six dishes served hot and steaming from the fire. All this. All this and more.

But when they came to Spuyten Duyvil, the Spitting Devil, at the crossing to the north end of Manhattoes Island, with the night coming down and the wind blowing a gale and the waters surging as if it were the Great Flood all over again, she couldn't go on. There was a bridge here, narrow and unreliable, perched high up out over the waters, and it was slick with a coating of ice that lay black and glistening in the fading light. She got down to lead her horse, because if she led him she'd be lower to the ground—or the planking— and wouldn't be at the mercy of his uncertain footing. Thomas Trowbridge, hulking in his coats, paid the gatekeeper the sixpence for the two of them, and started across, mounted and oblivious; Sarah held back.

He was halfway across to the far shore, nearly invisible to her in the accumulating dark and the hard white pellets of ice that seemed to have come up with the wind, and the gatekeeper was huddled back in his hut giving her an odd look. All she could hear was the thunder of the roiling water where the river hit the surge of the tide even as the skin of it, black and unforgiving, stretched taut beneath her and exploded again. She was going to die. She was certain of it. She'd come all this way only to have the horse panic and trample her or bump her over the rail and into the spume or the bridge collapse beneath her. Thomas Trowbridge was gone now, enfolded in the mist, and he hadn't even so much as glanced back. The city was on the far shore, somewhere to the south of the island, and it was what she'd come for. There was lodging there. Fire. Food. Die or not, she stepped out onto the bridge.

It quaked and quailed. The wind thrashed. The horse jerked at her arm like a dead weight come to life. But she steeled herself and put one foot in front of the other and never looked down, a whole eternity passing till she was halfway across and then another eternity till she made the far side in a hard pale swirl of spray thrown up off the rocks and frozen in mid-air. For a long while she just stood there looking back the way she'd come, the bridge fading away into the blow till it might not have been there at all. But it was there, because this was no child's tale struck with magic, and she knew, even as she turned her mount and swung out onto the road, that she would have to cross it again.

Up Against the Wall

MY CHILDHOOD wasn't exactly ideal, and I mention it here not as an excuse, but a point of reference. For the record, both my parents drank heavily, and in the early days, before my father gave up and withered away somewhere deep in the upright shell of himself, there was shouting, there were accusations, tears, violence. And smoke. The house was a factory of smoke, his two packs of Camels a day challenging the output of her two packs of Marlboros. I spent a lot of time outside. I ran with the kids in the neighborhood, the athletic ones when I was younger, the sly and disaffected as I came into my teens, and after an indifferent career at an indifferent college, I came back home to live rent-free in my childhood room in the attic as the rancor simmered below me and the smoke rose up through the floorboards and seeped in around the doorframe.

After a fierce and protracted struggle, I landed a job teaching eighth-grade English in a ghetto school, though I hadn't taken any of the required courses and had no intention of doing so. That job saved my life. Literally. Teaching, especially in a school as desperate as this, was considered vital to the national security and it got me a deferment two weeks short of the date I was to report for induction into the U.S. Army, with Vietnam vivid on the horizon. All well and fine. I had a job. And a routine. I got up early each morning, though it was a strain, showered, put on a tie and introspectively chewed Sugar Pops in the car on the way to work. I ate lunch out of a brown paper bag. Nights, I went straight to my room to play records and hammer away at my saxophone and vocals.

Then a day came—drizzling, cold, the wet skin of dead leaves on the pavement and nothing happening anywhere in the world, absolutely nothing—when I was in the local record store turning over albums to study the bright glare of the product and skim the liner notes, killing time till the movie started in the mall. Something with a monumental bass line was playing over the speakers, something slow, delicious, full of hooks and grooves and that steamroller bass, and when I looked up vacantly to appreciate it, I found I was looking into the face of a guy I recalled vaguely from high school.

I saw in a glance he'd adopted the same look I had—the greasy suede jacket, bell-bottoms and Dingo boots, his hair gone long over the collar in back, the shadowy beginnings of a mustache—and that was all it took. "Aren't you—Cole?" I said. "Cole, right?" And there he was, wrapping my hand in a cryptic soul shake, pronouncing my name without hesitation. We stood there catching up while people drifted by us and the bass pounded through the speakers. Where had he been? Korea, in the Army. Living with his own little mama-san, smoking opium every night till he couldn't feel the floor under his futon. And I was a teacher now, huh? What a gas. And should he start calling me professor or what?

We must have talked for half an hour or so, the conversation ranging from people we knew in common to bands, drugs and girls we'd hungered for in school, until he said, "So what you doing tonight? Later, I mean?"

I was ashamed to tell him I was planning on taking in a movie alone, so I just shrugged. "I don't know. Go home, I guess, and listen to records."

"Where you living?"

Another shrug, as if to show it was nothing, a temporary arrangement till I could get on my feet, find my own place and begin my real life, the one I'd been apprenticing for all these years: "My parents'."

Cole said nothing. Just gave me a numb look. "Yeah," he said, after a moment, "I hear you. But listen, you want to go out, drive around, smoke a number? You smoke, right?"

I did. Or I had. But I had no connection, no stash of my own, no privacy. "Yeah," I said. "Sounds good."

"I might know where there's a party," he said, letting his cold blue eyes sweep the store as if the party might materialize in the far corner. "Or a bar," he said, coming back to me, "I know this bar—"

I WAS LATE for homeroom in the morning. It mattered in some obscure way, in the long run, that is, because funding was linked to attendance and there had to be somebody there to check off the names each morning, but the school was in such an advanced state of chaos I don't know if anyone even noticed. Not the first time, anyway. But homeroom was the least of my worries—it was mercifully brief and no one was expected to do anything other than merely exist for the space of ten minutes. It was the rest of the slate that was the trial, one swollen class after another shuffling into the room, hating school, hating culture, hating me, and I hated them in turn because they were brainless and uniform and they didn't understand me at all. I was just like them, couldn't they see that? I was no oppressor, no tool of the ruling class, but an authentic rebel, twenty-one years old and struggling mightily to grow a mustache because Ringo Starr had one and George Harrison and Eric Clapton and just about anybody else staring out at you from the front cover of a record album. But none of that mattered. I was the teacher, they were the students. Those were our roles, and they were as fixed and mutually exclusive as they'd been in my day, in my parents' day, in George Washington's day for all I knew.

From the minute the bell rang the rebellion began to simmer. Two or three times a period it would break out in riot and I would find myself confronting some wired rangy semi-lunatic who'd been left back twice and at sixteen already had his own mustache grown in as thick as fur, and there went the boundaries in a hard wash of threat and violence. Usually I'd manage to get the offender out in the hall, away from the eyes of the mob, and if the occasion called for it I would throw him against the wall, tear his shirt and use the precise language of the streets to let him know in excruciating detail just who was the one with the most at stake here. A minute later we'd return to the room, the victor and the vanquished, and the rest of them would feel something akin to awe for about ten minutes, and then it would all unwind again.

Stress. That's what I'm talking about. One of the other new teachers—he looked to be thirty or so, without taste or style, a drudge who'd been through half a dozen schools already—used to get so worked up he'd have to dash into the lavatory and vomit between classes, and there was no conquering that smell, not even with a fistful of breath mints. The students knew it, and they came at him like hyenas piling on a corpse. He lasted a month, maybe less. This wasn't pedagogy—it was survival. Still, everybody got paid and they were free to go home when the bell rang at the end of the day, and some of them—some of us—even got to avoid the real combat zone, the one they showed in living color each night on the evening news.

WHEN I GOT HOME that afternoon, Cole was waiting for me. He was parked out front of my house in his mother's VW Bug, a cigarette clamped between his teeth as he beat at the dashboard with a pair of drumsticks, the radio cranked up high. I could make out the seething churn of his shoulders and the rhythmic bob of his head through the oval window set in the back of the Bug, the sticks flashing white, the car rocking on its springs, and when I killed the engine of my own car—a 1955 Pontiac that had once been blue, but was piebald now with whitish patches of blistered paint—I could hear the music even through the safety glass of the rolled-up window. "Magic Carpet Ride," that was the song, with its insistent bass and nagging vocal, a tune you couldn't escape on AM radio, and there were worse, plenty worse.

My first impulse was to get out of the car and slide in beside him—here was adventure, liberation, a second consecutive night on the town—but then I thought better of it. I was dressed in my school clothes—dress pants I wouldn't wish on a corpse, button-down shirt and tie, a brown corduroy sport coat—and my hair was slicked down so tightly to my scalp it looked as if it had been painted on, a style I'd adopted to disguise the length and shagginess of it toward the end of appeasing the purse-mouthed principal and preserving my job. And life. But I couldn't let Cole see me like this—what would he think? I studied the back of the Bug a moment, waiting for his eyes to leap to the rearview mirror, but he was absorbed, oblivious, stoned no doubt—and I wanted to be stoned too, share the sacrament, shake it out—but not like this, not in these clothes. What I finally did was ease out of the car, slip down the block and cut through the neighbors' to our backyard, where the bulk of the house screened me from view.

I came up the cellar stairs from the garage, my father sunk into the recliner in the living room with the TV going—the news grim and grimmer—and my mother rattling things around in the kitchen. "You going to eat tonight?" she asked, just to say something. I ate every night—I couldn't afford not to. She had a cigarette at her lips, a drink in her hand—scotch and water. There were dishes set out on the table, a pot of something going on the stove. "I'm making chili con carne."

I had a minute, just a minute, no more, because I was afraid Cole would wake up to the fact that he was waiting for nothing and then it would be the room upstairs, the hypnosis of the records, the four walls and the sloping ceiling and a gulf of boredom so deep you could have sailed a fleet into it. "No," I said, "I think I might go out."

She stirred the pot, went to set the cigarette in the ashtray on the stove and saw that there was another there, already burning and rimmed red with lipstick. "Without dinner?" (I have to give her her due here—she loved me, her only son, and my father must have loved me too, in his own way, but I didn't know that then, or didn't care, and it's too late now to do anything about it.)

"Yeah, I might eat out, I guess. With Cole."

"Who?"

"Cole Harman. He was in high school with me?"

She just shrugged. My father said nothing, not hello or goodbye or you look half-starved already and you tell me you're going to miss dinner? The TV emitted the steady whipcrack of small-arms fire, and then the correspondent came on with the day's body count. Four minutes later—the bells, the boots, a wide-collared shirt imprinted with two flaming outsized eyeballs under the greasy jacket and my hair kinked up like Hendrix's—and I was out the door.

"HEY," I SAID, rapping at the window of the Bug. "Hey, it's me."

Cole looked up as if he'd been asleep, as if he'd been absorbed in some other reality altogether, one that didn't seem to admit or even recognize me. It took him a moment, and then he leaned across the passenger's seat and flipped the lock, and I went round the car and slid in beside him. I said something like, "Good to see you, man," and reached out for the soul shake, which he returned, and then I said, "So, what's up? You want to go to Chase's, or what?"

He didn't reply. Just handed me the tight white tube of a joint, put the car in gear and hit the accelerator with the sound of a hundred eggbeaters all rattling at once. I looked back to see my house receding at the end of the block and felt as if I'd been rescued. I put the lighter to the joint.

The night before we'd gone to Chase's, a bar in town I'd never been to before, an ancient place with a pressed-tin ceiling and paneled booths gone the color of beef jerky with the smoke of a hundred thousand cigarettes. The music was of the moment, though, and the clientele mostly young—women were there, in their low-slung jeans and gauzy tops, and it was good to see them, exciting in the way of an afterthought that suddenly blooms into prominence (I'd left a girlfriend behind at college, promising to call, visit, write, but long distance was expensive, she was five hundred miles away and I wasn't much of a writer). My assumption—my hope—was that we'd go back there tonight.

But we didn't. Cole just drove aimlessly past bleached-out lawns and squat houses, down the naked tunnels of trees and into the country, where the odd field—crippled cornstalks, rotting pumpkins— was squeezed in among the housing developments and the creep of shopping malls. We smoked the joint down to the nub, employed a roach clip and alternated hits till it was nothing but air. An hour stole by. The same hits thumped through the radio, the same commercials. It was getting dark.

After a while we pulled up at a deserted spot along a blacktop road not two miles from my house. I knew the place from when I was a kid, riding my bike out to the reservoir to fish and throw rocks and fool around. There was a waist-high wall of blackened stone running the length of a long two blocks, and behind that a glimpse of a cluster of stone cottages through the dark veins of the trees. We'd been talking about something comforting—a band or a guitar player—and I'd been drifting, wheeling round and round the moment, secure, calm, and now suddenly we were stopped out on the road in the middle of nowhere. "So, what's the deal?" I said.

A car came up the street in the opposite direction and the lights caught Cole's face. He squinted, put a hand up to shield his eyes till the car had passed, and he craned his neck to make sure it was still moving, watching for the flash of brake lights as it rounded the curve at the corner behind us and vanished into the night. "Nothing," he said, a spark of animation igniting his voice as if it were a joke—the car, the night, the joint—"I just wanted you to meet some people, that's all."

"What people? Out here?" I gave it a beat. "You don't mean the little people, do you? The elves? Where are they—crouching behind the wall there? Or in their burrows, is that where they are—asleep in their burrows?"

We both had a laugh, one of those protracted, breast-pounding jags of hilarity that remind you just how much you've smoked and how potent it was. "No," he said, still wheezing, "no. Big people. Real people, just like you and me." He pointed to the faintest glow of light from the near cottage. "In there."

I was confused. The entrance to the place—the driveway, which squeezed under a stone arch somebody had erected there at some distant point in our perfervid history—was up on the cross street at the end of the block, where the car had just turned. "So why don't we just go in the driveway?" I wanted to know.

Cole took a moment to light a cigarette, then he cracked the door and the dark pure refrigerated smell of the night hit me. "Not cool," he said. "Not cool at all."

◆

I MADE A REAL EFFORT the next day, and though I had less than three hours' sleep, I made homeroom with maybe six seconds to spare. The kids—the students, my charges—must have scented the debauch on me, the drift away from the straight and narrow they demanded as part of the social contract, because they were more restive than usual, more boisterous and slippery, as if the seats couldn't contain them. There was one—there's always one, memorable not for excellence or scholarship but for weakness, only that—and he spoke up now. Robert, his name was, Robert Rowe. He was fifteen, left back once, and he was no genius but he had more of a spark in him than the others could ever hope for, and that made him stand out— it gave him power, but he didn't know what to do with it. "Hey, Mr. Caddis," he called from the back of the room where he was slumped into one of the undersized desks we'd inherited from another era when the average student was shorter, slimmer, more attentive and eager. "You look like shit, you know that?"

The rest of them—this was only homeroom, where, as I've indicated, nothing was expected—froze for a moment. The interaction was delicious for them, I'm sure—they were scientists dissecting the minutest gradations of human behavior: would I explode? Overheat and run for the lavatory like Mr. James, the puker? Ignore the comment? Pretend I hadn't heard?

I was beat, truly. Two nights running with less than three hours' sleep. But I was energized too because something new was happening to me, something that shone over the bleakness of this job, this place, my parents' damaged lives, as if I'd suddenly discovered the high beams along a dark stretch of highway. "Yeah, Robert," I said, holding him with my eyes, though he tried to duck away, "thanks for the compliment." A tutorial pause, flatly instructive. "You look like shit too."

The cottage, the stone cottage on the far side of the stone wall in the featureless mask of the night that had given way to this moment of this morning, was a place I felt I'd come home to after a long absence. I'd been to war, hadn't I? Now I was home. How else to describe it, what that place meant to me from the minute the door swung back and I stepped inside?

I hadn't known what to expect. We vaulted the stone wall and picked our way through a dark tangle of leafless sumac and stickers that raked at our boots and the oversized flaps of our pants, and then there was another, lower wall, and we were in the yard. Out front was a dirt bike with its back wheel missing, skeletal under the porch light, and there were glittering fragments of other things there too, machines in various states of disassembly—a chain saw minus the chain, an engine block decorated with lit candles that flickered like votives in the dark cups of the cylinders, a gutted amplifier. And there was music. Loud now, loud enough to rattle the glass in the windowpanes. Somebody inside was playing along with the bass line of "Ob-La-Di, Ob-La-Da."

Cole went in without knocking, and I followed. Through a hallway and into the kitchen, *obladi oblada life goes on bra!* There were two women there—girls—rising up from the table in the kitchen with loopy grins to wrap their arms around Cole, and then, after the briefest of introductions—"This is my friend, John, he's a *professor*"—to embrace me too. They were sisters, both tall, with the requisite hair parted in the middle and trailing down their shoulders. Suzie, the younger, darker and prettier one, and JoJo, two years older, with hair the color of rust before it flakes. There was a Baggie of pot on the table, a pipe and what looked to be half a bar of halvah candy but wasn't candy at all. Joss sticks burned among the candles that lit the room. A cat looked up sleepily from a pile of newspaper in the corner. "You want to get high?" JoJo asked, and I was charmed instantly—here she was, the consummate hostess—and a portion of my uncertainty and awkwardness went into retreat.

I looked to Cole, and we both laughed, and this was a laugh of the same quality and flavor as the one we'd shared in the car.

"What?" Suzie said, leaning back against the stove now, grinning wide. "Oh, I get it—you're already stoned, both of you, right? High as kites, right?"

From the living room—the door was closed and I had to presume it was the living room—there was the sudden screech of the needle lifting off the record, then the superamplified rasp of its dropping down again, and "Ob-La-Di, Ob-La-Da" came at us once more. JoJo saw my quizzical look and paused in putting the match to the pipe. "Oh, that's Mike—my boyfriend? He's like obsessed with that song."

I don't know how much time slid by before the door swung open—we were just sitting there at the table, enveloped in the shroud of our own consciousness, the cat receding into the corner that now seemed half a mile away, candles flickering and sending insubstantial shadows up the walls. I turned round to see Mike standing in the doorframe, wearing the strap of his bass like a bandolier over a shirtless chest. He was big, six feet and something, two hundred pounds, and he was built, pectorals and biceps sharply defined, a stripe of hard blue vein running up each arm, but he didn't do calisthenics or lift weights or anything like that—it was just the program of his genes. His hair was long, longer than either of the women's. He wore a Fu Manchu mustache. He was sweating. "That was hot," he said, "that was really hot."

JoJo looked up vacantly. "What," she said, "you want me to turn down the heat?"

He gave a laugh and leaned into the table to pluck a handful of popcorn out of a bowl that had somehow materialized there. "No, I mean the— Didn't you hear me? That last time? That was hot, that's what I'm saying."

It was only then that we got around to introductions, he and Cole swapping handclasps, and then Cole cocking a finger at me. "He's a professor," he said.

Mike took my hand—the soul shake, a pat on the shoulder—and stood there looking bemused. "A professor?" he said. "No shit?"

I was too stoned to parse all the nuances of the question, but still the blood must have risen to my face. "A teacher," I corrected. "You know, just to beat the draft? Like because if you—" and I went off on some disconnected monologue, talking because I was nervous, because I wanted to fit in, and I suppose I would have kept on talking till the sun came up but for the fact that everyone else had gone silent and the realization of it suddenly hit me.

"No shit?" Mike repeated, grinning in a dangerous way. He was swaying over the table, alternately feeding popcorn into the slot of his mouth and giving me a hooded look. "So how old are you—what, nineteen, twenty?"

"Twenty-one. I'll be twenty-two in December."

There was more. It wasn't an inquisition exactly—Cole at one point spoke up for me and said, "He's cool"—but a kind of scientific examination of this rare bird that had mysteriously turned up at the kitchen table. What did I think? I thought Cole should ease up on the professor business—as I got to know him I realized he was inflating me in order to inflate himself—and that we should all smoke some of the hash, though I wasn't the host here and hadn't brought anything to the party.

Eventually, we did smoke—that was what this was all about, community, the community of mind and spirit and style—and we moved into the living room where the big speakers were to listen to the heartbeat of the music and feel the world settle in around us. There were pillows scattered across the floor, more cats, more incense, ShopRite cola and peppermint tea in heavy homemade mugs and a slow sweet seep of peace. I propped my head against a pillow, stretched my feet out before me. The music was a dream, and I closed my eyes and entered it.

A WEEK OR TWO later my mother asked me to meet her after work at a bar/restaurant called the Hollander. This was a place with pretensions to grander things, where older people—people my mother's age—came to drink Manhattans and smoke cigarettes and feel elevated over the crowd that frequented taverns with sawdust on the floors, the sort of places my father favored. Teachers came to the Hollander, lawyers, people who owned car dealerships and dress shops. My mother was a secretary, my father a bus driver. And the Hollander was an ersatz place, with pompous waiters and a fake windmill out front.

She was at the bar, smoking, sitting with a skinny white-haired guy I didn't recognize, and as I came up to them I realized he could have been my father's double, could have been my father, but he wasn't. There were introductions—his name was Jerry Reilly and he was a teacher just like me—and a free beer appeared at my elbow, but I couldn't really fathom what was going on here or why my mother would want me to join her in a place like this. I played it cool, ducked my head and answered Jerry Reilly's interminable questions about school as best I could—*Yeah, sure, I guess I liked it; it was better than being executed in Vietnam, wasn't it?*—without irritating him to the point at which I would miss out on a free dinner, but all I wanted to do was get out of there and meet Cole at the cottage in the woods. As expeditiously as possible. Dinner down, goodbyes and thank-you's on file, and out the door and into the car.

That wasn't how it worked out. Something was in the air and I couldn't fathom what it was. I kept looking at Jerry Reilly, with his cuff links and snowy collar and whipcord tie and thinking, *No, no way—my mother wouldn't cheat on my father, not with this guy.* But her life and what she did with it was a work in progress, as unfathomable to me as my own life must have been to my students—and tonight's agenda was something else altogether, something that came in the form of a very special warning, specially delivered. We were on our third drink, seated in the dining room now, eating steak all around, though my mother barely touched hers and Jerry Reilly just pushed his around the plate every time I lifted my eyes to look at him. "Listen, John," my mother said finally, "I just wanted to say something to you. About Cole."

All the alarm bells went off simultaneously in my head. "Cole?" I echoed.

She gave me a look I'd known all my life, the one reserved for missteps and misdeeds. "He has a record."

So that was it. "What's it to you?"

My mother just shrugged. "I just thought you ought to know, that's all."

"I know. Of course I know. And it's nothing, believe me—a case of mistaken identity. They got the wrong guy is all." The fact was that Cole had been busted for selling marijuana to an undercover agent and they were trying to make a felony out of it even as his mother leaned on a retired judge she knew to step in and squash it. I put on a look of offended innocence. "So what'd you do, hire a detective?"

A thin smile. "I'm just worried about you, that's all."

How I bristled at this. I wasn't a child—I could take care of myself. How many times had her soft dejected voice come at me out of the shadows of the living room at three and four in the morning, where she sat smoking in the dark while I roamed the streets with my friends? *Where had I been?* she always wanted to know. *Nowhere,* I told her. There was the dark, the smell of her cigarette, and then, even softer: *I was worried.* And what did I do now? I worked my face and gave her a disgusted look to show her how far above all this I was.

She looked to Jerry Reilly, then back to me. I became aware of the sound of traffic out on the road. It was dark beyond the windows. "You're not using drugs," she asked, drawing at her cigarette, so that the interrogative lift came in a fume of smoke, "are you?"

THE FIRST TIME I ever saw anyone inject heroin was in the bathroom of that stone cottage in the woods. It was probably the third or fourth night I'd gone there with Cole to hang out, listen to music and be convivial on our own terms (he was living at his parents' house too, and there was no percentage in that). Mike greeted us at the door—he'd put a leather jacket on over a T-shirt and he was all business, heading out to the road to meet a guy named Nicky and they were going on into town to score and we should just hang tight because they'd be right back and did we happen to have any cash on us?—and then we went in and sat with the girls and smoked and didn't think about much of anything until the front door jerked back on its hinges half an hour later and Mike and Nicky came storming into the room as if their jackets had been set afire.

Then it was into the bathroom, Mike first, the door open to the rest of us lined up behind him, Nicky (short, with a full beard that did nothing to flesh out a face that had been reduced to the sharp lineaments of bone and cartilage) and the two sisters, Cole and me. I'd contributed five dollars to the enterprise, though I had my doubts. I'd never done anything like this and I was scared of the consequences, the droning narration of the anti-drug films from high school riding up out of some backwater of my mind to assert itself, to take over, become shrill even. Mike threw off his jacket, tore open two glassine packets with his teeth and carefully—meticulously— shook out the contents into a tablespoon. It was a white powder, and it could have been anything, baking soda, confectioners' sugar, Polident, but it wasn't, and I remember thinking how innocuous it looked, how anonymous. In the next moment, Mike sat heavily on the toilet, drew some water up into the syringe I'd seen lying there on a shelf in the medicine cabinet last time I'd used the facilities, squeezed a few drops into the powder, mixed it around and then held a lighter beneath the spoon. Then he tied himself off at the biceps with a bit of rubber tubing, drew the mixture from the spoon through a ball of cotton and hit a vein. I watched his eyes. Watched the rush take him, and then the nod. Nicky was next, then Suzie, then JoJo, and finally Cole. Mike hit them, one at a time, like a doctor. I watched each of them rush and go limp, my heart hammering at my rib cage, the record in the living room repeating over and over because nobody had bothered to put the changer down, and then it was my turn. Mike held up the glassine packet. "It's just a taste," he said. "Three-dollar bag. You on for it?"

"No," I said, "I mean, I don't think I—"

He studied me a moment, then tossed me the bag. "It's a waste," he said, "a real waste, man." His voice was slow, the voice of a record played at the wrong speed. He shook his head with infinite calm, moving it carefully from side to side as if it weighed more than the cottage itself. "But hey, we'll snort it this time. You'll see what you're missing, right?"

I saw. Within the week I was getting off too, and it was my secret— my initiation into a whole new life—and the tracks, the bite marks of the needle that crawled first up one arm and then the other, were my testament.

◆

IT WAS MY JOB to do lunch duty one week a month, and lunch duty consisted of keeping the student body out of the building for forty-five minutes while they presumably went home, downtown or over to the high school and consumed whatever nourishment was available to them. It was necessary to keep them out of the junior high building for the simple reason that they would destroy it through an abundance of natural high spirits and brainless joviality. I stood in the dim hallway, positioned centrally between the three doors that opened from the southern, eastern and western sides of the building, and made my best effort at chasing them down when they burst in howling against the frigid collapse of the noon hour. On the second day of my third tour of duty, Robert Rowe sauntered in through the front doors and I put down my sandwich—the one my mother had made me in the hour of the wolf before going off to work herself—and reminded him of the rules.

He opened his face till it bloomed like a flower and held out his palms. He was wearing a T-shirt and a sleeveless parka. I saw that he'd begun to let his hair go long. "I just wanted to ask you a question is all."

I was chewing tunafish on rye, standing there in the middle of all that emptiness in my ridiculous pants and rumpled jacket. The building, like most institutions of higher and lower learning, was overheated, and in chasing half a dozen of my charges out the door I'd built up a sweat that threatened to break my hair loose of its mold. Without thinking, I slipped off the jacket and let it dangle from one hand; without thinking, I'd pulled a short-sleeved button-down shirt out of my closet that morning because all the others were dirty. That was the scene. That was the setup. "Sure," I said. "Go ahead."

"I was just wondering—you ever read this book, *The Man with the Golden Arm*?"

"Nelson Algren?"

He nodded.

"No," I said. "I've heard of it, though."

He took a moment with this, then cocked his head back till it rolled on his shoulders and gave me a dead-on look. "He shoots up."

"Who?"

"The guy in the book. All the time." He was studying me, gauging how far he could go. "You know what that's like?"

I played dumb.

"You don't? You really don't?"

I shrugged. Dodged his eyes.

There was a banging at the door behind us, hilarious faces there, then the beat of retreating footsteps. Robert moved back a pace, but he held me with his gaze. "Then what's with the spots on your arms?"

I looked down at my arms as if I'd never seen them before, as if I'd been born without them and they'd been grafted on while I was napping. "Mosquito bites," I said.

"In November? They must be some tough-ass mosquitoes."

"Yeah," I said, shifting the half-eaten sandwich from one hand to the other so I could cover up with the jacket, "yeah, they are."

MIKE LIKED THE COUNTRY. He'd grown up in the projects on the Lower East Side, always pressed in by concrete and blacktop, and now that he was in the wilds of northern Westchester he began to keep animals. There were two chickens in a rudely constructed pen and a white duck he'd hatched from the egg, all of which met their fate one bitter night when a fox—or more likely, a dog—sniffed them out. He had a goat too, chained to a tree from which it had stripped the bark to a height of six feet or more, its head against the palm of your hand exactly like a rock with hair on it, and when he thought about it he'd toss it half a bale of hay or a loaf of stale bread or even the cardboard containers the beer came in. Inside, he had a fifty-gallon aquarium with a pair of foot-long alligators huddled inside it under a heat lamp, and these he fed hamburger in the form of raw meatballs he'd work between his palms. Every once in a while someone would get stoned and expel a lungful of smoke into the aquarium to see what effect it would have on a pair of reptiles and the things would scrabble around against the glass enclosure, hissing.

I was there one night without Cole—he was meeting with his

lawyer, I think; I remember he'd shaved his mustache and trimmed his hair about that time—and I parked out on the street so as to avoid suspicion and made my way over the stone wall and through the darkened woods to the indistinct rumble of live music, the pulse of Mike's bass buoyed by the chink-chink of a high hat, an organ fill and cloudy vocals. My breath steamed around me. A sickle moon hung over the roof of the cottage and one of the cats shot along the base of the outer wall as I pushed through the door.

Everyone was gathered in the living room, JoJo and Suzie stretched out on the floor, Mike and his band, his new band, manning the instruments. I stood in the doorway a moment, feeling awkward. Nicky was on keyboards and a guy I'd met a few times—Skip—was doing the drumming. But there was a stranger, older, in his late twenties, with an out-of-date haircut and the flaccid beginnings of jowls, up at the mike singing lead and playing guitar. I leaned against the doorframe and listened, nodding my head to the beat, as they went through a version of "Rock and Roll Woman," Mike stepping up to the microphone to blend his voice effortlessly with the new guy's on the complex harmonies, and it wasn't as if they were rehearsing at all. They could have been onstage playing the tune for the hundredth time. When the song finished, I ducked into the room, nodding to Mike and saying something inane like, "Sounding good, man."

As it turned out, the new guy—his name was either Haze or Hayes, I never did get that straight—had played with Mike in a cover band the year before and then vanished from sight. Now he was back and they were rehearsing for a series of gigs at a club out on Route 202, where eventually they'd become the house band. I sat there on the floor with the girls and listened and felt transported—I wanted to get up and sing myself, ask them if they couldn't use a saxophone to cut away from the guitar leads, but I couldn't work up the nerve. Afterward, in the kitchen, when we were all stoned and riding high on the communion of the music, Haze launched into "Sunshine of My Love" on his acoustic guitar and I lost my inhibitions enough to try to blend my voice with his, with mixed results. But he kept on playing, and I kept on singing, till Mike went out to the living room and came back with the two alligators, one clutched in each hand, and began banging them together like tambourines, their legs scrambling at the air and tails flailing, the white miniature teeth fighting for purchase.

THEN THERE WAS parent/teacher night. I got home from work and went straight to bed, and then, cruelly, had to get back up, put the tie on all over again and drive to school right in the middle of cocktail hour, or at the tail end of it anyway. I make a joke of it now, but I was tentative about the whole thing, afraid of the parents' scrutiny, afraid I'd be exposed for the imposter I was. I pictured them grilling me about the rules of grammar or Shakespeare's plays—the ones I hadn't read—but the parents were as hopeless as their offspring. Precious few of them turned up, and those who did looked so intimidated by their surroundings I had the feeling they would have taken my word for practically anything. In one class—my fifth period—a single parent turned up. His son—an overweight, well-meaning kid mercilessly ragged by his classmates—was one of the few in the class who weren't behavioral problems, but the father kept insisting that his son was a real hell-raiser, "just like his old man." He sat patiently, work-hardened hands folded on the miniature desk, through my fumbling explanation of what I was trying to accomplish with this particular class and the lofty goals to which each and every student aspired and more drivel of a similar nature, before interrupting me to say, "He gives you a problem, you got my permission to just whack him one. All right? You get me?"

I was stuffing papers into my briefcase just after the final bell rang at 8:15, thinking to meet Cole at Chase's as soon as I could change out of my prison clothes, when a woman in her thirties—a mother—appeared in the doorway. She looked as if she'd been drained of blood, parchment skin and a high sculpted bluff of bleached-blond hair gone dead under the dehumanizing wash of the overhead lights. "Mr. Caddis?" she said in a smoker's rasp. "You got a minute?"

A minute? I didn't have thirty seconds. I wanted nothing but to get out of there and get loose before I fell into my bed for a few hours of inadequate dreamless sleep and then found myself right here all over again. "I'm in a hurry," I told her. "I have—well, an appointment."

"I only want a minute." There was something about her that looked vaguely familiar, something about the staring cola-colored eyes and the way her upper teeth pushed at her lip, that reminded me of somebody, somewhere—and then it came to me: Robert Rowe. "I'm Robert's mother," she said.

I didn't say anything, just parked my right buttock on the nearest desk and waited for her to go on. Robert wasn't in any of my classes, just homeroom. I wasn't his teacher. He wasn't my responsibility. The fat kid, yes. The black kid who flew around the room on the wings beating inside his brain chanting *He's white, he's right* for hours at a time, the six months' pregnant girl whose head would have fallen off if she stopped chewing gum for thirty seconds, yes and yes. But not Robert. Not Robert Rowe.

She was wearing a dirty white sweater, misbuttoned. A plaid skirt. Loafers. If I had been older, more attuned, more sympathetic, I would have seen that she was pretty, pretty still, and that she was desperately trying to communicate something to me, some nascent hope grown up out of the detritus of welfare checks and abandonment. "He looks up to you," she said, her voice choked, as if suddenly she couldn't breathe.

This took me by surprise. I didn't know how to respond, so I threw it back at her, stalling a moment to assimilate what she was saying. "Me?" I said. "He looks up to *me*?"

Her eyes were pooling. She nodded.

"But why me? I'm not even his teacher."

"Ever since his father left," she began, but let that thought trail off as she struggled to summon a new one, the thought—the phrase—that would bring me around, that would touch me in the way she wanted to. "He talks about you all the time. He thinks you're cool. That's what he say, 'Mr. Caddis is cool.'"

Robert Rowe's face rose up to hover before me in the seat of my unconscious, a compressed little nugget of a face, with the extruded teeth and Coca-Cola eyes of this woman, his mother, Mrs. Rowe.

That was who she was, Mrs. Rowe, I reminded myself, and I seized on the proper form of address in that moment: "Mrs. Rowe, look, he's a great kid, but I'm not, I mean—well, I'm not his *teacher,* you know that—"

The room smelled of adolescent fevers and anxieties, of socks worn too long, unwashed hair, jackets that had never seen the inside of a dry cleaner's. There was a fading map of the United States on the back wall, chalkboards so old they'd faded to gray. The linoleum was cracked and peeled. The desks were a joke. Her voice was so soft I could barely hear her over the buzz of the fluorescent lights. "I know," she said. "But he's not . . . he's getting F's—D's and F's. I don't know what to do with him. He won't listen to me—he hasn't listened to me in years."

"Yeah," I said, just to say something. He looked up to me, sure, but I had a date to meet Cole at Chase's.

"Would you just, I don't know, look out for him? Would you? That's all I ask."

I suppose there are several layers of irony here, not the least of which is that I wasn't capable of looking out for myself, but I buried all that at the bar and when I saw Robert Rowe in homeroom the next morning, I felt nothing more than a vague irritation. He was wearing a tie-dyed shirt—starbursts of pink and yellow—under the parka and he'd begun to kink his hair out in the way I wore mine at night, but that had to be a coincidence, because to my knowledge he'd never seen me outside of school. It was possible, of course. Anything was possible. He could have seen me coming out of Chase's or stopped in my car along South Street with Mike or Cole, looking to score. I kept my head down, working at my papers—the endless, hopeless, scrawled-over tests and assignments—but I felt his eyes on me the whole time. Then the bell rang and he was gone with the rest of them.

I was home early that evening, looking for sustenance—hoping to find my mother in the kitchen stirring something in a pot—because I was out of money till payday and Cole was lying low because his mother had found a bag of pot in his underwear drawer and I felt like taking a break from the cottage and music and dope. Just for the night. I figured I'd stay in, read a bit, get to bed early. My mother wasn't there, though. She had a meeting. At school. One of the endless meetings she had to sit through, taking minutes in short-hand, while the school board debated yet another bond issue. I wondered about that and wondered about Jerry Reilly too.

My father was home. There was no other place he was likely to be—he'd given up going to the tavern or the diner or anyplace else. TV was his narcotic. And there he was, settled into his chair with a cocktail, watching *Victory at Sea* (his single favorite program, as if he couldn't get enough of the war that had robbed him of his youth and personality), the dog, which had been young when I was in junior high myself, curled up stinking at his feet. We exchanged a few words—*Where's Mom? At a meeting. You going to eat? No. A sandwich? I'll make you a sandwich? I said no.*—and then I heated a can of soup and went upstairs with it. For a long while I lay on the floor with my head sandwiched between the speakers, playing records over and over, and then I drifted off.

It was late when I woke—past one—and when I went downstairs to use the toilet, my mother was just coming in the door. The old dog began slapping his tail on the carpet, too arthritic to get up; the lamp on the end table flicked on, dragging shadows out of the corners. "You just getting in?" I said.

"Yes," she said, her voice hushed. She was in her work clothes: flocked dress, stockings and heels, a cloth coat, no gloves, though the weather had turned raw.

I stood there a moment, listening to the thwack of the dog's tail, half-asleep, summoning the beat of an internal rhythm. I should have mounted the stairs, should have gone back to bed; instead, I said, "Late meeting?"

My mother had set her purse down on the little table inside the door reserved for the telephone. She was slipping out of her coat. "We went out for drinks afterward," she said. "Some of us—me and Ruth, Larry Abrams, Ted Penny."

"And Jerry? What about him—was he there?"

It took a moment, the coat flung over the banister, the dog settled back in his coil, the clank of the heat coming on noisy out of all proportion, and then she turned to me, hands on her hips, and said, "Yes, Jerry was there. And you know what—I'm glad he was." A beat. She swayed slightly, or maybe that was my imagination. "You want to know why?"

There was something in her voice that should have warned me off, but I was awake now, and instead of going back upstairs to bed I just stood there in the dim arc of light the lamp cast on the floor and shrugged my shoulders. She lifted her purse from the telephone stand and I saw that there was something else there, a metal case the size of the two-tiered deluxe box of candy I gave her for Christmas each year. It was a tape recorder, and she bent a moment to fit the plug in the socket next to the phone outlet. Then she straightened up and gave me that look again—the admonitory look, searing and sharp. "I want you to listen to something," she said. "Something a friend of Jerry's—he works for the Peterskill police department, he's a detective—thought you ought to hear."

I froze. There was no time to think, no time to fabricate a story, no time to wriggle or plead, because my own voice was coming at me out of the miniature speaker. *Hey,* I was saying, *you coming over or what? It's like past nine already and everybody's waiting—*

There was music in the background, cranked loud—"Spinning Wheel," the tune of that fall, and we were all intoxicated by David Clayton Thomas and the incisiveness of those punched-up horns—and my mind ran through the calendar of the past week, Friday or Saturday at the cottage in the woods, Cole running late, the usual party in progress . . .

Yeah, sure, I heard Cole respond. He was at his mother's—it was his mother's birthday. *Just as soon as I can get out of here.*

Okay, man, I said. *Catch you later, right?*

That was it. Nothing incriminating, but incrimination wasn't the point of the exercise. It took me a moment, and then I thought of Haze, his sudden appearance in our midst, the glad-handing and the parceling out of the cool, and then I understood why he'd come to us—the term "infiltrated" soared up out of nowhere—and just who had put him up to it. I couldn't think of what to say.

My mother could, though. She clicked off the tape with a punch of her index finger. "My friend said if you knew what was good for you, you'd stay clear of that place for a while. For good." We stood five feet apart. There was no embrace—we weren't an embracing family—no pat on the back, no gesture of any kind. Just the two of us standing there in the half-dark. When she spoke finally her voice was muted. "Do you understand what I'm telling you?"

As soon as I got out of work the next day I changed my clothes and went straight to the cottage. It was raining steadily, a cold gray rain that drooled from the branches of the trees and braided in the gutters. Cole's Bug was parked on the street as I drove up, but I didn't park beside him—I drove another half mile on and parked on a side street, a cul-de-sac where nobody would see the car. Then I put my head down and walked up the road in the rain, veering off into the woods the minute I saw a car turn into the street. I remember how bleak everything looked, the summer's trash revealed at the feet of the denuded trees, the weeds bowed and frost-burned, leaves clinging to my boots as if the ground were made of paste. My heart was pounding. It was a condition we called paranoia when we were smoking, the unreasoning feeling that something or somebody is about to pounce, that the world has become intractably dangerous and your own vulnerability has been flagged. But no, this wasn't paranoia: the threat was real.

The hair was wet to my scalp and my jacket all but ruined by the time I pushed through the front door. The house was quiet, no music bleeding through the speakers, no murmur of voices or tread of footsteps. There was the soft fading scratch of one of the cats in the litter pan in the kitchen, and that was it, nothing, silence absolute. I stood in the entryway a moment, trying to scrape the mud and leaves from my boots, but it was hopeless, so finally I just stepped out of them in my stocking feet and left them there at the door. I suppose that was why Suzie and Cole didn't hear me coming—I hadn't meant to creep up on them, hadn't meant anything except to somehow come round to tell them what I knew, what I'd learned, warning them, sparing them, and as I say my heart was going and I was risking everything myself just to be there, just to be present— and when I stepped into the living room they gave me a shock. They were naked, their clothes flung down beside them, rolling on a blanket in sexual play—or the prelude to it. I suppose it doesn't really matter at this juncture to say that I'd found her attractive—she was the pretty one, always that—or that I felt all along that she'd favored me over Cole or Nicky or any of the others? That didn't matter. That had nothing to do with it. I'd come with a warning, and I had to deliver it.

"Who's that?" Suzie's voice rose up out of the stillness. Cole was atop her and she had to lift her head to fix her eyes on me. "John? Is that you?"

Cole rolled off her and flipped a fold of the blanket over her. "Jesus," he said, "you picked a great moment." His eyes burned, though I could see he was trying to be cool, trying to minimize it, no big thing.

"Jesus," Suzie said, "you scared me. Do you always creep around like that?"

"My boots," I said. "They just—or actually, I just came by to tell you something, that's all—I can't stay . . ."

The rain was like two cupped palms holding the place in its grip. The gutters rattled. Pinpricks needled the roof. "Shit," Cole said, and Suzie reached out to gather up her clothes, shielding her breasts in the crook of one arm, "I mean, shit, John. Couldn't you wait in the kitchen, I mean, for like ten fucking minutes? Huh? Couldn't you?"

I swung round without a word and padded out to the kitchen even as the living room door thundered shut at my back. For a long while I sat at the familiar table with its detritus of burned joss sticks, immolated candles, beer bottles, mugs, food wrappers and the like, thinking I could just write them a note—that would do it—or maybe I'd call Cole later, from home, when he got home, that was, at his mother's. But I couldn't find a pencil—nobody took notes here, that was for sure—and finally I just pushed myself up, tiptoed to the door and fell back into my boots and the sodden jacket.

It was just getting dark when I pulled up in front of the house. My father's car was parked there at the curb, but my mother's wasn't and it wasn't in the driveway either. The rain kept coming down—the streets were flooding, broad sheets of water fanning away from the tires and the main road clogged with slow-moving cars and their tired headlights and frantically beating wipers. I ran for the house, kicked off my boots on the doorstep and flung myself inside as if I'd been away for years. My jacket streamed and I hurried across the carpet to the accompaniment of the dog's thwacking tail and hung it from the shower head in the bathroom. Then I went to the kitchen to look in the refrigerator, feeling desolate and cheated. I didn't have a habit despite the stigmata of my arms—I was a neophyte still, a twice- or three-times-a-week user—but I had a need, and that need yawned before me, opening up and opening up again, as I leaned over the sink. The cottage was over. Cole was over. Life, as I'd come to know it, was finished.

It was then that I noticed the figure of my father moving through the gloom of the backyard. He had on a pair of galoshes I'd worn as a kid, the kind with the metal fasteners, and he was wearing a yellow rain slicker and one of those winter hats with the fold-down earmuffs. I couldn't quite tell what he was doing out there, raking dirt or leaves, something to do with the rain, I guessed—the driveway was eroding, maybe that was it. It never crossed my mind that he might need help. And Robert Rowe never crossed my mind either, nor the fact that his speech had been garbled and slow at the noon hour and his eyes drifting toward a point no one in this world could see but him.

No. I was hungry for something, I didn't know what. It wasn't food, because I mechanically chewed a handful of saltines over the sink and washed them down with half a glass of milk that tasted like chalk. I paced round the living room, snuck a drink out of my mother's bottle—Dewar's, that was what she drank; my father stuck with vodka, the cheaper the better, and I'd never acquired a taste for it. I had another drink, and then another. After a while I eased myself down in my father's chair and gazed around the room where I'd spent the better part of my life, the secondhand furniture, the forest-green wallpaper gone pale around the windowframes, the peeling sheet-metal planter I'd made for my mother in shop class, the plants within it long since expired, just curls of dead things now. Finally I got up and turned on the TV, then settled back in my father's chair as the jets came in low and the village went up in flames.

LOOK FOR T.C. BOYLE'S NEWEST NOVEL
TALK TALK
COMING IN HARDCOVER FROM VIKING IN JULY 2006

As T.C. Boyle's suspenseful new novel opens, Dana Halter, a young deaf woman, is in a courtroom, her legs shackled as a list of charges is read out—assault with a deadly weapon, auto theft, passing bad checks. Clearly there has been a terrible mistake—someone has been impersonating her. As Dana and her new boyfriend set out to find him, they begin to test the limits of the life they have started to build together.

Talk Talk is both a thrilling road trip across America and a moving story about language, love, and identity, from one of America's finest novelists.   *ISBN 0-670-03770-2*

After the Plague
These sixteen stories display an astonishing range, as Boyle zeroes in on everything from air rage to abortion doctors to the story of a 1920s Sicilian immigrant who constructs an amazing underground mansion in an effort to woo his sweetheart. By turns mythic and realistic, farcical and tragic, ironic and moving, these new stories find "one of the most inventive and verbally exuberant writers" (*The New York Times*) at the absolute top of his form.   *ISBN 0-14-200141-4*

Budding Prospects
All Felix and his friends have to do is harvest a crop of *Cannabis Sativa* and half a million tax-free dollars will be theirs. But as their beloved buds wither under assault from ravenous scavengers, human caprice, and a drug-busting state trooper named Jerpbak, their dreams of easy money go up in smoke. "Consistently, effortlessly, intelligently funny."
—*The New York Times*   *ISBN 0-14-029996-3*

Descent of Man
A primate-center researcher becomes romantically involved with a chimp. A Norse poet overcomes bard-block. These and other strange occurrences come together in Boyle's collection of satirical stories—his very first book—that brilliantly express just what the "evolution" of mankind has wrought.   *ISBN 0-14-029994-7*

Drop City

It is 1970, and a California commune devoted to peace, free love, and the simple life has decided to relocate to the last frontier—unforgiving Alaska—in the ultimate expression of going back to the land. Armed with the spirit of adventure and naïve optimism, the inhabitants of "Drop City" arrive only to find their utopia already populated by other young Alaskans who are successfully homesteading in the wilderness. As the two communities collide and winter sets in, unexpected friendships and dangerous enmities are born as everyone struggles with the bare essentials of life: love, nourishment, and a roof over one's head. Rich, allusive, and unsentimental, T.C. Boyle's ninth novel is a tour de force infused with the lyricism and take-no-prisoners storytelling for which he is justly famous.

A *New York Times* bestseller and Finalist for the National Book Award
ISBN 0-14-200380-8

East Is East

Young Japanese seaman Hiro Tanaka jumps ship off the coast of Georgia and swims into a net of rabid rednecks, genteel ladies, descendants of slaves, and the denizens of an artists' colony. *The New York Times* called this sexy, hilarious tragicomedy a "pastoral version of *The Bonfire of the Vanities*." ISBN 0-14-013167-1

A Friend of the Earth

"America's most imaginative contemporary novelist" (*Newsweek*) takes a provocative new turn with a brilliant, timely, darkly funny novel about love, activism, and the future of the planet. Ty Tierwater, failed ecoterrorist and ex-con, ekes out a bleak living managing a rock star's private menagerie of scruffy hyenas, jackals, warthogs, and three down-at-the-mouth lions, some of the only species remaining after the collapse of the earth's biosphere. ISBN 0-14-100205-0

Greasy Lake and Other Stories

Mythic and realistic, these masterful stories are, according to *The New York Times*, "satirical fables of contemporary life, so funny and acutely observed that they might have been written by Evelyn Waugh as sketches for . . . *Saturday Night Live*." ISBN 0-14-007781-2

If the River Was Whiskey

Boyle, winner of the 1999 PEN/Malamud Award for Short Fiction, tears through the walls of contemporary society to reveal a world at once comic and tragic, droll and horrific, in these sixteen magical and provocative stories. "Writing at its very, very best." —*USA Today*
ISBN 0-14-011950-7

The Inner Circle

T.C. Boyle's tenth novel is narrated by John Milk, who in 1940 accepts a job as assistant to Alfred Kinsey, an extraordinarily charming professor of zoology known around campus as "Dr. Sex." As a member of Kinsey's "inner circle" of researchers, Milk is called upon to participate in sexual experiments that become increasingly uninhibited—and problematic for his marriage—as Kinsey ever more recklessly pushes the boundaries both personally and professionally. While Boyle doesn't resist making the most of this delicious material, *The Inner Circle* is at heart a very moving and loving look at sex, marriage, and infidelity that will have readers everywhere reassessing their own relationships.

ISBN 0-14-303586-X

Riven Rock

T.C. Boyle pens a heartbreaking love story taken from between the lines of history. Millionaire Stanley McCormick, diagnosed as a schizophrenic and sexual maniac shortly after his marriage, is forbidden the sight of women, but his strong-willed, virginal wife Katherine Dexter is determined to cure him. "As romantic as it is informative, as colorful as it is convincing. Boyle combines his gift for historical re-creation with his dazzling powers as a storyteller."—*The Boston Globe*

ISBN 0-14-027166-X

The Road to Wellville

Centering on John Harvey Kellogg and his turn-of-the-century Battle Creek Spa, this wickedly comic novel brims with a Dickensian cast of characters and is laced with wildly wonderful plot twists. "A marvel, enjoyable from the beginning to end." —Jane Smiley, *The New York Times Book Review*   *ISBN 0-14-016718-8*

T.C. Boyle Stories

"Boyle has the tale-teller's gift in abundance," writes the *Chicago Tribune*. And nowhere is that more evident than in this collection of sixty-eight short stories—all of the work from his first four collections, as well as seven tales that have never before appeared in book form—that comprise a virtual feast of the short story. "Seven hundred flashy, inventive pages of stylistic and moral acrobatics." —*The New York Times Book Review*   *ISBN 0-14-028091-X*

The Tortilla Curtain

Winner of France's Prix Medicis Étranger for Best Foreign Language Novel, *The Tortilla Curtain* illuminates the many potholes along the road to the elusive American Dream. Illegal immigrants Cándido and América cling to life at the bottom of Topanga Canyon, dreaming of a privileged existence of the sort endured by L.A. liberals Delaney and Kyra. When a freak accident brings these two couples together, darkly comic events leave them wondering what the world is coming to.

ISBN 0-14-023828-X

Water Music

Funny, bawdy, full of Boyle's inimitable flights of imaginative and stylistic fancy, *Water Music*, his first novel, follows the wild adventures of Ned Rise, thief and whoremaster, and Mungo Park, explorer, through London's seamy gutters and Scotland's scenic Highlands—to their grand meeting in the heart of darkest Africa. There they join forces and wend their hilarious way to the source of the Niger. ISBN 0-14-006550-4

Without a Hero

With fierce, comic wit and uncanny accuracy, Boyle zooms in on an astonishingly wide range of American phenomena in this critically-applauded collection of stories. "Gloriously comic . . . vintage Boyle . . . [these] stories are more than funny, better than wicked. They make you cringe with their clarity." —*The Philadelphia Inquirer*

ISBN 0-14-017839-2

World's End

Set in New York's Hudson Valley in three time periods—the late seventeenth century, the 1940s, and the late 1960s—this fascinating novel, for which Boyle won the prestigious PEN/Faulkner Award for American Fiction, follows the interwoven destinies of three families and showcases the author's "ability to work all sorts of magical variations of literature and history" (*The New York Times*). ISBN 0-14-029993-9